THE UNQUIET GRAVE

THE UNQUIET GRAVE

STEVEN DUNNE

headline

First published in 2013 by
HEADLINE PUBLISHING GROUP

1

Cataloguing in Publication Data is available from the British Library

ISBN (HB) 978 0 7553 8370 2
ISBN (TPB) 978 0 7553 8371 9

Typeset in Hoefler New by Avon DataSet Ltd, Bidford-on-Avon, Warwickshire

Printed and bound in Great Britain by Clays Ltd, St Ives plc

Headline's policy is to use papers that are natural, renewable and recyclable
products and made from wood grown in sustainable forests. The logging
and manufacturing processes are expected to conform to the environmental
regulations of the country of origin.

HEADLINE PUBLISHING GROUP
An Hachette Livre UK Company
338 Euston Road
London NW1 3BH

www.headline.co.uk
www.hachette.co.uk

For Susan
Love and thanks for all you do

Acknowledgements

Love and gratitude go to my wonderful wife Carmel for her continuing support and encouragement and to the far-flung McKenna tribe who spread the word about the DI Brook case files. The same goes to my lovely sister Susan Dunne to whom this book is dedicated. My two biggest fans.

As well as providing regular practical support, Jeff Fountain supplies insightful editorial comment on the content and direction of my work. Thanks also to Patrick Raggett for his razor-sharp observations and instinctive understanding of what my novels are trying to achieve – two indispensable friends.

I couldn't reach such a wide audience without the work of all the quality people at Headline. Many thanks to Ali Hope, Sam Eades, Anna Hogarty and all the team for their efforts on my behalf. And I can't let pass a final opportunity to say a big thank you to the departed Martin Fletcher for his help and guidance and for believing in the potential of my work.

David Grossman, my agent, continues to provide his expert guidance through the choppy waters of publishing and his editorial input is always invaluable. Thank you.

My gratitude also goes to fellow Weekenders' cricketer Joseph McDonald for taking the time to produce thoughtful advice on police procedures and criminal practices as well as chipping in with valuable runs down the order.

Finally a big hug of appreciation to all Waterstone's branches up and down the country for putting up with me in-store, as I hawk my wares at book signings. The welcoming and knowledgeable staff, too numerous to mention, are an invaluable resource to all book buyers and readers and long may you continue.

I can't finish without a special mention of Sean Heavens and the team in Derby Waterstone's and Glenys Cooper and the staff in the Burton-on-Trent branch. Without their longstanding support, I wouldn't have been able to establish such a strong readership base in the East Midlands and, now, beyond.

Steve Dunne

T'is I, my love, sits on your grave,
And will not let you sleep;
For I crave one kiss of your clay-cold lips,
And that is all I seek.
(Anon.)

One

Saturday, 22 December 1973 – Derby

THE BOY LOOKED UP FROM sorting through his football cards to watch his mum light another cigarette. Her hands were tight and clumsy as she fumbled for her props but, eventually, the hiss of gas and a guttering flame signalled job done. Tossing her gold lighter on to the coffee table, she took a quivering draw, holding the blue-grey poison in her lungs for a beat before exhaling across the room.

Jeff watched in silence as she tried to ease back and relax but she couldn't manage it, at once pulling back her frame to the edge of the sofa, her legs bent double, her tension-wracked shoulders invisible under the uncombed hair. She played with her housework-reddened hands, sometimes picking at a jagged nail, sometimes swivelling the two rings round her wedding finger.

'I'm hungry, Mum,' said Jeff, in that way children have of asking for things without actually posing the question.

Without looking over at him she answered, her voice hoarse and strained. 'Dad's home in an hour.'

Jeff gazed unblinking, waiting for her to crack. It didn't happen. 'But I'm hungry now.'

'You can have a sandwich when Dad gets home,' she replied, trying to keep the rising emotion from her voice. She glanced his way to reassure but it didn't take.

'But—'

'You'll have to wait,' she snapped, her face turned away again, longing to return to her reverie, a land of unblinking vacuity where she could hide from present pain and the prospect of more to come.

'Well, can I have a slice of dripping and bread to put me on?' His mum didn't answer. Just stared at the bearskin rug as though her son wasn't there and hadn't spoken. But he was there and he wanted an answer, sensing one more push might do it. 'Can I . . . ?'

'Help yourself!' she barked, twisting her rings like she was trying to unscrew her finger. 'Help yourself,' she repeated softly, eyes closed, a blind nod to tell herself she had control.

Jeff stared impassively at her pale drawn face, trying in vain to make contact with her red-rimmed eyes. Eventually he laid down his cards in two piles – keepers and swaps – then dragged himself to the kitchen. OK. He'd have to get his own food. Not the best outcome but still a small victory, a chink of light and acknowledgement in the wall of silence his mum and dad had erected around him and what had happened.

It was yonks ago, for God's sake. You've still got me.

He turned at the kitchen door, and glued his eye to the crack, watching his mum who, after his departure, looked briefly up to the fireplace before resuming her inspection of the rug and pulling a balled handkerchief from her sleeve.

Jeff had been expecting as much and mimicked her quick glance to the *only* photograph on the mantelpiece, the picture of his dead brother, little Donny. The clumsy black ribbon across one corner obscured an ear and part of his lopsided dopey grin, Donny's grin, the grin that conquered all, that drew the lion's share of parental love.

Don't deny it, Mum. Donny was your favourite. Always had been. Mum always took Donny's word that Jeff should shoulder the blame and Jeff could almost hear Donny's whining voice, accusing. *Jeff did it. It was him.*

Jeff sighed. Yes, he had done it. He *had* sat on Donny until he could barely breathe, he *had* nicked Donny's toy, he *had* spat in Donny's food, poked him in the eye, pulled his pants down with his

2

back turned – plus a million other things, some involving insects. But did that give Donny the right to tell tales?

Jeff scowled from behind the door, watching as his mum opened the floodgates and sobbed silently into the tight, damp ball of cotton, her shoulders convulsing as if puking.

Happy now, Don-kee? You made Mum cry, Don-kee. Happy?

He glared at his dead brother's picture with his grin and his quiff and his too-big Dennis the Menace jumper. Mum had kept the jumper, he knew. She'd hidden it under the stairs but one night, soon after the drowning, Jeff had snuck down and watched her bury her face in it, trying to catch a whiff of Don-kee's stink, what was left of it after the river had washed away him and his stupid smell forever.

He turned away, miserable. Three days to Christmas. This should be an exciting time. The decs were up, the tree was up (though not as carefully dressed as in years past, he'd noticed) and there was decent telly on all three channels, with good films on as soon as he jumped out of bed. Incredible.

But instead of excitement, this – boredom and tears. No telly. No noise apart from the clock and his mum's muffled sobs. At least Dad would be home soon, finished for the hols. At least *he* made an effort to be normal. He worked all day, plus Saturday mornings, not like Mum, and on top of that, he'd had to do all the decorations, the tree, even cook meals. And still he made time to get out in the yard and help his son make a snowman. That's a proper parent.

Jeff cheered up at the thought of his presents. *Double bubble this year 'cos they'd already bought and wrapped Don-kee's presents before he fell in the river reaching for his stupid balloon. Afterwards, Mum couldn't face taking them back so I get the lot.*

Smiling now, Jeff reached for the dripping pot on the kitchen window sill and pulled a slice of Mighty White from the bread bin. He dug around in the dripping with the knife to get past the hard grey fat on top to the meaty brown sludge below. Yummy. He shook some salt on to the slice and took a large slimy bite, peering out at the harsh winter weather outside. It was beginning to snow again. Brilliant.

3

His eye wandered round to the snowman as he jammed the rest of the bread into his mouth. The snowman had started to look tired and dirty but now it was snowing again maybe he could rebuild it with fresh snow when his dad got home. As he chewed, he noticed with dismay that its nose was gone. The carrot must've fallen off. He rushed back to the stifling lounge. 'Going outside, Mum.' Statement, not question, but his mum barely noticed.

She straightened momentarily but didn't turn round as she made a stab at parental responsibility. 'Wrap up warm,' she croaked.

'I know,' groaned Jeff, grabbing coat, hat and gloves from the rack in the hall and rushing outside, slamming the door behind him. His orange leather football was right outside the kitchen door. He flicked it up to head and nearly went flying but young supple limbs managed to keep him upright. Taking heed, he crunched more carefully round the side of the house over the frozen patio, catching the full hit of the sub-zero wind howling across the countryside, snow corkscrewing along in its grip.

Jeff stood to contemplate the white wonderland before him, soft undulating layers of snow calling him to take their virginity. First things first. He scuffed over to the snowman to pick up the carrot only to discover that it wasn't there. It wasn't screwed into the face and it wasn't on the ground below. He puzzled over this. Maybe a bird had taken it. Or an animal. But then, with a start, he saw the footprints that had walked up to the snowman then turned away, returning to the back gate from where they'd come.

'Mmmmm.' Jeff hovered a boot over the prints thinking they must be his. No, too small – he had big feet for his age. He put his weight down in the snow to confirm that his feet were two or three sizes bigger than the print and he knew his dad's feet were bigger still.

'Illogical, Captain,' he reasoned, using a line from his all-time favourite TV programme. (Don-kee's favourite was *Magpie*. What a loser.) Jeff followed the trail of footprints from the gate as they headed off into the woods and, beyond, the golf course.

After a few yards he stopped to raise his head, allowing his sharp eyes to plot the course taken by the carrot thief out across the field of white to the horizon. The wind dropped for a moment and with it the swirls of snow that limited his vision. There, in the distance, a diminutive figure was standing on the edge of a small copse that bordered the golf course. Although some way away, the figure seemed to bridge the expanse of ground between them, reaching out to squeeze the heart with an invisible hand and Jeff found his pulse racing, his breath arriving in spurts.

'No,' Jeff panted. 'Can't be.' He rubbed his eyes in time-honoured fashion and looked again but there was no mistake. The outline of a small boy stood statue-still against the elements and, worse, appeared to be staring straight back at him. The bright red and black hooped jumper seemed to dwarf the lightly framed form as though it was a mid-length skirt and not a woollen jumper.

'Dennis the Menace,' gasped Jeff, turning in confusion to the house where he knew the garment was hidden, squirrelled away in the shoe cupboard when it wasn't covering his mum's tear-streaked face.

'Don-kee,' he muttered under his breath, returning his stare to the distant form. He tried to see the face of the boy but snow stung his eyeballs so he shielded his eyes with a gloved hand. The figure hadn't moved, standing motionless, one arm hanging by his side, one arm bent, hand in mitten, clutching a balloon that danced in the swirling wind.

'Don-kee!' he repeated, this time shouting across the fields at the apparition. No reaction. Jeff moved slowly, reluctantly, towards the image of his dead brother then hesitated before tracking back towards the snowman, dragging his feet through the alien footprints until all traces were gone – all the way back through the gate, all the way back to the snowman. No one else could know.

Spinning back, Jeff's mood turned to anger and his fist clenched. He thought of all his presents. He thought of having to share. He thought of the lopsided grin. A second later he began to jog towards the trees, stomping heavily across the scarred white ground. 'Don't you tell, Don-kee,' he shouted when only a hundred yards away. 'Don't you tell.'

At that moment, a gust of snow blew across Jeff's face and he missed his footing, slipping clumsily on a tuft of grass. When he surfaced, the figure had gone. Jeff stood, brushing himself down, wondering if his eyes were playing tricks, like when you could see water on a hot road in the distance. But then he saw the balloon jogging up and down in the breeze, before its owner disappeared out of sight over the hill towards the ninth fairway.

'Wait!' screamed Jeff, quickening his pace. 'I'm coming!' He set off again, following the clear trail over the frozen ground, shouting to the darkening sky as he clambered after the sure-footed figure. 'Don't you tell, Don-kee. I'm coming.'

DI Walter Laird crunched across the slippery white ground towards the hive of activity a hundred yards up the slope. Looking around at the snow-filled hollows and sparse brown trees lining his path, Laird realised he was on an actual fairway of the Allestree Park Golf Course. And though he was no sportsman, he also surmised that the crime scene officers, working furiously on a raised plateau ringed by more trees, must be working on a putting green. Green in summer perhaps but, everywhere he gazed, the colours of deepest winter assaulted the eye; blinding white snow dominated, leavened only by the soothing washed-out brown and pale green of dormant shrubs and trees, dotted around the landscape to trap the unskilled and delineate the path of play.

As Laird approached the throng of technicians that attended the aftermath of every violent death, a single bright colour stood out from the drabness. A shiny red and black balloon had snared in the branches of a bare tree, a few yards above the hastily erected crime scene tent. Its presence jarred and the detective was lost in private contemplation until a fresh-faced young man emerged from the tent.

Detective Constable Clive Copeland's face was as white as the ground around him, the victim's fate seared on his eyeballs. Staring blankly at Laird and unable to speak, he acknowledged his DI with a tiny drop of the head.

'Clive,' said Laird, fighting off the unworthy smile curling at the edge of his mouth. 'You'll get used to it,' he added, for once omitting the usual quip about Copeland's inexperience.

The younger man's saucer-eyed stare was broken, his head snapping towards Laird. He took a second to assess his superior's words. 'I hope not, guv,' he replied.

'Hold that thought,' said Laird. 'What have we got?'

'A kid called Jeff Ward, guv. We've not done a formal ID yet but it's him, all right. Went missing yesterday lunchtime. He's been strangled.' He paused, biting at a lip as though about to convey crucial information. 'Twelve years old.'

Laird shook his head. 'Bastard. Any . . . ?'

'Nothing sexual that we can see. Clothes seem intact.'

'Thank God.'

'I don't think God's involved here, guv. WPC Langley took the details from the parents. Seems the family was already in mourning. They buried their other kid a couple of months ago – younger son. He drowned.'

'Ward,' murmured Laird, looking to the heavy sky to think. 'Not little Donny Ward that was in the papers?' Copeland's faint nod confirmed it. 'Jesus Christ. Two kids lost in the space of two months . . .'

'I know.'

'Merry bloody Christmas,' growled Laird.

'And I thought my family had it rough with Tilly,' muttered Copeland.

'Steady, lad,' said Laird, glancing sharply at the young man. 'We've a job to do.'

Copeland smiled weakly. 'Guv.'

'Walk me through it?' continued Laird, remembering *his* first dead child. *Concentrate on the facts. Keep the mind busy.*

'Right,' agreed Copeland, seeking sanctuary in the specifics. He swept an arm up to his left, indicating the horizon where a suited SOCO was kneeling on the ground, measuring barely visible marks in the fresh snow. 'The Wards live a mile or so over there on West

Bank Road. You can just about make out some of the dead kid's footprints heading away from home down to here.'

'And then the bastard sneaks up and grabs him,' concluded Laird.

'I don't think so, guv.'

'Oh?'

'It's weird. There seem to be two sets of footprints leading from the house but they're hard to make out, like they've been trampled over . . .'

'Trampled over?'

'It's hard to tell under the fresh snow but it's like somebody has made an effort to obliterate any clear prints by dragging his feet through the marks.'

'A chase?'

'I don't think so.'

'Could be the doer leaving the scene, covering his tracks?'

'Maybe. But we have a faint set of single prints leading in the opposite direction that we think are more likely the killer's. SOCO reckon it was the Ward kid following his killer, obliterating all his footprints as he went.'

'So he must have known him.'

'Looks that way,' agreed Copeland.

'The dad did it,' said Laird. 'Fiver on it.'

'Can't take your money, guv,' said Copeland regretfully. 'The father was still at work when Jeff walked off. He's alibied.'

'You've checked that?'

Copeland's expression was reproachful. 'I'm not that wet behind the ears.'

Laird grinned. 'Yes, you are.' His levity faded. 'All right, it's not the dad. But some pervert got hold of the lad and strangled the life out of him. Witnesses?'

'Uniform are going house to house. Nothing yet. One thing.' Copeland gestured Laird to follow and set off to one of the clearer lone footprints disappearing into the distance. 'The marks are from a small shoe. Size five.'

'Are you thinking this was another kid's handiwork?' said Laird.

'I wouldn't rule it out,' said Copeland. 'It's becoming more common.'

'OK, so check the Ward boy's school friends. See how many live local and bring them in. What about other witnesses? Dog walkers, tobogganists, arctic explorers?'

'No one even heard him scream, guv.'

'Can you scream with someone's hands round your throat?' asked Laird.

'I suppose not,' replied Copeland. 'And the bruising on his neck shows the killer used a rope.'

'Show me.'

They walked back towards the crime scene tent and gazed past the two SOCOs busy in their work. On a flash of the camera, Laird saw the line of the rope on the skin.

'Not good,' said Laird, stepping past the younger man to spend a quiet couple of minutes looking at Jeff Ward's lifeless body, flopped like a rag doll on the snow. 'A rope smacks of planning. Let's hope we can wrap this up sharpish.'

'Weird thing,' said Copeland over his shoulder, looking at the lifeless boy. 'There's no sign of a struggle.'

'We all react differently, Clive.'

'But if it were me I'd be trying to break away, do something.'

'You can't predict what people will do,' explained Laird. 'Some are paralysed with fear when they know they're about to die.'

'But no fight *or* flight,' said Copeland.

'Which makes it more likely it was someone the Ward kid knows,' said Laird.

The pair stepped out of the tent, back out into the wintry chill. Only mid-morning and already it felt like dusk. Once clear of the hive of activity, Laird fumbled in vain for his cigarettes but Copeland failed to pick up on the hint.

Laird gave up the search for cigarettes, his expression grim. 'I hate domestics. OK. Work up the father's alibi until it's cast in bronze then widen it out to other relations and ask about friends and neighbours. Maybe we've got a closet paedo in the area.'

'But Ward wasn't raped.'

'If it's a first-timer, the perv might have got off on it before he was ready. Doesn't mean he didn't *want* to violate him. If there's a next time, the victim may not be so lucky.'

'Lucky?' exclaimed Copeland, turning to leave.

'You know what I mean,' said Laird. 'Clive!' Copeland glanced back. 'Gently does it. We don't want any more weeping and wailing than necessary. And make sure we've got plenty of girls to do the hand-holding.'

Copeland was about to depart when his eye caught a figure marching over the horizon. He took a sharp intake of breath and nodded at the distant form. 'I hate to tell you this . . .'

Laird turned to look. 'What in God's name is Bannon doing here?'

The two officers watched the heavily layered man with a wild grey beard and wilder silvered hair striding towards the crime scene. He walked with difficulty and Laird surmised that the underfoot conditions were not the only factor.

'Jesus,' said Copeland. 'He's gone downhill fast. He's not long retired, is he?'

'Keep your voice down, Clive,' mumbled Laird. 'That's a friend of mine and he used to be the finest detective on the force.' He shouted in greeting at the approaching Bannon, his smile aping normality. 'Sam! What are you doing here?'

Bannon panted to a halt, his thin pockmarked face red from the exercise. Laird could see he'd lost a lot of weight since he'd last seen him and, even at this early hour, his breath smelled of whisky.

'Walter,' said Bannon in return. He glanced at Copeland and narrowed his eyes. 'I know you.' Copeland squirmed under the older man's cobalt-blue stare.

'DC Copeland,' interjected Laird.

Bannon's eyes narrowed, as though sifting evidence in his pomp. 'Clive Copeland – Matilda's brother. I'm sorry for your trouble.'

Copeland blanched, the wound still raw.

'Sam,' said Laird quickly, stepping in front of Copeland. 'You shouldn't be here.'

Bannon fumbled in his heavy coat for cigarettes, pulling out a squashed pack of Capstan Full Strength and offered them round, his sudden grin exposing black and yellowed teeth. Both officers refused a free smoke though Laird plucked the cigarette from Bannon's mouth and put it in his pocket for later.

'This is a crime scene, boss,' said Laird softly.

Bannon nodded in remembrance of procedure. 'Crime scene. Right.'

Laird sounded out the words as though addressing a child. 'Boss. Sam. You have to leave. You can't be here.'

'Come off it, Walter,' said Bannon with a wink. 'You can't hide it from me. It's another one, isn't it?'

'Another one?' asked Laird and Copeland in unison.

Bannon touched his nose with a finger. 'You can't fool me, Wally.' He nodded towards the canvas. 'I heard it on the radio. It's the missing Ward kid, right?' Their silence confirmed it. 'Thought so. How long has he been dead?'

'Sir,' began Copeland. 'I don't think—'

'How long?' shouted ex-DCI Bannon in sudden and violent frustration. The noise was deadened by the canopy of snow but still activity stopped, all heads turning to the drama.

Laird sighed then nodded at DC Copeland.

'About twenty hours at a rough guess,' said Copeland reluctantly.

Bannon found his smile again. 'Killed yesterday then.' He beamed at Laird. 'December the twenty-second.'

'Oh, Jesus,' exclaimed Laird. 'Not this again.'

'But was I right?' beamed Bannon.

'I don't want to hear it, Sam,' said Laird.

'But—'

'Enough!' shouted Laird. 'Now get yourself away from here before I have you escorted away.'

Bannon's expression was dismayed. 'You'd do that to your old guv'nor?'

Laird stared at him, his jaw set.

Bannon nodded unhappily before turning to stumble away. 'All right, Wally. But you'll see,' he muttered over a shoulder. 'You'll see I'm right.'

When Bannon was fifty yards away, Laird turned back to the crime scene.

'Guv?' ventured Copeland.

'Don't ask,' ordered Laird.

Two

Sunday, 22 December 1963 – Kirk Langley, Derby

'SAY CHEESE, EVERYONE.' BERT STANFORTH squinted at the group through the viewfinder of his shiny new Kodak Instamatic 100, one leg kneeling on the carpet.

'Cheese!' screamed the assembled youngsters. The noise was cacophonous and the children – grinning, gurning and gap-toothed – clung to each other, many off balance in contortions only young bodies could allow, their hands clutching at friends' garments for ballast.

Stanforth tried to hurry as every second that elapsed increased the certainty of chaos, inevitable when the young are invited to be still.

'Hang on.' Stanforth lowered the small camera from his face and looked at the flash cube before making an adjustment. He smiled apologetically at the assembly. This was his first ever camera, specially purchased for the occasion, and his discomfort with the technology was evident.

'Ready this time. Cheese!'

'Cheese!'

Awaiting the flash, the youngsters wriggled like eels against the confinement of proximity, some leaning on a quivering leg, kept upright by other bodies as they leaned towards birthday boy Billy Stanforth, arm in arm with best friend Teddy Mullen, at the centre of shot. Others grinned shyly, hiding their bashfulness behind the

13

shoulders of friends while Charlotte Dilkes just stared dreamily at Billy, her features wreathed in adoration.

Party hats, made from yesterday's newspaper, fell to the floor or were grabbed and held to the head, causing further commotion. Others, boys in particular, railed against being demoted to the back row and pushed down on the front row's shoulders, straining to be centre stage in this pictorial record of William Stanforth's thirteenth birthday.

'I'm Hillary on top of Everest,' shouted one boy, raising his head above the rest.

'And I'm Sherpa Ten Pin,' shouted another, trying to join him on the backs of others.

'Just a minute,' tutted Bert Stanforth, checking the flash again. The noise amongst his subjects ramped up further.

'Hurry up, Bert,' said his wife from the kitchen doorway, from where the delicious smell of baking sausage rolls wafted. 'The kids are starving.'

'OK, this time,' shouted Stanforth. 'Cheese.'

'Cheese!' screamed the young voices, even louder than before.

To one side of the scrum of giggling kids stood Billy's elder sister, fifteen-year-old Amelia, looking on indulgently at the squirming mass of youth, urging her father to take the photograph. Her lips-only smile tightened when she glanced at the grandfather clock, her mood darkening with every second of captivity.

Take the flipping picture, will you, Dad? Brendan will be waiting for me.

She looked round at her escape route but it was blocked by her mother, smiling happily, her hands habitually hidden in a crumpled tea towel. Ruth Stanforth was a plump woman in her late forties. Her only respite from delivering and raising three children was standing in front of a stove cooking the meat her husband brought home from his butcher's shop. The constant standing, combined with the protein-rich diet, had made her legs fatter at the ankle than the calf.

Amelia caught her mother's eye and was forced to fake joy for the second it took to turn away in frustration.

He won't wait if I'm late and then what? The rest of the day babysitting these flipping nippers. She gulped back her emotions. *I'm losing him. Plenty of girls after my Bren. He won't wait. And he won't come up to the house to see me. Not after Dad sent him packing that time.*

'You're not to speak to that young man again, Amelia,' he'd said. 'Do I make myself clear?'

Amelia shuddered at the memory of her father's tone and the subsequent overheard conversation with her mum.

'That Brendan's a wrong 'un, Mother.'

'But Bert, she's nearly sixteen and old enough to live her own life,' her mum had replied.

'She's not sixteen yet.'

'But Bert—'

'Not while she's under my roof, Mother. Not with him. The McClearys are criminals, no-good gypsies. Walter Laird tells me young Brendan is already on their radar for thieving.'

'I know he's a bit wild, Bert, but he's only young.'

'He's seventeen, Mother, and Walter says he smokes and drinks and God knows what else. Do you want your daughter ending up in the family way like that trollop Vivienne what's-her-name down in the village?'

Amelia tried not to scowl at her father, his face hidden behind the camera. *Have you never been in love, Dad? If so, you wouldn't make me suffer like this, forbidding me from seeing my Brendan.* Forbidden love. Amelia knew about that. She'd been close to tears during a reading of *Romeo and Juliet* last month. According to her Lit teacher, Romeo's lover was even younger than she was and yet, barely old enough to have her monthly cycle, Juliet had allowed nothing, not even death, to come between her and the boy she loved.

Amelia looked again at the clock, ticking down to her sixteenth birthday as well as her rendezvous in Kirk Langley. In a few short weeks she'd be a woman. Then there'd be no good reason to resist Brendan's coaxing. If only she could keep him happy until then. Already her young body ached, physically ached, to be near him and, once enfolded in his strong arms, Amelia Stanforth had felt temptation stirring within her. She loved Brendan and, before she'd let him put his hands under her jumper, Brendan had been forced to confess his love in return.

Once she would have felt dirty but not any more. Temptation was in the Bible. She'd learned that in RE. Only a week ago, they'd studied the story of Adam and Eve and their encounter with the serpent in the Garden of Eden. And although the teacher had explained their fall from grace with thin-lipped disgust, Amelia had begun to understand their folly in a way that Sister Assumpta would never be able to appreciate if she taught the subject until she was a hundred.

Amelia glanced at the clock again. Her eye was taken by her younger sister, standing beside her at the end of the front row. Billy's twin, Francesca, was the only child not grinning or fidgeting with impatience at their father's incompetence. Instead she looked coolly at Amelia's private smile of anticipation and leaned over to her. 'Missing Brendan, I bet.' Amelia blanched at her sister's taunt. 'Well, he's not missing you.'

'Shut up,' whispered Amelia.

'Was that his new dolly bird earlier?' murmured Francesca, out of the side of her mouth.

Amelia turned to her, face like thunder. 'I said shut up, Fran.'

'Nearer my age than yours, the dirty old man,' continued Francesca, under her breath.

The sudden explosion of the camera caused a whoop of excitement and rubbing of eyes before the roiling mass of young bodies attempted disentanglement.

'OK. One more,' joked Bert Stanforth, unleashing a chorus of protest. He laughed as he wound on the film. 'Just kidding.'

'Brendan loves me,' insisted Amelia to her sister's leering face. 'It's Billy's birthday. Better not start a barney, Fran.'

The grin on Fran's face disappeared and she turned white. 'It's my birthday too,' she spat.

Amelia grinned, sensing swift retaliation. She looked round with mock interest. 'So tell me, sis. Which of these nippers are *your* friends? Oh, wait a minute. None of them. You haven't got any.'

Mrs Stanforth reappeared at the kitchen door, tea towel in hand once more. She smiled maternally at the assembled party. The feast was ready. Ham sandwiches with the thinnest scrape of butter, homemade egg and bacon tart, sausage rolls, tinned peaches and Carnation milk to follow, topped off by trifle and a plate of Jammie Dodgers for those keen to force as much of heaven's bounty down their throats as they could manage.

'Go through to the dining room and help yourself to cordial, children,' she said to an answering hoot of pleasure. 'I'll bring in the food.'

'Let's eat,' said Mr Stanforth, ushering the eager mass of youth towards the dining room with its brand-new, extended drop-leaf table and borrowed chairs. 'Make sure your hands are clean,' he chided, as he shooed them along.

'Want to sit next to me, Billy?' breathed Charlotte Dilkes, grinning bashfully at Billy.

'No, thanks,' replied Billy, brushing abruptly past her scrawny frame. Teddy Mullen, cruising in Billy's wake, smiled cruelly at her and she gulped back a tear before sullenly following the others into the dining room.

The hall was nearly empty and Amelia waited for her father's back to turn before sidling towards the door.

'Where are you going, Amelia?' called Francesca, a malicious grin returning to her features.

Bert Stanforth turned to see Amelia's retreating frame. 'Amelia?'

Amelia turned, a pallid smile fixed to her face. 'Going to round up the strays, Dad.'

'But the gang's all here,' beamed Mr Stanforth. 'Come on, give us a hand.'

Amelia dutifully followed him to the dining room, glancing fiercely at Francesca as she passed.

Amelia stood in the lean-to conservatory at the side of the house, occasionally looking out into the dark windy countryside. Through the rattling windows, she hoped to catch sight of Brendan walking back down Moor Lane from Kirk Langley to his father's rented bungalow on Pole's Road. She should have met him an hour ago and, in her heart of hearts, she knew he wouldn't have waited more than ten minutes.

Amelia was always on time to their secret trysts and this would be the first time she'd stood him up. At least she was still in credit there – Brendan had stood *her* up three times. And when he did turn up, he was always late.

'My turn,' shouted Billy.

'Move up,' moaned Teddy. 'You've got more room.'

Amelia turned back from the darkness, the damp bath towel hanging limp in her hand. Billy and Teddy Mullen dunked their heads in unison into the barrel of water, trying to get what teeth they had into the apples bobbing on the surface. After several unsuccessful attempts, Billy took his hands from behind his back and gripped the side of the barrel. A few seconds later, he tossed back his wet hair and bit down hard on the green apple.

'I win!' shouted Billy, grabbing the towel from Amelia. 'I win.'

'You cheated,' gasped Teddy, emerging from his fruitless trawl of the water. 'You're supposed to keep your hands behind your back.' Teddy turned to Amelia. 'He didn't keep his hands behind his back, Amelia. You saw. He cheated.'

Amelia bridled under Teddy's beseeching gaze, the reluctant referee of these childish pleasures. Her dad was in charge of blind man's buff in the lounge and Mum was organising pin the tail on the donkey.

'No, I never,' insisted Billy. 'I kept my hands behind my back. Tell him, sis.'

'He did,' confirmed Amelia, unable to look at Teddy.

Billy began to jump up and down, punching the air to celebrate his victory. Teddy ignored his friend's goading and stared at Amelia, struck dumb by the decision.

'It's not fair,' he croaked, when he could finally speak.

Billy threw the sopping towel at Teddy's head. '*It's not fair,*' he mimicked. 'Dry up and dry off, dumbo. It's *my* birthday, after all.' He marched off to the next game while Teddy pulled the towel limply across his hair, training his gaze on Amelia once more.

Silently he handed her the wet towel and shook his head. 'It's not fair,' he muttered, before turning to follow his crowing friend back into the house.

A blindfolded Edna Hibbert steadied herself after three dizzying turns. Equilibrium restored, the spindly legged girl took a hesitant step then paused to brush a strand of blond hair away from an ear to listen for clues. The other children looked at each other, barely containing their glee. Some held their breath, trying not to give away their position but the more attention-seeking made little noises to spin Edna in their direction then became giddy with excitement at the prospect of the limelight. The rustle of a child's clothing, a suppressed giggle, a chair moving – Edna's sightless head jerked round at every sound. Finally she took a decisive pace, hands exploring ahead, and came to a halt virtually standing on top of Charlotte Dilkes, cowering behind a chair, her tears over Billy forgotten in the thrill of the chase.

A second later, Edna pounced on the girl and pulled off her blindfold as Charlotte screamed. 'Got you.'

'You're it, Charlotte,' chuckled the portly Bert Stanforth, snapping on the big light and fiddling with his unlit pipe. Edna handed him the knotted blindfold to untie.

'What's that?' said Charlotte, pointing through the window at thick grey smoke and the orange glow of flames. She ran to the back door and into the back garden for a better view.

'Bonfire,' shrieked the diminutive Roger Rawlins, jumping up and down with delight. 'Bonfire, bonfire.'

Bert Stanforth ran out into the darkness, followed by Edna and the other blind man's buffers, while children arrived from the conservatory with wet hair, squealing and pointing at the flames, breathless in their exhilaration.

'Mother, the shed's on fire,' Stanforth shouted at his wife above the noise of the inferno as she arrived with more excited children. 'Ring the fire brigade.'

'It's too late, Bert,' retorted Ruth, the tea towel gripped tight around her hands.

Stanforth turned back to the towering flames just yards away. She was right. The blaze was out of control. The paint thinners were kept in the shed, a jerry can of petrol too. Mentally Stanforth stood down, stepping back and stretching out his arms to keep the goggle-eyed pack of excited children at a safe distance. Luckily the old shed stood on its own in the middle of the garden, away from the house. 'You're right, Mother. At least it's not likely to spread. Just keep everybody back.'

'I wonder how it started.'

Amelia came running up unnoticed by all except Francesca who was holding on to her father's trousers. Amelia's face looked hot and streaked as though she'd been crying. But this time Francesca decided not to risk her wrath and said nothing.

'What happened?' screeched Amelia over the roar and crackle of destruction.

Stanforth shrugged. 'I wish I knew, love.' He turned back to his wife, a look of confusion on his face. 'Have you left something in the oven, Mother?'

'No. Why?'

'I can smell roasting meat.'

'The oven's off, Bert.'

Stanforth processed the information before snapping his head back towards the flames, a look of horror on his face. 'Oh, my God . . .'

At the same time, Charlotte Dilkes looked away from the blaze, her eyes darting across the gallery of gleaming, excited faces, their eyes gorging, hypnotised by the flames as the shed hummed and spat.

'Where's Billy?' she wondered aloud.

Three

Monday, 23 December 1963

THE SUN WAS ABSENT FROM the leaden sky when DCI Samuel Bannon reached Kirk Langley ten minutes after setting off from his Derby home. He turned off the A52 on to Moor Lane and had no difficulty finding the scene. He pulled across to the kerb in his smart Jaguar and parked behind the line of police vehicles.

Before pulling the door handle, Bannon extracted a flask from his pocket and spun off the cap. With a furtive look round, he took a long swallow of the fiery liquid before returning the flask to his overcoat pocket. As a final act of courage, he kissed his fingers and then touched the grainy snap of his recently deceased wife taped to the dashboard.

The acrid smell of wood smoke and burnt chemicals greeted his nostrils as he stepped from the car and walked along the path to the house. Resisting eye contact, he nodded briefly at various uniformed officers standing around looking for something to do, while the crowd they were there to control slept in their warm beds. A couple of interested dog walkers had briefly watched proceedings from the lane but with nothing to see, they'd soon lost interest and drifted away to alert their neighbours.

Bannon walked round the house to the back garden, where there was more purposeful activity. He spotted Detective Constables Walter Laird and Graham Bell chatting to a fire brigade officer and automatically reached for his packet of Capstan Full Strength cigarettes, pausing to light one with a strong hand cupped around the match. DC Graham Bell nudged Laird who turned and, after muttering something unheard to his colleague, waved a greeting.

Bannon didn't need to hear the muttering to know the gist of what was said. *You shouldn't be here, boss. Not yet. Not until you're over it*. Instinctively he reached towards the flask of whisky in his overcoat but managed to stay his hand. Maybe they were right.

He approximated a return smile, the packet of cigarettes still in his hand. As Laird and Bell approached, he glanced across at the smouldering heap of blackened ash barely peeping above ground level. 'I hope you've not dragged me out of bed on a Sunday morning for an illegal bonfire, Wally.'

Laird's laugh was forced, a gesture of normality intended for every eye watching Bannon for signs of grief and turmoil. Laird could already smell the drink. His grieving boss hadn't yet recovered from the death of his wife while giving birth to their first child a couple of months before. There'd been complications; Bannon's wife had never made it out of theatre, never held her newborn daughter. To be honest, Laird wasn't sure if Bannon had either.

'Didn't expect you, boss,' said Laird amiably. 'Not with a new baby at home.'

Bannon's expression soured. 'My sister . . .' He waved a hand to explain away his neglect.

'How is little Rosie?' asked DC Bell.

As Bannon looked away, tight-lipped, Laird was able to fire a warning glance at Bell. *Too soon, Graham.*

'Oh, *she's* fine,' snapped Bannon.

Laird's eye drifted down towards the pack of cigarettes in Bannon's hand, spotting a chance to move away from awkward subjects. 'Can I borrow a gasper, boss? Mine are in my—'

'Other coat,' finished Bannon, happy to accept the offer of well-grooved banter. He tossed the brown pack at him. 'I don't know how you can afford so many coats on your take-home.'

A grinning Laird pulled out a cigarette and lit up. 'Funny.'

'So,' said Bannon, feeling the need to announce his participation. 'What have we got?' He struck out towards the blackened ground, Laird and Bell falling in step beside him and flicking open notebooks.

'William Stanforth burned to death in the garden shed. He was thirteen years old yesterday and they were throwing a birthday party for him.'

'Many happy returns,' said DC Bell.

Bannon flicked a contemptuous glance at Bell. 'Keep it down, soldier. What happened, Wally?'

'It seems Stanforth went missing some time in the late afternoon/ early evening and the alarm was raised when the shed caught fire,' said Laird. 'No one knew the lad was inside until it was too late.'

'No screaming?'

'Nobody heard it if there was.'

'How are the parents taking it?' said Bannon.

Laird shrugged his reply.

'Sorry, stupid question.' They arrived at the mound of saturated ashes being carefully probed by a man wearing a white coat, white overalls and a face mask. 'Where's the body?'

Laird's expression betrayed a glimmer of the horror witnessed. 'What's left of him has gone to the mortuary. They'll need to do tests. There were flammables stored in there – petrol, paint thinners. It was all over in minutes.'

'Tragic.'

'Tragic, yes,' said Laird, leading his superior to a canvas sheet. Spots of rain tapped out a rhythm on the canvas. 'Accidental? We don't think so.' The detective constable pointed at the mound of blackened, twisted metal on the ground. 'That's the hasp and the padlock.'

Bannon narrowed his eyes, inverting his salt and pepper eyebrows into a wishbone. The padlock was closed through the ring of the hasp. 'They're intact.'

'Exactly.'

'The kid was locked in from outside?'

'With a key. No sign of the key,' added Laird.

'So it was murder.'

'At least manslaughter, assuming the culprit is legally chargeable,' confirmed Laird. 'It was mostly kids at the party. Mr and Mrs Stanforth were the only adults. They were busy organising party games inside the house for the half-hour leading up to the fire. All the kids confirmed it.'

'You've already spoken to the children?' inquired Bannon, impressed, if a little put out. 'What did they say?'

Laird hesitated. 'Are you sure you wouldn't prefer to be at home with your daughter, boss? Graham and me can handle this.'

Bannon glared at him. 'What did they say?'

Laird shook his head. 'Nothing relevant. No fingers pointed. No confessions. They were enjoying the party and then they saw the flames. They thought it was a bonfire.'

'How many kids are we talking about?'

'Twenty.'

'And you've interviewed the lot?'

'We thought it best to speak to them all briefly while their memories were fresh.'

'And?'

'Like I said.'

'How hard did you go?' asked Bannon.

'Hard enough, boss. They're young. There were a lot of tears.'

'How young?'

'Apart from big sis, between eleven and thirteen. In fact, William and his twin, Francesca, were the oldest.'

'His twin?' said Bannon. 'So it was her party too.'

Laird shrugged. 'I guess so.'

'Where are they now?'

'I sent them all home,' said Laird, producing a list. 'They're all local to Kirk Langley and they were all exhausted. I can re-interview if need be.' Bannon caught his eye. 'We can,' Laird corrected.

Bannon nodded. 'So if *we* buy their collective testimony, the parents are in the clear.' He pondered for a moment. 'We'll need to dig deeper on that. Parents *do* kill their children.' He paused then added in barely a murmur, 'And vice versa.'

Laird flipped his notebook closed. 'And if we clear the Stanforths?'

Bannon shrugged. 'The best we can hope for is some drifter wandered past, lured Billy into the shed and torched him after doing God knows what.'

'Let's hope that's it,' said Laird. 'Kids shouldn't be killing kids.'

'Any of them seem wrong to you, Wally?'

'Wrong, boss?'

'Kids argue. Kids fight.' Bannon shrugged as though the rest was obvious.

'No one stood out,' answered Laird. 'And they mostly alibi each other.'

'Mostly?'

'One lad, the deceased's best friend, Edward Mullen, known as Teddy, was the only one alone when the fire started.'

'Where?'

'In the house. Or so he says.'

'Any reason to disbelieve him?' asked Bannon.

'Not from the reaction to his friend's death,' said Laird. 'He was beyond distraught, wailing and crying like a girl.'

'Guilty conscience maybe,' ventured Bannon.

'There was talk of an argument between them but it was pretty minor,' added Laird.

'It may seem minor to us,' commented Bannon. 'Look into it. Any other possibilities?' He sensed Laird had more to say and was keen to get to it.

'William Stanforth's older sister, Amelia. She's nearly sixteen, though why she'd kill her little brother, God alone knows.'

'Forget motive, Wally,' said Bannon. 'And you can ask God later. What about her alibi?'

'Also unclear. No one saw her until the fire had started.'

'Then she's a suspect.'

'She doesn't seem the type, boss.'

'There's a type now?' snapped Bannon. His expression softened at once. 'Sorry. It's been . . .' Bannon shook his head, unable to go on.

'Forget it, boss. You should go home.'

'I will,' nodded Bannon. 'But I want to be kept in the loop.' He eyed his detective constable. 'There's something else, isn't there?'

Laird affected reluctance before grinning. 'Amelia has a boyfriend,' he answered. 'Older.'

'Who?'

Laird smiled suddenly, savouring Bannon's coming reaction. 'We're in Kirk Langley, boss. And it's a small place.'

Bannon stared at his colleague for a moment before realisation started to work on his face. 'Not young McCleary?'

Laird grinned again. 'The very same. *And* he was seen by neighbours standing in the lane before the fire. Apparently he was supposed to be meeting Amelia last evening but she was busy at the party and stood him up.'

'Which might make someone like him angry,' reasoned Bannon.

'Maybe even vengeful,' added Laird.

Bannon smiled for the first time. 'I suppose with a father like Malcolm, it was only a matter of time before young Brendan stepped up to the big leagues. Pick him up.'

Malcolm McCleary staggered into the kitchen in his stained long johns, running a hand through his unkempt, greying hair. Barefoot, he was forced to avoid the discarded beer bottles on the sticky floor before slumping on to a chair at the flimsy dining table. The surface was covered in dirty plates and full ashtrays and McCleary poked through the remains of discarded butts for enough stray tobacco to fill a cigarette paper. While doing this he raised a bleary eye towards his son lying on the too-small couch, puffing away on his own roll-up.

'Give me a cigarette,' ordered McCleary senior.

'I got mine where you're getting yours,' said Brendan, with barely concealed disdain.

McCleary senior's grizzled features were deformed by hate. 'You cheap little bleeder. Can't even buy some gaspers for your old man after all I've done for you? What about breakfast?'

Brendan shook his head slowly, avoiding eye contact. 'Parlour's empty.'

'You ate those two eggs I was saving?' replied an exasperated McCleary.

'You had them for your tea last night.'

McCleary senior narrowed his eyes in disbelief. 'I don't remember that.'

Brendan raised a sarcastic eyebrow. *That's not surprising.*

McCleary caught the scorn, adding quietly, 'Not hungry anyway.' He continued to root around amongst the dead cigarette butts, emptying singed, stale tobacco on to his rolling paper. 'Get me a cup of tea.'

'There's a fresh pot on the side,' answered Brendan, concentrating on reviving his own dormant roll-up.

McCleary's weasel eyes flicked around the debris on the table, before alighting on a teaspoon. He flung it at his son, hitting him on the top of his head and producing a cry more of shock than pain. The spoon glanced off and plopped into the ash-filled grate of a dead coal fire. 'Then get off your arse and pour me some, you ungrateful little sod.'

Brendan hauled himself off the sofa and poured tea, ignoring the beady eye trained on him. He plonked it sullenly down on the Formica table and tried to withdraw but the old man grabbed him by the wrist with a powerful hand and stood up to swing his other fist at the side of Brendan's head.

Caught flush on the ear, Brendan staggered back against the gas cooker, dislodging several used pots and pans standing dirty on the hob. Trying his utmost to avoid showing the pain, he gathered himself, keeping his eyes glued to his father, and retreated to the safety of the couch.

'Of all the bloody nerve,' muttered an aggrieved McCleary, sitting back down to take a noisy swig of tea. 'Kids these days don't know they're born. No wonder that whore of a mother didn't take you with her.'

'She's not a whore!' screamed Brendan, jumping to stand square on to his father.

McCleary slammed his chair back with unexpected vigour, sloshing some of his tea on the table. He made no further move, instead raising an arm, his hand stiff and straight. 'Talk back to me again and there's more where that came from, my lad,' he shouted, glancing at the back of his hand.

Brendan glared with hate-filled eyes but said nothing, his chest heaving as he tried to control his rage.

'Didn't think so.' McCleary sat down again, a sneer contorting the stubble on his sagging, wrinkled face. He pulled open a drawer of the table and took out a half bottle of Navy rum. Removing the cork, he poured a large measure into his tea without taking his amused eyes from his son glaring back at him. 'That's right,' he said quietly. 'You keep thinking it, son. One day your old man will be too old and you'll be too big and then . . .' his laugh was more of a snarl. 'That day's a long way off, you little guttersnipe, and don't you forget it while you're under my roof.'

'Not as far off as you think,' mumbled Brendan.

'What you say?'

'I said it's not your roof unless you pay the rent.'

'And that's my fault, is it? The Social can't get their bleeding act together and I'm to blame.' McCleary sneered again with unconcealed violence but then his expression softened into pleasure and he sought the right words. 'You see that ripe little virgin last night then?'

'Don't talk about her,' muttered Brendan.

'Who? That stuck-up Stanforth girl with the juicy little knockers?' McCleary chuckled.

'I said don't talk about her.'

'When you bringing her round here to meet your old man?' leered McCleary.

'Never. I threw her over, see.'

'You mean she ditched you 'cos you didn't know what to do with it.' McCleary grinned, and finally managed to ignite his patchwork cigarette. 'Shame. I could have taught you a thing or two about how to handle those cock-teasing little whores. Maybe even break her in for you, you ask nicely.' He stuck out his tongue at an invisible ice cream and laughed as Brendan jumped from the couch and ran to grip the other side of the table, his knuckles white with the effort, face red with anger.

'You disgusting old bastard,' he screamed. '*Teach me something?* You couldn't break wind without sleeping it off for half a day, never mind telling me what to do with a bird.' He thrust a finger in McCleary's face. 'And that's why Mum left.'

'You bleeding little . . .'

McCleary made a grab for his son, but Brendan yanked his arm out of reach and headed for the front door, pulling his coat from a chair as he opened it.

'One day I'll do for you, old man,' he screamed then jumped back in shock at the burly figure filling the doorway.

'Going somewhere, Brendan?' inquired a smiling DC Laird.

Four

31 October 2011 – Normanton, a suburb of Derby

THE TWO LIGHTLY BUILT HOODED figures pelted along the wet pavements for all they were worth, a free hand holding up their tracksuit bottoms, usually slung halfway down their hips. After rounding a bend, they slithered to a halt behind a privet hedge, and crouched down out of sight of imagined pursuers. Both boys flipped back their hoods and dropped their hands to their knees to suck in much needed oxygen.

Scott Wheeler grinned from ear to ear, looking up at his friend, Joshua Stapleton, for approval. 'Well sick, bruv.' His grin tempered when he saw doubt on his friend's face. He managed to pant another inquiry. 'S'up, bruv?'

'What's up,' panted Josh in return, 'is people could get hurt.'

'Naw,' scoffed Scott. 'It's just a bit of fun. Anyway, what do we care? It's not like we know 'em. They can die, far as I'm concerned,' he continued, hardening his heart to emotions that would weaken him. 'Shit, Josh. We're under age, I told you. We can do what we want. Remember Boffo, from my brother's crew? He reckons Five-o can't touch us 'cos we're too young to know what we're doing. All they can do is tell us off and let us go.'

'Is that why we're wild? Proving you a G so you can hook up with Cal's crew?' said Josh. 'DBI, bruv.'

'Don't beg it?' said Scott, affronted. 'What you chattin'?'

'You said it, Scoot,' panted Josh. 'We're just kids. Don't try too hard. Let it come to you. Ain't no good to your bro's crew, 'cept they want someone to hold for 'em.'

'What's wrong with that?' argued Scott. 'That's how you start. The Gs can't hold 'cos they're too old. That's what gets us in.'

'Mug's game,' said Josh. 'All you get is a rap sheet and your ass RO-ed for a year.'

'They can stick their referral orders up their fucking arses,' spat Scott. 'When you got a crew that's got your back, that's respeck, man. Proper respeck.'

'You mean people we know shit bricks when they see us,' retorted Josh. 'That's called fear, bruv.'

'Bring it on, yo,' drawled Scott, throwing his arms in front of him like his *best* rapper, 50 Cent, two imaginary guns held across his chest.

'Yeah, great, but what if someone saw us tricking that guy up?' said Josh, nodding back down the street. 'And he died.'

'So what?' snarled Scott. 'Din't you hear me? We get a free pass.' He shrugged. 'Sides, any stiff who clocks us gets a visit from our fam. They soon forget they seen us, you hear what I'm sayin'.'

'I hear,' replied Josh, looking no happier. He glanced up at the steady drizzle falling from the gunmetal sky. 'Look, Scoot. It's freezing . . .'

'I fucking knew it,' howled Scott. 'Yer bailing on me.'

'Quit dekin' me out.'

'It's trick or treat, man,' wailed Scott.

'Yeah, it is,' agreed Josh. 'And you know what? We're only supposed to kick over bins and bang on windows. Give 'em a scare, is all.'

'A scare? What you chattin', pussy?' snarled Scott. 'These fuckers get plenty of warning. If you don't get us no sweets, there's rules. Everyone knows. No treat means a trick, right?'

'There's a limit.'

'A limit?' snarled Scott. 'Why you talking gay? No limits, remember. Like Cal.'

'Cal's in Juvey for two years,' pointed out Josh.

'So what? He's a big man. He got his rep an' he gets respeck.'

Josh smiled. 'Which *big man* you know gets told when to take a piss and hit the sack?'

Scott's expression darkened. 'Well, no one tells me what I can and can't do,' he shouted. 'Anyone gets up in my grille, got a serious beef comin'. That's what No Limits means or have you blanked it?'

Josh glanced briefly at Scott. No, he remembered all right – he still had the scar on his palm where the pair had cut themselves to allow their blood to mingle. He'd told his dad he'd cut it taking a header off his skateboard. *Weren't no biggie, Dad.* And Scott was right. They'd both pledged. *Blood brothers. No limits.* Josh hadn't known what it meant until tonight, until Scott had looked at him with those cold blue eyes and told him what they were gonna do, like it was stealing sweets from the Paki shop. But it weren't. Somebody could die and then what? Is that what Scott wanted? Take a life then strut round Juvey with a gangsta's rep?

Josh looked down now at the scar on his cupped hand.

'You deaf as well as gay?' shouted Scott.

Josh decided against an answer. He kept his eyes to the ground and shrugged. Over the last few weeks, he'd realised his best mate had changed. Worse, his short fuse had got shorter since scoring that skunk. Now the flex was all wrong. They weren't mates no more. Scott made the running and he didn't expect no backchat.

'I said, are you deaf as well as gay?' repeated Scott, bristling with aggression. Josh couldn't meet his eye and Scott was pleased. Eyes down meant he was top dog and Josh knew it. 'How many fags you got left?' he demanded coldly.

'Couple,' mumbled Josh.

'Gimme one,' ordered Scott, waggling a hand as a hurry-up.

Josh stared at his friend. Yeah, he was different. Taking it all too serious.

'*You're just kids, Joshua,*' his dad had always told him. '*Have a childhood.*' Josh had feigned ignorance but the point had hit home.

He would have reached it by himself anyway. All this gang stuff was for kids. Unless you *wanted* to be a criminal the rest of your life, getting out was part of growing up.

He fumbled in the pocket of his hoodie and slapped the packet into Scott's hand. 'You have 'em both, bruv. I'm gettin' back to my block.'

He hunched himself against the cold and set off along Carlton Road towards Whitaker Road.

'You can't,' Scott shouted after him.

'Watch me,' said Josh over his shoulder.

'It's trick or treat,' pleaded Scott.

'It's also pissing down.' Josh gave reason one last try. 'There's no one about, Scoot. What's the point?'

'It's me and you, bruv. That's the point.'

Josh walked away.

'Don't turn your back on me,' screamed Scott. 'I'm connected.' No response from the retreating Josh. Scott played his last card, his voice rising to a whine. 'Your dad said we had to stick together, remember?'

Josh turned, steam rising from him. 'Then come with me. Let's go mine, have a pizza and play MW3.'

Scott hesitated. He *was* wet. Cold too. And pizza sounded good. But there was a principle involved. They had a pass to do whatever they wanted and his pussy mate wanted to go home to Mummy. Decision made, his young face deformed into a scowl. 'You're a faggot, Stapleton. We still got shit to do. Text your dad you're staying mine or we never speak again.' No response. 'Fucking omerta, man.'

Josh hesitated. Scott was his friend. They'd taken an oath. Omerta was right. He'd taught Scott the word. Found it on Wiki. He stood to attention and gave Scott their special salute, the one they'd copied off a game on Xbox. 'Laters.'

'Pussy,' spat Scott at Josh's retreating frame. He looked up into the night sky at the rain now falling harder in the sulphurous glow of the street lights. 'It's always down to me,' he shouted. 'I'm the leader.' He pulled out a cigarette and lit the end, pulling in such a long belt of smoke that it burned his throat. He wanted to shout something more cutting while Josh was in range but thought he might start coughing like a girl, so he settled for a V sign towards his friend, now splashing into the distance.

Can't count on nobody, even blood. 'Always down to me.'

The man watched the two boys from the cover of an overgrown garden. 'Scoot,' he repeated with soft relish, not sure he'd heard the name right in the din of the rain. He looked back to the pair. Scoot's friend had given him an odd salute and was stomping away, shoulders hunched, hood yanked back over his head. The man raised his right arm to ape the salute, still watching.

They'd argued, he was sure, because Scoot stayed behind, shouting something at the other boy which the man couldn't pick up above the noise of the strengthening deluge rat-tat-tatting on his canvas poncho. He was tempted to lower his own hood to try and catch the gist but the dialogue was clearly over and the other boy was nearly invisible in the downpour.

He watched as Scoot continued to shout insults which his disappearing friend ignored as he walked away without a backward glance. A smile began to broaden around the man's mouth. Two boys – the right age, the right profile. They'd argued and now each was alone in the dark and deserted streets.

'Perfect,' breathed the man. He kept his gaze on Scoot, taller and more powerful than his absent friend. He was smoking a cigarette like he'd been on sixty a day for years then started posing, arms crossed, fingers splayed into gun shapes. A fit of coughing curtailed the posturing.

'Didn't your parents ever tell you smoking is bad for your health?' The man smiled faintly in the darkness, not taking his eyes from the prize, almost sniffing the air like a wolf on the scent of a deer. 'Course not. They only told you how special you were. And one day you actually started to believe it. Now no one can tell you what to do because you think you're a man.'

The man looked around for hurrying pedestrians or hardy dog walkers on the way to Normanton Park. There was no one. Cars were all dormant, curtains all drawn against the elements.

'Perfect.'

Ahead of him, Scott threw his butt into the road and marched away in the same direction as his absent friend. The man heard the boy utter a single word, 'Omerta,' then stepped softly out of the shadows.

Five

3 November 2011 – Normanton

DETECTIVE SERGEANT JOHN NOBLE TOOK another long look at the pale corpse of the boy, his shattered head at right angles to a torso that lay twisted on the rubble-strewn ground. The dust and grime of the concrete base had partially absorbed the black puddle of old blood lying like a halo around his head. For the first time, Noble managed to bypass the boy's milky eyes that seemed to glare back at him, rebuking the voyeur in him.

Getting down on his knees, Noble gazed at the jagged edge of another injury in the midriff where the boy had landed on something sharp. Without rolling the body on to its back, it was impossible to tell what had gouged the long gash across his stomach. But whatever had corrupted the integrity of the boy's stomach had allowed the merest peep of viscera to push against the lips of the lesion.

Noble couldn't look directly at the youngster's slim, smooth legs and bared buttocks, naked below the waist, his tracksuit bottoms pulled down to his ankles and bunched against his stockinged feet. *God alone knows what the boy's been through.*

Far from heaven though he was this night, Noble was confident he could fill in the blanks although he took temporary comfort from the lack of visible bruising around the anus.

'Where are your shoes, son?' Noble mumbled, righting himself, hand twitching in his ache for a chemical friend. He took out a cigarette from beneath his protective layers and, without lighting up, jammed it behind his ear to let the virgin tobacco's earthy aroma promise future comfort.

Like lightning striking, the flash of the camera heightened the drama of the desolate tableau as scene of crime officers went about their grisly work. Noble stepped back for the bigger picture as DI Brook had taught him. It didn't matter. Whichever way he faced, his eye returned to the boy.

Some mother's son. So young. So dead. And no balm to pour on parental wounds, no comfort to take from a quick and painless death. This poor kid had died in humiliation and distress over the course of many hours – maybe days – the story of his final moments evidenced by the tear tracks on the undamaged side of his face as the cries for help went unheeded. In this grim place the boy had died in agony, able to feel his young life ebbing away before it had really begun.

Noble nuzzled the cigarette, shaking off an image of the young man pleading in vain for his mummy. He stared at the first-floor landing to plot the body's trajectory, the handrail long since torn down and used for fuel by squatters and other indigents. Judging by the distance of the corpse from the top of the stairs, the boy hadn't merely fallen or stumbled. He had been thrown, launched even, from the upper storey to where he still lay, immobilised by a broken neck and maybe a collarbone and pelvis too.

Emerging from his detection bubble, Noble turned away, becoming aware of others waiting for him to finish.

'Let me know if you find the kid's shoes,' he said, gesturing to the nearest SOCO to commence the bagging and tagging before stepping outside on to Whitaker Road, fingering the cigarette with more urgency. He smiled briefly as he imagined Brook standing next to him, darting a glance first at the cigarette, then up at his face until he cracked and offered his DI the pack. But Brook's comforting presence was missing and, until DI Ford managed to drag himself out of bed, Noble was on his own.

Far enough from the scene, he lit up with a deep sigh as he watched uniformed officers setting up the crime scene tape around the large plot of scrubland, while others stood around their flashing vehicles, waiting in vain to control a non-existent crowd, not yet awake to the drama in their midst at three in the morning.

A black Mercedes drew to a halt behind the line of emergency vehicles and Dr Higginbottom, the duty police surgeon, already decked head to toe in protective coveralls, stepped from the vehicle. After a brief reconnoitre he made for Noble at the front of the derelict building.

'Sergeant,' said Higginbottom. The doctor's eyes looked tired from lack of sleep despite the wind and rain trying to rouse him.

'Doc. Through the entrance then second door on the right,' said Noble. 'Follow the lights.'

Higginbottom glanced at Noble's cigarette. 'Next time you see me in the mortuary, remind me to show you a smoker's lungs.'

'Look forward to it.'

'Are you the lead?' asked Higginbottom, with little semblance of interest in Noble's reply.

Noble shook his head. 'DI Ford.'

'Brook still on leave, is he?'

Noble's smile made a reply unnecessary.

'Is DI Ford with the body?' asked Higginbottom mischievously.

'No. He's . . . been delayed,' muttered Noble.

Higginbottom affected surprise. 'Really?' With a sly grin, the doctor moved towards the building. 'Must be traffic,' he said, before taking his leave.

Noble's minute grunt of appreciation was barely audible. The doctor must know Ford lived less than half a mile away, barely across the ring road in upmarket Littleover. He'd been alerted two hours ago and could have walked to the scene in fifteen minutes.

Noble pulled his coat tighter against the cold and drew on his cigarette again, his frozen hands struggling to obey. Then he walked a few paces back towards the house to check Higginbottom had found his way. Keith Pullin, an emergency worker wearing a bright orange bib, was coming in the opposite direction.

'Got a spare, John?' he asked, sidling over to Noble.

Noble inhaled and looked at him, wondering whether to unfurl the banter he'd imagined with Brook a moment ago. Instead he shook out a cigarette and soon Pullin was blowing his own smoke rings into the damp night air.

'Lucky break, eh?' said Pullin. Noble raised an inquiring eyebrow. Pullin nodded over to the response car where two uniformed constables, Jacques and Penrose, had finally cajoled their near-comatose handcuffed prisoner into the back seat of the squad car. 'Beavis and Butthead putting the collar on Rasputin over there,' he added by way of explanation. 'They found the boy's underpants on the mattress where the perv was sleeping. Torn to shreds.'

'Torn or cut?' asked Noble.

'Does it matter?'

Noble pulled a face at Pullin. He could almost hear Brook pontificating. *Everything matters until it doesn't, John.* 'It matters.'

'Well, I wouldn't put it in the report before the lab gets them but I'd say they were cut off,' conceded Pullin.

'And did you find a blade?'

'Not yet,' replied Pullin.

Noble set off for the patrol car to talk to Jacques and Penrose. When the two PCs had closed the door on the wild-haired vagrant, he'd promptly lost consciousness, his head lolling against the steaming window, oblivious to his surroundings. Neither officer made to get in the front of the car, instead walking towards Noble, eyeing his cigarette.

'He say anything?'

'Nothing intelligible, Sarge,' said Penrose. 'He's out of it.'

'There was gauze and blackened bottles all over his doss,' continued Penrose. 'Needles too.'

'Not surprising,' added Jacques. 'They'll take whatever they can get their hands on, this lot.'

'Don't generalise,' said Noble to the surprise of all three of them. 'We don't know for sure it's his gear,' he added in an attempt to mollify.

'Well, he stinks of paraffin too,' added Penrose, somewhat miffed to have his street smarts questioned.

'And we couldn't see any mixers,' chipped in Jacques, sniggering.

'At least it covers the stench of shit coming off him.' Penrose and Jacques now sniggered in harmony.

Beavis and Butthead was right. 'What about a knife or a blade?' asked Noble. 'Is he carrying?'

'Don't think so, Sarge.'

'Should we wait for the van?' asked Penrose.

Noble's eyebrow headed north. 'Why? You put a sheet down, didn't you?'

'Yeah, but he stinks like a fresh cowpat,' complained Jacques.

'Then get him to the station sharpish and get a tech to process him. We want clothes, fingernails, DNA, the lot. And assuming he's not carrying a passport and credit cards, get him printed so we can get an ID. Do you two know the routine or do I need to write it down for you?'

'Yes, Sarge,' said the pair in unison, dragging themselves back to their vehicle like naughty schoolboys.

'And do a thorough search for a blade,' Noble shouted after them.

A yell from the house and Pullin waved an evidence bag at Noble. Before the squad car could leave, Noble held up a hand to prevent departure. 'Hang on.' He jogged back to the gutted building.

'They found the boy's trainers under a coat in an old shopping trolley,' said Pullin. 'Same room as Rasputin's mattress,' he added significantly.

Noble took possession and darted back to the squad car. 'Open the back door,' he said to Penrose. When the locks clicked, Noble opened the door and, kneeling, leaned into the vehicle, to hold the trainers against the vagrant's feet. Noble puckered up his nose at the smell coming off the virtually rotted boots on the suspect's left foot. He could even see the blackened flesh of a heel visible where the sole hung off.

A second later, Noble slammed the door on the bewildered prisoner, banging on the roof for the patrol car to pull away. He returned to Pullin, examining the smart trainers through the bag.

'Yeah, lucky break,' muttered Noble.

'Not for the kid obviously, poor bastard,' said Pullin. 'Fancy having that hanging out of your backside . . .'

'We don't know for certain he was raped, Keith.' Noble took out another cigarette to avoid another conversation about making assumptions.

'You saw the body,' said Pullin. 'Time was,' he continued, drawing closer as though imparting some great secret, 'when a kiddie was raped and murdered, your lot took whoever done it on a little detour and kicked the living shit out of him. After he got sent down he'd have his card marked for the screws and his fellow inmates to keep up the good work.'

'Happy days, eh?' replied Noble tersely.

'Not any more,' bemoaned Pullin, missing the sarcasm. 'Now these perverts get three squares a day, soft loo paper and a thirty-two-inch TV for their romper room. Where's the justice?'

Noble couldn't think of a suitable answer so he gave voice to his own thoughts. 'The training shoes were a size nine.'

'So?'

'The suspect's feet looked the same, maybe slightly smaller,' continued Noble. He shrugged as though the rest was obvious.

'Then he must have raped and killed the lad and nicked the shoes for himself – fucking obvious.'

Unexpectedly, Noble found himself wincing at Pullin's profanity. 'You saw the state of his boots?'

'Yes,' replied Pullin, as though spelling it out for a child. 'That's why he took the trainers.'

'Then why didn't he put them on?' demanded Noble, using the same patronising tone.

Pullin was quiet for a moment. 'Maybe he was too out of it.'

'But not too out of it to hide them,' rejoined Noble.

Pullin thought it through. 'You got me there.' After finishing his cigarette, he marched off to gather his team.

A Volvo pulled up to the rear of the convoy and Detective Inspector Frank Ford hauled himself out. A tall man, with thinning grey hair, pinched mean features and a slight stoop, Ford ducked under the tape and ambled over to Noble, a sour expression distorting his face.

'Couldn't this wait till morning, Johnny?'

'Sorry, sir,' Noble replied. 'But you're on call.'

'Well, it better be worth it.'

'It's a dead child, sir,' Noble explained. 'Didn't I say?'

Ford tried to look interested and made his way into the building, picking his way delicately around the detritus common to the floors of all derelict houses.

Noble followed, his heart sinking. He didn't know DI Ford that well, except that he was two years away from retirement and didn't seem overly keen to put himself out. In fact, on the phone, Ford had asked more than once whether his presence at the scene was required.

After a quick inspection, Ford and Noble watched Higginbottom finish up then followed him back to the fresh air.

'Well?' said Ford.

'The boy's been dead two or three days, I'd suggest. Poor chap. Can't be much more than twelve or thirteen . . .'

'Was he raped?' inquired Ford. Noble shot the doctor a tired glance, fairly certain the question was unanswerable at this stage.

Higginbottom smiled patiently. 'We can't determine that here, Inspector. His trousers were pulled down and his underpants are missing, yes—'

'They were cut off and found on an old mattress in the room above,' chipped in Noble.

'Raped then,' said Ford with a kind of grim satisfaction.

Higginbottom caught Noble's eye. 'Like I said, we'll know soon enough. SOCO are bagging hands and feet, and swabbing for other trace,' he said, 'but we'll have to wait for the autopsy. As for CoD,

I can say that the boy's neck is broken and the right side of his face and body are crushed. Lividity shows he died where he fell though I'm fairly certain he didn't die instantly. There was some limited movement around the landing site. He has internal bleeding and would have choked on his own blood. Eventually. Might have taken twelve hours for the poor lad to go. Maybe longer.'

'So what are we thinking?' asked Ford, looking at Noble.

'We think there was a struggle upstairs and the perpetrator, possibly a vagrant, threw the boy off the upper floor to the ground below.'

'Vagrant?'

'On his way to processing,' said Noble.

Ford nodded with satisfaction. 'And the lad couldn't have fallen accidentally?'

'His body is some distance from the first-floor landing,' said Noble. 'If he'd fallen he would have been closer to the wall. There's no banister. It wouldn't have been difficult.'

'I see,' nodded Ford. 'Can we rule out suicide?'

'Suicide?' exclaimed Noble.

'Maybe the kid threw himself off after being raped,' answered Ford. 'Couldn't stand the shame of it.'

Noble managed to hide his surprise. 'I don't think so, sir.'

'But we can't rule it out,' Ford persisted.

'Child suicide is still rare,' observed Noble. 'But when kids do top themselves, they try and do it quickly and painlessly. Hanging and pills are favourites. And if hiding his shame was the reason, don't you think the lad would have pulled his tracksuit back up?'

Ford grunted in agreement.

'Noble's right,' said Higginbottom. 'And people rarely dive to their deaths head first. It's always feet first and from a greater height.' He excused himself, promising his report at the earliest opportunity and headed for the entrance. Members of the SOCO unit swarmed back towards the body.

'This vagrant was living in the house?' inquired Ford.

'Looks like it.'

'Sounds like our perp.'

Noble stifled a smile, remembering Brook's stock reply to anyone who referred to a *perp* in his presence. *Have you got indigestion?*

'Pity you didn't tell me you'd made an arrest before I dragged myself from a warm bed,' grumbled Ford. 'On his way, you say?'

'A few minutes ago.'

'Also a pity,' replied Ford.

'Sir?'

Ford looked Noble up and down, sizing him up. 'You got kids, Sergeant?'

'No, sir.'

'I've got two boys. Grown up, thank God.'

'Very nice for you, sir,' said Noble in a monotone. He knew a retread of Keith Pullin's sentiments was on its way.

'And this is every parent's nightmare,' continued Ford, gesturing back towards the house.

Noble didn't know how to react to what was hardly news, even for a single man. 'Of course.'

'And when some homeless paedo pulls a kiddie off the streets and does that . . .' Ford nodded back towards the corpse. 'Probably a blessing he did kill him after that.'

Noble's answering smile was thin-lipped. *Tell that to his parents.*

'Do we have an ID?'

'We've got a likely victim from Missing Persons,' answered Noble. 'Joshua Stapleton, local lad, twelve years of age. He was out trick or treating with a friend three nights ago . . .'

'Halloween,' exclaimed Ford shaking his head. 'I might have guessed. All those kids wandering around on their own. It's a fucking finger buffet for these creeps. When will parents learn? Go on.'

'Joshua didn't return home that night and his parents thought he'd slept over at his friend's but when they rang the next morning he wasn't there. Dad reported him missing the same day. According to Joshua's friend,' Noble referred to his notebook, 'Scott Wheeler, they were supposed to stay together but obviously that didn't happen. Scott said they separated not far from here and he last saw

Joshua walking along Carlton Road in this direction. That would be around nine-thirty p.m. on the thirty-first.'

'No one else saw him?'

'Cold night, sir.'

'And so uniform finally got off their arses and had a poke around here,' finished Ford. 'Well, at least it's a clean result.'

'Clean? Sir, it's a little early—'

'What condition was that down-and-out?' demanded Ford, glancing surreptitiously towards his car.

'Not good. It'll be a while before we get any sense out of him.'

'Mmmm,' grunted Ford. 'I might as well be off then.' He yawned. 'We can put the seal on this first thing tomorrow.' Noble didn't answer and Ford stole a glance at him. 'Pity you didn't keep hold of the bastard. We could have tuned him up a little. Got what we needed.'

'Sir, if he's our killer, there's going to be trace all over him.'

Ford looked down his nose at Noble. 'But it wouldn't have hurt to take him somewhere and give him a good hiding.'

'It might have hurt our case,' replied Noble.

'That's a dead child in there, Johnny. That bastard deserves more than to spend the rest of his days being fed and housed by the state. And I'm sure we could have found a few caring fathers to lend you a hand.'

'No doubt.' Ford made to leave but was halted by Noble's voice. 'Just for future reference, if I had organised a *tune-up* for the suspect and he'd died as a result, should I have assumed our conversation never took place and shoulder the responsibility myself? Sir.'

Ford turned to sneer at Noble. 'You know, Johnny, you sound more like that cunt Brook every day.'

Noble smiled frostily. 'Thank you, sir.'

Six

'HAPPY BIRTHDAY, CHELSEA,' SHOUTED ADAM Kramer, above the hubbub of his classmates, as Chelsea Chaplin blew out the thirteen candles on her cake amidst a round of cheering and whooping. 'That's thirteen snogs you owe me, girlfriend,' he added, to general laughter from the assembled children. Chelsea's mum suspended her photographic duties to glare at him, her party grin fading for a moment.

When Mrs Chaplin resumed her task, Adam put a hand to his mouth and muttered to his friend standing slightly behind him, 'Bet Chelsea could pull my train all night long, know what I'm sayin', blood.' He giggled suggestively. 'Choo choo.'

Behind Adam, Scott Wheeler was the only one among the throng of Chelsea's schoolmates not smiling or laughing. Cherubic of face, he whispered sourly in his friend's ear, 'Like she'd look twice at a spongebob like you.'

Oblivious to the insult, Adam ploughed on. He glanced sideways at his friend and winked suggestively. 'As for Chelsea's mum,' he continued, gesturing at Mrs Chaplin's tight red blouse, 'she's one sick MILF.' He turned to leer at Scott and stuck out his tongue, mock-panting like a dog. 'I'd tit-fuck her any day.'

'You mean, you would if you had a dick,' replied Scott, refusing to look at him.

'Fuck off!' mouthed Adam. 'I don't get no complaints.'

'That's because you're a virgin,' sneered Scott. 'The only pussy you ever seen was down Cats Protection.'

Adam cast around for a sassy comeback but it wouldn't come and, unable to dispute the facts, he had to take it on the chin. *Dread. Scoot was bang on. There'd been plenty of tit squeeze and the occasional fish finger but nothing worth sexting about.* Defeated, he glanced at Scott's impassive features. 'Why you being dread, man?'

Scott made brief eye contact with his friend for the first time. 'Like you don't know.'

'I know it's not the best party evs but we can still have a blast,' muttered Adam, looking round furtively. When certain he was unobserved, he pulled a small Pepsi bottle from his pocket and eagle-eyed Scott to look. 'Got some vodka into my Coke when Mum wasn't watching.' He sniffed self-importantly. 'Let's me and you take a trip to the coat room and get wrecked.'

Scott stared at him, coming to a decision. A second later he beckoned Adam to lead the way and followed, looking around to see they weren't being observed.

'Don't hog the lot, bitch,' complained Adam.

Scott took another pull on the vodka and Coke and handed it back to his friend sitting on the bed. He walked to the window and looked down the two storeys to the dark garden below. He turned back to Adam, his expression severe. 'I know it was you, Ade. Couldn't be no one else.'

'Me what?' retorted Adam, grinning.

'Play dumb if you like,' growled Scott, pulling a Stanley knife from his pocket. As he advanced towards the bed, he slipped his thumb along the stock to expose the blade. 'You know what I'm on about. Following me around.' He pressed his face close to Adam. 'And other stuff.'

Adam paused in mid-drink, his eyes glued to the blade. 'Are you joking me?'

'I look like I'm joking you?' retorted Scott.

Adam shifted uncomfortably as the blade was held in front of his eyes. His voice began to tremble. 'Scooter, I don't know what you're chatting. Swear down.'

Scott gazed at Adam's drained face, the first doubt softening his own expression. A moment later, he lowered the blade. 'You didn't send me no note?'

'A note?' said Adam, blowing out a breath in relief. 'Why would I send you a note when I can BBM you? Old people send notes, you div.'

Scott's eyes dropped to the floor. Fear and confusion invaded his features. He returned to look out of the window, face hidden from his friend. Couldn't show fear to his mate. Fear was death. Fear was for victims. Scott Wheeler was a G.

'Someone sent me a note,' breathed Scott on to the glass. When Adam didn't react he continued, 'Pretending to be Josh.'

'Josh. You mean Josh Stapleton?' exclaimed Adam. 'He's dead, Scoot.'

Now Scott gurned back at his friend and threw his arms in the air. 'Think I'm a mong? I know he's dead, shithead. That's what I'm on about. Someone's fucking with me and whoever's sending me notes knows he's dead and it's not fucking funny.'

Adam stood up in case Scott lost his cool and produced the Stanley knife again. 'Chill, man. I'm your bredrin.' When Scott seemed calmer he asked, 'What did the note say?'

Scott exhaled. 'Saying it was Josh, asking me to meet him.'

'Where?'

'I'm not sure,' he said with a covert glance towards Adam, unable to meet his eyes.

'Anything else?'

Scott took a deep breath. 'Josh said I should be careful because he wants me next.'

'Who wants you next? You mean that tramp what merked Josh?'

'Maybe. Dunno. It just said I'm next.'

'But that don't make no sense. The feds caught the skell and banged him up. How can he be after you?'

Scott shook his head. 'Dunno.'

'The note, where is it?'

'Home. Why?'

'Maybe we can trace the handwriting like they do in *Criminal Minds?*'

'OMG – stop being a div. We're kids, you knob. 'Sides, it weren't written by hand. It were bits of newspaper stuck together.'

Adam's mouth fell open. 'Just like in the movies. Creepy.'

Scott turned back to the window, 'Creepy if you're a girl.' He stared blankly at the Stygian gloom below, only a rectangle of light falling on one corner of the overgrown lawn, itself corrupted by the moving silhouettes of partygoers, dancing to some gay music. Poker Face.

A movement caught Scott's eye and his head turned like a frightened bird. A figure in a hoodie stepped out of the bushes and stood in the shadow of the largest tree. The fat lettering across the chest reading LEGEND, the baggy tracksuit held up by the thighs and the white trainers all caught the eye in the millisecond it took to process the information.

'Josh!' exclaimed Scott, gripping the sash window as though trying to pull his face through the glass for a closer look. Though hidden in the shadow of the hood, Scott felt certain the figure was looking up at him. When the figure raised an arm to touch one finger against his head, Scott turned, ashen-faced, to Adam and let out a whimper. *Our salute.*

'What you say, Scoot?'

Scott turned back to the window, his legs buckling, his fingers gripping the frame to stay upright. The figure had gone.

Adam moved towards Scott who was mumbling incoherently. He peered down over Scott's shoulder to the garden.

'What is it? What did you see?'

Scott gathered himself and wrestled his way past Adam, brandishing his Stanley knife again. He hurtled out of the room and down the stairs.

'Scoot!' shouted Adam. He ran to look out of the window again but, seeing nothing, followed his friend down the stairs at a safer lick. 'Scoot! Wait up.'

Seven

DETECTIVE INSPECTOR DAMEN BROOK WOKE from a familiar dream with a violent shudder. After running his hands over his face, he sat up to get his bearings, staring at the splayed palm of his right hand. Unlike Lady Macbeth he was unable to find any blood and after a moment's contemplation, Brook let his hand fall.

It was gone midnight. The TV was on and the trailer for the DVD was playing over and over. He felt for the warm remote under his body and switched off both machines.

He picked up the empty case for *Don't Look Now*, one of the hundred favourite films his daughter Terri had sent him at the start of his suspension, her misguided apology for almost losing him his job. Brook tossed the case on to the top of the DVD player. It was a good film – atmospheric and chilling.

Donald Sutherland and Julie Christie played a married couple living in Venice, trying to work through the numbing grief that followed the loss of their daughter, drowned in a pond as a young girl. Then the husband begins to see her – in slides he's shot for his work, in glimpses out of the corner of his eye – and suddenly the couple can believe that their daughter is with them again to comfort them, if only from the afterlife.

Brook had fallen asleep at that point, certain that the couple's new-found sense of contentment and purpose would end badly. He smiled groggily. *Or maybe that's just personal experience kicking in.*

He clambered unsteadily to his feet and rustled around in his tiny kitchen, readying the tea things for morning. Tomorrow would be his first day on duty for five months. 'Today,' he croaked in a voice unused to conversation. For the first time in his career, the prospect filled him with dread and he thought of his resignation letter, sitting on the printer in his office. The same internal debate that had disturbed his sleep for the last week rose in him again.

Maybe it's time to get out of the force and get on with life.

And he'd made a good start. He'd finally given up smoking, for one thing. And having spent the entirety of his suspension hiking around the Derbyshire Peaks by day and sitting on his garden bench by night, whisky and water in hand, examining the stars, Brook wanted more. Five months of rest and recuperation from his injuries. Five months of isolation in his Hartington cottage – easily his longest absence from the job since his breakdown over twenty years ago.

The irony, not lost on Brook, was that only three of those months covered his suspension for gross misconduct; the other two months had been taken up by his recovery from the burns sustained to his hand on his last case, hunting the Deity killer.

Were he ever to break the habit of a lifetime and engage colleagues in conversation, Brook was certain many would tell him he got off lightly, that he should have lost his rank and maybe even his job. It was hard for Brook not to agree with them, not that he felt his offence deserved to end in dismissal, more that such an outcome would at least have simplified everything, made his life easier, his future choices clearer.

And losing his job would have cauterised the seeping loss of his moral authority at a stroke. It would have lanced the sense of shame he had experienced, that for the first time in his career, encompassing all his brushes with superior and junior officers, he'd never been so clearly in the wrong. And with the ringing endorsement of the disciplinary panel, his detractors would be able to look down their noses at him for a long time to come.

Brook padded wearily upstairs to bed, expecting no sleep, settled in his decision. Again.

Early that morning Brook tossed his smartcard on the passenger seat, relieved to see the barrier swing up. He hadn't been to the car park of Derby Division's headquarters at St Mary's Wharf in many months, and he'd got it into his head that his parking privileges might have been withdrawn as part of his suspension.

Brook drove under the barrier to park his elderly BMW in the nearest empty bay, aware that, sooner or later, he'd have to run the gauntlet of derisive remarks from local officers. He killed the engine, at least content that the first wave had been postponed; he was hours early for his reinduction meeting. He poured tea from his flask and reclined, eyes closed, on to the cracked leather, listening to the Radio Derby news bulletin in the dark.

The search for Derby schoolboy, Scott Wheeler, continues and, four days after his disappearance on December the seventh, police are no closer to finding out what happened to the thirteen year old.

Scott, who is five feet eight inches tall with striking blond hair and blue eyes, was last seen by school friends at a party in St Chad's Road, Normanton, last Friday evening at around eight o'clock. He was wearing black jeans, black Nike training shoes, a camouflage T-shirt with matching baseball cap and a blue hoodie with the words RIP CURL on the front.

A pupil at Derby Community School, Scott disappeared during a birthday celebration at the house of classmate Chelsea Chaplin. The party finished at nine p.m. and Scott's mother, Beverley Wheeler, who lives in nearby Stone Hill Road, went to collect her son but when she arrived at the Chaplin house, Scott had vanished.

According to witnesses, Scott left the party of his own

accord, apparently in an agitated state, though police have yet to verify this. So far, there have been no sightings of Scott after he left the house.

Mrs Wheeler said she was unaware of any problems her son might have been having or why he might have been agitated. She told Radio Derby that Scott is a popular young man and there is no suggestion that he was a victim of bullies. However, gang involvement has not been ruled out because Scott is the younger brother of Callum Wheeler, who was convicted last year of racially aggravated assault and wounding in a fight between rival Normanton gangs.

Needless to say, police are desperate to find witnesses to Scott's disappearance and although there is no direct evidence of abduction, police say it cannot be ruled out.

At this stage, investigators have denied any connection with last year's murder of Scott Wheeler's friend and classmate, Joshua Stapleton, who died thirteen months ago, after an evening spent trick or treating with Scott. Joshua's body was later found on the ground floor of a derelict house in Whitaker Road, Normanton. He had suffered severe head and spinal injuries.

Noel Williams, a fifty-five-year-old vagrant known to shelter at the house, was found guilty of the boy's manslaughter and began a twenty-year sentence in April this year.

Chief Superintendent Mark Charlton says Derby Constabulary are interviewing everyone connected with the party but they urgently need witnesses to come forward, especially if they remember seeing a young man fitting Scott's description in St Chad's Road or Stone Hill Road or the wider Normanton area. Any sightings of Scott will be vigorously investigated.

When we spoke to Chief Superintendent Charlton earlier, he told us that officers on the task force are also keen to hear about other unusual occurrences in the area that night.

Brook braced himself for Charlton's sickly smooth media voice.

'Scott Wheeler is a happy and well-liked young man. We would ask the people of Derby, particularly in the Normanton area, to rack their brains about last Friday evening.

'Even if you don't remember seeing this young man walking the streets that night, maybe you saw something else, something that might have struck you as odd but, at the time, you dismissed it. We're particularly interested in the hours between eight p.m., when Scott was last seen, and midnight. Did you see something that may have seemed trivial but which could yet have a bearing on the case? Maybe you spotted a car that you haven't seen before; perhaps you saw a stranger in the neighbourhood, or even someone you know, behaving in a suspicious manner.

'Did such a person catch your eye? If you can think of anything, no matter how unimportant it might seem, please contact us immediately. All information will be treated in the strictest confidence and it's imperative . . .'

'. . . that I get myself on the TV and radio a lot more.' Brook depressed the button to silence his superior.

'Four days missing.' Brook didn't need to look at the statistics to know the Wheeler boy was almost certainly dead. He knew nothing about the case except what he'd heard from the local media. And DI Frank Ford was in charge, a fact which didn't fill Brook with confidence. As a result, and despite misgivings about resuming his career, Brook had even emailed Charlton to ask if he wanted him to return to duty early to help the investigation. The Chief Superintendent hadn't seen fit to respond.

'At least Noble's on the case,' said Brook, surprised and a little miffed his DS hadn't been in contact for advice about the missing boy.

Glancing up at the building, Brook allowed his eyes to wander to the third floor and the window of the office he'd shared with

Noble. A light was on. The churn of police work never ceased.

He peered across to the well-lit entrance of D Division, trying and failing to see who was on the reception desk, pondering whether to make a dash for the sanctuary of his office while the station seemed quiet and the sun was still no more than a suggestion in the east.

More chance of avoiding Sergeant Hendrickson and his ilk if I go now.

In the end, Brook made no move to get out of the car. He poured more tea and flexed his damaged hand, almost good as new, the evidence of skin graft invisible to the eye, and only a slight tingling to remind him it had ever been injured. His head wounds had healed even earlier and only Brook knew about the scar and slight bump under his hairline.

As he drained his tea, Brook caught sight of headlights in his mirrors. A second later, a squad car drove under the barrier, followed by a civilian vehicle and another squad car bringing up the rear of the convoy.

Brook watched. Criminals tended to be night owls; they liked a lie-in after a long night's lawbreaking which meant arrests were simpler in the early hours. He craned his neck to watch the vehicles drawing to a halt at the front steps and passengers begin to disgorge. The two police vehicles were full and contained eight officers in total. Their car doors opened and closed quickly as the officers jumped out to wait for the civilian car to empty. Three of the officers were CID, Noble amongst them. Brook also recognised DS Rob Morton and DC Dave Cooper, who opened the doors of the civilian car. A slightly built woman stepped from the passenger side and the male driver met her in front of the car and tentatively linked his arm with hers before all ten jogged up the steps to the glass vestibule that was reception and disappeared from sight.

No handcuffs. No separation of the couple. This wasn't an arrest. They were 'helping with inquiries'. Brook's eyes narrowed. He'd seen the man before but couldn't place him. He stepped from the car and walked with flask and laptop towards the smoked-glass doors. Once inside the glass entrance hall, Brook fixed his eyes to the floor and marched quickly to the lifts.

Sergeant Harry Hendrickson, on duty at the front desk, caught a glimpse of Brook's retreating frame and smiled malevolently. 'Snuck past me, did you, mental boy?' he muttered under his breath. 'Not to worry. I'm not going anywhere.' He turned to a uniformed colleague sipping coffee at the back of the office and grinned. 'Guess what the cat just dragged in.' Taking out his mobile, Hendrickson scrolled down to the name Brian Burton and began thumbing out a text: 'Christmas has come early.' He sniggered, face creased like a leather accordion.

Brook eased back behind a potted palm and watched Noble, Morton and DC Cooper emerging from a door that led from the detention area, heading up the stairs towards CID. The two civilians and the five uniformed officers were nowhere to be seen.

When he was alone, Brook descended to the refurbished custody suite. Opposite the entrance, he slipped into an adjoining toilet. It was deserted so he dumped his laptop and flask in the furthest empty cubicle, hoping no one would need to use it.

Two minutes later, Brook pushed through the shiny new door of the custody suite and stopped cold, his face a mixture of admiration and dismay. As a consequence of his suspension, he hadn't yet seen the results of the recent modernisation. The suite was now light and airy, where once it was forbidding, the decor soothing when once it was austere. No more cold tiles, narrow corridors or doors with security grilles in these enlightened times. The ambience suggested he was in a supermarket rather than a place of confinement. It was profoundly worrying.

Instead of discouraging those who might be teetering on the brink of a life of crime, today's wrongdoers, brought to this place for interview, were to be treated like customers rather than potential offenders. Someone in authority, who had never been on the receiving end of the vitriol and violence that was de rigueur in any detention area, had decided it was important that an arrested felon's *experience* of arrest and custody be user-friendly.

'Help you, sir?' inquired the young PC behind a monitor at the elevated booking-in desk.

Trying not to stare, Brook approached the counter, hoping to identify the officer. He failed but for once felt confident the young man was unknown to him.

'DI Brook,' said Brook, flashing his warrant card. 'Yes, Constable, I—' he began before giving in to interruption. He fished out his antiquated mobile from a jacket pocket, not even checking to see if it was turned on, and put it to his ear.

'Chief Superintendent? Yes, I'm there now.' He covered the inert speaker with his free hand and locked eyes with the young officer. 'Is DS Noble in with the happy couple?'

'Sir?'

'DS Noble.' Brook sighed with impatience. 'I know it was all of five minutes ago, Constable, but it can't be that hard to remember a man and woman being processed at this hour of the day.'

'You mean the Stapletons, sir. Yes, I mean no, sir. DS Noble's not in with them yet. Back in five, he said. Might I ask who you are?'

'The Stapletons.' Brook nodded, ignoring the constable's query. 'Right. Letting them sweat, I expect. Has anybody taken a drinks order?'

'Er . . .'

'Never mind. I'll do it myself. Where are they?'

'Interview Two, sir.'

Brook walked into the interview room and, though they'd never met, he recognised Mr and Mrs Stapleton from press conferences the year before, appealing to be left alone to grieve for their murdered son, Joshua. They were visibly on edge, with their hands interlocked, their knuckles white with tension.

'About time,' said Mr Stapleton, a tall balding man who dwarfed his tiny bird-like wife. He pushed his chair back with his calves as he stood.

'Sit down please, sir,' said Brook.

'Why have we been brought here?'

Brook indicated the chair. 'Please.'

'I want to know why we're here,' insisted Stapleton.

As Brook didn't know the answer he decided not to start his first day back with a lie. 'I can't discuss that.'

'Is this about Scott Wheeler?' asked Mrs Stapleton.

'As I said—'

'You're that DI Brook. You were on the telly in the summer,' said Stapleton. 'About those students who disappeared.'

Brook smiled faintly. He'd never got used to the recognition his job sometimes afforded him. 'Yes.'

'Are you responsible for us being here?' demanded Stapleton.

'No.'

'Then who is? And how long will we be here?'

Brook shrugged. 'It's not my case, Mr Stapleton, but not long, I hope.'

'Then why are you here?'

'This *is* about Scott Wheeler, isn't it?' insinuated Stapleton's wife, trying to stand.

Her husband pushed her back down and sat himself. 'Easy, Jen.'

'Again, I don't know,' replied Brook truthfully, beginning to wish he hadn't intruded.

Appearing not to hear Brook, Stapleton said, 'Whatever I said, I said it in the heat of the moment. It was months ago, for Christ's sake. I wouldn't hurt Scott, no matter how badly he let down our son.'

'Don't give them the satisfaction, Greg.' Mrs Stapleton glared up at Brook. 'This is typical. We've had to listen to the world and his wife singing the praises of that nasty little shit the last four days. He disappears and suddenly everyone thinks he's an angel. Well, he isn't.' Present tense, Brook noted. 'Scott Wheeler is a foul-mouthed little thug and if we'd known what he was like before Joshua befriended him . . .' she sighed heavily at the floor and looked to her husband for support.

Stapleton tightened his jaw and looked Brook full in the face. 'We've lost everything, Inspector. Our boy is dead because Scott Wheeler abandoned him that night. Yes, I had some harsh words to say to Scott *and* his mother and I wish I hadn't said them. But that's all they were – words. We were devastated—'

'Greg could never hurt a child,' interrupted his wife. 'Not even Scott Wheeler.'

'And we certainly don't know where he is or what happened to him.' Stapleton stared defiantly at Brook. 'Though I won't shed any tears if . . .' he halted, suddenly ashamed.

'Your son's killer was tried and convicted, Mr Stapleton,' said Brook. 'No matter how difficult, isn't it time to move on?'

'But it was Scott who put Josh in harm's way,' spat Stapleton's wife, on the verge of tears. 'That doesn't mean . . .'

'I understand,' said Brook softly, when she couldn't continue. 'How about I get you a hot drink while I hurry up DS Noble?'

Brook opened the door of his outer office and put his flask and laptop on a chair. Noble was on the phone but still managed to wave a greeting which Brook acknowledged. He'd missed Noble. Not enough to invite him out to the cottage for a drink. Not enough to arrange to meet in one of the city centre bars Noble frequented. But he'd missed him nonetheless.

When Noble's phone conversation was over, he stood to give Brook a lingering examination and threw in an awkward handshake for good measure.

'You're early.'

'You were expecting me?' remarked Brook.

'I've been counting the days.' Noble grinned. 'Seen anyone else?'

Brook lowered his eyes. 'Sergeant Hendrickson was on the desk.'

'But you scuttled past him so he wouldn't see you.'

Brook didn't answer.

'And that's why you're in so early,' added Noble, with sudden realisation. 'Avoiding people.' He shook his head. 'Honestly, you were making such good progress before you . . .' he tailed off.

'Before I disgraced the force,' finished Brook, remembering the Chief Superintendent's phrase from the summer.

Noble laughed. 'The force will get over it.'

'I dare say,' agreed Brook. 'But will I?'

'You're a DI,' said Noble. 'You shouldn't be worrying what clapped-out desk sergeants think about you.'

'No,' agreed Brook.

'How's your hand?' said Noble.

'It still needs ointment occasionally but it's a lot better, thanks.'

'Never seen you looking so fit,' said Noble, still scrutinising him. 'Suspension seems to agree with you.'

Brook managed a thin smile. 'Does it?'

'I didn't mean . . .'

Brook held up his good hand. 'I know what you meant.'

'Glad to be back?'

Brook took a deep breath. 'Honestly, no. I hardly slept a wink last night.'

'And you make it sound so unusual,' teased Noble.

Brook emitted his one-note laugh, insomnia contributing to his unaccustomed levity. 'How are things with you?'

Noble blew out his cheeks. 'Hard. Sixteen-hour days at the moment. We could've used you this week.'

'The Wheeler kid?'

Noble confirmed with a dip of the eyes. 'Even Charlton's been coming in before eight to deal with all the garbage.'

'I did offer,' said Brook. 'My suspension finished two months ago but Charlton insisted on medical clearance.' He held Noble's eye. 'Four days now.'

'Four days,' repeated Noble. 'Four nights.'

Brook pursed his lips. They both knew if the first forty-eight hours passed without finding a missing child, then things were unlikely to end well.

Noble looked at his watch and then at the door. 'Well . . .'

'You've cleared the Wheeler boy's parents?' said Brook, keeping Noble on the subject.

'I think so,' replied Noble. 'Mum and Dad are separated and, though they're not Charles and Camilla, they're solid working people who've walked into every parent's nightmare.'

'A bit careless walking into two,' observed Brook.

'Sorry?'

'Their eldest boy's already in the system,' said Brook.

'Callum, right,' nodded Noble. 'Career criminal in the making.'

'A chip off the old block?'

Noble hesitated and Brook realised that he might be under orders not to discuss the case with his disgraced senior officer. Before the younger man could stumble into an evasion, Brook let him off the hook. 'You can't talk to me about it, John. I understand.'

Noble sighed, coming to a decision. 'The father's got a cast-iron alibi so we're looking at everyone connected with the party, all the other parents and everyone at Scott's school. A few parents have got some minor previous, but we're talking twocking and D and D from fifteen, twenty years ago. We look long enough we might dig out some benefit cheats but so what? There's not a stand-out child killer anywhere on the horizon.'

'You've widened the checks?' asked Brook.

'We're looking into *everyone*, digging deeper on all male adults in the area but nobody's jumped out at us yet.'

'So you think it's sexual.'

'We don't know.'

'You've been through the SO Register?'

'Not a sex offender within miles,' said Noble. 'Normanton's a solid, working-class area, racially relaxed – everyone minds their business.'

'What about leaning on Social Services?' suggested Brook. 'They can be slow to put clients in the frame, in case it comes back to bite them.'

'I . . . we've done everything you would have done, sir.'

Brook nodded. 'I'm a bit rusty, John. What would I have done?'

'You would have knocked on every door within a mile of the party, checked every resident's background, searched every garden, every outhouse and been over every local CCTV film with a fine-tooth comb. You would check hospital records for all the kids at the party, thirty of them, going back ten years, to see if we couldn't scare up some unseen pattern of violence in any parent likely to be on or near the scene.'

'I sound like a good copper,' smiled Brook. 'And what would I have found?'

'Nothing,' replied Noble.

'You've been on Facebook and—'

'We're trawling through all the social network sites and all Scott's personal accounts. Cooper's been monitoring Facebook, MSN, Bebo and the rest. Nothing but the usual tribute pages and nothing jumps out from the kid's emails.'

'Mobile?' suggested Brook, getting to the end of his mental checklist.

Noble sighed. 'Nothing on his text or call records and he's not on Twitter because he's got an old model. His mum *had* bought him a new phone for Christmas, all the bells and whistles, including GPS, but she decided to wait until the twenty-fifth to give it to him. You can imagine how much she's beating herself up for that decision.'

Brook lowered his head in parental sympathy. That was the kind of 'if only' detail that would tear what was left of the Wheeler family to shreds when the body was found. 'Sorry, I shouldn't be grilling you like this.'

Noble's answering smile was bleak. 'Keep your apology. It was you that taught me to challenge superiors who wouldn't take advice just because they hadn't thought of it themselves. And that counts double when lives are at stake. Remember?'

'It rings a bell.'

'"Don't be afraid to step on toes," you said. "Ego is the enemy of detection," you said.'

'Did I?' laughed Brook. 'How pompous of me.'

'Maybe so but if you've got an angle we haven't covered, then . . . forget Charlton and tell me now because there's a thirteen-year-old kid out there who should be at home looking forward to Christmas.'

Brook studied Noble for a second. 'Soft living has made me forget how good you are at your job, John. Let me apologise for that, at least.'

'Apology accepted,' said Noble, glancing at the door then his watch.

'The radio mentioned there might be a gang connection.'

Noble spoke quickly, impatient to leave. 'Not that we can see. A few rival crews talking some trash but that's all it is. Scott's not in a gang yet, which makes him a civilian. Besides, a gang wouldn't abduct him, they wouldn't know what to do with him. And if they'd killed him, they wouldn't hide the body and they certainly wouldn't be able to keep from bragging about it.'

Brook wondered whether to broach the next subject. 'How's DI Ford? Good SIO?'

'He's OK,' answered Noble, unable to meet Brook's eyes.

'Is he around?' asked Brook innocently.

'Not yet.'

'He was always a good delegator,' observed Brook, with a rare diplomatic touch.

Noble wasn't fooled. 'He's got a year left. Do you blame him?'

'Not with you watching his back, John, no.'

'Now I really have to . . .'

'Of course,' said Brook, stepping aside. 'Don't let me keep you from the Stapletons.'

Noble froze, hand on the doorknob. He turned back to Brook, a mixture of admiration and annoyance distorting his features. 'How do you do that? You're back five minutes and already . . .'

'I can't lie,' said Brook. 'I was in the car park when you brought them in.'

'And you remembered them from last year?'

'No, I was out of the country when their son was murdered, remember? I recognised them from the trial in the spring.'

'I'm impressed.'

'Don't be. I'd forgotten their names until I went down to Interview Two to ask if they wanted coffee.'

Noble pursed his lips. 'And?'

'Milk and two sugars,' replied Brook.

'Sir . . .'

'Bad joke,' conceded Brook. 'But the Stapletons seem tense, John. Should they be?'

Noble closed the half-opened door. 'You remember Joshua's murder.'

'A little. He was killed last Halloween, thrown off the upper floor of a derelict house in Normanton somewhere – broke his neck.'

'Whitaker Road,' said Noble, staring at his mind's eye. 'It wasn't pretty. Ford picked up the case. You were away so I was assigned to him. We found the boy's body as well as a comatose vagrant, asleep in an upstairs bedroom.'

'Noel Williams,' said Brook, remembering the radio broadcast.

'That's right. He'd been living in the house for a while.' Noble shrugged. 'It was an open-and-shut case. He confessed and pleaded diminished responsibility; got off with manslaughter. Case closed.'

'OK,' said Brook doubtfully. He sensed there was something else, something Noble didn't want to tell him. 'That doesn't explain why the Stapletons are downstairs.'

'There were some issues surrounding the death. Joshua and Scott Wheeler were thick as thieves, inseparable. They were only twelve-year-old kids but the day of the murder, somehow they persuaded their parents to be allowed out on their own to go trick or treating, on the strict understanding that they stick together.'

'But they didn't,' said Brook.

'There was an argument about something and nothing and Joshua stormed off and ended up in a filthy squat with his neck broken. After his son's death, Greg Stapleton turned on the Wheeler boy, said his son would be alive today if Scott hadn't abandoned him.' Noble held out his hands. 'Push came to shove and, just before the trial, Stapleton threatened Scott.'

'He'd just lost his son, John.'

'I know.'

'Any parent could have an outburst like that.'

'I know,' repeated Noble. 'No way Greg Stapleton's going to abduct a young kid to get even for his son's death, not after so long. Even Scott's mum said it was ridiculous.'

'But you have to look into it,' nodded Brook.

'Especially as a witness at the party, a friend, said something spooked Scott really badly. Said he was scared out of his mind just before he disappeared.'

'So any reported threats have to be followed up,' said Brook. Noble lifted a confirming eyebrow. 'Then they're not under arrest.'

'No,' said Noble. 'We just need to straighten it out and tick it off as a dead end. I thought it best to bring them in early so the media wouldn't get wind of it. At the moment, everyone in the area is looking sideways at their neighbours, not sure if they're living next door to a child killer or a paedo. Any reports about the Stapletons being brought in and they'll be . . .' he cast around for a suitable word.

As usual Brook came to the rescue. 'Demonised.'

Noble jabbed a finger in Brook's direction. 'So the sooner I get to speak to them . . .'

'Mind if I give you one more piece of advice, John?' ventured Brook.

'Go on.'

'If you want to protect them, get them out of here now.'

'Why?'

'Hendrickson's on reception.'

Noble's brow furrowed. 'Sir, I know you and Hendrickson don't see eye to eye—'

'Remember the leaks to the local rag about the Plummer rape a few years ago?'

'You don't know that was Hendrickson.'

'I couldn't prove it, no. But Brian Burton splashed sensitive details on the front page of the *Telegraph* the next day and the prosecution collapsed. And that wasn't the only time it's happened in a big case.'

'Sir, why—?'

'Hendrickson's close to retirement, John. And local coppers of his generation . . . did things differently. Briefing a journalist for a drink was accepted practice in their day.'

'Most of the time it's harmless.'

'It wasn't during the Deity inquiry.'

'What do you mean?'

'We brought in one of the parents, remember?'

'So?'

'Who turned up out of the blue with a photographer when we picked him up? Brian Burton. The next day, front-page news.'

'Yeah, but the father was cleared.'

'He committed suicide, John.'

'You can't blame Brian Burton for that. Or Hendrickson.'

'And you can't prove Burton's coverage didn't have an effect on how things ended. The man's a lowlife.'

Noble was deep in thought. 'So you think Burton could be on his way now?'

'Photographer in tow,' added Brook.

Noble opened the door to leave. 'Your first day back, in *your* shoes, don't you think you should worry about your meeting with Charlton?'

'Would you want to be in the Stapletons' shoes if I'm right?'

After a brief hesitation, Noble took out his mobile, marching out of the office as he spoke. 'Rob, get the Stapletons' car round to the dock and get them off home, stat. Don't ask questions, just do it.'

Eight

BROOK SAT AT NOBLE'S DESK and fired up his laptop, nearly choking when he saw the number of unopened internal emails in his Inbox. 'Five hundred and thirty-seven!' As he had no pending court cases, he deleted them all, trying to suppress the absurd sense of satisfaction it gave him.

Noble re-entered the office. 'What's so funny?'

Still smiling, Brook answered, 'Nothing's funny. Success?'

Noble nodded sombrely at Brook. 'They're on their way home.'

'Any sign of Burton?'

'None,' said Noble emphatically. 'Why do I let you talk me into these things?'

'Because you've got good instincts, John.' Brook logged off and closed his laptop. 'Sorry, I'm keeping you from your desk.'

Noble looked uncomfortable suddenly, glancing towards Brook's adjoining office. The desk was stacked high with files and papers, with used plastic cups and mugs dotting what little surface area was left. 'I'm sorry about your office. It became a bit of a dumping ground. I was going to tidy up but you know how it is.'

'Hardly your fault, John. I wasn't here to keep it clear.'

'I can—'

'Forget it,' said Brook. 'It's not as though I'm going to need it where I'm going.'

'No,' conceded Noble. There was a sudden awkwardness as Brook's colleague cast around for more to say. 'I'm sure that's just temporary – until Charlton gets his payback. You'll soon be back in the saddle. We're stretched pretty thin.'

Brook could tell he wasn't convinced. 'We'll see.'

Again Noble had to be first to find a new topic of conversation. He'd forgotten Brook's aversion to small talk. 'How's your lovely daughter?'

'Terri's fine,' said Brook. 'I think.'

'You've not seen her?'

'Not since my suspension, no. After I was discharged from hospital, she went to Greece for the rest of the summer and now she's back at university.'

'Think she's avoiding you?'

'I don't know,' replied Brook honestly. 'But she still thinks it was her fault I got suspended.'

'You put her straight, I hope?' replied Noble.

'Several times,' said Brook.

'It might have been her idea but *you* should have known better,' continued Noble, suddenly stern.

Brook smiled feebly. 'Believe me, I know.'

'OK then,' said Noble, a little sheepish after admonishing a DI. 'Maybe you'll see her at Christmas.'

'You never know,' said Brook softly. 'Any news about your promotion?'

Noble was surprised and impressed. 'You remembered?'

'Counting off the days,' teased Brook.

Noble emitted a short laugh. 'It's between me and Jane Gadd as you said. Though we don't find out until tomorrow.'

'You should both have made DI after Greatorix retired,' said Brook. 'It should never have come to this.' Noble's expression wasn't one of optimism and Brook looked away, fiddling with his coat, trying to ignore the elephant in the room.

Of course, if I'd done the decent thing and resigned five months ago, it wouldn't have. For something to do, Brook stepped into his office to clear the debris and unlock the drawers.

Noble followed him in. 'I can always apply for promotion

elsewhere if Jane gets the nod,' he said. 'Though I'd rather not leave Derby.'

'Any division would be lucky to have you,' said Brook, making an effort to be upbeat.

'Thanks,' mumbled Noble.

Brook decided against a further rallying call. Both men knew that positive discrimination, and his loyalty to Brook, might cost Noble a deserved promotion. 'So, DCI Copeland. What can you tell me about him?'

'I hardly knew him,' said Noble. 'I was just a lowly DC when he retired. Seemed OK, if a bit up himself.'

'Up himself?' repeated Brook, aware he was being mocked. 'Could proud be the word you're looking for? Or pompous? Or arrogant?'

'Could be,' replied Noble, laughing. 'My vocabulary's suffered while you've been away.'

'At least you haven't called me *guv* yet.'

'Never happen,' answered Noble. 'And I've stopped swearing for ever, promise. I think you've finally beaten that out of me.'

'Glad to hear it,' smiled Brook.

The door opened and Chief Superintendent Charlton popped his head round. 'Sergeant, I need the latest on Scott Wheeler. I'm briefing . . .' He straightened when he saw Brook, trying to achieve more than minimum regulation height, then nodded a greeting to the two CID officers, both several inches taller. But instead of bridling with habitual discomfort at their differences in height, the Chief Superintendent was fighting the curl of his lip at the sight of Brook, barely able to keep the smugness in check. 'Inspector Brook. Welcome back,' he said without an ounce of sincerity.

'Thank you, sir.'

'You're early,' Charlton observed.

'Tardiness is one problem I've managed to avoid. Sir.'

'Humility,' exclaimed Charlton. 'From you, Brook. Heartening – let's hope it stands you in good stead for the future,' he added coldly. 'My office, five minutes.' He turned briskly on his heel and left without another word.

'He's really got it in for you this time,' said Noble.

'As you say, it'll blow over.' Brook opened and closed a drawer. There were three unopened cartons of two hundred cigarettes each. He left them where they were. 'Anything else on the books, John?'

'Nothing major. Burglaries are up so we've got a small unit chasing around after housebreakers.'

'Operation Why-Don't-People-Get-Proper-Locks?' observed Brook. 'I won't have to suffer that, at least.' Looking around for his flask, he swung his laptop back over his shoulder and prepared to leave.

Noble looked quizzically at him. 'You really are going to suck it up, aren't you?'

Brook winced but didn't rise to the bait. 'I really am. Until one of us thinks I've suffered enough. Did you think I'd fall on my sword?'

'It crossed my mind.'

'Too *up myself* to take my punishment.'

Noble laughed. 'No, but you and Charlton . . . he's like a cat with a mouse. Besides . . .' Noble hesitated then decided not to finish.

Brook raised a mocking eyebrow. 'Go on.'

'Well, you are the wrong side of fifty,' Noble shrugged. 'Not that you can't still cut it but nobody would have blamed you for taking the easy way out.'

Brook pictured the resignation letter sitting on the printer at home. 'Never entered my head, John.'

Brook marched into Charlton's office on command and stood in silence, looking over the Chief Superintendent's hunched frame towards the window. Outside, the pale sky was heavy with clouds.

Charlton didn't look up but continued to feign deep interest in the document in front of him. Brook felt the tug of levity in the face of such cheap, psychological tricks but managed to maintain a serious expression.

After a suitable interlude, Charlton looked up with mild interest, as if just becoming aware of Brook's presence. He sat back in his chair to consider him and Brook could see Charlton had been practising his posture and expression for weeks, preparing to revel in the full majesty of his office.

'You look very well, Brook.'

'Thank you, sir.'

'Inactivity seems to agree with you.'

'I'm fit and well-rested, sir,' replied Brook. 'Ready to work.'

'How's the hand?'

'Much better.'

'That's good,' said Charlton. His expression tightened. 'Looking forward to your new role?' He gazed intently at Brook for any sign of discontent.

'Can't wait, sir.'

The Chief Super narrowed his eyes to detect any sarcasm. 'Good.'

'Unless you think I'd be more use in the Wheeler task force.' Brook kept his eyes on the wall behind Charlton's head. 'I have had some experience—'

'I don't think so,' interrupted Charlton. 'And don't take your new assignment lightly. This is important work. Very good for our PR. Shows the people that we never forget, never let unsolved cases drift.'

'No, sir.'

'We've cobbled together a couple of rooms for you and Clive Copeland to work from. I hope you'll enjoy working with him. He may be retired but he was an ex-DCI and I'm sure he'll be a big help to you. He has a lot of experience in this precinct, being a local man.' *Unlike you* remained unsaid.

'No doubt.'

'And I know I don't need to remind you, you're on very thin ice in this division, Inspector.'

Brook finally met Charlton's eye. 'I'm ready to redeem myself, sir.'

'A viable prosecution was sabotaged by your unfathomable decision to pass off your daughter as a police officer, to conduct an illegal search of a suspect's home—'

'The *suspect* wasn't a suspect at that time.'

'Are you arguing with me, Brook?' demanded Charlton.

Brook took a discreet pull of oxygen and returned his eyes to the wall, annoyed at getting drawn into a war of words that the Chief was clearly trying to provoke. Charlton had thrown the book at Brook when his misconduct had been discovered and he had been certain his career was in jeopardy. But, oddly, Charlton had made no effort to eject him from the service and Brook had finally figured out why. Charlton was keen to keep him around so he could gloat at how far and fast Brook's star had fallen. At long last the Chief Super had seized the moral uplands, so often ceded in the past and, clearly, he was still enjoying the view. Further, he now had a hold over Brook's career and he wasn't about to relax it until he'd extracted maximum payback for all the perceived slights received during their shared history. On the upside, until such time as Charlton had sated his appetite, Brook assumed his job was safe.

'No, sir.'

'Good. Now your duties are strictly defined,' said Charlton. 'Clive has specialised in cold case work since his retirement and you'll be guided by him.'

'How long will I be working these cases, sir? I gather we're stretched pretty thin until this boy is found.' Brook regretted his question at once. This was his first day back from suspension and so far he'd only spoken to DS Noble. Charlton was certain to know from where Brook had received his information.

'Don't fret about staffing, Brook,' said Charlton frostily. With a touch more aggression, he added, 'Not that I need justify myself to you. And don't forget, tomorrow there'll be a new DI promoted from your own team, so I'm sure we can manage our current caseload without you for a while.'

Brook nodded impassively.

'Now let me take you down to meet Clive.'

Brook sat in the stark windowless room across the corridor from Clive Copeland's equally dismal office, trying to ignore the stench of stale tobacco and the merciless glare of the strip light. Despite the relative modernity of the building, the small magnolia-coloured suite of rooms that housed the newly created Cold Case Unit in the basement felt damp and chilly and the two rooms, being slightly below ground level, were appropriately dingy. At least Copeland had a glimpse of the outside world through the mottled glass of his tiny ceiling-high window, even if the most he could ever see were the legs of officers slipping away to the car park for a crafty cigarette. Even that meagre concession had been denied Brook.

He sighed and emptied the last of his tea from his flask and looked around at the bare surroundings from the discomfort of his metal chair. Like the chair, the metal table in front of him was cold to the touch. The only thing on it, apart from an old marmalade jar full of pens and pencils, was a bulky old computer fed by wires which emerged from a crude circular hole cut into the top of the table. And although Brook had logged on to the system five minutes earlier, a glance at the monitor showed his machine still trying to load the relevant software. He switched it off, pushed the keyboard away and picked his laptop case from the floor to unpack.

When he'd finally logged on, Brook cleared his Inbox of a further half-dozen internal emails without reading a single one then stood and paced around his cell to warm up. He paused at the metal filing cabinet and opened a drawer. It was empty. All the other drawers were empty too.

Brook slumped back down on his unforgiving chair. 'Welcome to hell.'

'Hell is a trifle warmer than our offices, I think.'

Brook looked to the door where Copeland's jaundiced grin drew the eye. The former detective chief inspector wheeled a trolley into the room, still amused. He wasn't a pleasant sight, even at second viewing. Apart from the yellowed teeth, Copeland was colourless. His eyes were grey, his clothes were chosen to match and there was a faint odour of decay about him. He had dust-coloured hair and skin like greaseproof paper and his current merriment looked like it might cause permanent scarring around the eyes.

'You've been there, have you?' said Brook.

Copeland's smile froze around his mouth and a glimpse of humanity invaded his features. 'Many times,' he said, before resuming his journey towards Brook, pushing the trolley. It had a squeaking wheel.

The noise stopped and Brook glanced over at the half dozen bulging manila folders sitting snugly on the top rack. They had seen better days.

'As I explained earlier, this is where we start. These are called files, Inspector.' Copeland fixed Brook with a mocking stare. 'They contain reports on *paper*, like coppers used to use before computers came along.' Brook raised a weary eye to Copeland. 'Paper reports not a problem for you, are they?'

Brook's expression glazed. 'No problem, Clive.'

Copeland bridled slightly at the use of his Christian name. 'I used to outrank you, Brook. I was a DCI,' he said, as though his meaning were obvious.

'And now you're a civilian,' retorted Brook, 'employed on a daily rate to supplement your pension and get you out of the house. You're here to help me rake over old cases that no one can close and no one cares about. Neither of us needs to be called sir, but if you'd prefer I call you Mr Copeland, I'm happy to oblige. You can call me whatever you want as long as it's not guv.'

Copeland was mute for a moment, working on his riposte. 'Reminds you too much of your time in the Met, does it?'

Brook's eyes narrowed, trying to read Copeland's meaning. What did Copeland know about his problems in the Met? *Of course he knows. Hendrickson knows, which means everyone knows.*

Copeland realised he'd said the wrong thing. His expression softened as he came to a decision. 'Clive's fine, Brook,' he said. 'Want me to walk you through the process?'

'I'm all ears,' replied Brook, without enthusiasm.

Copeland was unfazed by Brook's lack of zeal. 'Good. As you said, what we're about in the CCU is reassessing some of the oldest unsolved murders on the books. But we don't have to solve them, Brook, just vet the files properly to reassess whether they're worth transferring on to the computer.'

'I thought we uploaded all cold cases on to HOLMES a few years back,' said Brook.

'We?' inquired Copeland.

'Someone,' said Brook, leaving out the rank he deemed worthy of such menial work.

'That's what everyone thinks but it varies. You see, most divisions don't have a dedicated Cold Case Unit, so normal procedure, as I'm sure you know, is to get full-time or retired officers to revisit cases every few years, when things are quiet or when a significant anniversary crops up. What people don't realise is that even an old murder won't be uploaded as a matter of routine because it all comes down to an individual officer's judgement. Some cold cases get lost in the shuffle because they lack what we call "resolution potential".'

'Resolution potential?' repeated Brook, fighting a smile. 'You're kidding.'

'Far from it. All the cases we look at have limited potential for reinterpretation of the available evidence.'

'You mean there's no DNA to test,' said Brook.

'And no possibility of obtaining any, right. See, priority was often given to uploading those cases where advances in DNA techniques and fingerprint retrieval might yield results in the future.'

'And so those cases that didn't have potential for either may not have been entered on the database,' concluded Brook.

'Correct,' confirmed Copeland. 'Rightly or wrongly, they were deemed unlikely to yield results and downgraded. We're then left with folders full of papers and reports and maybe some artefacts in a distant warehouse.'

'Assuming they haven't been routinely destroyed,' suggested Brook.

'They often have been, unless a special request for retention from the case officer is received.'

Brook nodded. 'So where do I come in?'

'You assess,' said Copeland. 'Go through the files and update them as appropriate. Find out which witnesses are still alive then update their details – address, occupation, that sort of thing. If deceased, enter a cause and date of death on the top sheet and move on. In the unlikely event you think the case has—'

'Resolution potential,' muttered Brook.

'In that case, update the file to say you've assessed it positively, do the paperwork to say why and then pass it on to me for uploading on to the database.'

'Sounds simple enough,' said Brook. *If deadly dull.*

'It is,' replied Copeland. 'But it's deadly dull – usually.'

Brook looked up. 'Usually?'

Copeland shrugged, unable to meet Brook's eye for some reason. 'Sometimes an old case grabs you and won't let go because you see something that no one's ever seen before. That can happen with a fresh pair of eyes and none of the baggage investigating officers carry into a case.' He looked at Brook, managing a smile. 'I won't talk down to a man of your experience. You'll soon pick it up. I always start with the oldest case and work my way forward chronologically. You can create your own method.'

'Do we know when and who last looked at a file?'

'First thing you check. There should be a list of officers' names and review dates on the front page. The second thing to do is—'

'Check which suspects and witnesses are alive for re-interview.'

Copeland smiled. 'You're a natural, Brook.'

'Next stop chief constable,' snorted Brook. 'Should I bother re-interviewing witnesses?'

'If you like wasting your time. Memories fade and even if you know what to ask, you're unlikely to get a better version of events than the one in the file. But sometimes it can bear fruit. Circumstances change and a witness who lied in the past might forget the details of what they said at the time. Or they might suddenly find a good reason to tell you the truth.' He shrugged. 'Either way, it can get you out of the office for a few hours, so please yourself. Otherwise just record all the information you can. Any questions?'

'How long have you been doing this kind of work?'

'I set up my first CCU in Nottingham about nine years ago so you can imagine how much work that was, with their murder rate.'

'Most of those would be drug shootings though, surely.'

'Of course,' said Copeland. 'But with that many guns on their doorstep, serving officers were usually too busy to look over traditional unsolveds.'

Brook nodded. 'Do you enjoy the work?'

Copeland considered for a moment. 'It supplements my pension and gets me out of the house.' Brook managed to crack a smile. 'Honestly, it's pretty dull, most of the time, but occasionally you catch a break which can lead to a resolution. Pretty rare, though.'

'And why leave Nottingham to come back here?'

Copeland hesitated, as though he hadn't thought about it. 'I still live near Derby and I've already reviewed a lot of the cases as a serving officer so I know the lie of the land, the people involved.'

Again Brook nodded. There was something in Copeland's manner that told Brook he wasn't being totally candid. 'And when did you start the CCU? In Derby, I mean.'

'Chief Superintendent Charlton recruited me a month ago. We attend the same church, so he knows me and my work. I've been setting up the unit for the last couple of weeks.'

'Two weeks?' said Brook, his smile fading. 'He's gone to a lot of trouble.'

'What does that mean?'

'Never mind,' said Brook. He yawned involuntarily.

'Am I keeping you up?' asked Copeland.

'Sorry. I didn't sleep so well last night.'

'I'm not surprised, kicking your heels at home for five months.' Brook caught his eye. 'No, Charlton didn't tell me, if that's what you're thinking. But everyone else I've talked to did. Are you surprised?'

Brook shrugged. 'I suppose not. You know the details?'

'You searched a suspect's home with your daughter in tow.'

Brook prepared to repeat the objection he made to Charlton but decided not to bother. 'Something like that.'

'If it's any consolation, I sympathise. What you did . . . well, a lot of coppers won't go that extra mile for a result.'

'And you will?'

Copeland smiled with mouth only. 'In my younger days, maybe.' He locked on to Brook's eyes. 'Though nothing came back to bite me. Guess I must have been a bit luckier than you, Brook. A word of warning. If you think you're just going to sit in here and catch up on your sleep, be advised. I'm to give Charlton weekly reports on your progress. He wants to know how you're doing and he wants me to play tittle-tattle if you fuck up.' Brook winced. 'Oh, I'm sorry, I forgot. I gather you have an aversion to swearing.'

Brook's answering smile was tight. 'Not to the swearing as much as what it tells me about the person doing it, Clive.'

'And what's that?'

'It's a symptom of a mind that's not under control,' replied Brook quietly. 'And control is what they pay us for.'

Copeland hesitated as though he wanted to say something further but decided it wasn't the right time. Brook knew then that Copeland had been made aware of the mental breakdown he'd suffered serving in the Met.

'I'll try and mind my Ps and Qs,' said the older man eventually.

Brook was sombre. Obviously Copeland had decided to fling that particular barb at a later date. 'And are you going to?'

'Going to what?'

'Play tittle-tattle.'

'I haven't decided yet but I'll have to tell him something.' Copeland made to leave but turned back at the door. 'Just so you know, Brook, I'm a fair man. I'll make up my own mind about you.'

'That's nice to know. Presumably you've sought other opinions.'

Copeland grinned. 'Excuse my language but almost everyone I've talked to thinks you're a prick.'

Brook nodded. 'Including the Chief.'

Copeland's answering smile was tight. 'Like I said, I'll make up my own mind.'

'Don't bother,' replied Brook. 'Charlton's right.'

* * *

Brook picked up each of the folders on the trolley in turn and skimmed the front pages. Some senior investigating officers on the files were unknown to him, some weren't. His heart sank when further inspection revealed which officers had subsequently revisited the cases. Brook found that, down the years, ex-DCI Copeland had reinvestigated all but one of the six cases. It was telling that he'd reviewed only two of the cases more than once so Brook put those in a pile with the case he hadn't reviewed at all. The three cases Copeland had reviewed just once were tossed on to the bottom shelf of the trolley.

Brook returned to the first three files. In one, he saw the name of Detective Inspector Robert Greatorix and let out an involuntary moan, sagging back on to his chair and recoiling immediately from the unforgiving metal.

Nine

Detective Sergeants Noble and Morton were deep in conversation when Brook pushed open the door with his knee. The metal chair appeared over the threshold first, Brook following a moment later.

'Don't mind me,' said Brook. He retrieved the padded office chair from behind his old desk and replaced it with the metal one.

'Back already,' said Noble. 'Those cases weren't cold for long.'

'Funny,' said Brook. He nodded at Morton. 'Rob.'

'Getting on OK with Copeland?' inquired Noble.

Brook stopped wheeling his chair towards the door. 'We're feeling each other out. He seems viable.'

'Rob knew him.'

'Oh?' said Brook, raising an eyebrow to Morton.

'Not well, I should say,' said Morton. 'But he was a good sort. Loyal to his team, good at his job.'

'Worth knowing,' nodded Brook. 'Ever on his team?'

'He was only a couple of years off retirement when I started here and I never worked under him,' answered Morton. 'But I rarely heard a bad word.'

Brook held his eyes. 'Rarely?'

Morton looked around, as though the room had suddenly filled with spies. Then, his voice lowered. 'Copeland has a temper, especially if the case . . .'

'What?' asked Brook, when Morton showed signs of finishing there. 'We're talking in confidence, Rob.'

'Well, he has a blind spot,' continued Morton. 'His teenage sister was murdered when he was a kid and they never found the killer. Hilda, Matilda or something. It was why he joined the force. After that, if he was on any case with a young female victim and you messed up, he could be a bit twitchy about it, as though you were letting down his own sister.'

'Never solved, you say,' said Brook.

'No,' said Morton. 'He looked at the case often enough, on the QT, but never got anywhere with it.'

'Copeland reviewed the case?' exclaimed Brook.

'You ask me, he was never off it,' replied Morton.

'You're telling me Brass let Copeland investigate his sister's murder?'

'That's just it,' said Morton, lowering his voice again. 'Brass never knew. Not officially. Copeland knew personal involvement would disqualify him so he'd review the file then get another officer to sign off on it.'

'And these officers would put their names to Copeland's work even if they hadn't re-interviewed a single witness,' said Brook, tight-lipped.

Morton shrugged. 'To be fair, Copeland wouldn't let any other detective near it once he was in CID. We're talking about his sister. He was obsessed. Who was going to argue? He was a DI at thirty and a DCI five years later.'

'Even so . . .' Brook halted, declining to pontificate further after his own fall from grace.

'Maybe you'll get to see the file,' suggested Noble.

'You think?' replied Brook doubtfully. 'I've got six cases. He reviewed five of them but only two of them more than once.'

'Was he SIO on any?' asked Noble.

'Not one,' replied Brook.

'He'd keep those to himself,' added Morton.

Brook raised an eyebrow in mock incredulity. 'Really?'

Morton smiled sheepishly. 'I mean, obviously. Who wouldn't?'

'So what cases are you looking at?' inquired Noble.

'I've not got that far,' said Brook.

'I'd forget the cases he only reviewed once. They're almost certainly duds,' said Noble. 'Stick to the two he investigated more than once, he must think there's some mileage there.'

'My thoughts exactly,' said Brook. 'Although there's one drawback. Ex-DI Greatorix also looked at one of those cases before he retired.'

'He's in the files?' queried Noble. 'Not as SIO, I hope.'

'No, thank God!'

'Which means a result isn't completely out of the question,' laughed Noble.

'In the Cold Case Unit we prefer the term "resolution potential",' replied Brook drily, wheeling his chair out of the office.

Brook picked up the first folder from the heap and pulled out a three-inch stack of cheap, now yellowed, paper. He glanced at the date on the dog-eared top sheet and his heart sank: 1963.

He read quickly through the first couple of pages, soon realising the reason for the file's thickness.

William 'Billy' Stanforth had died on 22 December 1963, burned to death in a garden shed at his parents' home on his thirteenth birthday. The party had been attended by twenty school friends so the number of potential witnesses that had to be interviewed, no matter how fruitlessly, had contributed to the mass of paperwork. Brook skimmed through the papers for nearly half an hour before turning back to the typewritten summary on the top to begin a more detailed read-through.

Billy had gone missing at the party while his sisters, Amelia and Francesca, and invited friends were eating jelly and trifle and playing party games inside his parents' house in Kirk Langley, a small village a few miles north of Derby. He was last seen playing a party game in the house at around four thirty on the fateful afternoon by his elder sister Amelia and his best friend, Edward Mullen. Nobody present – including the only adults, Billy's father and mother – had seen him leave the house and certainly nobody had seen him arrive at the shed where he perished in the flames.

The initial theory was that Billy might have slipped away to have a cigarette – he'd just begun to dabble, according to Edward Mullen's statement – and once inside the shed, Billy had knocked over a jar of paint thinners which may have been ignited by the cigarette.

The old shed had burned down to the ground within minutes, with Billy trapped inside. To add to the pathos, the Stanforth family and all the party guests were soon alerted to the fire and stood watching the blaze, unaware, at first, that Billy was dead or dying inside. Initially no one thought the fire anything serious. Nothing of value was stored in the shed, and it stood alone in the large garden with no chance of the flames spreading. When it was discovered that Billy was missing, the alarm was raised and the dreadful realisation that the young man had been trapped in the blaze began to dawn.

In the early hours of the next morning, forensics officers had found Billy's blackened, charred remains amongst the smoking ruins. But what appeared to be a tragic accident took a sinister turn when officers searching the debris found the metal hasp of the shed door, which, though misshapen by the blaze, was clearly still attached to the staple by the locked padlock. Billy had gone into the shed and been padlocked in from the outside. Although there was no clear indication as to how the fire inside the shed had been started, the coroner had been left with little choice but to record a verdict of unlawful killing.

Brook turned to the autopsy report which confirmed that Billy Stanforth had died of smoke inhalation as the fire took hold inside the shed. The presence of toxic chemicals had accelerated both Billy's suffocation and the intensity of the inferno.

Brook returned again to the front of the report. The SIO was a DCI Samuel Bannon. Next to the typed text of his name was the handwritten addendum DECEASED in brackets. The junior officer on the investigation was a DC Walter Laird. There was no report of his death. The file had last been updated and amended four years previously by Brook's former colleague, DI Robert Greatorix.

'And what did you turn up, Bob? Let me hazard a guess. Nothing.'

Brook continued reading. In the days following the fire, DCI Bannon and DC Laird interviewed Billy's parents, Bert and Ruth Stanforth, and cleared them of any suspicion, even though talks with occupants of neighbouring houses revealed Billy was a wayward child and often in trouble with his parents for fighting and not getting to school on time.

Brook couldn't prevent a smile at what passed for anti-social behaviour in 1963. He wondered at the reaction he'd get if he were able to transport some of the drug-taking, knife-wielding teenagers he encountered in Derby back to those times.

After ruling out the Stanforths, who by all accounts did not leave the house that afternoon, until the fire, Bannon and Laird had then interviewed every child at the party including Billy's twin sister Francesca and fifteen-year-old elder sister Amelia. After interviewing Amelia, DC Laird did eventually identify a suspect.

Seventeen-year-old Brendan McCleary was a local petty criminal. He'd left school at fourteen without a trade and been unable to hold down a job for more than three months. At the time of Billy's party, he was unemployed. He was also Amelia's boyfriend and was seen in the vicinity of the house during the hour between the last sightings of Billy playing party games and the fire. Other witnesses claimed that Amelia had left the party around that time, presumably looking for McCleary, and had arrived at the fire after everyone else.

At the station, according to the reports, Bannon and Laird had questioned McCleary closely. Brook frowned, imagining what *closely* might imply in the days before taped interviews. Whatever the tactics used by investigating officers, it was all to no avail. No matter what pressure was brought to bear on the young man, he refused to be cajoled into a confession to Billy Stanforth's murder and was released a day later after making a statement.

Yes, he'd admitted to being outside the Stanforth house a half hour before the fire. Yes, he'd had cigarettes and matches with him. Yes, he sometimes supplied Billy with the odd one if asked, but Brendan insisted he hadn't seen Billy that day and he hadn't set the fire, claiming to have left after a brief conversation with Amelia. He claimed he didn't know there'd even been a fire until the next day when DC Laird called at his father's house to question him.

His girlfriend, Amelia Stanforth, had supported his testimony and, try as they might, Bannon and Laird couldn't budge either from their version of events. In the end, they were forced to take McCleary's word, though obviously he remained a *person of interest*.

Brook skimmed through the statements taken from the schoolchildren. Most were cursory and translated into police-speak; *no recollection*, was a common phrase, presumably supplied by the interviewing officer. Most were only capable of testifying as to their whereabouts when the alarm was raised about the fire.

Francesca Stanforth's initial statement was more detailed than the rest. Like others she had not seen her twin brother leave the party and had no idea why he might have slipped away. However, Francesca claimed to have seen Amelia running to join the throng already gathered around the burning shed and, significantly, her older sister appeared to have been crying.

'Boyfriend trouble,' was Brook's immediate assessment. Reading on, he saw that Bannon and Laird had come to the same conclusion – her assignation with Brendan McCleary had ended in some form of disagreement. Subsequent to this, Brendan McCleary had refused to confirm that Amelia had been in tears when he'd left her but he did admit he'd told her he didn't want to see her later that night for a scheduled date and she'd been angry. He'd then watched her go back towards the house before setting off for home.

Brook reread Amelia's statement but it confirmed Brendan's version of events exactly. She denied, however, that she'd been crying and after further questioning, young Francesca was forced to admit that she may have been mistaken about seeing her sister in tears.

Brook turned to the statement given by Edward Mullen, Billy's best friend. Shortly before Billy's disappearance, Mullen had admitted having a row with Billy. Mullen had been angry that Billy had cheated during a party game and had stormed off upstairs to sulk under a pile of coats in one of the bedrooms.

Significantly, Mullen was the only person at the party, adult or child, who, by his own admission, was alone around the time the fire was set. That, coupled with the recent argument with his friend, no matter how childish and pathetic, had served to briefly make him the prime suspect. Certainly Bannon and Laird had concluded as much and had interviewed him extensively. A further handwritten assessment was clipped to Mullen's statement.

Edward Mullen is a strange and introverted boy with (to my way of thinking) an unhealthy obsession with his late friend. Talking to him you might be forgiven for thinking Billy Stanforth hadn't died at all. Every time we mention his name, Mullen's face lights up as though his friend had just walked through the door. Odd. However, the only time we see Mullen upset or tearful is when we accuse him of murdering Billy. He becomes hysterical at the idea that we'd think he'd hurt his friend. Doesn't appear to be faking. DCI SB.

On the next page were details which threw doubt on Mullen as a suspect. He had an alibi. One of the party rooms fed directly out on to the bottom of the stairs. In Mrs Stanforth's statement she remembered seeing Mullen stomping up the stairs with a face like thunder, and didn't see him come down again until the alarm was raised for the fire.

But Mullen was still alone in the minutes leading up to the fire.

With Mullen's alibi, the murder inquiry began to peter out. There was no eyewitness or forensic evidence against any of the main suspects and, without a confession, Bannon and Laird had little option but to widen the net. Brook then read several pages of fruitless information about a couple of not-so-local pyromaniacs who were questioned and found to have watertight alibis.

Bannon and Laird then investigated the possibility of a sexual angle, even though the autopsy had found no evidence of what was discreetly referred to as 'interference'. Nonetheless, several known sex offenders from the Derby area were brought in for questioning but nothing came of this line of inquiry either, and gradually the intensity of the investigation wound down.

For something to do, Brook turned back to the autopsy report. The pictures of the dead boy made for grim viewing and Brook tried not to linger over them. Billy Stanforth's blackened mouth was fixed and contorted into an oval of mortal agony and Brook almost imagined he could hear him screaming.

Despite the charred condition of his young corpse, forensic scientists were able to conclude that young Billy had tried desperately to escape the flames. His knuckles were damaged and three of his fingernails had been ripped off as he tore frantically at the shed door. What wasn't clear was why he hadn't attempted to escape through the small window on one wall and the detectives had attributed this to the height of the window and panic. Had Billy remained calm, he might have noticed a small wooden stepladder that would have allowed him easy access to the window.

Brook emptied out an A4 wallet crammed with crime scene photographs showing serious-looking men with baggy trousers, white lab coats and thick, round spectacles sifting through the wreckage of the shed. The blackened, locked padlock, attached to the twisted remains of the metal hasp, was photographed on the ground next to a twelve-inch ruler.

Brook wondered aimlessly if the padlock was still in storage anywhere. Not that seeing it would be of any value. No fingerprints, partial or otherwise, had been discovered on any of the metal components.

Brook took out his notebook and a pen from the jar on his table but hesitated over the blank page. 'Nineteen sixty-three! Am I really going to do this?'

After an internal debate, Brook wrote, 'Screaming?' then skimmed back over the witness statements of Billy's parents, sisters and fellow partygoers. Not one report of anyone hearing screams. Had Billy already inhaled a lethal dose of toxic smoke by the time the fire was discovered? Possible. If he had screamed, had the noise in the house been so loud that Billy couldn't be heard? What about neighbours? None of them had mentioned screaming in their state-ments either. Given the struggle evidenced by the damage to Billy's hands, screaming in panic would be a natural response. But perhaps the intense toxic fumes had made it impossible to inhale sufficiently for an audible cry.

Brook reread the statements from four of the Stanforths' neigh-bours. Several had seen Brendan McCleary walking along Moor Lane towards the Stanforth house before the fire. No one had seen him entering or leaving the Stanforth property or walking back to his home in Pole's Road less than a mile away.

'But it was winter and it would be dark and cold, so curtains would be drawn.'

Brook scanned the witness list at the front of the file again, stopping at Charlotte Dilkes's name. Next to her entry, DC Walter Laird had recorded the date of her death – June 1964.

Only six months after Billy Stanforth's death. Interesting.

Brook thought no more of it before coming across a further note about her demise. He checked the signature at the bottom of the page. Again Walter Laird, now a DS, had written it.

Brook skimmed the account of Charlotte's sad but banal death. She had gone out to play on her own in nearby fields and had fallen into a pond. The pond wasn't large or particularly deep but Charlotte was small for her age and, unable to swim or clamber out, had drowned in just five feet of water. She was only thirteen years old. There were no witnesses and no signs of force or trauma on her little body. The inquest had returned a verdict of accidental death.

Interestingly, in spite of the inquest, DS Laird had seen fit to interview Brendan McCleary and Amelia Stanforth in an attempt to establish a connection between the deaths of Billy Stanforth and Charlotte Dilkes. Brook sat back to ponder this. Perhaps Laird had been convinced that one, or both, of them had murdered Amelia's brother, Billy. Why they might then have decided to kill Charlotte was unknown but if she was a witness to Billy's murder they might have decided to cover their tracks.

A moment later, Brook shook his head. It was a bit thin. If Charlotte Dilkes had witnessed something during Billy's murder, presumably she would have given evidence to that effect during the original inquiry.

Brook finished reading Laird's notes – neither Brendan McCleary nor Amelia Stanforth had an alibi for the approximate time of Charlotte's death. McCleary, by then an eighteen year old, claimed he was out fishing, though nobody could be found to corroborate that, and sixteen-year-old Amelia said she was alone in her bedroom. So at the time of the drowning, the two were less than half a mile from the scene, although this wasn't enough to affect the coroner's verdict.

Brook turned to the final wallet in the file – photographs of the partygoers taken *before* the fire. He took them out and picked through them. There were only a dozen, mostly taken by Mr Stanforth because he was only in one of them – a family shot taken of Bert and his wife Ruth, smiling happily with Billy and his twin Francesca, each sitting on a parent's knee. Presumably elder sister Amelia had taken this snap because she was missing from the family group.

All four wore a folded newspaper, in lieu of a party hat, and the kind of jovial, crooked-toothed grins that traditionally made Americans bemoan the complete absence of dental surgeries in the UK.

Other pictures showed bright-eyed, thin-limbed children enjoying the luxury of orange squash and trifle, playing various party games and generally grinning happily for Bert Stanforth's camera. Unlike digital cameras, however, there was no data that could give a clue as to what time, and in what order, these pictures had been taken so Brook had to piece them together the best he could.

He turned to the back of each photo. There was a developer's stamp on all of them, J.E. Browns of Derby, and a date – 20 January 1964 – nearly a month after Billy's death. Assuming it wouldn't take as long as a month to develop photographs, even in those days, Brook surmised that these pictures had been forgotten about in the aftermath of the tragedy. Later, they must have been sent for processing, whether by the Stanforths or detectives, Brook couldn't be sure.

The final three photographs in the pile were shots of the entire gathering, much like schools would take an end-of-year picture of an entire class. One had been taken inside the house and two had been taken earlier in the afternoon, in the garden, while still light. Bert Stanforth was absent from all three and presumably behind the camera. The rest of the family, including Amelia, were in shot, as were all of Billy's friends and schoolmates. Billy was arm in arm with one particular lightly built boy as they leered at the camera.

One of the garden pictures was similar to the image taken in the house – a group shot. The other picture was clearly a dry run, a failed attempt to take the ensemble photo, which had ended in disarray. The assembly had broken up and children were scattering in all directions, looking towards a dog which had run across the garden and distracted them. The dog was visible at the edge of the shot being collared by a young arm out of the frame. The arm sported a bracelet so – assuming boys didn't wear jewellery in 1963 – must have belonged to one of the girls.

In both outdoor pictures, the sky was darkening and the wind was getting up. Several people were hanging on to their paper hats and some girls were pushing down their billowing skirts.

Brook plucked a large fist of used Blu-Tack from a drawer and arranged all the photographs on a large whiteboard, putting them in the best chronological order he could come up with. He looked carefully at each picture in turn.

Brook found a sheet of tracing paper at the bottom of the packet of photographs. It had been used to trace around the figures in one of the group photographs and, helpfully, whoever had gone to that trouble had put a name to each member of the shot. Brook looked at the three group photographs then Blu-Tacked the sheet of tracing paper above the second picture taken in the garden. Everyone but Bert Stanforth had been named on it.

When he'd finished, he turned again to the list of witnesses at the front of the file. In the fifty intervening years, the list had been amended many times by reviewing officers, as people who were there that afternoon had passed away.

Brook scrolled down the list of names. Amelia Stanforth and Edward Mullen, Billy's best friend, were both still alive four years ago when Greatorix had reviewed the case. So were three other school friends of Billy's though only Edna Spencer (nee Hibbert) still lived in Derby. Brendan McCleary was also alive and living in the city. All the other people in the photographs were either dead or untraceable.

Bert Stanforth had died, in 1976, at the age of sixty-five. His wife Ruth had followed in 1981. Beside both their names and dates of death were the initials 'NC' – natural causes.

Brook's finger came to rest on the name of Billy's twin sister, Francesca Stanforth. She had died in 1968 at the tender age of just eighteen. Significantly, she had died on her birthday which, as Billy's twin, was also the fifth anniversary of her brother's death – 22 December. Her date of death was followed by the initials 'AD' – accidental death. There were no other details, which suggested that her death had been properly investigated before being deemed an accident.

Brook was solemn. Mr and Mrs Stanforth had buried two of their three children – the unspoken dread of all parents. Worse, they had both died on their shared birthday, five years apart. Brook's thoughts drifted to his daughter, Terri. It was against nature to outlive your offspring. They were the future. They carried the torch forward when you fell. Brook resolved to ring Terri to arrange a visit at the earliest opportunity.

He gazed again at the group photographs from the party – all those happy smiling faces just hours before tragedy had struck.

Correction: assuming Billy's killing had not been spur-of-the-moment, maybe one of them was not happy, maybe one of them was harbouring murder in their heart. Yet, apart from Mr and Mrs Stanforth, all the suspects were children. Today, though still horrifying, thirteen year olds committing murder was all too plausible. In the sixties, the idea would have been greeted with shock and disbelief.

Brook's pen hovered above the notebook. With a sudden shake of the head, he tossed both aside. *Interesting case but see it for what it is, Damen – bureaucratic form-filling.*

He looked once more at the three group pictures on the display board on his dingy wall then at Billy Stanforth's grinning, leering face. 'Sorry, Billy,' he said. 'I'm sure better men than I have tried to give you justice.' He shook his now empty flask, hauled himself up and stepped wearily into the corridor.

He knocked on Copeland's door and marched in without waiting for a reply. He caught the tail end of Copeland's arm moving to cover something on the table. Under his arm Brook could see the spine of a folder much newer than the ones he'd been handed.

'I'm just going to get a tea from the vending machine,' said Brook. He eyed Copeland, his arm still held self-consciously across the folder, although his demeanour tried to convince Brook that his position was natural. 'Want one?'

Copeland glanced beyond Brook to the far corner of his room and Brook followed his gaze to a kettle, a packet of tea bags and a carton of milk that he hadn't spotted earlier when Charlton had brought him down to meet his new colleague.

'Help yourself,' said Copeland. 'I get through about twelve cups a day. You don't want to be drinking filth out of a vending machine.'

'That's why I bring a flask,' answered Brook. 'But I'm empty.'

'Boredom,' said Copeland. 'Pointless denying it,' he added, when Brook began to prepare a rebuttal. 'It's the nature of the beast – sitting around in grimy rooms reading ancient history makes you thirsty.'

'But you get used to it.'

'Give it a few months,' Copeland replied.

'God forbid,' said Brook before he could stop himself. He glanced at the single picture frame on Copeland's desk. A string of rosary beads was draped over it. Brook edged round to see the photograph's subject but couldn't get a good angle without going to stand beside Copeland. 'You've cracked one of these cases without DNA, you said.'

'I wouldn't do the job otherwise,' replied Copeland.

'How does that work?'

'Like I said, sometimes a killer forgets what lies he's told and gives himself away or an eyewitness remembers some apparently unimportant detail.'

'Deathbed confessions?' suggested Brook.

'That can happen as well and it's good to get closure but it doesn't count as a win,' said Copeland. 'To chalk up a result, there has to be some notion that the doer faces earthly justice as a result of our inquiries.'

'Earthly justice?' said Brook, glancing again at the rosary. He tried to keep the cynicism out of his voice. 'You mean, before God has his say.'

Copeland's answering smile was thin. 'You're not a religious man, I think.' Brook declined to answer. 'Nor was I, once. Not until . . .' Copeland halted, before smiling more effusively. 'There comes a point in every man's life when he realises he has to make amends.' He glanced sadly at the picture on his desk before closing his eyes to remember.

'Death closes all: but something ere the end,
Some work of noble note, may yet be done.'

Brook studied him briefly. 'Tennyson.'

Copeland looked up in surprise. 'You know "Ulysses". I'm impressed.'

Brook raided his own memory.

'Come, my friends,
'Tis not too late to seek a newer world.'

93

'They said you were bright,' said Copeland softly. 'Too bright to believe in God?'

'It's not that,' said Brook. 'I was raised a Catholic.'

'What then?'

Brook wasn't sure he wanted to be drawn into a theological discussion. 'Like Tennyson, I believe redemption has to be earned in life. Religion condones the worst sinners performing appalling acts by allowing them to wipe the slate clean with one act of contrition, one deathbed confession.'

'So you don't believe in forgiveness,' said Copeland.

'Not from a third party,' said Brook. 'We can forgive ourselves once redemption is earned through deeds, not mumbling a few words at a priest as you slip away.'

'My God,' said Copeland. 'What happened to harden your heart against us poor sinners?' He smiled at Brook. 'Or was it something you did?'

'What do you mean?'

'The worst poachers make the best gamekeepers, Brook.'

'Do they?'

'And have you?' asked Copeland, a thin smile on his lips.

'Have I what?' inquired Brook.

'Forgiven yourself.'

Brook was uncomfortable but held Copeland's gaze. 'Have any of us?'

Copeland blinked and his eyes flicked towards the photograph on his desk, before returning to Brook, a tentative smile appearing on his face. 'Help yourself to tea whenever you like, Brook.'

'Tomorrow perhaps.' Brook turned to the door, glad to be leaving. 'I didn't bring a mug. Besides, I need to see daylight at least once before I go back to my dungeon.'

'They're not the best rooms, are they?' said Copeland. 'Not a lot of money floating around the budget for this kind of work.'

'Not a lot of staff either,' said Brook.

'Don't tell me you're missing the warmth of human companionship,' mocked Copeland. 'I was told you were a loner.'

'I'm used to having a partner to throw ideas at.'

'You mean a dogsbody to show off to,' grinned Copeland. 'Don't deny it, Brook. I was a DCI. I know how much ego can influence the clear-up. It's pointless having skills if there's no one around to appreciate them.'

Brook threw another discreet glance at the folder under Copeland's arm and left the room.

Ten

BROOK SIPPED HIS BITTER TEA in the car park, determined to enjoy the cold fresh air and fading daylight in spite of the gunmetal sky and dipping temperature. He was unaware of the two men, one a photographer with a telescopic lens at the perimeter fence, the other, a small rotund man grinning maliciously as he pointed at Brook. The cameraman responded by training his camera on the DI as he drained his cup and turned to walk back into the building, oblivious to the scrutiny he was under.

Noble walked round the corner, lighting a cigarette in a cupped hand. 'Three times in one day.' He smiled. 'You might as well have kept your old office.'

'I wish,' retorted Brook.

'How goes it?'

'It's like being in prison,' said Brook, repeating his earlier grumble to Copeland.

'You'll get used to it. Cigarette?' asked Noble, making no move to produce the packet.

'I've given up, John. For good this time.'

'It won't last,' retorted a grinning Noble. 'And it's expensive for me from the day you're smoking again until the day you *accept* you're smoking again.'

'Thanks for the vote of confidence,' replied Brook. He crushed his plastic beaker and set off back into the building. Before he was out of sight, he turned back to Noble. 'By the way, John, a word to the wise. Expect a visit from Copeland soon.'

96

'Don't worry,' said Noble. 'I've already spoken to him. I bigged you up, good and proper.'

Brook closed his eyes in pain. 'Meaning?'

Having found his target, Noble grinned again. 'I gave you a glowing testimonial – nearly had *myself* in tears, I can tell you.'

'That's nice but he won't be asking about that.'

'Oh?'

'I think he's looking over the Wallis and Ingham files.'

'He's re-opening the Reaper killings?' said Noble, suddenly animated. 'Those are our cases. At least the Derby murders.'

Brook shrugged. 'They're unsolved. That's what he does.'

'And he had the brass neck to tell you he was looking.'

'Not exactly. I went in to speak to him and he covered up the file he was looking at.'

'Then how do you know it was the Reaper file?' asked Noble. 'Maybe he was looking over his sister's murder again, like Rob said.'

'Possible, but the file looked too new for that. Besides, why hide it unless he was embarrassed?'

'He might be embarrassed looking over a file that's personal to him.'

Brook conceded with a gesture. 'You could be right. But best to be forewarned.'

'Makes no difference,' said Noble. 'He can look all he wants; he won't find anything at our end. We did everything we could and we did it by the book.' Remembering Brook's recent suspension, Noble's eyes betrayed a glimpse of doubt. 'Didn't we?'

Brook's answer didn't reassure. 'I think so.'

'You don't sound convinced,' observed Noble. 'Anything you want to tell me?'

Brook smiled. 'Just be aware. There's often something on a case you don't see because you're too close.'

He shivered as he walked through the front entrance to be greeted by the sight of Sergeant Hendrickson, leaning on the front desk, grinning at him like a Cheshire Cat.

'Sergeant,' said Brook icily, avoiding his eye and hurrying his step towards the lifts.

'Inspector,' replied Hendrickson. 'We thought you'd retired,' he shouted gleefully at Brook's retreating frame.

Brook's pace didn't slacken and he pushed through the double doors a second later.

'Still, not long now,' muttered a chuckling Hendrickson. 'And seeing you about to get royally fucked over is just as good, mental boy.'

Brook headed back down the stairs to the basement, a feeling of gloom growing with each step of his descent. Winter was here and the days were too cold and dark to sit in his cottage garden when he got home from work. Worse, what little daylight on offer at work was being denied him. It wouldn't have concerned a younger Brook, but advancing age brought with it the instinctual dread of winter's cold embrace that he'd once observed with bemusement in the elderly.

He opened the door to his bare office and slumped down, at least able to draw a measure of comfort from a familiar chair. He resisted picking another cold case file from the trolley and spent the rest of the afternoon searching the usual sites to confirm the continued well-being and last known addresses of the remaining living witnesses in the Stanforth murder. By the end of the afternoon, Brook had a list which included ex-DI Walter Laird, now in his seventies, Edward Mullen, Edna Spencer and Amelia Stanforth.

His final search was for Brendan McCleary. It proved more difficult as there seemed to be large gaps in his National Insurance and tax records, which usually meant one thing.

'Prison,' muttered Brook. He yawned and looked at his watch. It was nearly five. Not a long day by his standards but he'd hardly slept the night before and felt close to exhaustion when he left the office and trotted out to the darkened car park with his laptop and empty flask.

'Good first day back, Inspector?'

Brook turned from unlocking his car to see the squat figure of Brian Burton grinning at him from behind the safety of another vehicle. He prepared an insult but kept it to himself when he saw the recorder in Burton's hand.

'You've just missed me, Brian,' said Brook, opening the car door. 'I left two minutes ago.'

'Same old Brook, too arrogant to say a few words to the local taxpayers,' commented Burton with a sneer.

'Where's the photographer you usually hide behind, Brian?' said Brook.

Burton could scarcely contain his glee. 'He's back at the paper looking through the shots we got of you this afternoon, loafing around in the car park while there's a kid missing. Good story that.'

Brook paused then stepped away from the car. 'That's a story? I'm not even on that case.'

'Everyone's on that case,' insisted Burton. 'Everyone who cares, at least.'

Brook was speechless for a moment. 'This is harassment. We have laws.'

Burton clicked off the recorder for a moment. 'Harassment, my arse. I'll let my readers decide. They have a right to know how you spend your time and they'd like to know how you've got the nerve to draw your pay sitting on your backside at home for five months.' Burton clicked the recorder back on, hoping for an indiscretion, an insult, possibly even an assault. 'Still no comment, *Inspector* Brook?'

Brook felt his fist tighten and his mind unconsciously plotted the optimum route to his prey. A second later, he had control. 'I spent part of that time in hospital because I was injured on duty, protecting the people of Derby.'

'You were fucking suspended as well.' Burton's smirk afforded a glimpse of yellow teeth. 'It's a matter of record. But never mind,' he said, clicking off the recorder. 'I'm sure I can think of something better for you to say.'

'You do that,' said Brook. 'And while you're composing our fictional chat, Brian, think about what *you* do for the good of this city – that is, apart from pressuring vulnerable people to commit suicide.'

Burton's grin faded and Brook returned to the driver's seat and drove away.

When Brook reached the village of Kirk Langley he pulled off the A52 on to Moor Lane and slowed to a crawl looking for the Stanforth house in the dark. Amelia Stanforth had never married and had lived her entire life in her parents' house – the same home, overlooking the same garden, where her younger brother had perished in an unexplained fire. Brook found it hard to imagine living nearly fifty years within sight of the spot where a loved one had died. Unless, of course, Billy Stanforth wasn't as loved as a younger brother ought to be and Amelia had stayed out of a warped sense of guilt.

When he found the house, Brook stepped from the car and approached the gate. The front garden was large, though details were difficult to pick out in the pitch black of a country night. The paved path to the door wound round the front of the house to the rear garden where Billy Stanforth had died.

The building itself was a weathered, redbrick structure, solid and spacious, built in 1952, when homes were not yet designed to shoehorn occupants into box-sized rooms. Although somewhat tired and shabby now, it must have been a desirable residence fifty years ago. Clearly Bert Stanforth, a master butcher, earned decent money although good housing wasn't ludicrously overpriced in the sixties.

Brook walked carefully over the damp, weed-encrusted paving stones, drawing his overcoat around him in the chill winter wind. He rapped on the glass door and a cheerful young woman appeared, struggling to balance a baby in her arms. A blast of heat and light hit Brook and warmed him.

'I'm DI Brook, Derby CID,' he said, not bothering to show his warrant card. 'I'm looking for Amelia Stanforth. I'm told she lives here.'

The woman shook her head. 'Not any more. My husband and I have lived here for the last three years. She was the nice old lady who lived here before us.'

'Any idea where she went?'

'She went to St Agatha's Care Home. At least that's where I forward any mail. I assume she's still there if she's still alive. She seemed quite frail. I gather she had heart trouble.'

Brook thanked her and walked away from the welcoming glow of family life. On a whim, he walked around the low wall of the garden boundary and peered into the unlit grounds at the rear. There was nothing to see except a rough lawn with a child's multicoloured plastic bike abandoned on its side to the elements. Retracing his steps, Brook fancied he could see a Victorian greenhouse-cum-conservatory on the other side of the house but the light was too poor to be sure.

He was returning to his car when a blood-curdling screech rent the air. He turned back to the house but didn't venture past the gate. He could see the woman in the well-lit kitchen preparing the evening meal. Through the large window at the front, Brook could also see a small boy standing entranced in front of a large television showing cartoons. Both were oblivious to the noise. It hadn't come from the house.

Brook listened for further cries. Nothing. Deciding the noise had been made by a distressed animal or more likely an owl, he got into the car and drove on through the light rain to Hartington.

Brook chewed his way mechanically through his dinner of cold rice, smeared haphazardly with cream cheese. His daughter, Terri, had left a cupboard full of staples for him to consume and Brook had nearly exhausted them. The pasta was gone but he had enough rice left for about three more meals of rice and cream cheese and then he'd be on to the few tins of pulses she'd laid in. Unless he wanted to eat lentils with cream cheese next week he was going to have to do the unthinkable and go food shopping.

After his austere meal, Brook lit the wood burner and sat down in his small sitting room to watch the end of *Don't Look Now*. As he'd suspected, the end of the film brought no comfort for the grieving family, just more death and suffering at the hands of an evil, almost supernatural entity. At the final death scene, as Donald Sutherland's throat was cut, Brook looked deep into the embers of the burning wood, recalling his conversation with Copeland.

Have you forgiven yourself?

As the end titles played, Brook's eyelids began to droop but he was roused by the distant vibrating of the mobile in his jacket. He dragged himself through to the kitchen and read the text from DS Noble. DS Jane Gadd was now a DI. Noble had been passed over for promotion.

'I'm sorry, John,' muttered Brook. After a few seconds composing suitable consolation, Brook began to thumb out a painstaking reply, but was halted by the phone vibrating again in his hand. Only two contact numbers on his speed dial and both were contacting him at the same time. If this kept up he was going to need a secretary.

'Terri.'

'Dad, how are you?'

'I'm fine.'

'How was your first day back?'

'How did you know that?' asked Brook.

'Because it's important, Dad. Don't you have an app on your phone for birthdays and stuff?' She laughed then answered her own question. 'Course not. If your phone were any older it'd be a plastic cup with string through the bottom.'

'I use my memory, girl,' announced Brook. 'Keeps the cobwebs off.'

'That explains all the missed birthdays. How was it?'

'I've had worse days.'

'What did your boss say?'

'Charlton? Not much. He thinks he can bore me out of the profession. He hasn't a clue about my threshold for staring at walls.'

'Go, Dad,' laughed Terri. 'Don't let the bastards grind you down.'

Brook pulled a face. 'Is that Proust?'

'Never mind Proust, are you still eating right?'

'I had pasta with cheese sauce last night and tonight I had rice.'

'Good.'

'Did you get my message about Christmas?'

There was an awkward pause. 'I did but I'll struggle to get over for Crimbo, Dad.'

'If it's about coming back to the cottage, Terri . . .'

'It's nothing to do with what happened, Dad.'

'You could have been killed.'

'But I wasn't and I'm not scarred for life or anything so stop worrying on that score.'

'No nightmares?'

'No, I told you.'

'At least tell me you've stopped blaming yourself for my suspension.' Silence. 'Terri, I'm an experienced detective. I should've known better.'

'But it was my idea.'

'And I should've said no. What happened was my fault. Accept it.'

'If you say so,' she said quietly.

'I do say so. Does that mean you'll come? Just for a couple of days.'

There was a pause at the other end of the line. 'I'll try but it's my final year, Dad, and I want to pull out all the stops.'

'I understand. Do what you have to do, Terri. I'll manage.' He smiled at her as if she were sitting across the table from him. Terri rang off. 'I always have,' he said to the silent phone.

Eleven

Wednesday, 12 December 2012

BROOK ENTERED HIS OLD OFFICE before seven the next morning. It was empty, prompting equal measures of relief and disappointment. Part of him was happy to avoid all contact at an hour when he wasn't the best communicator. However, another part of him wanted to make Noble aware of his brush with Brian Burton the previous evening, the result – he was in no doubt – of a tip-off from Hendrickson.

He retrieved an old mug from a desk drawer and headed down to the basement with it, proud that he'd managed to avoid taking any of the cartons of cigarettes that had forced themselves so alluringly into his field of vision.

After making tea in Copeland's empty office, Brook picked up the photograph on Copeland's desk. A striking young girl's doomed smile gazed back at him, her arms draped around her younger brother Clive, their dog between them. He replaced it and looked around the office for the files he'd seen Copeland covering with his arm the day before. They were nowhere to be seen. He tried the desk drawer but it was locked.

'Taking no chances, eh, Clive?'

With little enthusiasm, Brook returned to his office and picked up where he'd left off the night before, tapping Brendan McCleary's name into the PNC database. The screen filled with his record. Theft was prominent and McCleary had served several small terms for burglary and shoplifting. But what drew Brook's eye was the single charge of murder for which McCleary had served twenty years of a life sentence from 1969 to 1989.

Details were basic but there wasn't a lot to report. In 1969 23-year-old Brendan McCleary had arrived home drunk one evening and must have got into a row with his father, Malcolm. After blowing his head off with a shotgun, McCleary had gone to bed and slept soundly until the next morning, when the body was discovered. With blood and viscera all over his clothing, McCleary had been charged and convicted with ease. Since his release in 1989, he hadn't reoffended or at least hadn't been caught doing so.

Brook clicked on a link to the Probation Service and found a current address for him on their database. Something about the address rang a bell so Brook double-checked his notebook. McCleary lived in the same sheltered housing complex as Edna Spencer, one of the young children at Billy Stanforth's fateful party in 1963.

Brook loaded Google maps on to the screen to reconnoitre the surrounding area. Mount Street was in Normanton, less than a quarter of a mile away from St Chad's Road, where young Scott Wheeler had disappeared five days previously. Brook flicked at his mobile then sifted through the Stanforth file with his free hand. He removed and folded a document into his pocket, while he waited for an answer to his call.

'John, it's me,' said Brook, a moment later. 'Listen, have you interviewed a Brendan McCleary about Scott Wheeler? He lives on Mount Street and has a record longer than my arm, including murder.'

There was a pause at the other end. 'Didn't you get my text last night?' asked Noble.

Brook closed his eyes in self-reproach. 'John, I . . . commiserations. It's a hard blow and totally undeserved.'

'Well, thanks for thinking of me at least,' came the sarcastic reply.

'Sorry I didn't respond. I thought you might want to be left alone,' Brook lied, his eyes still closed. He regretted it immediately.

'No, that was a lie, John. Terri rang me and I got distracted. I've no excuse.'

Strangely Noble seemed to perk up at this admission of Brook's failings. 'No, you're right. There's nothing to be said. What was the name again?'

'Brendan McCleary.'

'I'll check. Anything with kiddies?'

'Nothing and only one incidence of violence on his whole record but that was a murder and he served twenty years for it.'

'Why the interest?'

'He's a name from one of my cold cases. A thirteen-year-old boy died at a party in nineteen sixty-three—'

'Nineteen sixty-three!'

'Tell me about it,' complained Brook.

'And this McCleary was there?'

'Sort of, well, unknown. It's a cold case, remember,' said Brook.

'He'd be how old?'

'Late sixties?'

'Got him,' said Noble. 'He's on our radar but only because he's on the DB and in the area. And the murder was a domestic. Nose clean ever since. Cooper called round but he wasn't there. No reason to suppose he's off the straight and narrow but we flagged him for a call back . . .'

'Is that it?'

'Well, he's pushing seventy and, as you say, there's nothing even close to fiddling on his jacket and if he was a paedo it should have shown up before now.'

'Do we still not know whether Scott's disappearance was sexually motivated?'

'No. We don't even know whether someone took him, but if they did . . .'

'Without a ransom demand, it's unlikely to be a kidnapping,' finished Brook.

'Exactly. And so sexual perversion moves to the top of the list. Hang on.' A pause and muffled voices as Noble spoke to someone else. 'Rob says Cooper spoke to the warden at the sheltered flats. To us he didn't stand out as anything other than a broken-down old lag. Unless you know something different.'

'No, John. It was just a thought.'

'Well, thanks for the information. I'll get Cooper back round there.'

'It's just that I'm on my way there now, unless you want me to hold off.' Brook couldn't be sure but he thought he heard an impatient sigh at the other end. *Am I becoming a nuisance in my old age?* Brook detected more than a trace of indulgence in Noble's exhaled reply.

'What's the address?'

Mrs Gross ascended the concrete stairs with discomfort, Brook and Noble averting their eyes from her huge backside. And each other. The rotund woman sidled rather than walked but Brook guessed this was more a function of her weight than any actual disability. The two officers trailed in her wake, breathing in the dual scent of stale tobacco and pickled onions that accompanied her. They reached a rotting, white-framed wooden door with a mottled security-glass window. The interior was further screened by a blind inside the apartment. She gestured superfluously at the door. 'Four A – this is it.'

Noble rapped hard on the glass and waited, ear cocked. He knocked again. No noise from within.

'Like I told the other officer, Mr McCleary's hardly ever here these days,' she wheezed, still recovering her breath.

'Do you see him coming and going, Mrs Gross?' asked Brook. Out of the corner of his eye he noticed Noble smiling.

'Sometimes,' she replied, flicking a glance at Noble who looked away. 'But about six months ago he moved a few things out and now he don't spend much time here. See him maybe once or twice a month to pick up his letters. That's it.'

'Is he allowed to just use the flat as a mail drop?' asked Brook, remembering to omit her name for Noble's sake. 'There must be plenty of people waiting for sheltered accommodation.'

She shrugged. 'None of my business until he snuffs it.'

Noble knelt to look through the letter box. 'I can see some post,' he said.

'Do you ever collect his post for him?' asked Brook.

'Not my business unless we're clearing a place.'

'And nobody else would have a key?'

'Nothing to stop him making a copy but I've never seen nobody else,' she said.

'Did Cooper check if he's on benefits?' Brook asked Noble.

'He's on Attendance Allowance on top of his pension and his cheques are posted,' said Noble. 'Does he pick up his cheques himself?' he asked the warden.

'Your guess is as good as mine.' She shrugged, her disinterest reaching critical mass.

'Maybe you see him on Thursday when he can collect his benefits and draw his pension at the same time,' suggested Brook.

'I don't remember what day I seen him last,' said Mrs Gross with a touch of impatience.

'Which post office would he use?' asked Brook. She shook her head, her chin waddle drawing the eye.

'Then which is nearest?' persisted Noble, his own patience beginning to thin.

'Normanton Road, I guess,' she said.

Brook produced his notebook and Noble's face broke into a wide grin. 'You're making your own notes!' he laughed.

Brook didn't join in. 'I don't have a lot of choice.'

'Well, I can't stand around all day,' said Mrs Gross, preparing to withdraw.

Brook glanced down at the bunch of keys swinging from a hook in her belt. 'Can you smell that?'

Noble was puzzled for a split second then pursed his lips in disapproval.

'I can't smell anything,' said Mrs Gross.

'I thought I could smell gas,' suggested Brook, unable to meet Noble's reproachful glare. 'Maybe when Sergeant Noble opened the letter box . . .'

'Gas?' The large woman became animated. 'I can't smell it,' she repeated.

'Maybe it's nothing,' said Brook. 'Still, you'd better get on to the supplier. Can't take the chance.'

'That's all I need,' said the large woman.

'I know,' sympathised Brook. 'They might have to break the door down. Evacuate the whole building.'

'Oh, dear God, no.'

Brook imagined Mrs Gross was someone who regularly poked around in people's apartments when they weren't there. He made his bid. 'If we could get in, I suppose we could take a quick look, put your mind at rest,' he offered solicitously.

'Well, we're not supposed to,' she frowned.

'Of course not,' soothed Brook. 'But we *are* police officers.'

The prospect of further inconvenience spurred her and she fumbled for her keys before slipping the selected one into the lock and pushing the door open.

'Better step back,' said Noble, striding into the bare front room. 'It might not be safe.'

'Won't be long,' added Brook, following Noble inside and closing the door on the woman craning to see inside.

Once out of earshot, Noble turned to him. 'I don't believe it. A day back from suspension and you're pulling these kinds of stunts. What if Charlton gets to hear about it?'

Brook shrugged. 'What else can he do to me?' He ran his eye quickly round the room which contained only a single armchair propped in front of a small TV on a lone dining chair.

'He could have your job,' retorted Noble.

'True,' conceded Brook. 'But that wouldn't grieve me. Having a limited future in the force is kind of liberating.'

Noble shook his head and turned to survey the apartment. 'Let's hope McCleary doesn't find out.'

'About what?' smiled Brook. 'We didn't demand to be let in. She volunteered so she's hardly likely to tell him.'

Noble grunted his sceptical reply.

'And frankly, Mrs Gross should be the one complaining – about your manners,' said Brook. 'Don't you know better than to laugh at people's names?'

Noble made his way to the kitchen. 'Then people shouldn't have names that describe them,' he said over his shoulder. 'She's got a chin like a Christmas turkey.'

Brook began a search of the single tiny bedroom. He searched the pockets of the few shabby clothes hanging in the built-in wardrobe then turned over the mattress and knelt to look under the bed.

'Nothing,' shouted Brook through to the kitchen.

'Same in the kitchen,' said Noble, meeting him back in the lounge. 'There's a packet of butter in the fridge – that's it. The gas is off,' he added wryly.

'That's a relief,' replied Brook, sifting through the pile of junk mail and leaflets on the armchair. He isolated the brown envelope, no doubt containing a benefit cheque, and pocketed three brightly coloured direct mail envelopes addressed to McCleary. 'Help with the recycling,' he explained when Noble raised an eyebrow. He examined a shrink-wrapped magazine before showing it to Noble.

'*Sporting Gun – the complete shooting resource*,' read Noble. 'A gun nut?'

'It may just be more junk mail,' said Brook.

'It's got McCleary's name on it.' Noble took the magazine. 'No harm in checking. He gunned down his father, after all.'

'Leave the benefit cheque?' offered Brook.

'I think so.'

Brook threw the brown envelope on to the doormat and, for authenticity, dropped the fast-food leaflets on top. 'Well, it's clear Scott Wheeler's not here.'

'You'd better make a note of that,' teased Noble. 'Two Ts in Scott.'

Brook smiled sarcastically and headed for the door. As Noble followed, he walked over a loose floorboard. He retraced his step and knelt to prise up the board. He extracted a large padded envelope from under the floor. Brook followed him to the armchair where Noble emptied out the contents. A smaller envelope contained photographs. Noble tipped them out and spread them around the cushion, his face souring. The pictures were of young naked boys, most masturbating for the camera. The photos were poor quality, old and dog-eared. In addition to the snaps there were three unmarked DVDs in blank cases with the handwritten titles, Little Squirts 1, 2 and 3.

'Looks like you were right,' said Noble. 'McCleary's a secret paedo.'

'John, those pictures are ancient,' said Brook. 'They could've been there for years.'

'Don't think so. The envelope's new and the state of that floorboard, whoever lived here would've found them as easily as us. They must be his or he'd have dug them out and binned them.'

'OK, but even if we tie that lot to McCleary, it doesn't put him next to Scott Wheeler.'

'Not yet,' said Noble. 'But he's local, he's got a record, he's got kiddie porn in his flat and he's done a runner.'

'You don't know that.'

'Maybe not,' conceded Noble. 'But he's a killer out on licence. Even if he can convince me he had nothing to do with Scott, this stuff gets him off the streets.' Noble's face tightened as he reached the bottom of the pile of photographs. 'It gets worse.' He held up a flattened box which had once contained ammunition. 'An ex-con paedo with a rifle. That's all we need.'

Brook massaged his chin, staring at the gap in the floorboards. 'This feels wrong.'

'How so?'

'This stuff was awfully easy to find.'

'Most criminals are stupid. Didn't you once tell me that?'

'I suppose,' admitted Brook.

'And this *was* your idea.'

They heard a tapping on the door followed by Mrs Gross's muffled voice. 'Is it safe?'

'Just a minute,' shouted Brook at the door. 'How do you want to play this?' he asked Noble. 'Search warrant?' Noble was taken aback for a moment, unaccustomed to making the decision. 'It's your case, John.'

'Search warrant,' confirmed Noble. 'We don't want to give his brief any wiggle room.'

Brook gathered up the photographs and returned them to the envelope with the DVDs and handed the package to Noble who replaced them under the floorboards. Back outside they waited for Mrs Gross to lock up the apartment and shuffle away before Noble flipped out his mobile to arrange the warrant.

Brook knelt down to examine the simple latch. 'A five year old could get past this.'

'Let's hope not,' replied a grim Noble.

'Funny there was no computer to view the DVDs,' said Brook.

'He might have a laptop with him.'

'In which case he'd have access to the internet,' observed Brook. 'And it's a pervert's playground.'

'Your point?'

'The photographs, John. They were pretty old hat. There's much harder stuff on the net. Why would he have such poor quality stuff when he can surf for up-to-date material in minutes?'

'He's an ex-con,' said Noble. 'Maybe he can't afford a laptop. Or maybe he doesn't want to leave a trail.'

Brook grunted his acknowledgment. 'Will you get SOCO to check if the Wheeler kid's been here?'

'That's up to DI Ford,' said Noble. Brook was about to reply when the younger man continued. 'But it'll be hard to object if they're already in the flat.'

Brook managed a half-smile as he left. 'I've got another call.'

Noble's voice turned him back. 'Sir. Good catch.'

Brook shook his head. 'No, John, it's wasted on me. I was never here. This is your prize.'

It was sleeting when the two detectives parted outside and Brook decided not to stand around in the cold. Instead he watched Noble jog to his car to wait for his search warrant then followed Mrs Gross's directions to Edna Spencer's ground-floor flat.

* * *

'Fucking coppers,' spat the man, through broken, blackened teeth, slamming a palm violently down on to the steering wheel. From his battered Land Rover, Brendan McCleary watched, seething with anger as the two plain-clothes detectives spoke briefly in the street outside his flat, before going their separate ways. He'd never come across these two during his many skirmishes with the filth but he could smell coppers a mile away.

'New faces,' said McCleary, kneading the ache in his knee. 'Same old problem.' But for once he'd been lucky. Another minute and he'd have walked straight into their hands. *Lucky? That'll be the day*. Through his misshapen mouth, between sagging, grey-whiskered jowls, he chuckled at the thought, tarry and bitter.

He slid down into his seat as the younger man walked towards the Land Rover, but the blond-haired young man got into his Audi before McCleary could begin to worry about being spotted. When the Audi didn't drive away, McCleary sat upright, ready to leave. But before he turned the ignition, his eyes followed the older man. The middle-aged detective wasn't waiting in the car with the young one. Instead he strolled to the next walkway and back into the complex. He was looking for another flat and McCleary instantly knew which one it would be. 'Edna,' he growled.

He was right. The policeman did a quick survey of the outside of her ground-floor flat then rapped on the door. McCleary had a flash of recognition at Brook's profile. He reached for the afternoon edition of the *Derby Telegraph*, sitting under his bottle of tablets, and stared at the picture of Brook on the front page, then back at the man banging on Edna's door.

'Hello, Inspector Brook.' He fingered the cold steel handle of the hunting knife strapped to his calf, still grubby from its last kill. 'Nice to meet you.'

Brook followed the path, now slick with drizzle, to a front door identical to all the others in the building, including McCleary's. But this time no blind blocked Brook's vision and he stared through the mottled security glass, gleaning from interior lights that someone was at home.

He knocked, feeling immediate guilt at a blurred image of an old woman rocking herself upright to answer his summons. With no little difficulty, the figure eventually got out of her chair and was able to stand. An outside light came on despite it being mid-afternoon and the door opened to reveal a milky blue eye blinking at him through the straggles of grey hair and deep wrinkles. Brook had his ID ready.

'Mrs Spencer, Detective Inspector Brook,' he shouted, enunciating more than usual.

The door opened wider. 'Why are you shouting, young man? You'll have the whole block looking out of their windows.'

Brook smiled. 'Sorry.' He noticed the old woman's piercing gaze move over his right shoulder and turned to see a net curtain fall in the opposite apartment.

'Don't worry, Dotty,' she called out. 'It's just the police. I've robbed another bank, dear.' She chuckled. 'Come in, come in.'

With the aid of her stick, she shuffled back to her chair, Brook following behind at a funereal pace. Eventually Edna fell back into the well-padded armchair with a grating sigh, pressing her hand against her hip to alleviate the pain. She opened her eyes again when the discomfort passed. At once, she wriggled arthritically to get up again. 'Where are my manners? Would you like a cup of tea?'

'No, thank you.'

'No, you must.' She pulled herself forward, nodding at the china cup full of tea on an occasional table next to her chair. 'I've just made a fresh pot. It'll go to waste.'

'Thank you, then,' said Brook quickly, holding up a hand to halt her exertions. He knew from experience that the elderly and infirm set great store by the little rituals that populated a dull and seemingly relentless struggle against pain and loneliness. One of the most important of these was being a generous host, the more so when the opportunities became less frequent. 'I'd love a cup but I can help myself.'

Edna beamed back at him. 'Thank you, young man. My hip's not good at this time of year. Arthritis does love the cold. There are biscuits in the barrel. And please excuse the mess,' she shouted after him a second later. 'I wasn't expecting visitors.'

Brook poured his cup of tea in the small kitchen at the rear of the apartment. It was bare and spotless. Even the empty stainless steel sink shone like a mirror. He ran his eye and a finger over the cheap decor. Every surface, from floor to ceiling, was washed, wiped, hoovered or dusted.

Like most decent old people, Edna Spencer spent her days and what little energy she had available preparing to leave the world. This involved fighting a continuous war against grime that would leave her conscience as clean as her home. Only constant vigilance against the forces of filth could leave the aged unencumbered by worries that they might be thought slovenly or dirty when the undertaker arrived to remove them. Even untidiness was a habit that might flag up bad character to other members of their generation and most avoided it scrupulously.

It didn't take long for Brook to see everything there was to see in her pitifully tiny apartment. There was a tiny windowless bathroom at one end and a bedroom off the lounge. It was the mirror image of McCleary's flat in the next block, only with a lot more knick-knacks.

Brook opened the fridge. Apart from a carton of milk and a small block of dried cheddar cheese, it was empty. He poured his milk and reluctantly helped himself to a Rich Tea biscuit from the barrel, knowing it would please Mrs Spencer to be feeding a guest. Sitting down in her compact lounge wasn't easy. As well as an armchair, Mrs Spencer had the matching sofa shoehorned into her living space and there wasn't much room for anything else except a TV in one corner. She'd already muted the programme about antiques she'd been watching and she lifted her own cup to her mouth with a chubby hand.

'Lovely tea,' said Brook, raiding his memory for small talk. 'Just what I needed in this terrible weather.'

'Oh, don't get me started on the weather,' she said.

Brook realised she was right and determined to get quickly to the point before he got drawn into the nation's favourite conversation. 'I'm here because—'

'I can barely get down the road for my pension as it is,' continued Edna. 'If it's not snowing, it's raining and if it's not raining—'

'I'm re-investigating the Billy Stanforth case,' announced Brook, quickly. Edna stopped cold and Brook realised the absurdity of his last utterance.

Edna Spencer laughed in disbelief. 'Billy Stanforth?' She shook her head in wonderment. 'Billy Stanforth? What are you thinking? Leave it be, young man. You're never going to find out who killed that poor boy after all this time.'

'Probably not,' admitted Brook. 'But we have to try.'

'Don't take me wrong, Inspector. I'm not trying to get rid of you. I'm glad of the company.'

'Me too,' replied Brook, before he could stop himself.

She grinned mischievously. 'You're a polite young man. Dotty will be very jealous. I don't get many handsome young men calling on me.' She smiled up at a picture on the mantelpiece. 'Not since my Eric passed.'

'Your husband?'

Edna nodded. 'Husband, best friend . . .' her voice began to falter but instead of indulging herself in the modern way, her upper lip stiffened and, demonstrating a dying British art, she pulled herself together. 'What happened to that great big detective who called last time?'

'DI Greatorix?'

'That's him. A very big man. I hope he didn't die of a heart attack. I told him to cut down. Had half a dozen of my biscuits. Ginger nuts, they were, an' all.'

'He retired,' said Brook. 'Four years ago.'

'Four years?' she exclaimed, shaking her head. 'Where does the time go?'

'What did DI Greatorix ask you?'

'Do you know, he didn't mention Billy or the fire. Not once.

He just sat where you're sitting now, drinking tea and eating biscuits and then he wrote something down and was off. Quick as you like.'

'He didn't ask *any* questions?'

'I tell a lie, he wanted to know the way to Brendan's flat.'

'Brendan McCleary? So you know him.'

'We're both from Kirk Langley so, yes, I know him, have done for years. Only to speak to, mind. Say hello of a morning. We don't have a lot in common with him being . . .' she hesitated.

'A career criminal?' suggested Brook.

Edna smiled her agreement. 'Poor boy. He's not had the best of times.'

'And did Inspector Greatorix manage to see him?'

'I wouldn't know about that. Brendan and me aren't on those familiar terms. Last time he came round was to borrow a fiver, a year or so ago, but I don't have that kind of money to spare. Still,' she said with a gleam in her eye, 'Dotty gets very excited about my gentlemen callers. Very excited.'

'When was the last time you saw Brendan?'

'He's not been round since then and I don't see him in the neighbourhood much any more. I only get out twice a week myself. For my pension and suchlike.'

'The warden says Brendan's pretty much moved out.'

'If you say so, dear.'

Brook took a sip of tea. 'What do you think of him?'

'Brendan? He's a very sad old man,' she said. 'Very sad. And bitter. He wasted his life, I mean a lot do these days, don't they? So much love he could have had from poor Amelia.' She shook her head. 'She loved Brendan with a passion, would have done anything for him.' She glanced slyly up at Brook, suddenly aware of the implications of what she'd said.

Brook latched on. 'Anything? Would that include lying for him?'

For the first time a frown appeared on her face. 'Amelia?' She shook her head. 'I'd say no but if you live long enough you realise anything's possible. She loved him for years; even when he went to prison she defended him around the village. And when her sister and her parents died, she had that big house all to herself and no man to share it.'

'An odd way to live,' observed Brook. 'Alone in a house with so much death.'

'I know,' agreed Edna. 'It doesn't do to live with ghosts for so much of your life. At least poor Francesca had moved out before she passed. That would have been too hard for Amelia to bear.'

'Do you remember how Francesca died?'

'She drowned in a bathtub, dear. Slipped and banged her head, they say, but I know the truth of it.'

'Truth?'

Edna waggled her wrist in the internationally recognised code for an alcoholic. 'Drank like a fish, did Francesca. The day she died in nineteen sixty-eight was her birthday. Billy's too. She must have took to her bath, drunk as a skunk. Celebrating? Mourning? Who knows? But the rest you can work out for yourself.'

'How did Amelia take her sister's death?' asked Brook.

'Hard,' said Edna. 'Amelia tried to get away but she never could. Her parents needed her. And also she couldn't bear to leave her Billy like that. Then, when Bert and Ruth went, she could've moved away. She had money from the insurance. But it was too late by then.'

'Too late?'

'Brendan was already in prison up in Leeds. He'd killed his father,' she explained. 'He got drunk one night. When he came home there must have been a row with his dad and there was a shotgun nearby, like there would be in the countryside in them days. Well, drink and guns . . . not a good combination, is it? The next day the police found his dad downstairs with his head blown off and Brendan asleep in his bed, blood all over him. There wasn't a long investigation, put it that way. Very sad. They might as well have taken Amelia to prison that day as well, instead of leaving her in that house, like Miss Havisham, with all those memories. Both their lives ended that night as far as I can see.'

'What about Billy's party? Did you see Brendan that afternoon?'

Edna gave a little laugh at Brook's persistence. 'No. He wasn't there, far as I could tell, though I've heard said he passed by.'

'Where were you when the fire broke out?'

'In the lounge with Mr Stanforth. There were a few of us playing blind man's buff.'

Brook sipped his tea. 'You've got a good memory, Mrs Spencer.'

'It's not so hard when all you do each day is sit and reflect. When you have a shrinking future, memories become your present as well as your past. You'll get there, young man.'

Brook's smile managed to mask the dead hand of existential terror suddenly constricting his heart. *I hope not.* He took out the folded sheet he'd extracted earlier from the file. 'Edna, this is a plan drawn up by DCI Bannon and—'

'Who?'

'DCI Bannon. He was the policeman in charge of investigating the fire.'

'Was he? I never met him. The other one took my statement.'

'DC Laird?'

'That's the one,' smiled Edna, turning her gaze on to the A4 sheet.

'This shows where everyone was when the fire broke out.' Brook leaned over to point to various details. 'BMB would have been blind man's buff in the room where you were playing. Is that right?'

She read out the names. 'Me, Charlotte Dilkes, Roger Rawlins, Francesca Stanforth . . .' She paused over the last name and tried to think.

'You don't remember Francesca being there?'

'I think so, at least part of the time.' She handed back the sheet to Brook with a smile. 'We were playing blind man's buff, remember. The lights were off. That's why we were the first to see the fire. We saw it through the window.'

'What happened when you saw the flames?'

'We ran outside, screaming and shouting, made a terrible racket, as you can imagine. Funny. It was exciting at first.' A tear pricked one eye. 'We never knew our friend was burning inside.'

'Did you hear anything? A scream, maybe.'

'No, nothing like that.'

'And according to most accounts, those playing with you arrived at the burning shed first. Is that right?'

'Yes, well, the lounge was closest,' said Edna. 'I got there at the same time as Francesca. We were just behind Charlotte.'

'Charlotte Dilkes was first there? The girl who drowned the year after.'

'Yes, poor little thing.'

'And then the other children came to see what all the noise was about.'

'That's right.'

Brook nodded. 'Was there anybody not in your room who seemed to arrive before you or even at the same time? Perhaps someone from the dining room or the conservatory.'

Edna looked at the plan, trying to remember. 'I don't think so. It was all very confusing.'

'Nothing that struck you as odd in any way?'

She thought for a moment. 'Nothing relevant.'

'Nothing relevant,' echoed Brook, finishing his tea. 'What about something irrelevant then?'

Edna's milky gaze pierced him for a moment. Brook got the impression she was taking a decision. 'No.'

Brook drained his tea. 'Well, thank you. You've been very helpful.'

'No, I haven't,' she smiled. 'I've not told you anything new.'

Brook took the floor plan of the Stanforth house from her and returned it to his pocket. 'So what do *you* think happened to Billy?'

'I couldn't tell you, Inspector.'

'Not even a bit of wild speculation?' prompted Brook. 'It won't go any further.' She smiled her reluctance so Brook threw her a conversational lifebelt. 'DC Laird and DCI Bannon were convinced it was McCleary.'

'Brendan kill Billy?' She shook her head. 'I can't see it. I mean, why would he?'

Brook thought about the pictures in McCleary's flat. 'Maybe Brendan was interested in Billy . . . in a different way.'

'Different?'

'I'm not sure how to ask this.'

'Straight out with it works best for me,' said Edna.

Brook smiled sheepishly. 'Did Brendan ever seem like he was sexually attracted to Billy?'

Edna Spencer's eyes widened in shock. 'Good lord, no. Brendan was a ladies' man through and through. Flocked around him, they did, and he loved it. Whatever made you ask that?'

'Just looking for a different angle,' lied Brook.

'It's different, all right. I never saw anything like that in Brendan. And the idea he'd set a fire as well . . .'

'What?'

'Well, it wasn't his style. If Brendan had a quarrel with some-one, he'd just march up to them and punch their lights out, he was that straightforward – not that he was especially violent. But to burn his girlfriend's brother to death, that's too measured for young boys.'

'You think maybe this was a woman's crime?'

'Well Amelia and Charlotte had some kind of a motive but it's harder to see why Francesca—'

'Sorry,' interrupted Brook. 'Amelia had a motive?'

'Well, not one you'd think she'd kill her brother over.' Brook egged her on with a gesture. 'See, it was Billy who told their parents about Amelia stepping out with Brendan. Caused a right kerfuffle, I can tell you. Mr Stanforth wouldn't have Brendan anywhere near the house and forbade Amelia to see him.' She smiled. 'But forbidden fruit, eh?'

'And Charlotte?'

'Charlotte was sweet on Billy,' said Edna. 'Followed him every-where. Course he was a year older and much more grown-up. He wouldn't give her the time of day. That has to take its toll, I imagine.'

'And she was first to arrive at the burning shed.'

'Yes, she was. And the first to notice Billy was missing. She cried for weeks after they found the body, though. Hard to imagine her setting the fire and locking Billy inside.'

'Hell hath no fury . . .' Brook broke off when he realised Charlotte Dilkes had been a long way from womanhood. 'What about Edward Mullen?'

Edna smiled with pleasure. 'Teddy? What about him?'

'He was the only child who was alone when the fire was set.'

'And you think . . . ?' She shook her head. 'No, Inspector. Teddy didn't kill Billy. He loved him. He couldn't kill Billy in a million years.'

'But they'd argued . . .'

'Teddy didn't kill Billy, Inspector.'

'You seem very sure.'

'Just want to save you the time and trouble.'

Brook nodded then tore a page from his notebook and wrote down his mobile number. 'If you remember anything else about that day, Mrs Spencer, please give me a call.'

'I will, Inspector.'

'Or even if you just want a chat,' he added.

'A chat?' Confused at first, Edna gave him a searching look before smiling, almost overcome. Brook rose to leave, glancing at the muted TV. The local news was on, showing a picture of Scott Wheeler. Instead of turning it back up, Edna closed her eyes in pain and made the sign of the cross. 'Poor boy,' she said. 'No child deserves to die before they've had a chance at life.'

'We don't know he's dead yet,' said Brook from the door.

'That's how these things always end,' said Edna softly. Brook considered contradicting her but decided against it. 'Inspector,' she called, as Brook made to leave.

'Yes?'

The old woman hesitated, glancing at the television. She seemed on the verge of tears, unable to speak. A second later, she shook her head so Brook thanked her for the tea and walked out into the gloom.

* * *

On his way home, Brook called into Sainsbury's at Kingsway's Retail Park to buy desperately needed groceries, unaware of McCleary's Land Rover pulling into a nearby spot. He didn't get past the newspaper stand where the *Derby Telegraph* front page stopped him in his tracks.

DISGRACED DI TAKES TEA WHILE SEARCH FOR SCOTT WIDENS. Brook picked up the top copy. Below the headline was a picture of him, drinking from a plastic beaker in the station car park as Burton had promised.

Brook didn't bother to read the article, dropping the paper back on the pile. He glanced over at the tobacco kiosk as he turned towards the exit but managed to drag himself back to his car without buying a pack.

Back at the cottage, Brook was also able to ignore the culinary attractions of a can of lentils; instead, he poured a large whisky and water which he nursed in a chair. He texted Noble to inform him of his plans for the morning and asked about developments from McCleary's flat.

Five minutes later Noble replied. 'Seen paper ☹ SOCO still working. Ford to go public, tipping off BMc ☹☹ Watching flat until. Why PO if benefit ck still in flat.'

'You missed your question mark,' mumbled Brook, tapping out his scrupulous reply. 'It's still pension day. He may go there first.' He finished with 'Nothing better to do' but deleted it.

'Want back-up?' replied Noble.

'No,' Brook sounded as he texted.

Twelve

THE NEXT DAY BROOK DROVE straight to McCleary's local post office on Normanton Road, glad of the chance to avoid the station and all those, including Charlton, who might feel inclined to comment on his unflattering appearance in the local paper.

There was a café nestled between all the Asian stores and Brook settled into a window seat with a tea, propping a printout of an old picture of McCleary against the salt cellar. Immediately his nostrils were assaulted by the smell of frying bacon and he realised how hungry he was. He'd eaten nothing but boiled rice smeared with Laughing Cow cheese the last few days and knew he had to take on board some proper fuel or risk falling victim to the winter weather.

Thirty minutes later Brook finished his all-day breakfast as though it was his death row meal, savouring every salty mouthful and chasing the last of the egg yolk round the plate with a triangle of white toast. After the hot meal, Brook became sleepy so he switched to drinking bitter powdered coffee while his gaze alternated between his notebook and the doors of the post office.

After a fruitless morning, Brook paid his bill and drifted out on to the street.

Having scanned the perimeter fence for photographers, Brook trudged wearily towards the station through the rain, only a full belly and a bag of Indian groceries in his boot to show for his morning's work. He might have hurried had he not been aware that he was saying goodbye to natural light for another day.

To dampen his mood further, Hendrickson was leaning on both elbows at reception, reading Brian Burton's puffed-up story on the counter. When the desk sergeant lifted his head, the grin began to form immediately.

'The Chief Super was looking for you,' he said. 'Sir.'

Brook nodded and quickened his step.

'You also had calls from *East Midlands Today* and Radio Derby wanting a word,' called Hendrickson to Brook's retreating frame. 'I told them you were on a tea break.'

Brook kept walking.

Barely able to keep the laughter at bay, Hendrickson added under his breath, 'That's right, mental boy. Run away.'

Brook, nearly at the double doors, stopped dead. After a few seconds he turned slowly to face his grinning tormentor. 'What did you say?'

Hendrickson's expression took on the innocence of the cornered schoolboy. 'Sir?'

'I asked you what you said,' replied Brook evenly, slowly retracing his steps towards reception.

'The Chief was looking for you,' replied Hendrickson with an air of insouciance.

'After that.'

'*East Midlands Today.*'

'After that.'

Hendrickson looked mystified. 'I don't know what you mean. Sir.'

Brook arrived back at the counter and rested his hands lightly on the polished wood. He looked coldly at the grey-haired sergeant and fancied he detected a sliver of doubt flash across his flabby face. 'Yes, you do. You called me mental boy.'

They were quite alone so Hendrickson swivelled round, his arms wide, seeking corroboration from non-existent witnesses. 'I think you must have imagined it.' He smirked at Brook then inclined his head slightly back towards the empty office to imply a pressing need to work.

Brook grabbed Hendrickson's uniform lapels, pulling the sergeant's upper torso down towards the wooden counter so that his right cheek was pressed against the wood, heavy jowls spilling across the surface. At the same time his left hand twisted Hendrickson's thin black tie round his throat so he could do no more than splutter in shock and try to breathe normally. Then Brook pushed his own face into close proximity, his nostrils flaring, his eyes bulging with restrained violence.

'Doesn't an out-of-condition bag of guts like you worry that one day mental boy could lose his grip and do you some harm?' snarled Brook through gritted teeth. 'Think about that before you ever speak to me again.' Brook held the old man's gaze a second longer then released his hand and stalked away, looking calmer than he felt.

Hendrickson righted himself, rubbing his throat, his face borscht-red. 'You fucking nutter,' he spluttered. 'You can't do that to me, I'll have your fucking job for that.'

'For what?' asked Brook, turning back to Hendrickson, arms out, looking round for support from the same non-existent witnesses who'd backed up the sergeant a moment earlier. With a thin smile, Brook continued towards the stairwell.

Hidden from view at the top of the stairs, Brook pulled out Hendrickson's mobile phone, filched from the breast pocket of his uniform. It was new and expensive and it took him some time to find the text Hendrickson had sent to Brian Burton on the morning of Brook's return to work.

When he found it he read it, this time with genuine anger. He was about to put the phone back in his pocket when a thought occurred. He flicked to Burton's acknowledging text and pressed REPLY before tapping out a message in his usual painstaking manner but this time remembering to lower the standard of his grammar.

A moment later he re-read the text before sending.

'Brook flipped out. Taken to Stoke loony bin in straightjacket. Not sure which one. Under false name.'

Shortly after, the vibration of Burton's reply shook Brook's pocket.

'Big ta H. On my way. Another mega drink innit 4 you. Lol. Got him.'

Brook nodded in satisfaction then deleted both recent messages so Hendrickson would be unaware of the new communication when he was in possession of his phone again. The thought of how to return the mobile without an ugly confrontation soured Brook's sudden good mood and he continued down the stairs to the basement, deep in thought.

As he reached the bottom of the gloomy stairwell, he became aware of raised voices. He heard an angry, 'And I say no,' from a voice that sounded like Charlton's.

Brook froze at the bottom of the stairs, just able to hear the pair in the corridor leading to his and Copeland's CCU rooms.

'Did you see the evening paper?' the voice continued. It was definitely Charlton and the subject needed no explanation. 'He's already attracting negative publicity.'

'That's hardly his fault,' was the reply. Copeland.

'It's always his fault,' rejoined Charlton.

'Brian Burton has been a wart on this city's nose for longer than I care to remember,' declared Copeland. 'He's a sewer rat and you mustn't let someone like *him* decide how Derbyshire Constabulary is run.'

Charlton was as taken aback as Brook by Copeland's forcefulness. 'Mustn't?' inquired the Chief Super.

'Shouldn't, I mean,' replied Copeland with a little more diplomacy.

'That's better,' said a mollified Charlton. 'Clive, you don't know Brook like I do. He goes out of his way to rub people the wrong way. I'm sorry but you can't let him anywhere near it.'

'It's too late,' replied Copeland. 'I've already . . .'

Brook had kept very still but the creak of his weight on the step caused the conversation to halt. Despite tiptoeing to a quieter step

Brook's movement caught Charlton's eye and his surprise was picked up by Copeland, who turned to follow the Chief Superintendent's gaze. Brook had no choice but to continue towards them and both men smiled tightly at him as he approached, Hendrickson's phone still in his hand.

'Brook. How are you settling in?' Charlton asked stiffly.

'Very well,' said Brook, trying to sound enthusiastic. 'I like my new office. It's cosy and the work is interesting,' he added, avoiding Copeland's sceptical expression.

'Good, good.' The disappointment in Charlton's voice induced a small swell of triumph in Brook, though his unscheduled presence on the front page of the local paper would doubtless be the next topic of conversation.

Brook's sweaty hand nestled against the stolen phone, ready to produce it in his defence and both he and Copeland watched Charlton's mind ticking over as they waited for the inevitable. To Brook's astonishment the subject wasn't broached.

'Well,' said Charlton, turning away. 'Don't let me keep you from your valuable work.'

A commotion from the stairs drew their attention. 'You fucker, Brook. Give me my fucking phone,' screamed Hendrickson at the top of his voice. He jumped down the last two steps and came face to face with a dumbfounded Charlton and Copeland, Brook beaming politely behind them.

'What the hell do you think you're doing, Sergeant?' shouted Charlton. 'Are you out of your mind?'

'Sir, I'm sorry—'

'Sorry?' shouted Charlton even louder. 'Not as sorry as you're going to be. What's the meaning of this outrage? I want to know now.'

Hendrickson was panting, red-faced, looking from Charlton to Copeland to Brook, who was trying to maintain an inquiring expression. 'Sir, Inspector Brook's got my mobile.'

'I beg your pardon?' boomed Charlton.

'I said—'

'And you think that justifies shouting and swearing at a superior officer like that?'

'Sir, I—'

'You're not fit to wear that uniform. Get to my office, now.'

Hendrickson didn't move but eyed Brook instead. 'Sir, I—'

'Did you not hear me?' Charlton was almost screaming in his apoplexy.

The sergeant began again. 'Sir, I'm sorry but I must tell you—'

'Sergeant Hendrickson, I do apologise,' said Brook, theatrically examining his cupped hand. 'You're right. I must have picked up the wrong phone when we were chatting upstairs. Here.' He extended his arm to Hendrickson.

The uniformed officer, his breath almost regained, took the phone on a reflex.

'So, you've got your phone back, now get to my office, pronto,' barked Charlton, no calmer.

Again Hendrickson hesitated, looking from face to face. He turned to Charlton, his mouth open to speak.

Brook chipped in, the model of contrition. 'I should have seen from the names on your contact list that it wasn't my phone, Sergeant. I'm very sorry.'

'I don't think it's you who should be apologising, Inspector,' put in Charlton.

'Nevertheless, I owe the sergeant a *mega drink* for picking up the wrong phone.' Brook's eyes bored into Hendrickson's as he repeated Burton's phrase.

Hendrickson, crushed, lowered his eyes. He turned back to the stairwell and plodded slowly back up to the ground floor, shoulders hunched in defeat, as though dragging a bag of coal behind him.

Charlton looked at Brook. 'I'm sorry about that, Inspector. I'll see that you get a full apology, providing Hendrickson can convince me he still belongs in my division.'

'If you think it will help, sir,' said Brook. 'You'll excuse me.' He stepped quickly past the pair and headed down the corridor, listening for the resumption of whatever argument Copeland and Charlton had been having. If it did continue, he didn't hear it.

A few seconds later, Brook opened Copeland's door and stepped smartly inside, closing the door quietly behind him. He flicked at the full kettle and glanced across at the desk. There were two files on the blotter. Brook hurried over to Copeland's desk. The Wallis file was on top, the Ingham file underneath. Two Derby families brutally butchered in their own homes by a serial killer called the Reaper, the last crimes of a killer officially still at large after more than twenty years, since his first kill in London in 1990.

Brook hadn't been the SIO when he'd hunted the Reaper during his time in the Met, he was only a DS, but the case had obsessed him and by the end of 1991, his sparkling reputation had been tarnished and his marriage irretrievably damaged. To complete the set, Brook's failure to catch the serial killer in London had taken a toll on his mental health, culminating in a nervous breakdown and, eventually, a much-resented transfer to Derby CID – much-resented by local officers, that is, affronted that a burnout from the Metropolitan force could be dumped in their division and deemed fit for duty.

Brook hastily flicked through the two files, looking for any notes or addendums made by Copeland. He couldn't see any. Perhaps any holes he had picked in Brook's investigations were written separately. He returned the files to the desk, fighting the urge to rifle through the drawers and hastening back to the kettle just as Copeland walked in.

'Brook,' said Copeland, a little startled. His eye shot to his desk.

'Clive,' answered Brook. The kettle clicked at the right moment. 'Tea?'

'You found a mug then?' asked Copeland suspiciously.

'Left it next door,' tutted Brook, nipping across the corridor to fetch it. On his return he glanced discreetly at Copeland's desktop when his colleague's back was turned. The files were gone.

Brook poured hot water into two mugs, itching to ask why Charlton and Copeland had been arguing but he knew he couldn't introduce the subject without revealing he'd overheard their conversation. 'I suppose you saw the evening paper.'

'I saw it,' confirmed Copeland. 'What have you done to Brian Burton to deserve that?'

'He's a self-serving bloodsucker,' said Brook.

'And even knowing you so briefly, I'm guessing you couldn't help but tell him,' grinned Copeland.

Brook acknowledged with a lift of his eyes. Guilty as charged. He couldn't thank Copeland for his support against Charlton either so he tried to be subtle. 'I was expecting a harder time from the Chief Super,' he said casually.

'He's not as bad as you think,' said Copeland, looking at Brook. *If he did hear us, he's not showing it*. 'And I can't believe you're worried about his good opinions.'

'Only if it impacts on my work,' replied Brook.

'Is that why you told him how much you're enjoying your new role?' asked Copeland, suppressing a smile. Sheepish, Brook didn't answer. 'I take it Sergeant Hendrickson's another member of your fan club.'

'He's the secretary *and* treasurer.'

'You certainly pushed his buttons.'

'It's a gift,' said Brook modestly.

'I wouldn't worry about that bum,' said Copeland. 'Hendrickson's not fit to be on the force and wasn't even when I was still around.'

Brook nodded. Copeland was going up in his estimation. He picked up his tea and headed for the door.

'How are you *really* getting on, Brook?'

Brook pulled a face. 'I've been rooting around the Stanforth case. You reviewed it three times, so I'm not holding out much hope.'

'Was it three?' Copeland was lost in the memory for a moment. 'I'd be interested in your thoughts when you get a chance. If you solve that stinker you'll be straight to the top of my Christmas list. Old Sam Bannon and Walter Laird were two of the best detectives around but they got nowhere with it. Wally's still about.'

'I know,' replied Brook. 'He's on my radar for a visit.'

'Is he?' said Copeland. 'Go easy on him. I've known him since I was a nipper.'

'Really?'

'He used to be a neighbour when I lived in Mackworth and he's always been a good friend. He helped me a lot when . . . well.' Copeland became hesitant, almost unable to speak, and Brook realised he must be thinking of his sister's murder. It would have been the same era as Billy Stanforth's death so maybe Bannon and Laird had picked up her case as well. And perhaps a *good friend* like Laird had gone further and signed off on Copeland's clandestine reviews into her death.

Brook turned to leave but was halted by Copeland coming out of his reverie. 'I hope you don't mind but as a courtesy I told Walter you might be looking into the Stanforth case.'

Brook paused. He did mind. Witnesses were always best interviewed cold. He decided the damage was done, but he could at least make a point. 'No problem, Clive. An officer should *always* be informed if one of his cases is being reviewed.' Brook held Copeland's gaze but the retired detective looked away, declining the invitation to reveal that he was reviewing two of Brook's old cases.

Instead Copeland changed the subject. 'Re-interviewed anyone yet?'

'A nice old lady called Edna Spencer,' said Brook.

'I remember her. Edna Hibbert, as was. Her husband Eric died when she was quite young. Just the one child, thankfully.'

'Thankfully?'

Copeland's smile was sad. 'Sorry. You have a daughter.' He glanced towards the framed picture on his desk and Brook followed his eyes to the attractive young girl smiling happily, her arm round her gap-toothed little brother. 'I don't know if you know, my sister Matilda . . .'

'I heard,' said Brook gently to spare Copeland the difficult words. Nearly fifty years hadn't healed the scar. He was impressed. 'I'm sorry.'

Copeland nodded. 'I never married because of it. In case a wife might want a family. I envy you, Brook. Feeling able to bring a child into this ugly world . . .'

During the gap left by Copeland for an endorsement of parenthood, Brook kept his counsel, deciding not to elaborate on the traumas he'd endured as father to a daughter subsequently abused by her stepfather.

'I'll leave you to get on, Clive.'

When Brook had left, Copeland was statue-still for several minutes, staring at a spot on the wall that wouldn't distract him from his past. Filling his lungs finally, he took a bulging file from a drawer, caressing it like a lover. With a deep sigh he looked at the picture of his smiling sister on his desk. 'I've done my best, Tilly.' He closed his eyes to remembered pain. He placed the file on the desk with great ceremony. 'Don't worry, love. You'll be in good hands.' Copeland broke away from his sister's doomed gaze and stared at the door after Brook.

Thirteen

Sunday, 29 August 1965 – Mackworth Estate, Derby

'COME ON, EBONY. COME ON, boy,' called Detective Sergeant Walter Laird, a tall, angular man in his late twenties, moving to lean on the picket fence. His hand reached into his jacket and pulled out a dog biscuit and held it just out of reach of the black Labrador, teasing it to stretch out its black paws on to the top of the fence.

'Uncle Walter,' shouted young Clive Copeland, jumping up, as excited as the dog, leaping over a cluster of multicoloured marbles to join him.

'Wotcha, Clive,' replied Laird, keeping the biscuit away from the slavering dog. 'Your dad in?'

'Dad!' screamed Clive, running towards the open front door. 'Walter's here.' He raced back to the fence as Laird finally caved in and held the dog biscuit on his palm for Ebony to gobble up then ruffled his floppy ears.

'Good dog.' Laird grinned at the eager boy, looking him up and down, as he tossed the dog's ears around. 'Cor blimey, you're shooting up, Clive. You'll be taller than me in a year.'

Clive smiled happily, looking at the policeman's hands then expectantly at his face.

'Sorry, lad. Nothing for you, Barney's was closed when I swung past.' When Clive's face fell, Laird whipped out a paper-wrapped lollipop on a stick. 'Lucky I keep these for special occasions.'

Clive let out a delighted yelp and tore the lolly out of the officer's hand and set about the wrapping with frenzy.

'What do you say, lad?' said Clive's father, walking up the path towards Laird for a handshake.

'Thank you, Walter,' said Clive, finally able to plunge the orb of hard orange sugar into his mouth.

'Evening, George,' said Laird. With a rueful expression he handed over a sturdy door key. 'Well, that's the last of it shifted. Thanks for this, neighbour.'

'What are friends for?' smiled George Copeland.

'It's just for emergencies,' said Laird. 'There shouldn't be any problem but an empty house can invite bother. The new owners have got the other keys and should be moving in next weekend. Just give them the spares when they get settled, will you?'

'Will do. What are they like?'

'They're a nice young couple, George. Just got married.'

'Fellas never learn, do they?' chuckled Copeland, pulling out a pack of cigarettes. He saw Laird eyeing them. 'Want one?'

'Go on then. I left mine in—'

'Your other coat,' smiled the older man, striking a match. 'You all set then?'

'Aye,' said Laird, looking back down the road to the house with the SOLD sign outside. 'I'll certainly miss the place.'

'Pastures new, though.'

'Aye. Off to the new house now, do a bit of painting so it's nice for her majesty.' He gestured to the car, a metallic-grey Jaguar Mark X, and the blonde lady attending to her nails in the passenger seat.

'Nice,' said Copeland, impressed.

'The car or Linda?' asked Laird, chuckling.

'Both,' grinned Copeland. 'Though the motor's probably got a better engine.' The two men laughed long and loud.

'Whoa,' shouted Clive, removing the lollipop to gawp at the car a few doors away. 'A Jag,' he exclaimed then vaulted over the fence for a closer look.

'Don't put your grubby hands on it, Clive,' Copeland shouted after his son.

'He's all right,' said Laird.

'A Jag though – that promotion's moved you up in the world, Walter.'

Laird grinned. 'Not yet, George. It's not mine – borrowed it off the boss while my old banger's still in the garage.'

'Your DI not need a car then?' asked Copeland.

Laird's face strained, trying to find a delicate answer. 'He's not well, George, been off work for a week or so.'

Copeland raised a sceptical eyebrow. 'Again?'

'He lost his wife, George.'

'Aye, two years ago. You can't keep covering for him, Wally.'

Laird's expression hardened. 'I can and I will, if he needs me to. It's called loyalty.'

Copeland shook his head. 'It's your funeral, lad.' His smile reappeared. 'Speaking of funerals, when's your wedding?'

'Steady on,' laughed Laird. 'We've only just got engaged.'

'Who's just got engaged?' asked Clive, barely audible through the lolly.

'Young Walter here,' said Copeland. 'He's getting married.'

'Is that good?' asked Clive innocently.

Matilda Copeland, a striking sixteen-year-old, emerged from the house. She wore a tight sleeveless blouse and shorts and held a bare arm up against the waning sun. 'Uncle Walter's getting married?' she said.

'Aye,' confirmed Laird, beaming at her. 'That's me off the market.'

'Congratulations,' said Matilda.

'Thanks, pet,' said Laird. 'And how you enjoying life as a Barney's shop assistant?'

'Loving it,' she said. 'Be even nicer if I got to keep some of my wages,' she added for her father's benefit.

'Be nice if you helped your mother round the house a bit more, an' all,' said Copeland, winking at the grinning Laird. 'Bit of luck, you'll meet a nice young man like Walter here and start giving your mother some grandkids.'

'Mmm, sounds exciting,' retorted Matilda drily.

'Have you seen the car Walter's driving?' said her father. 'That's what hard work brings you, young lady.'

'Not his hard work, though,' said Matilda.

'Eh?' said Copeland.

'It's borrowed,' she explained. 'I heard him say.'

'Doesn't miss a trick, this one,' laughed Laird. 'She'll go far.'

'Aye, too far one day,' observed Copeland. 'Thought you had a headache, madam.'

'I'm feeling a lot better, Dad.' She knew what was coming and smiled to disarm her father.

'Just not well enough to go to church this morning, is that it?'

A sassy comeback played around her pretty mouth for a moment but she settled for, 'Thought I'd take the dog out. Get some air. You know how much I like to help out.' She stroked her curmudgeonly father's thinning hair. 'You should wear a hat in this sun, Dad.'

The two men laughed. 'Cheeky beggar,' said her father.

'What's funny about that?' said Clive, to cause more merriment. Confused, he looked from face to face.

Matilda called the dog to her and she set out along Radbourne Lane towards Station Road.

'Can I go with her, Dad?' pleaded Clive.

'No. Get them marbles cleared up and get ready for bed.'

The boy blew out his cheeks in dismay. 'O-kay.'

'And don't you be long, young lady, it's already half past eight,' Copeland shouted after Matilda. 'Just round the estate.' She raised an arm in acknowledgement without looking back. Copeland rolled his eyes at Laird. 'Kids today.'

'You don't need to tell me, George.' Laird straightened, preparing to leave. 'Half eight, you say. Didn't realise it was so late.' He looked at Copeland's wrist for confirmation but saw no watch.

Copeland noticed him looking and nodded towards an untidy figure, shambling along the pavement in the same direction as his daughter, a trail of cigarette smoke billowing behind him. 'Don't need a watch, Wally, when not-so-clever Trevor's on his way to the Northern for his four pints. Half eight on the dot. Every night without fail.' He laughed. 'And I'd be going with him if I lived on me tod.'

'You'd make a good detective, George.' Laird hesitated. 'Everything OK with Matilda?' he ventured, nodding at the retreating figure of Copeland's daughter.

'Don't worry, Walter,' said Copeland, his face suddenly severe. 'I keep more than a weather eye on that one, thanks to you.'

'A weather eye on what one?' asked Clive, the lolly stick hanging out of the side of his mouth, a box of marbles nestling under his arm.

'Never you mind,' replied his father. 'Ready for bed.'

'But I want a ride in Walter's car,' whined Clive.

'And what does wanting get you?' demanded Copeland. 'Bed.'

'Yes, Dad,' mumbled the boy, his shoulders slumping dramatically. 'See you Walter.'

'Night, Clive. Another time for that ride,' consoled Laird, giving him a pat on the head as he trudged away. With the boy inside, Laird and Copeland shook hands. 'Thanks for everything, George.'

'You'll be missed, Walter.'

'I'll pop back from time to time,' said Laird. 'And I hope you and the lovely wife will be coming to the wedding in five years.'

'Five years? You'll not get away with it that long, lad.' The two men's laughter was interrupted by the impatient honking of the Jaguar's horn. They laughed again.

Two minutes later Laird and his fiancée drove along Radbourne Lane, past the athletic, languid frame of Matilda Copeland as she guided Ebony off the main road and back into the estate. Laird sounded the horn as they passed and she raised an acknowledging hand, without turning to look. He watched her disappear in the rear-view mirror, the unkempt figure of Trevor Taylor shuffling along behind, his hooded eyes glued to Matilda's backside. Laird returned his eyes to the road ahead, a strange sense of foreboding washing through him.

Fourteen

BROOK TURNED ON HIS LAPTOP and wearily pulled the Stanforth file back towards him for another read-through. As the screen came to life and cast its light over the manila folder, Brook's eye was drawn to a series of indentations on the cover that he hadn't noticed before. He held the folder to the light and moved it around to decipher the marks. Something had been written on the folder and, later, vigorously erased, leaving a slightly lighter blue colour on the card.

A trace remained so Brook took a pencil and used the flattened point to rub lightly over the affected area. A couple of minutes later he was able to make out the faint outline of what had been removed.

Pied Piper
63 WS 1st?
22/12/73 JW 2nd or 3rd? Wrong MO
Dec 78? 3rd or 4th?
Others?
No 68. Why? FS?

'The Pied Piper,' mumbled Brook. A fairytale figure who played a magic pipe to entice rats away from a small German town.

He copied the note into his pad then removed all the documents from the Stanforth folder to search for any mention of a Pied Piper, missed first time round. He couldn't find a single reference. However, by comparing several handwritten reports against the mysterious message, Brook found a match against a report signed by DCI Samuel Bannon, SIO of the Stanforth inquiry.

The Pied Piper didn't just lure away rats, thought Brook, rubbing his chin. When the townspeople refused to pay, he lured the town's children away from their homes as well. According to legend they never returned.

Robert Browning had written a poem about the Pied Piper so Brook loaded it from the internet but, after reading all fifteen verses, was no closer to understanding why Bannon had scribbled the note on a fifty-year-old murder file.

'63 WS 1st?' read Brook. 'William Stanforth in 1963. The first.' Was Bannon speculating that Stanforth's murder was the first of a series, the second of which occurred in December 1973?

'JW on December the twenty-second, nineteen seventy-three,' said Brook. 'Billy's birthday, ten years later. That's a very long wait for a second kill, Sam. Even a third.' Maybe that's why he rubbed out the note.

Out of interest, Brook Googled the date of the second kill and soon found the story in archives of a murdered young boy, Jeff Ward, twelve years old. But instead of being burned alive, Jeff had been strangled on a golf course in the dead of winter. The killer was never found.

'Wrong MO,' said Brook, echoing the note. 'Although, I suppose both Billy and Jeff died from lack of oxygen.' He screwed up his face. 'Flimsy, Sam.'

Reading on, Brook learned that Jeff Ward was last seen kicking a football around the back garden of his family's home in leafy Allestree to the north of the city. As dark had fallen, his mother had called him but Jeff was nowhere to be seen.

The police were alerted and a search undertaken. It seemed the boy had wandered away but the police were able to follow his footprints in recent snow and it didn't take long to find the boy's remains, less than a mile away on the snow-covered putting green of Allestree Park Golf Course.

Brook logged into the PNC and loaded what details there were in the database. He smiled when he saw the SIO. Walter Laird, by now a DI, had picked up the case. Interestingly, Clive Copeland, then a callow DC, was on the investigation with him.

The facts of the case were a bit more detailed than the story in the local paper. Another set of prints were found besides Jeff Ward's leading to the crime scene. Heading away from the killing ground were the lone tracks of the murderer. Two things had struck the investigating team. It seemed Jeff Ward had followed his killer to the putting green where he'd died and, in so doing, had made a deliberate attempt to eradicate the footprints of the perpetrator.

Secondly, the lone tracks leading away from Jeff's body were small enough to have belonged to a child, though no witnesses were ever found to support this hypothesis.

Brook sifted through the crime scene and autopsy photographs but they shed no further light on an apparently brutal and senseless crime. He was puzzled. Why would Bannon connect the two deaths, especially as he had no investigative role in the Ward killing? And why was the only reference to Sam's theory an erased scribble on a folder?

Putting himself in Bannon's shoes for a minute, Brook tried to compile a list of common features that might have encouraged his premise. It wasn't long.

Pied Piper
1) Victim – young/teenage male (sporty/robust)
2) Possible child as killer?
3) Date of death – 22 December (ten years apart)
4) No witnesses to abduction (Lured away by Pied Piper?)
5) Walter Laird investigates (Bannon?)
6) Death by asphyxiation

Brook shook his head and turned his attention to the third date – *Dec 78?* This time only a five-year gap between kills. Brook's 1978 search for a murdered boy was more of a fishing expedition because this time there was no specific date in Bannon's notes, just the month. There were also no initials to identify potential victims. But assuming any murder consistent with Bannon's theory would have happened around the date of Billy's birthday, Brook searched for unlawful killings on 22 December. It was a short search. Nobody had been murdered in the Derby area on that date in 1978.

Brook widened his search to include the whole of December but this also proved fruitless. There was the odd murder but not one of the victims was a teenage boy. It was a dead end. But that prompted the obvious question. Why would Bannon theorise about a murder that didn't happen in 1978? And what was the connection to the Stanforth and Ward killings years earlier?

'No initials,' mumbled Brook, holding up an index finger. 'So maybe Bannon wrote this note before December 1978 because he saw a pattern that led him to *believe* there would be a murder committed on that date.' But there wasn't.

His eye moved further down the note. 'Others?' he read. 'No 68. Why? FS?'

As Brook typed 1968 into the search engine, he realised there *had* been a death in that year on 22 December – Francesca Stanforth had drowned in her bath after hitting her head.

'FS?' Was Bannon's note speculating that Francesca hadn't died accidentally, that she had in fact been murdered? It appeared so.

'But you weren't sure because her death had been classified as an accident and the other victims were young boys,' said Brook. 'Different victim profile to the other two – hence the question mark.'

Brook located his mug and finished his tea, now cold. 'Sorry, Sam, it doesn't hold together. A serial offender committing five-yearly kills on a preordained date. Where's the escalation? Where's the evidence?' Clearly Bannon's theory had foundered on the same problem.

Brook gave up and walked thoughtfully into Copeland's office to make another tea.

'Clive,' said Brook. 'When you reviewed the Billy Stanforth killing in the seventies, did you ever hear any mention of the Pied Piper?'

Copeland returned Brook's inquiring gaze. 'Pardon?'

'The Pied Piper?' repeated Brook.

'The only Pied Piper I know was a rat catcher in a German fairytale,' Copeland replied, a silly grin distorting his features.

'I was thinking more in terms of a nickname for a killer in Derby,' said Brook.

Copeland shook his head. 'In Derby? Can't say I've heard that one. Why?'

For reasons he couldn't put his finger on, Brook decided not to specify. After all, somebody had erased Bannon's jottings. Maybe it wasn't Sam. 'Just something I read somewhere.'

'Where exactly?' smiled Copeland. 'That might help me place it.'

Brook hesitated. He had the distinct feeling Copeland was ruffled and was trying not to show it. 'I found it on a scrap of paper in the Stanforth file.'

'Really?' Copeland did a good impression of someone racking his brains before shaking his head. 'I don't remember seeing it or hearing any reference. Sorry.'

Brook took a sip of his hot tea. 'It's probably nothing. Thanks anyway.'

Back in his office, Brook tore out a blank sheet from his notebook and wrote 'The Pied Piper?' with his left hand. He omitted the rest of the message he'd found on the cover. He popped it in the front of the file, so Copeland wouldn't waste too much time finding it, then erased his own pencil marks from the cover until Bannon's scribbling had disappeared again.

Leaving the file on the table for his colleague to find, Brook shouted a cheery goodnight through Copeland's door and headed for his car.

Fifteen

THAT NIGHT, BACK AT THE cottage, Brook ate the samosas purchased in Normanton earlier in the day and stared into the fire, brooding over his momentary lapse of self-control with Hendrickson that afternoon. If anyone else had seen the way he'd manhandled the sergeant – and it was a miracle that no one had – he could have kissed his career goodbye, on the spot.

That didn't worry him unduly; he'd embraced the notion often enough. What worried Brook more was that the act of assaulting Hendrickson had generated within him a pleasure that he knew was both addictive and unhealthy. It was the product of a volcanic anger that had first erupted in the Reaper investigation in the early nineties and culminated in his mental breakdown.

Brook examined his right hand, remembering that dark time. He wondered again if it was time to get out while he still had the semblance of a reputation. He retrieved his resignation letter, reading it for the hundredth time since writing it at the start of his suspension, five months before. He took out a pen and, for the first time, actually signed it, folded it into an envelope and, after sealing it, wrote Chief Superintendent Charlton's name on the front.

He couldn't deliver it yet, though. To abandon a case in midstream, even one as fruitless as the Stanforth murder, was anathema to Brook. But preparing the ground gave him a tremendous sense of relief. He put the envelope in his jacket for the right moment.

'You win, Charlton. You too, Brian.' *And by going at a time of my own choosing, perhaps I win too.* Brook lifted a foaming pint glass to his mouth and took a celebratory sip of his Indian lager.

As he padded into the kitchen with his plate, a knock sounded at the door. Brook instinctively looked at his watch. Visitors to his cottage in Hartington were rare, and non-existent during the dark nights of winter. And although Christmas was looming, he hadn't heard the singing of carols in the night. He peered out into the darkness before pulling open the door.

'John?'

Noble leaned on the door jamb and grinned ruefully back at Brook. 'I was just passing.'

Brook discharged his usual one-note laugh. 'Just passing?'

'If you're entertaining a lady . . .' said Noble, raising a mocking eyebrow.

Brook rolled his eyes. 'My juggling days are over, John. Come in.'

Noble removed his coat and put it round a kitchen chair, looking about him as he sat. 'Nice place. Quaint.'

'You've not been here?' said Brook, half-question, half-realisation. 'No, of course you haven't. That's my fault.'

'Don't worry,' said Noble. 'We used to see more than enough of each other before your suspension. Not got round to putting up the Christmas decorations yet?'

'No,' conceded Brook, unable to elaborate with an excuse. He hesitated, unsure what to do, his hosting skills atrophied over many years. 'Some news about McCleary?'

Noble shook his head. 'I think he's in the wind.'

'And Scott Wheeler?'

'Nothing to show he'd ever been in McCleary's flat but we're still waiting on tests. Post office?'

'No show.'

Noble nodded. 'You didn't expect him to, did you?'

'Not really,' admitted Brook.

'You were right. But I had an unmarked car there all day just in case.'

'You might have said.'

Noble shrugged. 'I figured you'd appreciate being under the radar after Brian Burton's antics. And after tonight's press conference, we won't be seeing McCleary any time soon either, if he's got any sense.'

'Ford really went public on the strength of those old photographs?' asked Brook

'Afraid so,' said Noble. He handed the evening paper to Brook.

'You told him to sit tight and watch the flat?' said Brook, skimming through the main points.

'Wasting my breath,' sighed Noble. 'It was all I could do to make him wait for the tests to shake out.'

Brook tossed the paper on the table.

'It gets worse,' Noble grunted. 'McCleary's been a subscriber to shooting magazines for a few years.'

'But he's an ex-con, he can't own guns.'

'Not officially, he can't,' replied Noble. 'But there's nothing to say he can't read about guns. Ford says we can't take the chance so he's putting an armed unit on standby.'

'Great,' said Brook, dismayed.

'How's life in the Cold Case Unit?' asked Noble.

'Not good. Staring at four walls . . . doesn't suit me.'

'I'm surprised,' teased Noble.

'Me too, actually,' smiled Brook. 'But Charlton's masterstroke is a life without daylight. That's the killer. I need to be out amongst the living.'

'As you stand over the dead.'

'At least I can see a victim's corpse, John. At the moment I'm chasing phantoms. Charlton's finally got my measure.'

'Never happen,' retorted Noble. 'You should tell him where to stick the Ghostbusters and get back to working cases. We need you. He'll back down, you'll see.'

Brook wondered whether to mention his resignation but couldn't think how to phrase it without sounding pathetic. *I'm worried about my self-control. I can't work in an office without daylight. I don't like taking my own notes.* He settled for, 'I doubt it.'

Noble spied Brook's pint glass. 'Anything to drink?'

'Aren't you driving?'

'I only knocked off an hour ago and I'm stone cold sober,' replied Noble.

Brook removed a bottle of Cobra from the fridge. 'How did you find the cottage?'

'I asked at the pub. Briefly,' Noble added as Brook hesitated with the bottle opener. 'I mean, Hartington's not big, is it?' He accepted his drink and poured the beer into a glass. 'Hadn't pegged you for a lager man.'

'As I was in Normanton Road this morning . . .' began Brook.

'Course. Good curry shops down there,' agreed Noble. 'And my nose tells me you picked up some spicy delicacies.'

'If you're hungry—'

'No,' interrupted Noble, downing a sizeable gulp of lager. 'This is fine.'

Brook sat down, curious to hear why Noble had ventured all the way out to Hartington so late. When Noble appeared reluctant to elaborate, Brook broke the ice. 'So no progress on Scott, you said?'

Noble looked at him over the rim of the glass, exhaling a beery sigh. 'We haven't found the body, if that's what you mean.'

Brook nodded sympathetically. 'McCleary aside, where are you at?'

'Six days in and we're at the fingertip-search dragging-rivers stage. Old ground to us, after the Deity murders.'

'You've—'

'We've done the appeals, knocked on every door, done the backgrounds, the parents, the relatives, the teachers, the ex-teachers, the friends, the parents of friends. Everyone and everything checks out.'

'And Greg Stapleton?'

'It's not Stapleton. I interviewed him this afternoon. He's got a watertight alibi for last Friday night – a dozen people were with him on a Christmas do until well after midnight.'

'And Mrs Stapleton?'

Doubt crept over Noble's face. 'She didn't threaten Scott.' Brook raised an eyebrow at Noble who conceded with a dip of his eyes. 'We'll check to be thorough. But after that all leads are dry.' He shrugged helplessly. 'Suggestions?'

'You need to go back to St Chad's Road, John.'

'Chelsea Chaplin's party,' said Noble.

'Right. If Scott was abducted, someone must have seen or heard something. And if they didn't . . .'

'Then maybe he wasn't abducted,' finished Noble. 'It is looking that way. We know Scott slipped away from the house under his own steam.'

'Any idea why?' inquired Brook.

Noble took a sip of lager and eyed Brook. 'Remember I told you he was scared?'

'I assume not because of Stapleton's threats.'

Noble shook his head. 'Something more recent. You remember Stapleton's kid, Joshua, killed by the vagrant in a derelict house?'

'Noel Williams,' said Brook. 'What of it?'

Noble fumbled for a folded piece of paper in a coat pocket. 'We haven't released any of this yet.' He held it out to Brook but withdrew it as Brook made to take it. 'Charlton can't know you've seen this.'

Brook was a little wounded that Noble needed to ask for his discretion. *But then he has a career to protect*. He nodded his agreement and Noble pushed the paper at him.

'This is a photocopy. Scott received the original and it's in for tests. We can't be certain but we think Scott received it a few days before the party because his mum noticed that he became withdrawn and nervous a few days before he disappeared.'

Brook opened out the paper.

Be cAreFul Scott. KeEp youR Eyes OPeN. HE WaNts
YOu neXt. IM CLOSE BY.
ItS DaRk. I cAnt sEE. come HelP ME. U kNOw WHERE.
JOSH

'Newspaper cuttings?' Brook smiled. 'A bit melodramatic. Found the source?'

'The letters are from a local free paper delivered all across the city,' said Noble.

Brook rubbed his chin. 'And you're testing for prints and DNA on the original.'

'No prints. I'm not getting my hopes up about DNA,' sighed Noble.

'Envelope?'

'Nope.'

'So you don't know *how* Scott received this?'

'No, though we're pretty certain it wasn't posted,' said Noble. 'Mrs Wheeler doesn't work and says she would've been first to see any letters mailed to her son.'

'I suppose it could easily have been slipped into his pocket or school bag,' agreed Brook, reading it again. 'I can see why Scott would be frightened – though he wasn't scared enough to avoid going to a party after dark.'

'That's because Scott thought one of the other guests sent him the note as a joke. He went there to find out.'

'Who?'

'Adam Kramer, his friend. Adam said Scott told him about the note then threatened him with a Stanley knife.'

'But this friend didn't send it?'

'Adam swears he'd never seen the note before we showed it to him,' said Noble.

'Do we believe him?'

'We do,' nodded Noble.

'But did Scott believe him?'

'Eventually.'

'Which is when he really started to get frightened,' concluded Brook.

'That doesn't cover it. According to Adam, he was terrified.' Noble paused for breath. 'There's something else. Adam thinks Scott saw something that night.'

'What?'

'We don't know for sure. During the party, the pair of them snuck off to a room on the top floor because Adam had vodka. Scott mentioned the note then pulled out the Stanley knife to confront Adam. When he realised Adam hadn't sent it, Scott got really edgy. He went to the bedroom window and looked out into the dark. He must have seen something or someone in the back garden because Adam says when Scott turned round he was as white as a sheet, almost frozen in terror.'

'Did Adam see what Scott saw?'

'No. And Scott didn't tell him. But he mumbled something before running out of the room in a panic. That was the last anyone saw of him.'

'What did he say?'

'Adam wasn't certain but he thinks it was *Josh*.'

'Josh?' said Brook. 'His dead friend.'

Noble shrugged. 'He may have misheard.'

'But?' prompted Brook.

'But we searched the garden. It's big, lots of trees and shrubs. There's one of those leylandii that neighbours are always going to court over. Massive.' He looked up at Brook. 'We found footprints in the soil next to it. Training shoes. The markings on the sole were from the same brand Joshua Stapleton was wearing the night he died – same size too.'

Brook said nothing for a few minutes, the silence broken only by the crack of wood in the burner and the gulp as Noble pulled on his drink.

'So someone else knew the trainers Joshua Stapleton wore the night he died and wore the same brand last Friday night. And if he was wearing similar clothes, you might conclude that someone was passing himself off as Scott's dead friend.'

'That's my thinking,' said Noble. 'And if I was thirteen years old, I think that would scare me rigid.'

'U kNOw WHERE,' said Brook, looking at the note again. 'The derelict house, you think?

'I don't see how. It was pulled down months ago.'

'Mmmm.'

'There's something else.' Noble pointed a finger at a part of the note. 'Whoever stuck these cuttings together left a bit of the date on one of them.'

'I noticed,' said Brook. 'The thirty-first – which month?'

Noble raised an eyebrow. 'Guess.'

Brook considered for a moment but didn't disappoint. 'October.'

'Halloween,' confirmed Noble. 'Not only that. The cuttings were taken from the edition published last year, not this. The same night Josh Stapleton went missing, after trick or treating with Scott.'

'Interesting,' said Brook, rubbing his chin. 'You'd better check the alibis of Stapleton's relatives again.'

'Why?'

'Who keeps a copy of a free paper from thirteen months ago unless it means something?' said Brook. 'But a grieving family might keep a copy from the day their boy died.'

'Maybe a killer too,' suggested Noble.

'Did you ask Stapleton about the note?'

'Without going into specifics, I asked if he, or his wife, had communicated with Scott in the month before his disappearance,' said Noble. 'They denied ever speaking to Scott after Greg threatened him at the trial.'

'Do you believe them?'

'It's not the Stapletons,' said Noble. 'They're decent people. Their world was turned upside down by their son's death and they lashed out verbally. But posting threatening notes? It isn't their style.'

'No,' conceded Brook. 'And I doubt they'd go round impersonating their dead son either.' He looked again at the note. 'Besides, this isn't a threat, it's a warning.' Brook stood and pulled a half-finished bottle of malt whisky from a cupboard. He poured a small measure into his only leaded tumbler and topped it up with water. Noble watched him walk around the kitchen while he sipped the contents. Eventually he sat down and looked hard at Noble. He tried to pick his words for maximum diplomacy. 'The existence and contents of that note imply the Stapleton boy's killer is still out there.'

Noble knew what was coming but didn't comment so Brook was forced to ask the question.

'Sorry to query one of your results, John, but how sure are you about the Williams conviction?'

'Noel Williams confessed to killing Joshua Stapleton,' said Noble slowly. 'Is that sure enough for you?'

'And you have no doubts?'

Noble looked at him tight-lipped. 'Why would I have doubts?'

'I don't know,' said Brook. 'I wasn't there. But the sentence . . .'

'What about it?' demanded Noble. Brook hesitated. 'Go on. I can cope.'

Brook looked hard at Noble. 'When a child is murdered and the killer gets off with twenty years, and could be out in ten, I think I'd smell a rat.'

Noble took a long sip of his lager and studied the foam draining down his glass. 'I didn't get to interview Williams.'

Brook nodded minutely. 'That's what I thought. We're the same. We want the right result or no result, even if it affects our clear-up. And that's what's worrying you now. You think DI Ford—'

'I didn't say that.'

'But you're thinking it.' Brook found Noble's eye. 'What happened?'

'We got a conviction.'

'You offered a child killer *manslaughter* with diminished responsibility. Why? Was it lack of evidence?'

'Noel Williams lived there—'

'Then forensics should have had a field day.'

Noble mulled it over. 'How does it look from the outside?'

'Without knowing the details, it looks like Noel Williams is an ideal fall guy – a homeless vagrant, probably a drink and drug abuser into the bargain. He's a suspect with no credibility.'

'But Williams confessed,' argued Noble. 'His brief offered no defence in court.'

'*Because* he's not credible, not even to his own defence counsel,' said Brook. 'When we arrest someone who doesn't know the time of day, more often than not the statement they sign is our version of events.'

'But he *did* sign it.'

'But was he competent to sign?' Brook pressed. Noble looked up, about to speak but couldn't. 'I know,' said Brook. 'You weren't there.'

'Look, we've written statements for suspects before and when we read them back we could be delivering the Queen's Speech, for all they know,' said Noble. 'Yet they still sign it.'

'Which is why you have to take extra care because someone like Noel Williams can be so out of it, he might actually believe he's guilty if someone tells him often enough. And even if Williams knew he was innocent, a vagrant doesn't need a lot of persuading to sign a piece of paper that gets him off the streets. Especially in winter. And now he spends his evenings watching TV in a warm prison, tucking into three hot meals a day, instead of shivering in ruined houses with only a bottle and a needle to console him.'

Noble searched for a way to contradict Brook. 'But Williams knew Joshua and Scott. They used to throw stones at him on their way home from school and break windows in the squat. He remembered them. Motive.'

'So Williams has a memory of being goaded by a couple of schoolboys. It changes nothing. Did he remember throwing Josh Stapleton to his death?'

'Not while I was present,' admitted Noble.

'Twenty years, John. For murdering a child. That's a slap on the wrist in this country.'

Noble was deep in thought.

'Look, I might be wrong,' said Brook. 'Have you listened to the tapes?'

'I have. I can't fault what I hear,' said Noble, seeming no happier.

Brook decided not to press too hard and let Noble brood. Finally,

'I'm the last person to cast doubt on Ford after what I did. But *you* showed me the note. You must have a reason for that.'

Noble blew out his cheeks in submission. 'I think Ford coached him off the record, offered him a reduction for a confession. Williams was left alone overnight. He'd been fed and had drunk a gallon of coffee so he could function by the morning. We were interviewing him early but when I went to pick him up, he wasn't in his cell. He was in Interview One – alone with Ford. The tape was off by now. Ford said the duty solicitor had just left and Williams had confessed.'

Noble went to take another drink but put the glass down. 'I knew something was wrong, even at the scene. Williams was completely gone when we brought him in. He could barely function. And there's something else.'

'Go on.'

'Joshua's underpants had been cut off . . .'

'I didn't know he was raped,' exclaimed Brook.

'That's just it,' said Noble. 'He wasn't. But after he'd been thrown off the stairwell, someone pulled his tracksuit down to his ankles, *cut* his underpants off and took his trainers. Both were found in the room Williams crashed.'

'And you don't think Williams could have done that?'

'He wasn't carrying a blade, for one thing.'

'He'd had three days to get rid of it,' said Brook.

'He'd also had three days to put on Joshua's trainers and three days to get out of there.' Noble shook his head, tight-lipped. 'But he was in no condition.'

Brook was silent for a moment. 'You had a confession, John. You had every right to square it away on Ford's say-so. Which brings us back to the note.'

'You think the killer's still out there?' asked Noble.

'*He wants you next*,' quoted Brook.

'And if the Stapleton kid's killer is still at large, he thinks Scott Wheeler might have seen him and wants to silence him.'

'Possible,' agreed Brook. Noble had a lot on his plate. There was no point muddying the waters further. Not without Scott Wheeler to interview.

'At least it's not a sexual motive,' added Noble, clutching at a straw. He drained his glass and stared into it, realising what Brook put into words for him.

'If Scott saw a killer, John, he's in even more danger.'

Noble rubbed his hands across his face. 'Oh, God, what a mess.' He looked at Brook through splayed fingers. 'What should I do about Williams? Ford will—'

'Do nothing. Yet. Concentrate on finding Scott then you can ask him the question.'

'And if he's dead?'

'Don't cross that bridge until it's in front of you, John. You've got enough to think about.'

Noble laughed. 'The thing is I haven't. We've done everything. If McCleary doesn't pan out all we can do is wait and hope.'

'Maybe the phones will come good. Nothing gets the public more involved than a missing child.'

Noble snorted. 'The public? You know better than me how much garbage they give us to wade through – people shopping neighbours who kicked their cat ten years ago or parked across their drive or trimmed an inch too much off their hedge. And that's just the nasty ones. The fruit loops are worse.' Noble managed a weary smile. 'But at least we get a giggle out of *them*.'

'Tell me,' smiled Brook.

'Can you believe someone actually rang in to tell us Scott had been abducted by the Pied Piper?' Noble laughed in spite of himself, unclear why Brook's smile had frozen on his face.

'All very interesting,' said Noble, tapping out a cigarette as they stood by his car. 'But the Pied Piper's a fairytale.'

Brook eyed the cigarette. He didn't want one but he loved the ritual – the cupped hand, the sound of the flame touching the tobacco, the first sullying inhalation – and muscle memory was itching his scratch. 'I know, John. But I'm looking for a killer who struck nearly fifty years ago so I'm feeding on scraps.'

'Well, I'm sure it's logged. I'll ask Morton.'

'Thanks. And keep it under wraps, will you? I don't want word getting out to the wrong people. I'm enough of a hate figure to the citizens of Derby as it is.'

Noble grinned as he unlocked his car. 'I heard about the hair-drying Hendrickson got from Charlton. I doubt he'll ever look you in the eye again.'

'And I suspect Brian Burton won't be getting any more tips either,' smiled Brook.

'How did you manage that?'

'I have my methods,' said Brook soberly, remembering how close he'd come to hitting Hendrickson.

Noble laughed. 'As well I know.' He opened the driver's door. 'Thanks for the drink.'

'Don't mention it,' said Brook. 'And maybe tomorrow you'll tell me why you came all this way to see me.'

Noble straightened, his brow wrinkled in confusion. 'How do you do that?'

'I'm a trained detective, John.' Brook smiled. 'If it won't keep, I'm still listening.'

Noble pulled on his cigarette, coming to a decision. 'Forget it. It's silly.'

'Then it'll make up for all the times you've listened to my drivel.'

Noble looked out into the cold night, suddenly embarrassed. Eventually he managed, 'I was thinking of jacking it in, resigning.'

Brook was genuinely surprised. 'Because of the promotion?'

Noble narrowed his eyes. 'I don't know. I don't think so. I hope not. It's just been getting me down, this case. It feels like I'm banging my head against a brick wall. I don't want to turn out . . .' He flashed an apologetic look at Brook then declined to continue.

'No, you're right, John. I didn't want to end up like me either. Fifty-one years old, divorced, alone, a daughter I hardly see, no friends . . .'

'Sir, I—'

'It's what our job can do to us, John. We see things that people shouldn't have to see. Victims, crime scenes, lost and wrecked lives. But it's not inevitable that you end up like me. This conversation shows it – you're aware in a way that I never was at your age. I took it home with me. I didn't make the effort to keep it separate. You're different.'

'Am I?' said Noble. 'I see Scott Wheeler's mum and know that one day soon I'm going to knock on her door with a WPC next to me. And when she sees my face, she's not going to need me to tell her why I'm there. From that moment on that poor woman is going to stop living. And I will have caused that.'

'No you won't, John. Whoever took Scott Wheeler's life will have caused that and someone with your empathy is the best person in the world to take that news to parents. I could never do it. And at the end of that day, if it ever comes, you're going to go home, have a beer and get up the next day and do your job as well as you can. You'll use that experience to make sure that the next Scott Wheeler, or the one after that, is returned home safely. And then you're going to remember why you became a policeman.'

'Maybe.'

'Definitely,' snapped Brook. 'Look, John, there's only one in a thousand can do our job. And the frightening thing is, some of the other nine hundred and ninety-nine are doing it as well. The force *cannot* afford to lose you so go home, have another beer and sleep on it.'

Noble nodded his appreciation. 'I'll do that.' He was about to duck into his car but held his ground. 'Better make that two.'

'Two beers then.'

'I meant two in a thousand,' said Noble, his face reddening. 'I've learned so much since . . . well. I can text you if I need advice?'

'As long as that's a two-way street, John,' said Brook.

With a curt nod, Noble climbed into his car and sped away into the night. Brook watched until the cold drove him back to the cottage. He picked up his whisky from the kitchen and headed back to the tiny lounge. The fire was almost out. He took a final sip from his glass and picked out the well-thumbed resignation letter from his jacket.

'I wish you hadn't said that.' Brook opened the small cast-iron door of the wood burner and dropped the letter on to the embers. He spent an enjoyable few minutes watching it smoulder as it turned brown and crinkly before finally catching fire and turning to ash within seconds.

Sixteen

Friday, 14 December 2012

THE NEXT MORNING BROOK PULLED his old BMW on to the steep forecourt of the sprawling two-storey building. A squad car from a local constabulary had parked in the last unrestricted bay so the only spaces available were for disabled drivers or cars carrying children.

Brook pulled into one of the latter, given that there were four such unoccupied bays and having long ago decided that to reserve parking space on the grounds of disability was laudable but to do so on the basis of lifestyle choice was perverse. Besides, he was visiting an old people's home on a school day and children would be thin on the ground.

He turned off the engine but didn't move. A few seconds later he turned it back on and reversed out of the space. He'd only been back on active duty for a few days and a complaint from an old people's home might just be the straw that broke the camel's back.

Following the signs to the deserted overflow car park, some three hundred yards away, he parked his car in splendid isolation then walked back up the slope, at least able to revel in the piercing winter sun after recent days of light-free confinement.

It was ideal walking weather, crisp and cold, and Brook was pleased to be outdoors in the countryside, breathing in the sweet perfume of wood smoke drifting past his nostrils. He heard the crack of a farmer's small-calibre rifle in a nearby field and yearned for the mild spring weather, when he could roam the Peaks with his tent and pitch up wherever he pleased.

As he approached the wheelchair-friendly ramp at the front entrance, he looked over to a paved rose garden where a handful of elderly residents were risking the cold bright weather. Some hardy souls sat on benches, others promenaded slowly around the flower beds with the aid of a white-uniformed member of staff or a walking frame. All were thoroughly wrapped up against the chill.

Brook stepped towards the glass doors as a uniformed officer emerged from the building. 'Sergeant,' said Brook, flashing his warrant card. 'DI Brook. Is there a problem here?'

The sergeant examined the warrant card. 'DI Brook? I know that name. You were in the paper—'

'I asked if there was a problem.'

'It's these old codgers,' replied the sergeant, omitting Brook's rank. 'They scare easy. Some old biddy reckons she's seen a prowler outside her window and thinks she's going to get raped. She should be so lucky, the dried-up old prune.' The uniformed officer laughed, anticipating a male bonding session. It didn't materialise and the sergeant's levity faded quickly.

'I'm here to interview an *old biddy*,' said Brook severely. 'What's the name?'

The officer peered down at the notebook in his hand. 'Jessica Pinchbeck. That her?'

Brook shook his head. After a pause, he added, 'I don't see any paperwork.'

The sergeant flipped his notebook shut and pulled a face as he walked past Brook. 'I can see why you made DI, pal. Good luck getting any sense out of this lot,' he added, thumbing over his shoulder at the building.

Brook stiffened in anger but felt incapable of speech or movement. He watched the unnamed officer return to his car, urging himself to intervene and take a position before the officer had strutted out of earshot. But before Brook could unglue his mouth and feet, the squad car had screeched out of the car park.

'I'm not your pal,' seethed Brook, finally regaining the power of speech. He suddenly felt very old and tired. Maybe the surroundings had sucked the will from him. More likely it was the aftermath of his suspension. After his own transgressions, Brook was stripped of the moral energy to demand better from subordinates.

Dejected, he approached the gloomy reception area, wincing at the hideously inoffensive music leaking from hidden speakers – soft tinkling piano, playing undemanding chords. Amazing how that which was designed to soothe could so readily raise hackles. He looked around at the dark black and gold wallpaper and outdated furniture. The few wall lights bestowed only the palest hint of illumination, like landing lights, designed to guide the infirm back to their rooms, clinging to the smooth brass handrail which disappeared into distant corridors. The smell of decay was omnipresent. At that moment, Brook's most fervent wish was that he never ended up in such a place.

'DI Brook, Derby CID,' he said, holding his warrant card up close to the young female receptionist in the dingy light. 'I'm here to talk to Amelia Stanforth.'

'We just had one of your lot in here about a prowler,' said the girl – her ID tag carried the name Sharmayne.

'I saw him outside,' replied Brook. 'This is another matter.'

'And what's Amelia been up to?'

'She held up HMV at gunpoint and demanded some decent music,' replied Brook, without expression.

The girl was momentarily confused before breaking into a hesitant smile. 'You're joking.' She smiled and flicked her head at the ceiling. 'Depressing, isn't it?'

'Very.'

'The annoying thing is only the staff can hear it. Sometimes I'm tempted to sling on some Slayer just to see what would happen.'

Brook nodded as though he knew what she was talking about. 'Amelia Stanforth?'

'Just a moment. I'll see if the doctor's available. Amelia has heart problems, you know.'

* * *

The old woman peered through her half-moon spectacles at Brook's ID. 'Inspector Brook,' she read, as though taking an eye test. 'You're new.' She sat back in the chair, swaddled in several nylon blankets that clicked on the rough skin of her hands as she moved. Once reclined, she closed her eyes and turned to face the temporary warmth of the winter sun. 'Is it that time of year again?'

Amelia Stanforth allowed her attached glasses to drop on to her chest before fixing Brook with a pale beady eye. She squinted beyond the rose garden to the trees dotted around the ample grounds, now naked under the assault of winter winds. 'Time for you to go through the motions for a few days.'

'So you know why I'm here.'

'I've not lost *all* my marbles yet, young man,' she said. 'You've come to arrest me for my brother's murder.'

Brook raised an eyebrow. 'Is that a confession?'

The old girl shook her head bitterly. 'Do you need one? Speak to anyone – my old neighbours, Billy's friends. Everyone knows I did it. They used to whisper as much whenever I walked by. Nice and loud so I could hear. "How can she live in the same house? She must have killed Billy."'

'And did you?' asked Brook, unable to pass up such an opening.

Now it was Amelia's turn to be surprised. 'Not shy, are you?' Brook shrugged. 'Of course I didn't. Why would I kill my brother?'

Brook cast around for a good reason. 'I'm told it was Billy who informed your parents you were seeing Brendan McCleary. And your father disapproved.'

'Oh, you were told, were you?' A tear formed in her eye. 'I suppose he did. You're well-informed. And so you think I could burn my little brother to death as payback? Dear God, I could never . . .' She began to sob gently. Brook spotted a packet of tissues in a cardigan pocket. She took one from the offered packet and daintily dabbed at her powdered cheek.

162

'I'm sorry it's still so painful,' said Brook.

She dried her eyes. 'It's not just for Billy. His death ruined so many lives. My parents. Francesca. Billy's friend.'

'His friend? You mean Edward Mullen.'

'Teddy, yes. He doted on Billy. I don't think he'll ever get over his death.'

'Sounds like you've seen him recently,' observed Brook.

'Not recently,' she replied. 'And now he's probably dead. Every few months another one goes. There'll soon be no one left.'

'Mullen's alive, according to my information,' said Brook. 'And I spoke to Edna Spencer two days ago. Maybe you remember her as Edna Hibbert.'

Amelia Stanforth's face lit up. 'Little Edna? How is she?'

'Frail but sharp,' replied Brook. 'And if it's any consolation, she was certain you didn't kill your brother.'

Amelia's face tightened into a bitter smile. 'That's nice of her.' Her thoughts drifted away to the past, bringing half-remembered pleasure, and pain.

Brook pressed on. 'Why *did* you live in that house after your parents died?'

Amelia raised the tissue and dabbed at another tear. 'Making amends,' she said finally. 'Keeping his memory alive, giving Billy the love I never showed him when he was still breathing.' She blew out her cheeks with emotion but the tears had dried. She suddenly glared fiercely at him. 'I thought you lot had given up. That Sergeant Laird was just here, poking his nose in again. But did he ask about Billy? Course not. He didn't even bother speaking to me. Probably just checking I'm still alive and filling his forms.'

'Amelia, DS Laird retired as a detective inspector years ago. He's in his seventies now.'

'He was just here, I tell you. I recognised him. He was wearing a uniform this time but I'd know him anywhere.'

Brook held his palms up to pacify her, looking warily at the orderly who'd warned him against upsetting residents. 'OK, take it easy.'

'Why are you here? Why can't you leave us alone?'

'Us?'

'Those left behind, picking up the pieces – me, Edna, Teddy . . .' she waved her hand as though trying to remember and Brook waited in vain for her to finish her list.

'I'm here because we never give up on a murder victim until we bring their killer to justice,' said Brook, adopting the party line, without excessive zeal.

Amelia Stanforth wasn't buying. 'Then why has it been so long? Someone used to call round every few years, once the snow was on the ground. It's been years since the last visit. Billy not so urgent now, is he?'

Brook tried to smile. 'Your brother's murder is an open case, Miss Stanforth. I wouldn't be here if it wasn't important.'

'Don't butter me up.'

'According to the file,' Brook ploughed on, 'the case was last reviewed four years ago. My colleague DI Greatorix might have called. You'd still have been living in Kirk Langley then.'

Amelia thought for a moment then shook her head.

'He was a large man with a round red face and breathing difficulties. He would have mopped his face quite a lot. Maybe you've forgotten.'

'I didn't see him, I tell you. Anyway, what's the point? My brother Billy died . . .' Amelia hesitated over information no longer as clear as it once was.

'Forty-nine years ago,' said Brook.

Amelia tried to hide her surprise. 'Is it really?' she exclaimed, narrowing her eyes to do the calculation. 'My little brother would've been sixty-two years old in a week.' She looked up at Brook and smiled suddenly. 'You have a nice face. That other officer who used to call . . .' she clicked a finger in frustration before it came to her. 'Inspector Coppell.' She beamed triumphantly.

'DCI Copeland,' suggested Brook.

'Copeland.' She nodded sombrely, her victory over Father Time somewhat diminished by Brook's assistance. 'Yes, that's the one.

He had a nice face too.' Her mood darkened suddenly. 'He had a sister, though. She died.'

'That's right,' said Brook, surprised at this tangent. 'Her death was in all the papers. She died two years after your brother.'

'I read about it. What was her name again?' asked Amelia.

'Matilda,' Brook recalled.

'Matilda,' she repeated, nodding in recognition. 'I remember. Murdered, she was. Worm's meat at sixteen.'

Worm's meat. Brook knew the phrase. Shakespeare. 'A cold way of referring to the death of a young girl,' he observed.

'It's from *Romeo and Juliet*,' answered Amelia, missing Brook's barb. 'I studied it at school.'

Brook never ceased to be amazed at how the elderly could lodge things in the memory for many years and recall them with crystal clarity, yet often not know what day of the week it was.

'A plague on both our houses,' said Amelia, another tear forming in her eye. 'A dead child from each. First Billy then Tilly Copeland.'

'Tilly? Was that Matilda's nickname?' asked Brook.

'That's what he called her.'

'So DCI Copeland spoke to you about his sister.'

For the first time in a while she looked at Brook. 'Poor man. He carried a lot of pain. And his sister was so young. When he first came to talk to me in . . .' she waved her hand in exasperation.

Brook raided his memory banks. 'Nineteen seventy-eight was the first time DCI Copeland reviewed your brother's case. He'd have been a DS back then.'

Amelia shook her head in wonder. 'Nineteen seventy-eight. Where does the time go? Yes. DS Copeland. He still seemed to be in shock about his sister when he came to visit. And he asked his questions but there was nothing I could say to help him. I wasn't there.'

Brook was confused. 'You weren't where?'

'Sorry, dear?'

'You said you couldn't help Copeland because you weren't there. Where do you mean?'

Amelia stopped to gaze at Brook. She seemed puzzled at first then smiled sweetly. 'Sergeant Copeland had a nice face,' she said finally. He couldn't be sure but for the first time Brook got the distinct impression she was trading on her age to appear befuddled to avoid the question.

'He wasn't a bit like that Sergeant Laird.' She took a deep breath. 'Nasty man – always insinuating things.'

'Murder isn't pleasant,' observed Brook, remembering how, as a DC and DS, he'd had to make the running, ask all the hard questions until promotion allowed him to delegate. 'I'm sure he was just doing his job.'

'And now Mr Copeland is worm's meat himself, isn't he?' Amelia said.

'Actually, no,' answered Brook. 'He retired as well.'

'Course he is,' she confirmed, not hearing. 'That's all we have to look forward to at our age – death amongst strangers. And I'm next. There's no one left. The whole family gone and the Stanforth name with it.' She looked up at him. 'I never married, never had children, you see. And Billy and Fran . . .' she shrugged and lapsed into silence.

Brook could see what Copeland meant about re-interviewing witnesses long after the fact. Resolution potential? Forget it. Amelia Stanforth's memory seemed clear one minute, foggy the next, leaving Brook unable to work out which utterance to trust. He glanced up at the cobalt sky. At least he was getting his fix of daylight.

He looked around to plot his escape then realised that he had nothing better to do, nowhere to go but back to his airless, artificially lit cell. For the next few minutes, he listened to her, nodding in that patronising way he'd always abhorred and sworn to avoid. He hoped no one behaved the same way when he became less able to see to his own needs and had to rely on the kindness of strangers.

A while later Amelia tired of Brook's undemanding demeanour. 'Did they tell you not to get me excited?'

Brook was sheepish. 'Actually they did. Something to do with your pills.'

'I thought so. I used to like a dance. Now look at me. Stuck in here. No family. No friends.' She chuckled and stuck her tongue out at Brook. He was taken aback until the old woman lifted it and picked out a blue tablet.

'They give me these to keep me calm.' She flicked it gleefully into the thickest clump of rose bushes and giggled at Brook. 'I'm sixty-four years old with a dodgy ticker and if I can't get excited now, I might as well step under a bus. Not that there are any out here in the middle of nowhere.'

Brook sighed. This was pointless. Perhaps Greatorix had taken the right approach. Just find out who's still alive, fill in the forms and move on to something useful. Brook put his notebook away and pulled his flimsy coat tighter.

'Aren't you taking any more notes?'

'I have everything I need.'

Amelia shrugged. 'You won't get another chance, young man. Though what would be the point – nothing will bring back my Billy, right?' She smiled. 'He could be a little shit, always getting into fights about something or other, coming home with skinned knuckles and shiners.' She smiled at the memory. 'Billy gave as good as he got, mind.' She looked into the distance again. 'Sixty-two this year – hard to believe.'

'Do you remember what happened that day?' said Brook, half-heartedly taking the opportunity to prompt.

'Hard to believe,' she repeated.

Brook's answering smile was thin. This was the coldest case on the books and dropping it into his lap was a waste of his time and skills.

'You've got a nice face, Inspector.'

'Thank you.'

'You're not married, are you?'

Brook raised an eyebrow. 'How can you tell?'

'When you've got a loved one at home, a part of you is always there with them. You can see that in someone's face. You could see it in my face when . . .' she hesitated.

'When you were with Brendan McCleary?' ventured Brook.

She said nothing for a while and her expression told Brook she was annoyed that she'd introduced the subject. 'We used to walk out together,' she acknowledged finally. 'My father told me Brendan was no good. I took no notice. Well, you don't at that age, do you? We were good together and I dare say we might have wed.'

'What happened?'

'Brendan didn't want me, is what happened. He wanted someone else instead.' She looked sadly into the distance. 'Or thought he did.'

'Who?'

Amelia roused herself to shake her head and dab a crooked hand at the corner of an eye. 'It's not relevant now.'

'This is hard for you. I'm sorry.'

'Don't be. It's not your fault. And Brendan knows he wronged me. That's some comfort.'

'He told you that.'

She hesitated. 'I could tell it from his face.'

'When did you last see him?'

She glanced slyly at him. 'Not for years. He went to prison.'

'But do you know where he is now?' asked Brook. 'We want to ask him some questions.'

'He knows he hurt me,' she said, apparently deaf to Brook's question. Her jaw tightened. 'Brendan didn't kill my Billy, if that's what you're implying. That's not how he hurt me. Don't say that. Don't ever say that.'

'I didn't. You already told me. He betrayed you with another girl.'

Amelia looked at the sky with her pale eyes. 'Another girl,' she repeated as though trying to deduce the meaning. She turned her face to his and covered his fist with her frail papyrus hand. 'I used to have nightmares about Billy, seeing him like that. There was nothing left. The shed burned down to ashes and Billy with it. What a blaze. Even in the cold and damp.'

'That's because there was an accelerant.'

'What's that, dear?'

'An accelerant – a chemical used to start fires and keep them burning.'

She nodded. 'You mean the paint thinners. I remember. Petrol too.'

'What about Brendan?' asked Brook, persevering. 'Did you see him that afternoon?'

She sighed. 'What a blaze.'

Brook produced a piece of paper to try another angle. 'This is a list of all those at the party. Most were Billy's friends – twenty of them, plus you, your parents and Francesca.'

She reached for the paper, scanning the list of names, in turn smiling and frowning. 'Charlotte Dilkes,' she said at one point. 'She was sweet on Billy. Always following him around, trying to get him to kiss her. What does D mean? Dopey?' she giggled. 'Charlotte was certainly that.'

'Amelia, Brendan's not on the list of guests but was he there? Did you see him?'

'You sound like that nasty man, Laird.'

'Do I?' said Brook. 'Then tell me. Did Brendan see Billy that day? Did you see Brendan?'

'Brendan. I remember he hurt me. I didn't deserve it.'

Brook sighed in frustration but decided he just had to go with the flow. 'What did he do?' he asked.

'Threw me over for some little trollop.'

'Your sister Francesca said she saw you crying. Is that why you cried? Because Brendan had another girl?'

Amelia glanced warily at him and Brook sensed she'd realised that her tears that day were a matter of dispute. 'Younger than me, she were,' she said, ignoring Brook's prompting. 'I would've given him the world but he wanted some child over me. Me!' she insisted, tapping a frail fist against her breast.

'Can you remember her name?'

'I told you, it's not relevant.'

'Tell me anyway.'

'Not relevant, he said. Forget about her, he said.'

'Who said forget about her? Brendan?'

'He hurt me.' She held the paper to her bosom and her eyes closed. Tears were squeezed on to her cheeks. 'Deceased. It means deceased. Charlotte's dead. She drowned. I remember. That nasty man thought we'd done it.'

'DS Laird? Why would DS Laird think you and Brendan killed Charlotte? And where is Brendan now?'

'He was my boyfriend. I loved him. He loved me.' She glanced up at Brook then looked furtively around. The sky was darkening and a cold breeze stirring. Most of the other patients had gone in. 'Do you have a cigarette? I'm not allowed.'

'I don't smoke,' replied Brook.

'Brendan always had cigarettes.' She smiled wistfully.

'Amelia, I need you to try and remember. What was Brendan's other girlfriend called?'

'I don't know where he got them. The newsagent wouldn't sell him any. Bit of a rogue, my Bren.'

Brook gave up. Even if Amelia could reply, her evidence just wasn't reliable. He fell into line with her topic of conversation. 'Did Brendan give Billy cigarettes?'

'Miss Stanforth, time to get you indoors into the warm,' said the young orderly in whites, walking towards them. 'You'll catch pneumonia if you stay out here much longer.'

'I'll be there in a minute, Craig.'

'See that you are.' He grinned. 'You'll miss out on the Bingo if you dilly-dally.'

Amelia smiled for Craig's benefit.

Brook tried again. 'The files said Billy was a smoker, according to the statement from his friend.'

Amelia returned her gaze to the piece of paper. 'Teddy,' she nodded after alighting on the correct name, 'little Teddy Mullen. There's no D next to his name. He's still alive, you said?'

'As far as I know,' said Brook.

'And they say the good die young.' She scanned the names again.

'He was a sensitive little thing. Didn't like losing at bobbing apples. Said I cheated him. Threw a right strop.'

'Edward Mullen?'

Amelia nodded. 'Nothing to him. A good breeze would have blown him over.' She laughed. 'The way he used to follow our Billy round. Like a lapdog. Worshipped the ground he walked on, did Teddy. Best mates forever.'

'Can you remember when you last saw Mullen?'

'Let me see. He was at the funerals at St Michael's – that's the local church. First Billy's, of course. Then he came to see Fran into the ground. Nice of him. It must have been quite a journey by then because he'd moved away to Derby. That would be in nineteen sixty-eight. No, Fran died on Billy's birthday in sixty-eight. The funeral was nineteen sixty-nine. Yes, January sixty-nine.

'Poor Francesca. Eighteen. What age is that to go and sit beside the Lord when I'm gone sixty? I wish Mum and Dad hadn't been alive to see Fran under the earth. Billy nearly did for the pair of them. But burying *two* of your children, well, it's not natural. Mum and Dad were never the same after Billy. They often used to say they died in that fire. Fran said the same.'

Amelia struggled to her feet and Brook went to help her. 'Fran got along as best she could after the fire but she was dead inside. They were twins, you see. They had a connection. All that love. But rivals at the same time. It must be difficult sharing everything. Mum's womb, birthdays, the same bedroom, new clothes – always having to share the attention, the love. When Billy passed, she couldn't cope. Barely spoke and left school early, and as soon as she was old enough to earn she started to drink. Gin and brandy, I think, and plenty of it. Drugs, too, I shouldn't wonder. Little by little she lost the will to live and killed herself . . .'

'Officially her death was an accident.'

'Well, there's accidents and there's accidents,' retorted Amelia. 'She drowned her sorrows with a bottle of gin. Afterwards she drowned herself in the bath. Isn't that a form of suicide? Getting drunk and putting yourself in harm's way.'

'I suppose. What about Edward Mullen? Was your sister's funeral the last time you saw him?'

Craig the orderly approached again and, without speaking, stopped a few yards away and pursed his lips. Amelia held out a hand for him to help her and Craig led her inside.

'I don't know, Amelia,' Craig chided her. 'You're going to get me the sack, staying out this long. I don't know where you get the energy. I wish you'd give me some of it.'

Amelia turned at the double doors leading back into the building and took a deep breath. 'I've seen him since the funeral, Inspector. He came to see me here and he scared me.'

'Who?'

'Teddy.'

'How did he scare you?' asked Brook.

She hesitated, looking up at the dark clouds beginning to gather. 'He told me he'd seen Billy.'

'Seen Billy? When?'

'Spoke to him after the fire,' continued Amelia, her eyes registering the significance of what she said. 'Do you see? After.'

'But Billy was dead,' said Brook.

'He *told* me he'd seen Billy,' Amelia insisted. 'He spoke to him.'

'Teddy Mullen spoke to Billy after the fire?' repeated Brook, trying to keep the scepticism out of his voice.

'That's right. And Billy told Teddy to come see me, to tell me it wasn't my fault. *Tell Amelia it wasn't her fault*, he said.'

'When was this?'

Amelia shook her head. 'I forget.'

She looked at her hand in Craig's then up at the orderly as he guided her back towards the building. 'Are you taking me for a dance?'

Craig turned away, one arm across Amelia's back. 'You wish,' he said indulgently, with a final roll of the eyes towards Brook.

'Can you tell me if Amelia Stanforth has had any visitors recently?' said Brook, back at reception.

Sharmayne logged on to her computer and tapped in a few commands. 'Not getting anything for the last year,' she said brightly. 'And she's only been in here three. She gets confused. They all do.'

'Could someone visit without you knowing?'

'Almost impossible. Visiting hours are very strict and if the patients aren't in their rooms, they're doing monitored activities.' She smiled. 'We occasionally get one of the sprightlier ones make a break for it, usually men, but there's nowhere to go except the village at the bottom of the hill and we always find them in the Heifer, having a pint and a bag of pork scratchings.'

'And Amelia's far from sprightly,' conceded Brook. 'Do the records go further back?'

'Just a minute.'

While she tapped out commands on her keyboard, Brook tore out a blank page from his notebook and wrote his name and number. 'I want to be contacted if she has any more visitors.'

'She's very popular all of a sudden,' said Sharmayne. 'That's what the officer from Ashbourne station asked before he left.'

'The officer who was here about the prowler?'

'That's right. Poor old Jessica, one of our residents, thinks she sees men prowling around outside her window.'

'But he asked to be kept informed about Amelia Stanforth?' said Brook.

'He did. He said it was official business and I'm to give him a call whenever—'

'Can I see the log?'

'I haven't had time to enter it yet.' Sharmayne rustled around for a piece of paper and handed it to Brook. The name next to the mobile phone number was for a Sergeant Laird. Brook stared for a moment before pocketing the paper.

'You don't need to worry about his number,' said Brook. 'I'm his superior officer.'

'So should I enter your number on Amelia's record instead?'

Reluctant though he was to bandy about his contact details,

Brook confirmed. 'So can you tell me if Amelia has had any visitors at all since she's been in here?'

Sharmayne scrolled down her screen. 'The last was two years ago. Just before Christmas.'

'Before? It wasn't December the twenty-second, was it?'

'Actually it was,' replied Sharmayne, impressed.

Brook nodded. Billy's birthday. 'Who?'

'Edward Mullen.'

On the way back to his car, Brook's mobile began to vibrate.

'Yes, John.'

'Notebook handy?'

'Pencil too,' replied Brook, fumbling in his jacket. He pictured the smirking on the other end of the line. 'Go ahead.' He listened and scribbled the name with difficulty, the phone held to his ear by a shoulder. 'What about an address?' Brook wrote hurriedly before the phone fell to the ground. Eventually he threw pen and notebook on to the roof of his car and held the mobile in his hand. 'Still there? Any breaks on the Wheeler case?'

'Yeah, we've cracked it wide open,' replied Noble, sarcastically. 'An eighty-year-old blind woman on St Chad's Road claims she heard a boy shouting the night Scott disappeared.'

'Whereabouts on St Chad's?'

'Are you serious? Did I mention she was blind?'

'Where?'

'Just before you turn on to Whitaker Road.'

'Whitaker Road?'

'Where the derelict house used to be.'

'Right location, at least. And just because she's eighty and blind doesn't mean she's unreliable,' added Brook without conviction, remembering his struggle to get answers from Amelia. There was a sceptical grunt from the other end of the line. 'What did she hear?'

'She said she heard a boy shouting, "Just wait!" Over and over. "Just wait!"'

'Was there a pause between the two words?'

There was a momentary silence from Noble. 'How did you know that?'

'Because maybe she heard Scott shouting, "Josh. Wait."'

More silence as Noble thought it through. 'That would make sense. But even assuming it's reliable, where does it get us?'

'I don't know, John. But we can't pick and choose our evidence. We can only gather it and follow where it takes us.'

Seventeen

ROOK ARRIVED AT HIS METAL desk just after lunchtime. Fortunately, Sergeant Grey was on duty at reception so he was spared having to face Harry Hendrickson en route. He knocked on Copeland's door but, for the first time since Brook had started working in the CCU, his office was locked. Entering his own room, Brook found an envelope on the table in Noble's handwriting.

Brook opened it and read Noble's thank you for last night's 'pep talk'. He grimaced as he read the invitation but resigned himself. 'OK, John, if I must.' Under his signature Noble had written, 'Nice office!'

Brook texted Noble about the invitation – 'I'll be there'. He sipped hot tea from his flask while he updated the Stanforth file with confirmation of Amelia's new address then mulled over his interview with her as well as his exchange with the uniformed officer outside the care home.

'How many coppers called Laird can there be in the county?' After a little digging and a couple of phone calls, Brook found his answer – Sergeant Darren Laird, forty-one years of age, working out of Ashbourne station, was indeed the only son of retired DI, Walter Laird.

No wonder Amelia thought she'd seen the original Laird that morning.

He loaded the electoral roll and confirmed father and son's separate addresses. Then he found the scrap of paper with Laird's phone number that he had pocketed at the care home.

A mobile number for official business? I don't think so.

What could justify Sergeant Laird checking out Amelia Stanforth's visitors unless it was part of the search for Brendan McCleary? And then an official contact number would be appropriate.

Brook resisted the impulse to simply ring the mobile number and ask.

The light was worsening as Brook arrived at the junction of St Chad's Road and Whitaker Road, the spot where a blind witness had heard a young boy shouting on the night of Scott Wheeler's disappearance. A pair of police vans along the road told him the house-to-house inquiries were ongoing.

Brook locked his car and retraced his steps along St Chad's to the large house, site of Chelsea Chaplin's birthday party. A small gate at the side of the building gave access to the rear; whoever had terrified Scott by imitating the late Joshua Stapleton would doubtless have used it.

Brook decided against wandering around the back garden unannounced; instead he walked back past his car and on up to Whitaker Road to the site of the derelict house, now demolished. A lone police officer stood guard outside the site's metal boundary fence.

A familiar-looking suntanned, grey-haired man in his mid-fifties wearing a sheepskin coat over shiny jogging pants and bright white training shoes was wagging a right index finger at the officer while a large husky strained at the leash in his left hand. Brook heard the man utter a forceful, 'See that you do,' before yanking on the leash and marching away. As he approached Brook, the man's eyes squinted in recognition but he looked away and kept walking.

'Constable,' said Brook, greeting the unknown PC with his warrant card.

'Sir.'

'Quiet in there,' said Brook, nodding towards the heavy plant vehicles sitting idle.

'Yes, sir.' The PC nodded at the grey-haired man crossing over to Carlton Road with his dog. 'But they'll be back to work on the new foundations tomorrow, thanks to Councillor Davison.'

'So the site was closed to search for the missing boy,' said Brook.

'DS Noble's idea,' replied the constable. 'But Davison owns the site and was livid. He's the chair of Police Liaison. You'd think he'd be more sympathetic.' The young man shook his head. 'Local politicians . . .'

'Thought I recognised him.' *And him, me.* Brook looked after the councillor. 'He lives in Normanton?'

The constable puckered up his lips to take a sharp breath. 'I wouldn't say that to him. The councillor lives in *Upper* Normanton.'

Brook was puzzled for a second. 'I didn't know there was an Upper Normanton.'

'It's not on the map,' grinned the officer. 'It only exists for them that think they're better than the rest of us.'

It was dark when Brook arrived back at his car. Looking around, his eye was drawn by a large wooden gate across an access road. The gate was chained and beyond lay darkness and vegetation into the distance. He pulled out his phone.

'John, what's that big padlocked gate at the top of St Chad's Road?'

'It's an allotment.'

'Did—'

'We did. We got them to open every shed. We looked in every greenhouse, poked around in every water tank, turned over every old bath. We got nothing except dirty shoes and a lot of earache from grumpy smallholders. And before you ask, we also checked for any freshly dug soil.'

'And?'

'There wasn't any. The ground's like iron. See you tonight.'

'See you . . .' began Brook but Noble had already rung off. 'And sorry to be a nuisance.'

A few minutes later, Brook turned off Carlton Road and pulled into a quiet side road, locating the address he was looking for. Staring at the house, he found it hard to believe that the redbrick, detached residence in front of him was occupied. In the sulphurous glow of street lights, it appeared as though it had been abandoned years ago.

From top to bottom the building spoke of decay. On the roof, the chimney was crumbling, the pointing almost skeletal. Brickwork and mortar had washed away, creating a channel of red silt which had stained the slate roof as it trickled down. Several slates were missing or had slipped away from their rotted fastenings to nestle against the sopping, sagging gutters which had decayed so badly, a large section hung down across the front of the house like an unkempt fringe.

What little paint Brook could see on the wood-framed windows was in the final throes of peeling away from the weather-bleached, warped timbers and the glass in the casement was caked with years of impenetrable dirt. On the upper storey, Brook spied yellowed net curtains, suspended lifelessly, shrouding occupants from prying eyes. Heavier curtains, brown and worn, barely visible behind the film of grime, hung from the large rectangular bay on the ground floor.

A movement drew Brook's eye back to the upper storey window on the corner of the house and he was in time to see a curtain shift slightly. *Someone at home.* Brook locked his car and strolled across the road.

'If you're thinking of knocking on Vlad's door, you're wasting your time,' panted a voice.

Brook turned to see Councillor Davison, in full tracksuit now, glide to a halt, pulling hard on the leash to restrain the eager husky.

'Vlad?'

'Dracula, Lord Lucan, take your pick, Inspector Brook.'

'You know me, Councillor?' said Brook.

'Only by reputation,' said Davison. 'Or the lack of it.' He was taken aback by Brook's one-note laugh. 'Something funny?'

'People who think I'll take offence are funny,' replied Brook.

'Aye, well, I was in Magaluf when your hearing came up in the summer so count yourself lucky you're still in a job. And you're no sooner back on duty than the negative publicity starts all over—'

'Do you live in Normanton, sir?' interrupted Brook.

'I live in *Upper* Normanton,' corrected Davison sourly. 'North of Carlton Road is Upper,' he explained to enlighten Brook's fake confusion.

'And do you know Mr Mullen?'

'What's he done?' asked Davison, nodding towards Mullen's house.

'I can't discuss that,' said Brook.

Davison raised an eyebrow. 'Is that right? You do know I'm on the PLC?'

'I do now,' replied Brook.

'Have you come about that missing lad?' said Davison, his tanned face lighting up. 'It were only a few streets over.'

'No,' replied Brook. 'I'm here on another matter.'

'What other matter?' snorted Davison. 'There's nowt so important as a missing kiddie.'

'Agreed,' replied Brook. 'But I'm not on that case.'

'I see,' said Davison, grinning. 'Cleaning out the stables, are you?'

Brook managed an answering smile. 'In a manner of speaking.'

'Well, you'll get nowt from Vlad. He's a weirdo and a recluse. I've been jogging down to Normanton Park for twelve year and I don't think I've seen the man more than twice and never outside.'

'Is he disabled?' asked Brook.

'Hard to tell,' replied Davison. 'He never comes out, never opens the door to visitors during the day, unless you're a Sainsbury's delivery man, and even then you'll only see an arm reaching out for the bags.'

'Maybe he comes out at night,' suggested Brook.

'To drink blood, you mean,' laughed Davison. 'Aye, well, I've never seen him but then I'm at the council chambers every night.' He sniffed self-importantly. He indicated the houses either side of

Mullen's, both sporting battered For Sale signs. 'Them poor buggers have been trying to move for years but as soon as the estate agent brings a client round...' He shrugged as though the rest were obvious. With a nod, he jogged away, reanimating the sitting husky with a low whistle.

Brook watched him go then stepped up to the remains of the gate. He fancied he could see a man's silhouette behind the same net curtain that had twitched a few moments earlier. At the same window, below the sill, a new cable ran neatly along the front of the house, round to the side then disappeared into the brickwork.

'A recluse with cable,' muttered Brook. 'That's cheating.' He pulled out his warrant card and picked his way past the inert wooden gate – rotted, bowed and immovable – and rapped on the mottled glass of the front door.

The door was in better shape than the rest of the woodwork on the house. Presumably Mullen was able to maintain it without leaving the house. Knocking again, Brook noticed an eye-level slab of wood by the side of the front door. It was rotting away from the retaining screws holding it to the brick. Four rotted holes gaped at each corner of the wood, as though something had once been attached.

Brook looked around and spotted a rusted metal nameplate almost hidden in the long grass of the tiny front garden. He picked it up by his fingertips to avoid noxious substances. It was completely oxidised but by holding it at an angle in the fading light, he could just about make out the words from the indentations: 'E. Mullen Psychic Medium'.

Brook held the plate to the wooden frame by the door. It was a perfect fit, right down to the fixing holes. There was a phone number at the bottom of the plate, the dialling code out of date. Brook took out his mobile and keyed in the number using the current 01332 code. The shrill ring of the phone echoed inside the house. No answer.

'Mr Mullen, I'm a police officer,' shouted Brook, dropping his hand. 'Please open the door.' No sign of movement. Only the ringing phone disturbed the silence. 'Mr Mullen. My name is Detective Inspector Brook from Derby CID. I'm investigating—'

The phone in the house stopped ringing. Brook lifted the mobile to his ear.

'Please stop shouting, Inspector. People might get the wrong idea.'

Brook waited. 'Are you going to open the door?'

'I told the other officer. I don't know anything about that missing boy.'

'I'm not here about that. I'm here about William Stanforth.'

'Billy?'

'Billy. Your friend. Please open the door so we can talk.'

'Are you alone? I have a problem with large groups of people.'

'You know I am.'

'I thought I saw someone with you.'

'One of your neighbours. He's gone.'

'I didn't mean him.'

Brook was becoming impatient. 'There's no one else here. Sir, if you don't open the door, I can return with more officers.' No reaction. 'I'll be back with a warrant and an enforcer ram and then you won't have a door.' Brook could hear the man's breathing quicken on the phone.

'How do I know you're really a policeman?'

'You're a psychic, aren't you?' quipped Brook. 'You must have known I was coming.'

'It doesn't work like that.'

Realising that sarcasm might not be the key to admission, Brook began to placate. 'Mr Mullen, I'm holding my ID against the glass.'

'Give me a minute to get downstairs. I'm disabled.'

The phone cut off and Brook threw the nameplate back into the tall grass and flattened his warrant card against the stained glass above the letter box. He heard the whine of machinery and a few moments later a dark figure on the other side pressed close to the glass. The door opened no more than an inch and Brook pushed it back and stepped into the dark hall.

As he crossed the gloomy threshold, Brook could smell wood smoke, not fresh but stale and damp from an old fire. The door slammed shut behind him. Despite the dark there wasn't a light on in the house and Brook struggled to see clearly. His foot kicked against something heavy and he felt water sloshing on to his shoe.

'Damn.' He strained to see an outmoded, circular light switch on the wall and flicked at it. Nothing.

'Go through,' said a soft voice from the shadows. 'I'll light a candle.'

Brook turned away from the black outline of Edward Mullen and edged into the large cold room off the hall, then stood aside for the small wiry figure to hobble past him, a walking stick in his left hand. Eventually Brook's reluctant host struck a match, throwing grotesque outlines against the walls, and proceeded to light a series of candles dotted around the room.

With a little more light, Brook could see the furnishings and general decor and, given the state of the exterior, he had to admit his surprise. Although the room seemed to have been frozen in time, it was neat, tidy and almost welcoming. The wallpaper was dingy and old-fashioned but in a good state of repair. The two armchairs arranged near the blackened Victorian hearth were covered in scuffed and severely cracked leather but appeared well-upholstered and comfortable.

In one corner, a long oak table with ornate carved legs had seen better days but was sturdy and reassuring. It was ringed by half a dozen matching, straight-backed chairs and was empty of all decoration save a single place setting at one end, and a chessboard at the other, the pieces scattered around the battlefield, taking a breather from combat commenced.

Unable to see more, Brook wandered over to assess the state of play on the chessboard. Mullen meanwhile bent over and put a match to some newspaper in the blackened wood-burning stove and the flames danced to life immediately.

'Electricity cut off?' ventured Brook, glancing up at the 1930s light fitting descending from an elaborately carved ceiling rose. He saw the bulb was missing. 'Apparently not,' he corrected himself.

'I try not to use it,' said Mullen, lighting another candle, before sitting at the table behind the white chess pieces, flopping down with the heavy sigh of the disabled. 'The expense,' he added, by way of explanation.

Mullen was a slim grey-haired man, with pale eyes and a closely shaven face. He was simply dressed in clothes appropriate to his age – a checked cotton shirt with a thin woollen tie and neat, nondescript trousers punctuated by black lace-up shoes. The aluminium stick rested against his thigh.

'Then I wonder why you bother connecting to the grid at all,' observed Brook.

Mullen grunted. 'I need it for the stairlift. And I'm not Cro-Magnon man, Inspector. I have a fridge, a computer and a couple of reading lamps.'

'But no television,' said Brook absently, keeping his approval under wraps.

'I prefer books.' He waved an arm at his teeming bookshelves on one wall.

'And the internet?'

Mullen paused for a beat, wondering how Brook knew. When he'd worked it out, he replied, 'My umbilical to the world. Or at least Sainsbury's,' he added. 'I don't eat cardboard yet, despite successive government attempts to impoverish me. The internet allows me to earn a modest income. And it helps me with my chess.'

'Really?' Brook returned his attention to the tussle between good and evil being enacted on the sixty-four-square board. 'The Sicilian Defence. Are you any good?'

'There's always room for improvement, Inspector. Do you play?' asked Mullen, glancing down at the game in progress.

'I did – in my youth.'

'You must have been an only child then,' observed Mullen. 'The world's grandmasters almost always are. Interesting that such solitary souls can become expert in a game designed for two. I've played since I was a boy, though opponents are harder to come by, these days.'

'Because you never leave the house,' said Brook.

'You talked to my unpleasant neighbour, I see.'

'Councillor Davison? A little. Why don't you go out? Mobility?'

Mullen bridled at the directness of the questions. 'As you see. But it's not the only reason. Hell is other people, Inspector. I could handle outside if it weren't for the teeming mass of cretinism populating the streets.'

'You do read books, don't you?' observed Brook wryly. Mullen maintained an inscrutable half-smile, declining to answer. 'What do you do for money?'

'I have a small number of clients on the internet,' answered the old man. 'I do readings for them. The house is paid for – it belonged to my parents – and I have some savings. My needs are simple.'

'So you live alone and frugally.' Until Charlton had cast him down into the bowels of the station, Brook might have envied Mullen's self-imposed isolation.

The old man stood to hobble over to a large sideboard and took out two small glasses and a dark bottle. 'Most of the time. But you're in luck, Inspector. Every Christmas I splash out and treat myself to the most expensive bottle of vintage port I can afford.' He examined the bottle before removing the cork. 'This year I've gone for the Fonseca – fruity and dense.' Mullen closed his eyes and drew a long nasal breath at the bottle. 'You can actually imagine you're outside picking blackberries at the end of summer.'

'A poor substitute for the outdoors,' said Brook, preparing to refuse but Mullen was already handing him a delicate glass of the inky black liquid.

'Merry Christmas, Inspector.'

Brook didn't quite know what to do so, after a minute sip of the drink, he thanked his host before setting the glass down. 'Good health,' he added, refusing to endorse the possibility of merriment over the most miserable part of any singleton's year.

Mullen sipped his glass of port with pleasure before a pained expression invaded his features. 'And now perhaps you can tell me why you people keep this farce alive? It's been nearly fifty years since my friend died. When are you going to let Billy rest in peace?'

'Peace?' said Brook. 'Is that what he has?'

'As much as he could hope for,' answered Mullen. 'Though all who die a violent death sleep in an unquiet grave.'

'An unquiet grave?' echoed Brook. The phrase rang a bell.

'Exactly.'

'So you've spoken to him, have you?' said Brook, trying to keep the sneer from his tone. 'In a séance or on the Ouija board.'

Mullen's features hardened briefly before his countenance transformed into the patience deployed for unbelievers. He meshed his hands together to await further scorn. 'I don't expect you to understand the ways—'

'Didn't happen to mention who locked him in that shed, did he?' said Brook. 'That would save some time.'

Mullen ignored the mocking tone. 'No, he didn't. I don't think Billy knows about the fire. He doesn't even know he's dead. All who meet an unexpected and brutal death are unaware. That's why they stay with us, to seek answers, discover what has befallen them.'

Brook snorted. 'So you *do* speak to him.'

'Why are you here, Inspector? And please don't tell me I should already know. As you saw from my sign, I'm retired.'

'You can do that? Just switch it off like a tap?'

'It depends. I can't speak for other members of my profession. But most of my . . . difficulties derived from engaging with clients in person. It's too painful, for me as well as them, so I stopped conducting my business face to face.'

'But I'm not a client so why refuse to open the door to me?' asked Brook.

'My abilities are as much a curse as a gift. I can't always turn off my powers and control what I'm seeing.' A smile played around Mullen's lips. 'And everyone has secrets they think they can keep from me, client or not. Secrets about things they've done in the past, people they've hurt.'

Brook was trapped in Mullen's gaze for a moment. 'I see.'

Mullen was the first to break away. 'I don't think you know what seeing means, Inspector. It can drive you to the edge of insanity.' He took a more contemplative sip on his port. 'You can't understand.'

Brook's smile was thin-lipped. 'And when you can't cope it's easier to shut out the rest of the world.'

'You sound almost envious,' chuckled Mullen.

'Once, I might've been,' replied Brook. He stared across at the comforting glow of the flames, licking around a dry log in the stove.

'But not any more?' probed Mullen.

Brook looked back at him, wondering how he'd let his own situation become the topic of conversation. He ignored Mullen's question. 'And yet you managed to drag yourself out to the country-side to visit Amelia Stanforth on Billy's birthday, two years ago.'

Now it was Mullen's turn to gaze into the flames. He carried his glass across to the fire and sank into an armchair, gesturing Brook to the chair across the hearth.

Mullen closed his eyes to the flames and Brook fancied his elderly host shuddered with remembered pain. He nodded, opening his eyes. 'You're right. I can get out if I absolutely have to, even during the day. If I take medication, I can. If it's important.'

'And what was so important you had to see Billy's sister on the anniversary of his death?'

Mullen hesitated. 'I had to tell her to forgive herself.'

'Why would she need to do that?'

'We all have to forgive ourselves at some stage, Inspector – even you. Billy forgave us. I've forgiven myself. I had to tell Amelia to do the same.'

Brook sat stony-faced in the candlelight and let the silence act upon Mullen.

'I know how this sounds but it was important to help her. Poor Amelia never left that house, you know, the house where Billy died. She lived with it every day until she couldn't look after herself. Can you imagine the levels of guilt that would drive you to sacrifice your peace of mind in that way?'

'Are you saying she killed her brother?'

Mullen was unblinking. 'You look like a man who understands guilt, Inspector. You don't need to be responsible for an act to feel guilt that it happened, even to blame yourself in some way. And Amelia blamed herself.'

'Was she a client of yours?'

'No.'

'Then did she tell you she blamed herself or did you just pull that out of the air using your *psychic abilities?*'

'No and no,' retorted Mullen tersely. 'A child could have seen the guilt Amelia carried. Not just the guilt of the survivor, but real guilt, if-only-I'd-done-something-different guilt.'

'And you know this how?' asked Brook.

'Because she never left that house, even after her father and mother died,' insisted Mullen. 'Francesca left when she was a teenager but Amelia didn't. She stayed on to serve her sentence. Don't you see what a sacrifice she made? She gave her life to live there all alone, to atone, even after her parents passed over, never marrying and never escaping the fire, not until she went into St Agatha's.' Mullen looked away. 'My parents died when I was young but I still live in their house so I know what that feels like. Do you? Amelia's brother died just yards from where she slept every night of her life. And yet she stayed there, as though waiting for something, as though watching over him. That's not normal, Inspector.'

'It might be if she'd killed him.'

Mullen shook his head. 'Amelia didn't kill Billy.'

'Then why should she feel so guilty? Why should you, for that matter?'

Mullen's head bowed. 'Because we weren't there when he needed us. Because my best friend died alone and, if I'd stayed with him, he might still be alive today.'

Brook was silent, remembering the file. 'What separated you?'

'It was all in my statement.'

'I want to hear it from you,' said Brook.

Mullen put his head in his hands but Brook waited and watched, refusing to relent. 'Very well. We had our first ever row – it was also our last,' added Mullen, with a bitter laugh, as though the thought had just occurred.

'About what?'

Mullen smiled, shamefaced. 'Nothing of importance.'

'About what?' Brook repeated.

Mullen couldn't look at Brook, instead staring saucer-eyed at the burning log. 'Something so stupid even now it makes me weep in frustration.' Finally he looked Brook in the eye. 'We were playing party games; bobbing apples, if you even know what that is. You have to pick up an apple from a barrel of water using only your teeth.'

'And?'

'And Billy could be so petty, such a baby.' Mullen's eyes suddenly blazed with fervour. 'But he was also funny and fearless and loyal.'

'What did he do?'

'He cheated,' mumbled Mullen, unable to give much volume to something so inconsequential. 'He put his hands on the barrel for leverage. Amelia was in charge of the game and she backed him. I think she was bored, she kept looking out to the road, I mean a fifteen-year-old girl having to look after us kids. Not surprising she wanted to get it over as soon as she could.' He took a sip of his port. 'So we argued and I stormed off.'

'But you say Billy's forgiven you?' said Brook.

'I think so. He knows I could never hurt him, no matter what he said or did to me. He was my best friend. I loved him too much.'

Brook chose his next words carefully. 'So when Billy . . . communicated, what exactly did he say to you?'

Mullen was tight-lipped. 'That's not how it works.'

'So they can't speak.'

'They can but not coherently. The dead,' Mullen stopped and looked searchingly at Brook, 'the murdered especially, are trapped and they don't know why. They're looking for someone, Inspector.'

'Who?'

189

'Someone who can see and hear them and can explain what happened to them.'

'You?'

'Sometimes.'

Brook waved a hand in the air, his scornful tone barely under control. 'So Billy didn't actually *say* he forgave you.'

'It's more like transmitting a feeling,' explained Mullen patiently.

'Which you pick up on.'

Mullen was unwilling to elaborate further. 'You don't understand. You're not a believer.'

'In what? Ghosts?'

'In the next incarnation,' answered Mullen drily.

'It's not my fault I've had a good education,' rejoined Brook, feeling immediate guilt for mocking this sad, deluded old man. He pressed on regardless. 'So you don't know who killed Billy?'

Mullen looked away. 'No.'

Something in Mullen's voice gave Brook pause. 'But you have an idea who did.'

'I've told you. I don't know.'

Brook smiled. He was an experienced DI. He knew about word games. 'That's not the same thing.'

Mullen stared off into a corner of the room. A second later he nodded at Brook. 'It's just an opinion. I have no proof.'

'Because there isn't any,' said Brook. 'That's why Billy's death is unsolved. It seems to be the perfect murder.'

'So it would appear.'

'Which makes your unproven theory just that. Something we talk about, a topic of conversation, no more. So tell me.'

Mullen took a sip from his glass and gazed into the flames. 'You understand this is just speculation.'

'I understand you were there and that you've had years to think about it and I'd like to know your opinion.' Brook waited while Mullen gathered his thoughts. Only the crack of the burning logs broke the silence.

Mullen looked guiltily into his drink. 'I've never told anyone this . . .' Brook acknowledged with a faint dip of the head. 'I think Francesca killed him.'

'His twin sister,' said Brook. 'Do you have a motive?'

'I think she was jealous of Billy.'

'Why?'

'They were twins, but everyone forgot that – even Mr and Mrs Stanforth at times. Billy was their only son, he was the favourite over Amelia and Fran. But it was harder to bear for Fran. They were born on the same day so the party that night was for Francesca as well but we all called it Billy's party. Are you going to Billy's party on Sunday? Have you got Billy a present? All the guests were his friends. All the attention was his.'

'Didn't Francesca have friends to invite?'

'Not really. She was strange, remote. She contained herself like you can't imagine a child could at that age. Billy told me how he used to tease her but she never reacted, never. He'd pinch her when she wasn't looking and Billy said she'd just grab his wrist and stare at him, completely expressionless.

'Actually Billy was in awe of her because of what she had to endure. When he was mean to her, she never ran to their parents to complain, she'd just stare. It used to make him very uncomfortable. He soon stopped plaguing her.' Mullen smiled. 'Well, if you don't get a reaction, there's not much point, is there? Fran seemed to know that, even so young.' He looked up at Brook with his pale sad eyes.

'At school, I know the older girls used to gang up on her and say things, spiteful things. You know what young girls can be like.' Mullen's expression deformed minutely from a hint of past humilia-tion. 'But here's the strange thing. Billy told me that no matter what happened to her at school, or anywhere, he never once saw Fran cry.'

'Fascinating,' said Brook. 'But so far I'm not hearing a good reason why she'd feel the need to kill him.'

Mullen took a sip of his port. 'I just think she'd reached a tipping point that night when she saw the two piles of presents.' He laughed.

'Not that you could call her presents a pile. Her parents had bought her a gift. It wasn't as expensive as Billy's.'

'What was it?'

'A cheap plastic watch. It had a cartoon character on the face. Donald Duck, I think.'

'And Billy?'

'Billy got a football and some boots. He was very pleased. And that was just from his parents. His friends bought him more stuff.'

'What did you get him?'

'Does it matter?'

'I'd like to know,' said Brook.

Mullen put down his glass to open a rather fine antique glass cupboard in the corner. He took out a cheap plastic box with a small metallic catch and handed it to Brook. 'It cost me all my pocket money that month, which wasn't much.'

Brook flicked off the catch and opened it out. It was a miniature chessboard, barely bigger than Brook's hand. Each square, black and white, had a small hole. The plastic pieces were tiny and sat in perfect formation, facing each other. Brook pulled out the black king. There was a 3mm plastic spike protruding, enabling it to sit in position or move to another square. 'Travel chess,' smiled Brook, remembering his own minuscule set, using magnetised pieces, with which he'd played on holiday as a child. 'And you got it back?'

'After the fire . . . I asked for it – a keepsake. Well, Mr and Mrs Stanforth were happy to see the back of it.' He looked wistfully into the fire. 'To this day, it's never been played on.'

'And you think Francesca saw all this love for her brother and just snapped.'

Mullen shrugged. 'That's my theory, for what it's worth.'

'It's different,' conceded Brook. 'The officers in charge of the investigation were convinced Billy was killed by Amelia's boyfriend, Brendan.'

'I know they were. DC Laird and his superior spent a long time trying to prove it.'

'But you don't agree.'

Mullen shrugged. 'It's possible. Anything is.'

'Did you see Brendan at the house that day?' asked Brook.

'No, but that doesn't mean he wasn't there. And Amelia kept looking at the clock and out of the window as though she had an appointment to keep.'

'And did she?'

'Who knows? But I'm sure Brendan wouldn't have come near the house in case Mr Stanforth saw him. Amelia's father didn't approve and forbade her to see him.'

'But Amelia could still have slipped out to meet him.'

Mullen shrugged. 'Of course. It still doesn't make either of them guilty of murder.'

'What was Brendan like?'

'Amelia's father was right,' said Mullen. 'Brendan was bad news. Billy told me Brendan stood up Amelia regularly. Either that or he'd turn up late just to see how much she'd tolerate. It didn't stop her going back for more.'

'So he was using her.'

'Oh, I still think he loved Amelia, in his way, but he treated her like dirt because he could. But then Brendan's father, Malcolm, was a brute and treated Brendan's mother the same way, by all accounts, so you can't really blame him for picking it up.'

'Did you know Malcolm McCleary?'

'Only by sight. And I'd moved into the city by the time Brendan blew his head off, though I followed the trial in the paper. Everyone knew Malcolm was an unpleasant and cruel man, a drinker too. He used to beat Brendan – or at least that's what Brendan's defence lawyer said.' He shrugged. 'Who knows? I do know Brendan would show up with fresh bruises and burns from time to time, even as a teenager.'

'What happened to the mother?'

'She left when Brendan was a small boy. And this was a time when people didn't split up as easily as they do now. That was his background, growing up listening to his father spitting bile over womankind because his absent wife couldn't take the abuse. I guess that's why Brendan used Amelia the way he did, other girls too, I reckon.'

'Were he and Amelia having sex?'

Mullen's face soured. 'Don't be disgusting. You couldn't possibly expect me to know that, let alone talk about it.'

'It's not easy to keep secrets in small communities,' said Brook. 'There must've been talk.'

'We were kids,' protested Mullen. 'There was always talk. You'd think we were international playboys the things we said to each other, but we only had to see a girl's knickers in PT and we'd be drooling over it for weeks. That's the level at which we operated, Inspector, so don't ask me about Amelia having sex, never mind a meaningful relationship. Our generation knew nothing about the opposite sex. The swinging sixties missed out Derbyshire.'

'What about Billy? How did Brendan get on with him?'

'Pretty well, considering the age difference. He was Amelia's brother so Brendan would usually make an effort. He'd give Billy cigarettes and sweets when he had them. And of course Billy was in awe. I mean Brendan was nearly a man and to take an interest—'

'Only because he was his girlfriend's brother.'

'Not just that. I think Brendan saw a lot of himself in Billy. He was wrong but that's what he thought.'

'So you think Brendan liked Billy.'

'Everyone did.' Mullen hesitated, conceding the obvious with a tilt of his head. 'OK. Someone didn't.'

'And did Brendan give Billy cigarettes on his birthday?'

'Like I said, I didn't see him and Billy didn't brag about having any, so I'm guessing not.'

'What about Francesca?'

'What about her?'

'You say she was remote. Was she like that after Billy's death?'

'Worse. After Billy died it was impossible to talk to her. She completely retreated into herself until she was old enough to numb the pain with alcohol and drugs.'

'The pain of having murdered her twin brother, you think,' suggested Brook. 'So maybe her death wasn't accidental. Maybe she killed herself on Billy's birthday.'

'Who knows?' said Mullen. 'But she left home as soon as she was able and self-medicated until her death. She never recovered from the fire.'

'I'm getting that impression about a lot of people,' said Brook.

Mullen smiled. 'You're not wrong. But you're a policeman. You must see the damage the death of a child inflicts on the people left behind.'

'They say the first fifty years are the worst,' replied Brook.

Mullen was stung and took a larger mouthful of port, swallowing it without savouring.

'Sorry, that was unkind.' Brook wasn't without compassion for this haunted shell of a man, but his best friend had died nearly half a century ago and there had to be an end to grieving. 'Looking through the file, according to Francesca Stanforth's initial statement, she said she saw Amelia in tears, just before the fire. And when I talked to Amelia—'

'You've seen Amelia? How is she?'

'She seemed OK.'

'What did she say?'

'Very little that wasn't in the files.' Brook paused to form his next line of inquiry. 'There was one thing she mentioned that interested me.'

'Oh?'

'She implied that Brendan was breaking up with her for another girl, younger than her. Might you know who that was?'

'Is it relevant?' asked Mullen.

'Is it relevant?' repeated Brook, a small alarm chiming in his brain. 'I don't know. I'm asking you.'

Mullen paused as though trying to remember. 'I can't recall. Brendan was a rogue. He had a lot of girls interested in him. Why is it so important?'

'Because Francesca initially claimed her elder sister had been in tears when arriving at the burning shed, although she later retracted that part of her statement.'

'And you think that Fran retracted under pressure, that Amelia *was* in tears because she knew about this other girl,' concluded Mullen.

'What do you think?'

'I wouldn't know.' Mullen stared into his glass to frame his own question. 'Did Amelia say who the girl was?'

'She said she couldn't remember,' said Brook.

Mullen nodded. 'It *was* a long time ago. Why is it important?'

'Well, it occurred to me that if he did have another girlfriend, maybe Brendan and Amelia broke up on the day of Billy's party, especially if she couldn't get away and he thought she'd stood him up.'

'Break up with Amelia the week before Christmas?' said Mullen. 'Yes, that's just the sort of thing Brendan might do.'

'Actually I was thinking more along the lines that, having found out about his new girlfriend, she broke up with him. From what I'm hearing about Brendan, that would be a red rag to a bull. Maybe he came back to the party in a rage . . .'

'And set the fire,' finished Mullen quietly.

'What do you think?'

'If he did, I didn't see him. I'd stormed off, remember.'

'To where?'

'Read my statement,' mumbled Mullen. He reached for the bottle of port and poured himself a larger measure.

'I'd prefer you to tell me.'

Mullen drank half a glass in one sip. 'To see if I've forgotten the lies I told DC Laird at the time of the fire,' he said sourly.

Brook could see the old man's eyes moistening with shame but he hardened his heart; the harder he pushed, the better the information. 'Something like that.'

'Very well. If you must hear me say it, I was sulking in Billy's bedroom, hiding under the coats, crying like a baby.'

'All because Billy cheated,' said Brook.

Mullen looked beseechingly at Brook, a tear rolling down his cheek. 'You have to remember. We were just children. These petty disputes seem like the end of the world when you're young. An hour later they're forgotten, resolved.' He hung his head. 'But this one never was. My last thoughts and words towards my friend were conceived in anger.'

'How long did you stay under the coats?'

Mullen dabbed at an eye with a folded handkerchief produced from a pocket. 'Until I heard the commotion and came down to the garden to watch the fire. And Mrs Stanforth saw me. You can check.'

'I have. Her statement confirms your alibi.'

'Then why are you putting me through this again?'

'I'm establishing the truth,' said Brook.

'And wasting my time.'

'Sorry, do you have to be somewhere?'

Mullen took a quivering breath and set down his glass. 'I apologise. You're right. I should be grateful someone still cares. It's just that Billy's birthday is coming up . . .' He broke off, staring back into the flames, past and present. A bitter laugh broke the gloom. 'You know the worst thing? At first the fire was exciting. Some of us were shouting and cheering. Nobody knew . . .' He rubbed his damp eyes with a thumb and forefinger and then looked back at Brook. 'There's not a day goes by when I don't think about my friend, Inspector, alone in that shed, frightened, confused, screaming in terror.'

Brook sat up. 'You heard him scream?'

'What?'

'You said you heard him scream. You didn't mention that in your statement – nobody did.'

'That's because I didn't hear it then,' said Mullen. 'I heard it later.'

'Later?'

Mullen looked up, threw his hands in the air in self-mockery and affected a ghostly wail. 'In my dreams.'

Brook smiled faintly and got to his feet, deciding against a parting shot at Mullen's psychic fantasies. 'OK. I think that covers it. For now.'

'You anticipate another visit?'

'I don't know.'

'I suppose finding other witnesses still alive and coherent is becoming more difficult,' said Mullen. 'If I can help with that . . .'

Brook paused. He still had the list of witnesses. 'I've got an address for Brendan McCleary – Mount Street – but he seems to have cleared out.'

'I know it,' said Mullen. 'It's not far from here, if you're able-bodied,' he added. 'He's gone, you say?'

'It seems so.' Brook gave Mullen the list of other partygoers and watched for any reaction.

'Nothing jumps out except poor Charlotte. She drowned, you know, the year after Billy. And Edna Spencer isn't in the best of health. She had a hip replacement a few years ago and she suffers with arthritis.'

'I know,' said Brook. 'Though she's not the type to complain.'

'You've spoken to her? Oh, I am glad. Poor thing lost her husband years ago. They lived a couple of streets over from me for a long time until Eric passed and Edna couldn't manage the house. They doted on each other. Very sad.' He handed the list back. 'Sorry I can't be more help.'

'No, you've helped a lot,' said Brook.

'And you've helped me, Inspector,' smiled Mullen. 'I feel better, talking things through. It's been a long time since anyone's *really* asked me about that night. DCI Bannon and DS Laird re-interviewed me in nineteen sixty-seven, then a different detective ten or eleven years later . . .'

'DS Copeland?'

'That's him,' nodded Mullen. 'I remember his visit. Nice man though carrying a lot of pain. I found out later that his sister—'

'His visit?' interrupted Brook.

'Sorry?'

'Visit – singular. Are you saying DS Copeland only came to see you once?'

Mullen looked uncertain. 'Is that a problem?'

'According to the file, Copeland reviewed Billy's case three times, in nineteen seventy-eight, eighty-two and eighty-six. By nineteen eighty-six he was a DI, soon to be a DCI.'

'I remember nineteen seventy-eight.' Mullen cast around for a recollection. 'But not the others.'

'Odd.'

'I'm sure he got all he needed from me the first time,' said Mullen.

'Possibly,' conceded Brook. 'So, when *was* the last time an officer conducted a proper interview with you?'

'Before today, DS Copeland in nineteen seventy-eight.'

'I see.' Brook's face was like stone. 'Thirty-four years ago.'

'Good lord, so long,' said Mullen, shaking his head in disbelief. 'You're surprised, Inspector. Don't be. I didn't kill Billy and those officers saw that. And remember, I had an alibi.' He smiled and got stiffly to his feet. 'I could never hurt Billy, I loved him.'

'Even so, thirty-four years . . .'

'Oh, I've had visits since,' said Mullen. 'Officers have knocked on the door occasionally to confirm my identity and that I'm not gaga.' He held up a mocking hand. 'I know – the jury's out on that one. But no one's interviewed me properly since then. Until today.'

'What about when Inspector Greatorix reviewed the case?'

Mullen thought for a second then slowly shook his head. 'I don't know him.'

'Why am I not surprised?'

Brook headed for the door. When he reached the exit, the smell of charred wood invaded his nostrils again. He followed his nose to the inside of the door. Beneath the letter box a large blackened scar fanned out across the panels.

'Had an accident?'

Mullen examined the door with Brook as though only just seeing it. 'A while ago now. I've been meaning to paint over it.'

In the flickering candlelight, Brook could see the sturdy plastic bucket he'd nearly kicked over on his entrance. It was filled to the brim with water. He looked curiously at Mullen.

'Someone put a burning rag through the letter box,' explained Mullen.

'When did this happen?'

'I forget. But don't worry, I'm a light sleeper. The smoke woke me. I've got a detector now.'

Brook glanced up at the smoke alarm on the hall ceiling. 'Did you report it?'

'No.'

'You should have.'

'Inspector, I didn't see or hear anything and didn't see the point of having busy officers wasting their time asking questions I couldn't answer,' said Mullen. 'These things happen occasionally.'

'It's happened before?'

'As you've discovered, my neighbours aren't fond of me,' he said. 'Usually it's dog excrement. The fire was a first but I woke up in time. No harm done. And now I put that bucket of water under the letter box every night so there's really no need to worry.'

Brook finally stepped across the threshold into the cold night air. 'It's your funeral.'

'Quite.' Mullen was cheered now that Brook was leaving.

Brook turned at the gate, his face in shadow. 'One more thing.' Mullen's head cocked with curiosity. 'Black checkmates in four moves.'

Mullen managed a watery smile as he watched Brook cross the road to his car. Without warning, Mullen closed his eyes, his hand moving to his temple as though in pain. His other hand moved to his throat and his mouth fell open, gasping for breath as though he was being choked.

'Who are you?' he croaked, panic written across his grey features. 'What do you want from me?'

As Brook sped away, Mullen's eyes opened. The constriction eased and the hand relaxed from his throat. Getting his breath back,

Mullen watched the BMW's lights turn the corner, continuing to stare long after the car had gone. Finally, feeling the cold bite of winter, he closed his door against the world and returned to the gloom of his home.

After a moment's contemplation, Mullen sat behind the chess-board, examining the pieces by the light of a guttering candle.

'Checkmate, eh? Think you're going to pull a fast one, do you?' Mullen studied the board before picking up the white queen, tapping the wooden base against his chin then moving it in front of his king for protection.

Having parked in a dark side street, Brook arrived at the bright and welcoming front door of the Duke of Clarence two minutes later. The pub, a short walk from St Mary's Wharf, was a hangout for officers celebrating a promotion, Christmas, or the cracking of a big case. Brook had never set foot in the place.

Instead of marching straight in, he tried to squint through the opaque window to confirm Noble's presence, straining to see through the misshapen glass like a neglected child, waiting for drunken parents to stagger out with a bottle of pop and a packet of crisps for supper.

To compound his discomfort, DI Ford emerged from the warmth and conviviality, the decibel level increasing briefly as he stepped outside, a cigarette already moving to his lips. He stopped when he noticed Brook. The heavy door swung back into place, silencing the din of companionship, and the two men were alone in their unease. But at least Ford had something to do with his hands.

'Brook,' he said, exhaling mightily after igniting his cigarette.

Brook caught the exquisite perfume and for the first time in months felt his resolve weaken. 'Frank,' he returned, unable to look Ford in the eye.

'Good to be back?' asked Ford, fighting the smile turning up the corners of his mouth.

'Fantastic,' replied Brook, completely deadpan.

At this, Ford's grin broke the shackles and was followed by a mocking laugh. 'Must be great, nosing around in all those dusty files, looking for—'

'How's the Wheeler investigation going?' interrupted Brook.

Ford's satisfaction dimmed and he looked hard at Brook. 'As well as can be expected.'

'It's just I thought you might be in there celebrating a break-through,' said Brook.

Now Ford's expression turned to pure frost as his mind groped for retribution. 'Just taking a little time out to support colleagues like a normal copper does. Not that I need explain myself to *you*.'

Brook lowered his head. Ford was right. Brook was in moral forfeit. And if even Noble could take time out to celebrate a colleague's promotion, Brook knew everything that could be done to find Scott Wheeler was being done. He turned away, suddenly tongue-tied, and regretted his next utterance immediately. 'Well, if you need any advice . . .'

'Advice?' snorted Ford, thrilled to find his path back to ethical supremacy handed to him on a plate. 'On what? Embarrassing the force. You toffee-nosed fucker. Why don't you go back to London? Let hard-working local coppers clear up your mess.'

Brook didn't answer, instead darting to the door and across the pub's threshold, now pushing eagerly towards the throng that, moments before, had caused him such trepidation.

The saloon was jammed with drinking officers. Brook's eyes searched for Noble, only too aware that his presence might be a cause for further comment and further embarrassment. When he spotted Noble he took a breath and made a beeline.

Noble's mouth fell open when he spotted Brook's uncomfortable, head-down passage through the scrum of drinkers, most glancing covertly at him as he passed. As he approached, Noble broke into a slow grin. 'You made it.'

Brook removed his rain-flecked coat. 'Didn't think I would?'

Noble's expression confirmed it. 'Must be because you've been cooped up in that dungeon all day.'

'Actually I've been out and about, John. Best way to avoid the photographers.'

Noble nodded in sympathy. 'That was below the belt. Burton needs a good hiding, you ask me.'

'He's just doing his job, John. It's serving coppers I can't excuse.'

Noble tilted his head. 'You still say Hendrickson tipped him off.'

'I saw the text to Burton with my own eyes, John. It was sent the morning I returned to duty.'

'You saw the text? How?' The inquiry in Noble's expression disappeared with Brook's reluctance to elaborate. 'You're taking chances someone in your position shouldn't be taking.'

'The point is, I was right, John. And I can prove it, if I have to.'

'So what are you going to do about Hendrickson?'

'There's not much I can do,' said Brook.

'But what if—'

'He won't, John. He knows I've seen his messages to Burton and he's already on thin ice with Charlton.'

'That makes two of you,' replied Noble.

'That's why we have a mutual interest in treading lightly around each other,' smiled Brook. 'Any developments?'

Noble sighed, his shoulders slumping. 'Nothing good. News about McCleary's stash of kiddie porn was all over the papers and local telly again.'

'Do you even know it was his yet?'

'The opposite,' said Noble. 'We can't find a single print of McCleary's on any of it. And I doubt we're going to be able to ask him anytime soon.'

'He might still pop up, John,' said Brook. 'Criminals don't always behave logically. He must be short of funds and nothing motivates ex-cons like money.'

'I know,' said Noble. 'We're maintaining surveillance on the flat and the post office but he won't show if he's got any sense.'

Brook nodded in sympathy, glancing at the newly promoted Gadd surrounded by well-wishers, enjoying her last day as one of the gang. 'How are you coping?' he said to Noble, tight-lipped in commiseration.

'Jane? Yeah, well. Who needs it?' said Noble. 'Let her take the strain. I'm happy as I am. I've seen what the pressure can do to people.' He stared down into his lager.

'You're not wrong,' agreed Brook. 'And CID could certainly do with less testosterone sluicing around.' He eyed Noble. 'And I meant what I said last night. If I ever stop chasing ghosts, I want you to know how much I value your work.'

'Well!' replied Noble, to draw a line under the matter. 'What are you drinking, *guv*?' he added in a Dickensian cockney accent.

Brook laughed and grimaced simultaneously. 'Don't. It's on me.'

Noble looked theatrically at his watch. 'Better remember the date – the first drink from my DI.'

'Excuse me,' protested Brook. 'According to my accounts, I've bought you at least three cups of tea over the years.'

'As many as that?' replied Noble. 'I stand corrected. I'll have another lager, thanks. Now you have been to a bar before . . .'

'Ye-es,' said Brook, setting off towards the counter.

Eighteen

Saturday, 15 December 2012

THE NEXT MORNING, BROOK WOKE later than usual and instead of dragging himself down to his small kitchen, his eyes barely open, he lay in bed for a few minutes, wondering whether he was expected to work weekends. He'd become so detached from the rest of his colleagues that following any kind of shift pattern had begun to seem irrelevant.

Recalling with dismay the exchange with DI Ford the previous evening, Brook decided to go to the station. If nothing else, he was determined to keep his nose to the grindstone, no matter how futile the work. No one would be able to criticise him on that score.

Before setting off, he sat down with a tea and scoured the anthologies on his bookshelves. 'The Unquiet Grave,' he muttered when he found what he was looking for. 'Anonymous.' He read the seven-stanza poem, giving voice to one of the verses.

> 'The twelvemonth and a day being up
> The dead began to speak:
> "Oh who sits weeping on my grave,
> And will not let me sleep?"'

An hour later, Brook parked at St Mary's Wharf. To avoid any chance of meeting Hendrickson, he decided to walk all the way round the building to the service entrance, which took him directly to the basement and, with a little effort, his new office in the depths of the building.

Finally, slumped in his chair, he poured himself a tea and glanced at the file on his blotter. It wasn't the Stanforth folder. He found it back on the trolley with the others. Brook flipped it open. Copeland had left the fake Pied Piper note, written by Brook, in the file. But carelessly he'd put the folder back in the wrong place. Even sloppier, Copeland had left a different file on Brook's desk.

'You're getting old, Clive,' said Brook, absent-mindedly picking up the new folder in front of him. His mood darkened when he saw the date: 1965.

'This is getting ridic—' Brook halted, mid-rant, when he saw the name at the top of the file. Matilda Copeland. *Clive Copeland's sister?* He took a quick peek at the first page to confirm it then looked at the cold case sheet which was nearly full and contained the names of several high-ranking detectives over the years.

Ex-DI Walter Laird had indeed been a good friend to Copeland, signing his name to reviews of Matilda's murder in 1969, 1973, 1977 and 1981.

Copeland was too young to be in the force in 1969 and, in 1973, would have been a callow 21 year old, so the first two case reviews were probably genuinely carried out by Laird. Brook suspected Clive Copeland would have first re-opened his sister's murder in 1977, when he would have been a Detective Sergeant.

And if DS Morton was correct, Copeland had performed every subsequent review until his retirement, persuading close colleagues to sign off on his work despite minimal involvement – first Walter Laird in 1977 and 1981 then a long list of other CID names, only some of which Brook knew. All were complicit in bending the rules for their obsessed colleague. Since Copeland's retirement, the case had been revisited only once, by Brook's former colleague Detective Inspector Robert Greatorix.

'This stinks,' murmured Brook, and if he hadn't been under a disciplinary cloud, he might have marched into Clive Copeland's office and told him so. All those reviews, taking place over decades, under the aegis of CID officers who didn't have a clue what had been actioned in their names.

Brook closed the file, unsure what to do. Was this a mistake? Had Copeland accidentally shuffled his sister's file into Brook's caseload? It seemed unlikely.

'No harm in having a look,' he reasoned, opening the file. He could take it back later as though he'd just discovered it. He could even pretend he hadn't made the connection between brother and sister, if this was a genuine mistake.

Matilda Copeland had been dead for over forty-seven years and her younger brother had lived with her unsolved murder all that time. According to Morton, Clive Copeland had joined the force as a direct result of her killing and the eleven separate occasions the case had been revisited were testimony to Copeland's dedication to his sister's cause. But despite all his efforts, her killer had escaped justice.

'You were too close to it, Clive. Too close to see, too close to think. That's why we have a rule.' Maybe Copeland knows that. Maybe he knows it's time for an impartial review.

Brook read on, skimming the wealth of material in the report before turning back to the beginning for a more methodical read-through. He had to admit, Copeland had been meticulous in compiling background on the case, over the years. Details rarely found in a murder book filled the page and, at times, Brook felt as though he was intruding on a private dialogue between Copeland and his sister.

To his credit, Copeland had forced himself to maintain a level tone throughout the written reports, even when touching on what must have been painful memories. It was as though he knew the day would come when he wouldn't be around to search for his sister's killer and that, to colour the facts in any way, might hinder a future investigation.

The late DCI Bannon had again been the original SIO, as in the Billy Stanforth case in 1963. Clearly, Bannon was – to use one of Charlton's irritating phrases – the *'go-to guy'* when it came to homicide. Walter Laird had accompanied Bannon again but this time as a detective sergeant.

In 1965 Clive Copeland and his family had lived on Radbourne Lane at the edge of the Mackworth Estate, overlooking fields to the north of Derby, and, even to this day, the lane was the dividing line between Derby's north-western suburbs and open countryside. At that time, according to Copeland's notes, Mackworth was a modern development of desirable homes, giving easy access to the country-side and providing a suitable location for a solid, well-to-do family.

George Copeland, Clive and Matilda's father, had worked in engineering for Rolls-Royce, one of Derby's main employers. During the Second World War, George had remained in Derby, maintaining Tiger Moths and Miles Magisters for the flying school at nearby RAF Burnaston. Later, when the Air Ministry needed a site to train glider pilots to deliver British Airborne Forces into combat, Burnaston was chosen and Copeland's father had worked on them too.

Copeland's mother, Mary, had met George working as a secretary for Rolls-Royce and had given up her career to be a housewife when the first of her two children had been born: Matilda, in 1949, and Clive two years later.

The Copelands were just another average family until Matilda Copeland's disappearance in the late summer of 1965. The story had been big news in Derby, and the local paper, then the *Evening Telegraph*, had led with it on several consecutive nights.

Brook skimmed through the chronological newspaper reports. Local journalists wouldn't have known more than CID officers so Brook restricted himself to looking at pictures of the Copeland home, maps of the area and a portrait of young Matilda taken the year before her murder, when she was fifteen.

According to family and friends, Matilda had been a normal, happy-go-lucky sixteen-year-old girl, fresh out of school with a good report and impressive exam results. She had recently started work in a local shop, Barney's General Store, on Prince Charles Avenue, just three streets away from the Copeland family home.

On 31 August, a warm Tuesday night, Matilda Copeland had taken the family dog, Ebony, for its evening walk around the estate. She had set off just after 8.00p.m. but never returned and the family never saw her alive again. At ten o'clock, the dog Ebony returned unaccompanied. Two hours of searching and shouting along all the usual walking routes had produced nothing and the police had been called in.

For four nights and three days, the search continued until, on Saturday, 4 September 1965, Matilda's naked body was spotted floating in Osmaston Park Lake by a couple of hikers. Osmaston Park was a local beauty spot, part of a large private park a few miles north-west of Mackworth, along the A52 past Kirk Langley towards Ashbourne.

Brook knew the lake well. It was on his way home and sometimes, when he was unable to get back to his cottage before dark, he would park his car outside the Saracen's Head in the village of Shirley and take the circular walk around the wooded grounds. In summer, the circuit would only take about ninety minutes but in winter, the ground around the lake became boggy and walking was difficult.

Brook checked the distance between Mackworth and Osmaston Park on his laptop. It was just over nine miles. 'Transport required,' he mumbled, flipping to a new page of his notebook and writing 'Van or car' under the heading 'Matilda Copeland'. Brook poured more tea from his flask and ploughed on.

The body of Copeland's sister was recovered and taken for autopsy, where she was found to have been strangled with a cord, before being dumped in the lake. Forensic scientists determined that she'd been in the water for around four days before her bloating remains were spotted on the surface amongst reeds. They further concluded from the lack of rigor mortis and discolouration of her neck that Matilda had died shortly after her abduction and must have gone into the water no more than a few hours later.

Unfortunately the long immersion in the lake had destroyed any evidence adhering to her corpse. Her fingernails were scraped but no evidence of the murderer's tissue was found beneath. No semen or foreign pubic hair could be detected in and around the vagina and no other clues were found on her body. Her clothes were never recovered.

With a naked corpse, determining whether Matilda had been raped before death was an important line of inquiry and here the case took a twist. It proved impossible to establish whether Matilda had engaged in sexual intercourse before her death. Apart from the lack of semen and pubic hair, the pathologist could find little in the way of bruising or other injuries around the sexual organs. However, this couldn't rule out the possibility that Matilda Copeland had submitted to sexual intercourse before death to try and save her life because, importantly, she had not been a virgin at time of death. Moreover, from the wording in the forensic report, it was made absolutely clear that Clive's sister had not lost her virginity on the night of her death. Matilda Copeland had been sexually active well before the night of her abduction.

As the father of an abused daughter, Brook closed his eyes to empathise. How painful it must be to Copeland every time he read the details of Matilda's death, especially as suspicion about her sexual partners would have been rife and, given her age, might have been stretched to include male members of the Copeland family.

After finding Matilda's body, search teams hunted for evidence in the surrounding woodland where Matilda might have met her end. However, the police were never able to identify any viable location where the killing had taken place, despite calling on extensive manpower, canine power and conducting a fingertip search of the dense woods.

According to Laird and Bannon's contemporary reports, the ground that summer was dry and firm, making it impossible to track the killer's movements around the heavily wooded park, even with dogs. No tyre tracks were found. No items of clothing were recovered. No scraps of torn material, no stray handkerchief, no detached buttons.

The absence of wounds on Matilda's body presented a similar problem, though that didn't prevent Bannon and Laird calling in the bloodhounds in the hope that, in her struggle to live, she might have drawn blood from her attacker. But again nothing was found. No blood, no fluids, sexual or otherwise were located by the dogs. There was no trace of human urine or faeces so often expelled during the death throes, making it impossible to determine the route taken by the killer to the lake's edge, despite having to carry a body. Indeed, there was no evidence to indicate that the murder had taken place in the woods at all.

Bannon and Laird were forced to conclude that the murder and any possible intercourse had happened elsewhere, before her naked body had been carefully packed then transported through the woods, possibly in some kind of body bag to contain fluids, before being dumped in the estate's lake. Somebody had been very careful to cover their tracks.

At the lake, attention focused on the estate's gamekeeper, John Briggs, and his seventeen-year-old assistant, Colin Ealy, who were both interviewed at length about their whereabouts on the night of Matilda's abduction. Both men had flimsy alibis, claiming to have been alone that night, Briggs at home and Ealy working on the estate until late. Neither could provide corroboration.

A boot print found on the shoreline was cast in plaster and found to be a match to the assistant's boot, but with Ealy employed as a woodsman, the evidence of the cast had to be set aside, especially as no other evidence that Matilda's body had been dumped from that spot could be found.

At this point, the two-pronged inquiry's emphasis switched from the woods around Osmaston Lake back to the site of Matilda's abduction in Mackworth. On the evening of her disappearance, several people who knew Matilda had seen her with Ebony, the family's black Labrador. Most were respectable neighbours and included an Arthur Barney. Brook wondered if Barney was connected to the general store where Matilda had just started working. He made another note.

To all who encountered her that night, Matilda had appeared to be her usual cheery self and no one had seen anything suspicious.

However, the last sighting of her had been at the top of Radbourne Lane, where the road swept up the hill towards Radbourne Common and then on in the direction of Kirk Langley, nearly three miles away.

Trevor Taylor, a local bachelor who lived alone, had been walking to a pub on nearby Station Road at 8.30p.m., and claimed to have seen Matilda running towards the common. Taylor hadn't seen the dog.

'Trevor Taylor,' said Brook, as though Noble was there to listen. 'The last person to see the victim is often the killer. What are the stats on that?'

Brook's instincts were right. Taylor's testimony was at odds with all the other witness statements gathered by Bannon and Laird. Every other witness who had seen Matilda had testified that they'd encountered her on the estate, with Ebony. And these sightings were all between 8 and 8.30p.m.

In addition, George Copeland testified that Matilda only walked the dog around the estate with its wide avenues and green spaces. The roads leading to the common had no pavements and no lighting and the Copeland children were forbidden from taking the dog along the lane in which Matilda had been spotted, especially in poor light.

To Brook it wasn't a surprise that Trevor Taylor became an immediate suspect. Even in today's enlightened times the unmarried loner is a red flag to officers hunting a sexual predator. In 1965, alarm bells would have been sounding long and hard in the heads of experienced detectives.

Trevor Taylor was subsequently arrested, interviewed under caution and forced to surrender his clothes from that evening for tests, as well as having his house searched. However, nothing to connect him to Matilda was ever found and eventually the police were forced to release him without charge.

But it didn't end there. Taylor was formally interviewed about Matilda Copeland's disappearance on three other occasions but, each time, experienced officers had been unable to punch any holes in his testimony. He insisted Matilda had been running up to the common that night. He'd recognised her, even in the failing light, by the way she moved and had checked his watch seconds after the sighting.

Brook ploughed on through the next few pages, providing painstaking background on Trevor Taylor. There were original documents from 1965, in addition to in-depth biographical reports compiled by a zealous Copeland on his first review of the case in 1977.

Taylor, a twenty-nine-year-old hospital porter at the time of Matilda's death, was an unremarkable man. He wasn't highly educated and had left school at fifteen to work in various menial jobs before joining the NHS as a porter in 1956, a job he kept until his death.

Taylor frequented pubs in the Mackworth area seven nights a week. This was nothing unusual in the fifties and sixties. Pubs were in their heyday as there was little in the way of home entertainment to keep people, particularly men, in the home. In addition, the cost of heating drove many to seek out the warmth of the tavern and it was Taylor's habit to walk to the pub at the same time every night, drink four pints of beer then return to his modest house in Mackworth on foot.

Bannon and Laird could find no evidence that Taylor indulged in any deviant behaviour; certainly he had no criminal record. And people who knew him said that he was quiet, kept himself to himself and was never drunk or aggressive when socialising.

Brook flipped back to the front of the file. Taylor had died in early 1978 at the age of forty-two. According to Clive Copeland's notes and a copy of the autopsy and inquest findings, Trevor Taylor had either fallen or jumped from a railway bridge in Derby, as a train approached. His body was mangled almost beyond recognition and his elderly mother was unable to recognise him. The railway bridge from which Taylor had fallen, or jumped, was on London Road, close to the hospital where he worked.

Even though suicide was indicated, an open verdict had been returned because 42-year-old Taylor had not left a note and medical reports and the autopsy had revealed nothing that might have led Taylor to take his life. He had no record of depression and no terminal diseases to push him to take the easy way out.

That didn't, of course, mean that Taylor couldn't have committed suicide for some other compelling reason; guilt maybe, especially if Copeland's review of the case had brought back memories of the night of Matilda's disappearance and subsequent murder.

Finally, Brook found the information he'd been looking for – a list of all the cars owned by friends, neighbours and businesses on the Mackworth Estate at the time of the abduction. There weren't many. Car ownership in 1965 was still the preserve of the few.

Brook looked down the short list. Trevor Taylor didn't own a car, though Bannon and Laird had been careful to note that his mother, who lived nearby, owned a ten-year-old Ford Zephyr Zodiac, which had sat undisturbed in the garage after the death of Taylor's father. They'd also made a note that when tried, the car had started first time. Brook looked either side of the report but couldn't find any notes on, or statements by, Trevor Taylor's mother. Odd.

Five other households on the estate were listed as car owners. At the bottom of the list was the name Derek Barney who had owned a Morris J-type delivery van. Brook flicked back through the file. Barney was indeed the owner of Barney's General Store where Matilda had just started to work. He was also the father of Arthur Barney, one of the eyewitnesses who saw Matilda on the night of her disappearance, walking her dog.

Brook underlined the name in his notebook. The Barneys lived close by, had their own transport and knew Copeland's sister well enough to approach her without setting off alarm bells. Brook rocked back on his chair, certain that he wouldn't be thinking anything that Bannon, Laird and subsequently Copeland hadn't considered before him.

'Plenty of suspects here, Clive,' muttered Brook, flicking through background reports on Derek and Arthur Barney. Derek Barney had been fifty-two years of age in 1965, a widower with two grown sons,

Arthur and Winston, aged nineteen and seventeen respectively. Both sons worked in the family business and both were old enough to be boyfriend material, although there was no mention of Matilda and boyfriends anywhere in the file. For an attractive sixteen-year-old girl who was no longer a virgin, this seemed another odd omission to Brook.

He ran a finger down the next report. At least Bannon and Laird had asked the right questions. According to statements given by Derek Barney, Arthur, the eldest son, drove the van on a daily basis, making deliveries to customers and collecting stock from various outlets. Also, younger son Winston was taking lessons and was capable of driving the van if necessary.

Brook alighted upon a photograph of the van and frowned. It was covered in a livery for Barney's General Store. Would any of the Barneys seriously consider abducting, murdering and disposing of Matilda Copeland using such a distinctive van? Even assuming one or all of them had a motive, it seemed unlikely.

Starting to tire, Brook turned a page. Derek Barney had died in 1985 and eldest son Arthur had followed in 2007. From the lack of further notation, Brook assumed both had died natural deaths. However, the file hadn't been updated since 2008: at least the official file hadn't. Brook had no doubt that Copeland, obsessed with finding his sister's killer, wouldn't just walk away from CID, shrugging his shoulders. Regulations or not, Copeland would certainly have made copies of all the material in the Derby Division files for use at home.

Brook had been in the same boat when he'd made the move from London; before his transfer to the East Midlands he had taken photocopies of all the Reaper documents held by the Met. There were some cases that detectives couldn't let go.

Brook looked sideways at the remaining pile of documents – he was only halfway through. He pushed back his chair and went to stretch his legs in the car park, glancing enviously at a pair of WPCs sucking joyfully on their cigarettes.

* * *

Scott Wheeler woke with a violent shudder, banging his head for the umpteenth time on the wooden roof of his tomb. He screamed and nursed his forehead, feeling delicately around the days-old swelling from that first blow on the night of Chelsea's party. Gradually the pain subsided and it took a moment to remember where he was but the awful realisation flooded in before the back of his head had come to rest on the damp plastic. The sunny light of his bedroom remained in his dreams; he was back in his damp, dark prison.

All was dark. All was quiet. It was night outside because the faint glow of daylight from the air pipe was gone. With a surge of panic Scott wondered if the pipe had been pulled up and he slithered on his back across to the reassuring flow of cold air. His breathing slowed in immediate relief. He could see stars. The universe was still there, though strangely it had decided that it could continue without Scott Wheeler.

How many days? Six? Seven? And how much longer would he have to be here? The passage of time brought a pinprick of a tear to Scott's eye but he brushed it away. *No more crying. Got to stay strong.*

To forget the ebbing of his life, Scott listened for the sound of anything other than the now-familiar trickle of soil dropping on to him through the cracks in the planks where the heavy plastic sheeting was holed. Nothing in the world at the other end of his air pipe stirred. Nothing suggested the noise of a search. *They must think I'm dead.*

A few days ago he'd heard, or imagined he'd heard, voices somewhere in the distance, somewhere above ground, shouting to each other. Shouting for him? The more he thought about it later the more he heard his name. People were looking for him. He was important. People wanted him back in their lives. Scott Wheeler mattered. He'd shouted back with all the strength he could muster, even risking pushing against the shaky wooden boards, but many hours later, when night had fallen and the voices had gone, Scott had sunk back on to the damp plastic, distraught and terrified that the soil he'd dislodged would engulf him.

After that day, he could fight no more. Without fail, every time he'd pushed and hammered his fists and feet against the wood, more soil had fallen, sometimes into his mouth, sometimes into his eyes, forcing him to sit up and bang his head again, freeing up more dirt to drop and fill his dwindling space.

After a long time screaming, hammering and kicking after he first woke in the tomb, he was defeated. There was no way around it. He was trapped. He couldn't move. He couldn't sit up. He couldn't go to the toilet. He couldn't wash. He couldn't even turn over without dislodging more soil. All he could do was lie on his back in almost perpetual night and exist, ignoring the stomach cramps, the pain from his spreading rashes, the stench of his waste soaking his clothes and steeping his once-soft skin in filth. He'd tried to pass the time rubbing his limbs to keep warm in the cold ground and occasionally even sleeping if he could ignore the smell from his soiled clothing. How long had he been here?

Don't think about it. Time passing was bad. Stop thinking about time, about anything.

He took a long slow breath of the cold clean air blowing down the pipe, the most important ally in his fight for life, and it calmed him. Keep still, he'd learned. Be like a robot, turned off for a while. Don't move. It's a game and the only way to win was to survive. With little choice, he'd adapted to his situation as far as possible, forced himself to abandon futile attempts to escape and finally cut out movement altogether. Even turning over on to his stomach was an issue, although he was young and supple and could do it at a pinch, at the cost of soil invasion.

But why bother? Stay still. Right. That was his ace. He was young and strong, a good footballer, a cyclist, good on a skateboard. Movement was everything to him. Even with the TV on, his mum complained he could never keep still. The TV. Scott had a surge of yearning. *Don't think about that. You're a robot, turned off for a while. Like a Transformer. Keeping still, waiting to show your power.*

Back at his desk, Brook started on the rest of Matilda's file. The two-pronged investigation into her death seemed to have hit a dead end when there was a sensational development which appeared to unlock the case. Five days after the discovery of Matilda Copeland's body, Colin Ealy, the estate's apprentice woodsman, disappeared and was immediately promoted from a person of interest to the inquiry's prime suspect.

'Why isn't this at the front of the folder?' Brook wondered aloud. He soon found out.

For the next two weeks, in tandem with a nationwide manhunt, Bannon and Laird proceeded to take Colin Ealy's life apart. His bedroom at his mother's house in Osmaston, his clothes, his tools and equipment, his workplace – all were methodically searched and all artefacts removed and subjected to detailed analysis, piece by piece, fibre by fibre, undergoing the most rigorous examinations available at the time. Nothing incriminating was found.

Unsurprisingly, Briggs and Ealy had access to a vehicle for their work, an old 1952 Bedford CA Panel Van, supplied by the estate owners. It had been in Ealy's possession on the night of the abduction and it had already been searched but now it was subjected to lengthy forensic and fingerprint tests.

Brook sat back. 'Why would a gamekeeper on a private estate drive nine miles to Mackworth on a Tuesday night to abduct a girl?' he asked himself. 'Did he know Matilda?' Unlikely. He read on, baffled.

Minute traces of blood found in Ealy's van had briefly raised hopes of a positive outcome but it was found to belong to one of the various dead animals that would sometimes be thrown into the back of the vehicle, appropriate to a gamekeeper's work.

In addition, extensive fingerprinting of all surfaces was compared to prints taken from the victim's bedroom but if Matilda Copeland had ever been in the vehicle, she'd left no trace. The van was clean and the reason for Ealy's departure was, and remained, a mystery to this day.

The rest of the documents dealt with case reviews and developments after the inquiry had petered out. In 1970, when the hunt for Matilda's killer had gone cold, Walter Laird had received and followed up an anonymous tip, claiming to be a sighting of Ealy in a remote part of Scotland. Unfortunately, the day before Laird arrived in Crianlarich in Stirling, the man in question had vanished again. Colin Ealy was never traced but remained a key suspect based solely on the fact of his disappearance.

Even Clive Copeland, who had focused on Colin Ealy's disappearance as soon as he joined the police force, spending two annual holidays in Crianlarich for good measure, had been forced to accept that it would never be proved that Ealy had killed Matilda without finding him and extracting a confession.

Brook ran a finger down the witness list one last time. Obviously Colin Ealy's status was unknown but gamekeeper John Briggs was dead. Barney's youngest son, Winston, was alive at the time of the last review. If Ealy and Winston Barney were still alive, they would both be in their late sixties.

Brook closed the file and turned to his laptop. He found Winston Barney's name on the electoral register and made a note of his last known address. He lived locally in Ashbourne, the attractive market town twenty minutes north of Derby, and on Brook's route home to Hartington. Cross-referencing on the PNC database, Brook found no criminal record. Of Colin Ealy there was no mention. He had effectively disappeared off the face of the earth in 1965.

Brook sat back. 'That's enough,' he muttered, tossing the mildewed folder aside and massaging his forehead. He pushed back his chair, gathered up the file and his laptop and left the room.

The corridor outside was in darkness save for a bar of light under Copeland's door. Brook had been so absorbed, he hadn't heard Copeland arrive. The ex-DCI was working on a Saturday. *Give the old boy credit. He takes his work seriously.*

Brook hesitated, knuckles poised. He wanted to speak to Copeland, find out why he'd been given Matilda's file or, at the very least, get Copeland to acknowledge that he'd left it for Brook to see. If it was a mistake, Copeland hadn't realised it yet since he hadn't asked for it back.

Brook knocked softly and entered. He was greeted by the sight of Copeland stretched out in his chair fast asleep. Instead of turning to leave, Brook tiptoed to the desk and took a peek at the tatty green folder sitting on it. Brook's heart skipped a beat. The name on the file was Jeff Ward, murdered on 22 December 1973, and identified by ex-DCI Sam Bannon as a victim of an unknown serial killer – the Pied Piper.

Brook stared at Copeland, asleep on his chair, wondering whether to wake him and ask about the Ward file and the Pied Piper. In the event, he opted to leave, closing the door softly behind him.

Copeland's eyes opened as soon as the door closed. He looked down at the Jeff Ward dossier. 'Damn.' He picked up his mobile phone. 'It's me. Brook's seen the Jeff Ward file. It was my mistake. It's *not* nothing. He knows about the Pied Piper. Sam left a note in the Billy Stanforth file and Brook found it, so I was checking the Ward file to see if we'd missed anything else. Agreed.' He replaced the receiver and looked thoughtfully towards the door.

At least Brook hadn't brought back Tilly's murder book to drop on his desk. So what did he want? To ask why he'd been given her file? Maybe even to ask questions about Tilly's death? Well, it was too soon for that. But at least he hadn't returned the file. Copeland smiled at the space vacated by his colleague. Brook was interested.

After driving back to his cottage in worsening weather, Brook hurried inside through the rain. He stooped to pick up a single Christmas card from the mat and dumped it on the kitchen table. Before preparing his evening meal of samosas and cream cheese, he lit the small wood burner in the tiny lounge and left the door open to listen to the soothing atavistic crackle of nascent fire, while he sat in the kitchen reading the final reports from Matilda Copeland's groaning file.

The last few documents were reports of tests carried out after the development of DNA profiling in the mid-eighties, including all subsequent advances. All tests had been unable to match Matilda

Copeland's genetic profile to any artefacts connected to the missing woodsman, Colin Ealy.

Brook finally closed the file and pushed it to one side, returning his thoughts to the Jeff Ward dossier he'd seen on Copeland's desk, his excitement at seeing it now dissipated.

Of course he's looking into it. Copeland and Laird were the investigating officers. And it's unsolved. That's what Copeland does. Even so, his reaction when I mentioned the Pied Piper seemed odd.

Brook shook it out of his head, his thoughts drifting back to his interview with Mullen, the lonely, troubled old man, haunted by the death of his friend half a century before – a man unable or unwilling to leave a house that was rotting around him because the outside world was too hard to face. Brook didn't know whether to envy or pity him.

After his meal, Brook went to stretch out in front of the fire. He remembered his Christmas card and tore it open. It was from British Telecom. *Season's Greetings.* He leaned towards the wood burner, opened the door and dropped the envelope on to the burning logs. Then he held the card above the flames. A second later, he withdrew it, closed the cast-iron door and placed the card on his bare mantelpiece.

The next day, the 16th, Brook decided not to spend Sunday morning at his metal desk in the station basement, preferring to do a little work from home. It was mainly the kind of legwork he routinely delegated to Noble and it was a chore having to hunt down the simple matter of a few addresses. Worse, he knew Noble would have found the information in half the time.

After a satisfying walk in the sharp cold air of a winter's morning, Brook drove the twelve miles to Bakewell and spent Sunday afternoon buying food to replenish his fridge-freezer. The market town was teeming with happy families, apparently enjoying pre-Christmas shopping, and Brook left restocked but thoroughly depressed.

In mid-afternoon, he drove up Monyash Road back to the A515

to Hartington but when he reached the turn-off, he kept going, arriving in Ashbourne twenty minutes later.

He double-checked the address of the imposing three-storey house in front of him then banged hard on the heavy door, stepping back to inspect the solid stone edifice. The front door pulled back to a chain and a well-groomed grey-haired man peered out.

Brook brandished his warrant card. 'Mr Winston Barney?'

A look of foreboding swept over the man's features. 'Yes.'

'DI Brook, Derby CID. I'd like to ask you some questions about Matilda Copeland.'

The man's face turned white and his eyes poured hate into Brook's. 'My grandchildren are here.'

Brook's eyes narrowed, trying to discern his meaning. 'It won't take long.'

'I'm finished answering questions about poor Tilly Copeland and you can tell her brother that from me. I wasn't her bloody boyfriend and neither was my brother. Now please leave.'

'Mr Barney, I—'

'Tilly's dead and she's not coming back. I didn't kill her and neither did Arthur or my father, God rest their souls. I wish to God Arthur had never seen her that night. Don't come back again, Inspector, or I'll report you for harassment.' Barney slammed the door, leaving Brook in no doubt that further knocking would be futile.

Arriving home, Brook poured a modest measure of malt and water and decided to hunt up the Christmas decorations from the attic to complement the small goose he'd purchased for Christmas dinner. He hadn't put the decorations up for three or four years but if Terri did make it to Hartington for the holiday, he had to be ready.

When he'd finished, he stepped back to admire his handiwork. It hadn't taken long. He only had a few streamers to drape on the wall, some of which he'd torn and had to discard. He found some coloured tinsel and wound it across the mantelpiece with a couple of sprigs of near-desiccated holly. At the bottom of the box he also found a folded piece of A4 paper covered in childlike crayon daubs in red and green. Terri's first Christmas card to her father had been homemade when she was a small child. There were remnants of gold sparkles on the front but most of the glitter had fallen away. Brook tried not to see it as a metaphor.

He placed the Christmas card on the mantelpiece next to the card from his 'Good Friends at BT' then took out his mobile to ring her. He decided against it. She might tell him she couldn't come for Christmas and not knowing her plans would at least give him hope. Instead he texted. 'Goose in freezer. Decorations up. No urgent cases. My time is your time. x.'

Nineteen

Monday, 17 December 2012

ROOK SIPPED HIS SECOND TEA of the day early the next morning, a blanket wrapped round his shoulders against the cold. When he was able to open his eyes, he took out his brief notes about the death of Copeland's sister and read through what he'd written. Three things had struck him. First, Trevor Taylor, the man who'd witnessed Matilda running towards Radbourne Common, the man that investigating officers Bannon and Laird had immediately picked out as a suspect, wasn't on the list of those owning a vehicle in 1965.

His mother *had* owned a car but, curiously, the file contained no reports or statements taken from her about her son's use of it. Whoever abducted Matilda would have needed transport to take her, dead or alive, to the site of the murder and then on to Osmaston Park Lake. And if Taylor was a suspect, as a matter of routine Bannon and Laird should have asked his mother whether her son had borrowed the car that night.

Brook gazed at the single word representing the other significant omission from the file in his eyes: 'Boyfriends?' He was not sure how he might broach the subject of Matilda's sexual activity with Copeland.

A few hours later, Brook parked in a pub car park off the A609 in Rawson Green, a hamlet near Belper, a small market town north of Derby. On closer inspection, Brook realised the pub was no more, another victim of the home entertainment industry and cheap supermarket alcohol. It had been converted into a private day nursery, which explained the full car park at eleven in the morning.

Brook locked the BMW, trying not to glance towards the nursery in case of reproachful looks from staff inside the building. He hurried along the main road to a terraced row of small, redbrick cottages, originally built to house workers at the long-abandoned rail yard round the corner. The wind blew cold droplets of winter rain into his face as he walked.

He rapped on the flimsy knocker of a white plastic door belonging to the end cottage in the row. While he waited, he looked around the neat front of house, defaced on the upper storey by a satellite dish turning its face to the heavens to seek the word of God. The small yard was paved and bare, devoid of plants, for minimal maintenance. This was the future for all who lived to infirmity, and the present for the growing underclass that aped such indolence. Brook resented it all the more as old age beckoned to him.

He banged down on the knocker again. It was shaped like a funeral urn which lightened his mood for a moment.

As he took a step to look through the front window, the door opened wide enough to tighten a door chain. A white-haired old man uncertainly pushed his face into the gap. Brook noticed the tobacco-stained left hand straining to maintain pressure on the rubber-tipped walking stick.

'I don't buy on the doorstep. On your way.'

'Walter Laird?'

'Who are you?' growled the old man, voice drenched in tar. He narrowed his eyes at Brook, who declined to reply, instead holding his warrant card close to Laird's face for inspection.

Laird squinted at the ID, nodded in recognition. 'Brook. Clive mentioned you might call. About the Stanforth boy.' He laughed suddenly, exposing unnaturally bright false teeth which shifted slightly as his jaw moved. 'You're not expecting to get anywhere with that donkey, are you, lad? It's been reviewed to death and if there was a result to be had, I would have closed it myself.'

'Can we discuss it inside please?' asked Brook. 'It's freezing out here.'

The ghost of a smile crossed Laird's features as various offhand replies came to mind. After allowing Brook to shiver in the cold for a few moments longer, the old man shakily drew back the chain and turned away to shuffle back to his tasselled armchair, using his stick for balance. Brook followed him at a necessarily sedate pace.

'Sit down,' said Laird through the tar, nodding at the small dining table by the window. There were two clean plates with knives and forks. A jar of Morrison's pickled beetroot stood next to the salt, pepper and malt vinegar. Laird saw Brook glance at them. 'It's fish and chip day,' he said.

'Isn't that usually Friday?' smiled Brook, pulling out a dining chair and crouching on the end while Laird readied himself to sink back into the sole armchair, in front of the single-bar electric fire.

'OAP discount on Monday.' He sank back, pulling a blanket over his legs, his breath whistling through his cheap teeth. 'Sorry it's not so warm. Fuel poverty. Not a lot of money in honest coppering in my day.' He looked across at Brook. 'Got any cigarettes, lad?'

'I gave up,' replied Brook.

'Gave up? On the job?' snorted Laird. 'Must be a desk jockey if you can get through the day without something to take your mind off it.'

'I *was* off work for a spell,' explained Brook, wary of opening the topic of his local infamy. 'But it's harder now I'm back working cases. Even cold ones.'

Laird produced a tobacco tin from down the side of his chair and proceeded to roll up for himself. When finished he snapped the lid back on his tin and shoved it down the side of his cushion. 'You'll not be wanting one of these then,' he said, lighting up and exhaling smoke towards Brook.

Laird sat back with a sigh and studied Brook, a smirk playing around his whiskered lips. 'Off work,' he chuckled through the lingering blue-brown smoke. 'Is that what you call it? I've not lost all my marbles, Brook. I read all about it. You got carpeted by Brass.'

Brook shrugged. 'I can't deny it.'

'But you felt the need to lie about it.'

'I didn't lie,' answered Brook softly. 'But I don't routinely volunteer my disciplinary problems to strangers.'

Laird picked a stray shred of tobacco from his tongue and flicked it at the hearth. 'You also don't share that you're that London fella who went doolally and transferred up from the Met a few years ago. Caused a right fuss in the local force, that did.'

'No,' replied Brook with a tight smile.

'No, what?'

'No, I don't share that either as my colleagues already know about it.'

'Does Clive?' continued Laird.

'Not from me,' said Brook. 'But I'm sure someone told him.'

'Typical,' opined Laird. 'The Met dropping their unfit officers in our lap like we're nothing. Arrogant southerners.' Like many people of advanced age, Laird rattled off the insults as though oblivious to the wounds inflicted, before giving the game away and looking coldly at Brook to check his barbs had broken the skin.

And this is why I never mention it. 'I do recall a little hostility when I arrived, now you mention it,' replied Brook drily.

Unexpectedly, Laird laughed at this though it was difficult to work out where his merriment started and his coughing ended. 'Good for you, Brook. Don't let the bastards grind you down, eh?' He grinned at his guest now, exuding sudden bonhomie. 'Call me Walter. I was never a fan of Brass either. Give 'em a committee to sit on and they'll chew your bloody ear off. Stick the buggers in front of a blagger with a knife and they'd soon be crying for Mummy. Why don't you make us a cup of tea, lad? Two sugars for me.'

Brook duly trotted off to the tiny dishevelled kitchen and made tea. 'I'm actually here about *two* of your old cases,' he said eventually, setting down a mug on the arm of Laird's chair.

'Two?' exclaimed the old man.

'It's a bit sudden,' said Brook airily, aware of the reaction he might get, 'but I'm also looking into Matilda Copeland's murder.'

'Tilly? Clive asked you to look at that?' Laird was uncertain for a moment but the suspicion soon returned. 'No chance. Clive wouldn't let anyone else near it in a million years.'

'You remember the case then?' said Brook.

'Like it was yesterday, lad. She died in sixty-five. Picked it up with Sam Bannon. I reviewed it in sixty-nine and again in seventy-three.' He shook his head sadly. 'We never closed it.' He shrugged. 'And as soon as Clive was old enough to join CID, it was all down to him. No one else got near.'

'That is odd,' said Brook, 'because according to the file, you also signed off on reviews into her death in nineteen seventy-seven and then again in nineteen eighty-one. Why would that be?' Brook paused. 'Walter.'

Laird's superiority complex evaporated along with his bonhomie and he studied Brook. 'A troublemaker like you is going to quote the rulebook at me? Clive's a friend, Brook. His sister had been murdered. You expect colleagues to keep him away from it?'

'That's the regulation.'

'I don't know what it's like in the Met, lad, but here in Derbyshire, coppers help their friends when they need it.'

'So you *didn't* actually review Matilda Copeland's murder in nineteen seventy-seven and eighty-one?'

Laird eyed Brook with distaste. 'No. And you won't make many friends with that attitude.'

'I'll withdraw my name from the popularity contests,' replied Brook.

The old man grunted – appreciative if unamused. 'Pity DI Ford's tied up with this missing kid. He knows how to treat an old colleague. What about Bob Greatorix? He reviewed the Stanforth file four or five year ago.'

'Retired,' said Brook. 'Ill health.'

Laird chuckled. 'Can't say I'm surprised. He was a big unit, all right. Nearly bust that chair you're sat on. Got himself a nice pay-off, did he?'

'I wouldn't know.'

'Course he did. Big money playing that game these days,' continued Laird. 'Still, good luck to him. He was a good officer, respectful, knew not to tread on toes . . .'

'That was always his strong suit,' replied Brook.

'. . . when to take advice and when to leave well alone.'

Brook shrugged in mock regret. 'Afraid I don't have his skills.'

'So I see,' said Laird, trying to reignite his tab.

'What advice did you pass on to Greatorix?'

'To stop wasting everyone's time,' growled the old man. 'The Stanforth boy's killer is likely dead. And if he isn't, there's not a scrap of proof available to put him in the frame. Believe me. We looked hard enough, me and Sam.' Laird made the sign of the cross. 'God rest his soul.'

'You had a male suspect at least.'

'We had several of each,' blustered Laird.

'Put *him* in the frame, you said,' pointed out Brook. 'Who are we talking about? Brendan McCleary? Edward Mullen?'

'Mullen?' laughed Laird. 'That little pipsqueak.'

'He's the only person we know who was definitely alone when the shed caught fire. And he'd had an argument with Billy . . .'

'Good God, man, the little pansy couldn't step on a spider without coming off worse.' Laird laughed again, though he seemed to be forcing it. 'And Billy's mum alibied him.'

'Who then? McCleary?'

'Who else?' snarled Laird. 'Born killer, that one. Murdered his own father in cold blood. Blew his head off with a shotgun then went upstairs and slept like a baby.'

'That was six years later,' remarked Brook. 'It doesn't prove he set the fire that killed Billy Stanforth.'

Laird sighed. 'And don't I know it. We would have put him down for it if we could and we went pretty hard at the scumbag, believe me.' He smiled. 'You could in them days, especially if the beggar was a known villain.'

'He wasn't much of a villain in nineteen sixty-three,' observed Brook. 'A bit of theft and affray.'

'He was a wrong 'un,' insisted Laird. 'You don't need a full jacket to know someone's not right. Decent coppers get a feel for it.'

Brook acknowledged with a hunch of the shoulders. 'But you didn't get a confession.'

'We couldn't shake him,' said Laird. He raised a thick white eyebrow. 'Surprising thing was we couldn't shake the lass, Amelia, neither, though we didn't pile into her as heavy, obviously. But we played the two against each other – separate interviews, gave them the old he-said-she-said routine. Nothing.' He fixed Brook with a pale eye. 'He wasn't a great loss to humanity but we might have saved Malcolm McCleary's life if we'd nailed Brendan back in sixty-three, though he was too young to hang. When we finally did nail him the bloody government had stopped stringing the buggers up, more's the pity. His sort need putting out of circulation permanent, like they do in China.'

'An enlightened country,' retorted Brook. 'With a fine record on human rights.'

'Mock all you want,' snapped back Laird. 'But people will wish we had the same system if McCleary's done for that Wheeler kid, like they're saying in the papers.'

'He's just a person of interest at the moment,' replied Brook. 'So they tell me.'

Laird's cackle turned into a rasping cough. 'Convicted killer, living in the same neighbourhood *and* he's done a runner – do me a favour, Brook. He's done for that kid, no doubt. The only shame is I didn't realise he was a kiddie fiddler back in the sixties or I'd have had his bollocks off.'

'McCleary killed his father in a domestic over forty years ago,' said Brook. 'Apart from that he's got no history of random violence and no record of abusing children, sexually or physically.'

'The news said they found kiddie porn in his flat,' growled Laird. 'What do you call that then?'

'They can't be sure it belonged to McCleary,' Brook said. 'Not definitely.'

'Just means he's been careful,' sneered Laird, fixing Brook in his sights. 'You dig deep enough, something'll turn up.'

Brook raised an eyebrow. 'And you didn't?'

'Like I said, we were all over McCleary for the Stanforth fire but we couldn't pin it on him, thanks to his girlfriend.'

'Girlfriend?' Brook saw an opening. 'Do you mean Amelia or the other one?'

Laird eyed him suspiciously. 'Poor Billy's sister, aye. Talk about misguided loyalties. And you're right, the silly bitch protected him even though Brendan had other girlfriends, some of them under age as well.' Laird raised a gnarled yellow finger at Brook. 'There's your history of child abuse.'

'It's only abuse if he had sexual relations with them.'

'Course he did. That's what he was like.'

Brook took out his notepad. 'Can you give me some names? If his other girlfriends are still alive, I'd like to speak to them.'

Laird looked off into the fire. 'I don't remember and that's a fact.' He took a pull on his roll-up.

'Please try.'

'It were near fifty year ago, lad,' said Laird. 'I'm an old man.'

'Funny how so many witnesses say they don't remember anything,' said Brook, sipping at his tea. He grimaced. The milk was turning sour. 'Then they tell you to leave them alone because they want to forget.'

Laird's customary grunt progressed to a tarry chuckle. 'Sounds familiar.'

'But here's the thing, Walter. In all my years in the job, that's never once applied to a detective. We can't seem to let go, especially if it's an unsolved murder. I know from personal experience, we can remember, and obsess over, the smallest details from decades ago.'

Laird glared at Brook, took a futile pull on his barely visible cigarette and tossed it aggressively into the hearth. 'I haven't forgotten, Brook. I remember everything that's relevant and whoever Brendan McCleary was knocking off on the side was *not* relevant to the inquiry. If it had been, I would've remembered.'

Brook's grin formed slowly but was all the more unsettling for the time it took. 'And there's the magic word.'

'Magic word? Have you got a screw loose?' inquired Laird.

'We've already established that,' answered Brook.

'Then what are you on about?'

'You're the fourth person I've interviewed about Billy Stanforth's death,' explained Brook. 'And every time I get to the subject of Brendan McCleary's *other* girlfriends, I've had the same response. *Not relevant.*'

'Because it wasn't and it isn't.'

'Four witnesses, including you, used that exact same phrase.'

'Who else you been speaking to?' demanded Laird.

'The only ones left,' said Brook. 'Edna Spencer, Edward Mullen . . .'

'Mullen? Waste of time.'

'And Amelia Stanforth.' Brook smiled. 'Oh, wait. You already know I spoke to Amelia, don't you? Because I bumped into your son at her care home.'

Laird was impressed. 'You're good, Brook, I'll give you that. Yes, my Darren was there. He's a local copper on a routine call. Some sort of prowler, he said.'

'Did that involve leaving his number to be notified in the event Amelia Stanforth has visitors?'

'There's no mystery there,' said Laird. 'If McCleary's in the wind, he may try and contact her, tap her up for money. The poor old girl might be confused enough to give it to him.'

'She was a *silly bitch* five minutes ago,' snapped Brook. 'What makes you think she's confused?'

The old man hesitated, forming his answer carefully. 'Because she was no different in sixty-three when she defended McCleary.' Laird's fists were clenched and his breath was harsh and rasping now. When it returned to normal he held up a hand. 'OK, maybe I'm being too severe on the lass. Let's say she was young and foolish back then. Easily led by career scumbags like McCleary.'

'She was easily led, I can agree to that.'

'What does that mean?' Laird's breathing shortened again. It was clear to Brook that he wasn't used to being challenged and didn't like it.

'It means someone fed her a line, Walter. And Edna Spencer. And Edward Mullen.' Brook waited for Laird to react but instead the old man turned to gaze at the electric fire, mouth tight, trying to breathe slowly. Brook knew he'd hit his mark. 'I don't know many twelve- and thirteen-year-olds who use the word *relevant*, do you? Yet three people, who were young children at the time of the fire, answered the same question with the same phrase, almost fifty years after the fact.'

'What question?' growled Laird, staring down at the hearth.

'Who was Brendan McCleary's other girlfriend?' Brook paused to tighten the screw. 'Know what I think, Walter. I think *not relevant* is the kind of phrase a CID officer would use to keep a witness on the subject when their mind begins to wander.'

'What you implying?'

'I think Edna, Amelia and Mullen were all coached.'

'Why would they be coached?' mumbled the grizzled old detective.

'That's what I asked myself,' said Brook.

'And?'

'When they were interviewed about the fire in nineteen sixty-three, I suspect they volunteered information about Brendan's *other* girlfriend. But for reasons unknown, someone didn't want to know and didn't want it on the record. Someone who was investigating that fire drummed it into everyone who mentioned her name, told them so often that it *wasn't relevant* that their reaction became automatic. The only question is, was it you or DCI Bannon?'

Laird pulled his tobacco tin from the side of the chair and proceeded to roll another cigarette. When he'd finished and lit up, he exhaled towards Brook. 'Sam wasn't there. Not at first. He had other things on his mind.'

'Then you coached them.'

Laird looked unswervingly back at Brook. Eventually, 'Yes. I coached them. But only because it *wasn't* relevant, Brook. They were just kids. I was trying to keep their minds clear.'

'Well, you drummed it in so effectively, even now it's their reflex answer,' said Brook quietly. 'Yours too.' Silence. 'So tell me now, Walter. Who was Brendan's other girlfriend?'

'I told you, I don't remember,' he growled.

'You're lying,' replied Brook softly.

Laird's breathing quickened and he found Brook's eyes again but the younger man's gaze didn't falter. Eventually Laird's breathing slowed. He nodded acceptance, his features becoming friendly, reassuring. 'Will you take it on trust, one copper to another, that whoever else Brendan was seeing had no bearing on the inquiry?'

Brook was surprised to be asked. 'I'll consider it if you tell me who she was.'

Laird shook his head. 'I can't do that.'

'Who are you protecting?'

'I don't want to discuss—'

'Is it DCI Bannon?'

'I said I can't tell you,' Laird snapped.

'If your SIO made an error of judgement . . .'

'Leave him out of it,' snarled Laird. 'Sam was my friend.'

'He was your friend and colleague, I understand that. But DCI Bannon is long dead. Nothing you say to me today—'

'I think you'd better leave now,' said Laird, struggling to stand on the threadbare carpet.

'We haven't discussed Matilda Copeland's murder yet.'

'And we're not going to until I speak to Clive. I can't believe he'd let you look at her file without speaking to me first. And yet you walk in here, bold as brass, riding roughshod over people's reputations . . .'

'When have I done that?'

'Sam Bannon was a great man and the finest detective I've ever served with.'

'I still need an answer.'

'The way me and Sam conducted our investigations is none of your business.'

'With respect, Walter, it's my only business until I get transferred back to active cases,' said Brook quietly. 'You know the routine. I ask the questions you asked at the time and then try to come up with some you didn't ask. I don't like it any more than you, but until I'm told to stop, that's my job.'

'Get out. I'm tired,' croaked Laird, beginning to pant again. 'Billy Stanforth died near fifty year ago. You can talk to me and all the other witnesses until we're blue in the face and we won't tell you anything new.'

'And Matilda Copeland?'

'What about her?'

'While we're on the subject of partners, I couldn't find a single reference in the file about Matilda's relationship with boys.'

'So?'

Brook sighed impatiently. 'So she wasn't a virgin when she died, Walter. She was sexually active. If she didn't have a boyfriend, you and Bannon must have given some thought to . . .' Brook hesitated, trying to find the right words, 'an abusive relationship.'

'You're disgusting,' panted Laird. 'George Copeland was a good father . . .'

'You checked?'

'Yes, I checked,' insisted Laird. 'Tilly wasn't abused by her father. He was a good man.'

'Well, someone was having intercourse with her,' replied Brook.

'You're wasting your breath until I clear it with Clive, understand?'

After a beat, Brook stood. 'Talk to Clive. But I'll be back.'

A door opened somewhere in the back of the house.

'Fish and chips, Dad,' shouted a voice with a strong Derbyshire accent. 'Get that kettle on. It's freezing out there. Haven't you put plates on to warm? Come on, me duck. Have I got to do everything meself?'

The uniformed sergeant Brook had encountered at the care home emerged from the kitchen carrying a parcel of steaming fish and chips wrapped in newspaper. Sergeant Laird was startled to see Brook.

'What the hell are you doing here?'

'Take it easy, son,' warned his father.

Brook realised his hands had balled into fists when he saw the officer who had been so offhand with him at St Agatha's. He took a few deep breaths, counting the seconds off in his head. It had been a while since he'd had to do the technique. 'I'm a detective inspector, Sergeant, so I suggest you mind your manners or you'll be up on a charge.'

Laird the younger stared at Brook, uncertain what to say, before finding his grin. 'You're that washed-up detective from London who nearly got canned a few months back.' He turned to face his father. 'What's he doing here, Dad?'

Brook answered for him. 'We were talking over old times, reviewing some of your father's old cases.'

'Which old cases?'

'You'll have to ask your father,' said Brook.

'Dad?'

'Billy Stanforth.'

'The Stanforth boy? After all these years? You've got to be joking me.'

'We're done now, son,' said Laird, putting a shaking hand to his brow.

'Are you all right, Dad?' His burly son rushed over to him.

'Tired out and that's a fact,' said the old man.

'Do you need a drop of rum?'

'Maybe a small one – we've been at it a while.'

'Have you now,' said the younger Laird. He turned to look at Brook with disdain. 'Time you were off, Brook.'

'Detective Inspector Brook,' replied Brook, enunciating clearly. He hesitated over his options but decided not to push too hard. He and Walter Laird still had a lot of ground to cover. 'I was just leaving.' He moved to the front door. 'We can pick this up later, Walter.'

'My dad can't pick nothing up later,' said the younger man. 'He's in his seventies and needs his rest so I'd advise you not to come back. Whatever business you had is done with. Got it?'

Brook had no fear of bullies and enjoyed cutting them down to size but he didn't want to poison the small pool of potential witnesses. He ignored the younger man, opening the front door to an icy blast.

'Did you hear what I said?' Laird advanced, unwilling to let Brook leave without an answer. The amused expression on Brook's face was not what he expected. 'What you grinning at?'

Brook's amusement was genuine. For reasons unclear to him, aggression always aroused in him the same reaction. Perhaps it was the sight of the less powerful trying to assert control in the only way they knew how, but whatever the cause, Brook had discovered that his apparent pleasure in the face of such hostility never failed to disconcert the aggressor.

He calmly held the younger man's gaze. Uncertainty lurked behind the belligerent façade and Brook knew he had his measure. 'Enjoy your meal,' he said from the front door. He turned but halted in the threshold. 'Oh, one more question, Walter. Have you ever heard of the Pied Piper?'

Sergeant Darren Laird sneered at Brook but his father's expression was blank as he shook his head.

'No.'

Just that. No curiosity, no amusement or contempt – a simple negative. Brook nodded and stepped out into the drizzle. The old man had heard the name before.

Twenty

BACK AT THE STATION LATE that afternoon, Brook knocked on Copeland's door and marched in. He wasn't there so Brook made a mug of tea and retreated to his stark office, suppressing the urge to search Copeland's office for the file about the death of Jeff Ward in 1973.

Sipping his tea, Brook mulled over his interview with Walter Laird. He wondered about the old man's relationship with the late DCI Bannon. What had happened at the time of the Stanforth investigation to cause an experienced SIO to delegate interviews with tricky witnesses like children to a detective constable?

'Or maybe he didn't,' mumbled Brook. 'Maybe it was Bannon who kept McCleary's mystery girlfriend under the radar.' *And, out of misguided loyalty, Walter Laird is covering for him.* 'And that's not all. You're talking to yourself, Damen. Please stop.'

'I will,' he answered a second later.

Brook took another sip of tea and turned on his laptop to hunt down DCI Bannon's personnel records. It took him much longer than it would have taken Noble but eventually Brook had the information he needed. He read with interest.

DCI Samuel Bannon's career was shorter than most detectives of the day but his record was distinguished nonetheless. Despite this, as he read Brook got the sense that something wasn't right. There was nothing actually on file but, reading between the lines, it seemed to Brook that something had happened in the sixties to blight Bannon's career. That there was no indication of a setback on the file didn't surprise Brook. Mistakes and poor performance were often glossed over and if you didn't actually know what the problem was, it could be difficult to spot. But Brook knew that chief constables often used coded shorthand on an officer's record to describe a career on the slide because similar references had appeared regularly in his own file.

Like Brook, Sam Bannon was initially much admired and often cited for excellent performance. He rose quickly through CID ranks and became a DCI at the tender age of thirty-eight. He was forty years old when he picked up the suspicious death at the Stanforth house in 1963, a case that was to be conspicuously unsolved, as was the even higher profile Matilda Copeland murder, two years later. Bannon was the SIO on both and Brook sensed that his career had started to turn sour around this period. It wasn't a nosedive, more a gradual falling-off of his clear-up rate and a sharp decrease in commendations. And according to the record, his health began to deteriorate at the same time because there seemed to be several long absences from duty which became a feature of his later years in the force.

Although there were few details, his absences were noted and this was reflected in the profile of cases he was allocated. From 1967 onwards, Bannon began to be assigned less important cases and he was shuffled into an administrative role in 1970. Two years later, Bannon took early retirement on health grounds at the age of just forty-eight and died at his home in the suburb of Littleover in 1978, at the age of fifty-five. There was no exact date of death.

Brook fumbled for his notebook, scrambling to find the right page amongst his notes.

Pied Piper

63 WS 1st?

22/12/73 JW 2nd or 3rd? Wrong MO

Dec 78? 3rd or 4th?

Others?

No 68. Why? FS?

Brook stared at Bannon's note then at the blank wall to think it through. 'If you're right, Sam, WS is William Stanforth, first Pied Piper victim on his birthday in nineteen sixty-three. Leaving out Francesca Stanforth, Jeff Ward was the second victim in nineteen seventy-three, also on December the twenty-second.'

Brook read and reread the fourth line. It made no sense. 'Dec 78? 3rd or 4th?' His brow furrowed. 'Third or fourth victim.' Brook sighed and his fingers twitched for a cigarette. 'Help me understand, Sam. If there was another victim on December the twenty-second, nineteen seventy-eight, why is there no record of any murders on that day in the Derby area?' Brook stared some more, his brain banging up against the facts.

'Or maybe it was just a theory and you died before you could confirm it.' Brook banged his head gently with a fist before looking sharply back at the screen. 'When did you die?'

He flicked through his pad and fumbled for his mobile, tapping out the number quickly. After a dozen rings, Laird picked up. 'Walter?'

'What do you want, Brook? I haven't spoken to Clive yet,' answered Laird sourly.

'It's not about Matilda.'

'What then?'

'Sam Bannon died in nineteen seventy-eight.'

'You rang to tell me that?'

'No. I need to know what date he died.'

There was a pause at the other end of the line. Brook got the impression Laird didn't need to search his memory for the details.

'My friend died in the early hours of December the twentieth.'

'The twentieth?' Two days *before* the anniversary of William Stanforth's death. As an afterthought Brook asked, 'How did he die?'

'A tragic accident,' said Laird quietly. 'He burned to death in a shed in his garden.'

Brook returned from the kettle in Copeland's empty office and wandered back to his chair. A shed fire. Coincidence? According to Laird, Bannon's death was a tragic accident, not a murder. And presumably it had been looked into by ex-colleagues.

Brook's laptop was still showing Sam Bannon's personnel inform-ation. Before he left the page, Brook noticed that Bannon's wife Alice had died fifteen years before her husband in 1963. Again there was no exact date but the odds suggested it would have been before the penultimate week in December.

'Nineteen sixty-three!' Brook sat back in his chair and sipped at his tea. The year of the Stanforth fire. The year Bannon had identified a young boy's horrific murder as the first strike of an unknown serial killer – the Pied Piper.

'Your wife's death might explain your negligence at the Stanforth crime scene,' mumbled Brook. 'But if you were distracted by grief, Sam, when did you get the idea that Stanforth was killed by a serial killer? And how do you know about a third or fourth victim in nineteen seventy-eight, if you died two days before Billy's birthday? Either you made a mistake . . .' Brook's eyes narrowed, 'or you were the next victim.' He shook his head. 'In which case, why didn't you die on the twenty-second?'

Brook banged his head with his hands, realising he was tired and hungry. 'This is nuts. I'm sorry, Sam. There's nothing here.' He stood, tempted to go in search of a vending machine but he didn't want to miss seeing Copeland. He had too many unanswered questions rolling around in his head and he was damned if he was going to write them all down.

McCleary reloaded and took aim again. He fired but the beer bottle remained resolutely on top of the crumbling drystone wall. At least dust from the stone had sprayed the bottle. Getting better. He took aim again, remembering to get his breathing right, and fired. The bottle disappeared from the stone. He took aim at the next bottle. It too disappeared, as did the next.

'Like riding a bike,' grinned McCleary, hitching his rifle and taking a roll-up from behind his ear.

He lit up then bagged the broken bottles and trudged back to the Land Rover through the mud.

* * *

Twenty minutes later, Brook woke in his chair, yawned and sat upright to massage his neck, feeling vaguely refreshed mentally, if not physically. Looking at his watch, he realised it would be dark when he dragged himself out to the car park so he sat still for a moment, enjoying the last call of that netherworld between sleep and consciousness, a foot firmly in both camps.

His bleary eyes came to rest on the small photo array of the Stanforth party gathered for a group shot, just hours before the fire that killed young Billy. He lingered on the two outdoor shots of Amelia and the younger children, posing in formation. Gazing blankly, he drank the details down into his semi-conscious mind. His eyes moved on but were drawn back. Then he stared harder.

A second later, he bounded from the chair and tore the formal shot of Billy and his grinning friends from its Blu-Tack fastenings. He also removed the tracing sheet that accompanied the group shot, identifying every partygoer where they stood. He counted the people in full view in both shots and compared them against the tracing paper and then against the guest list. 'Twenty. Plus the Stanforth family.' There was no mistake. All were accounted for.

Brook snatched the first attempted portrait from the board, the one ruined by the dog that had run across the shot. He peered at the willowy right arm reaching in from the edge of the frame to grab the black dog. There was a bracelet on the wrist.

'So if everyone else is in position, who the devil are you?' The question was answered before fully formed and his mouth fell open. He stared into space as he thought it through then scuttled over to the far wall to look at the large map of Derby. He found Kirk Langley then followed the single road south to Mackworth.

Radbourne Common was equidistant from both Kirk Langley and Mackworth. Brook tore across the corridor to Copeland's empty office and grabbed the picture of Matilda Copeland on the desk. It was her. The dog, the bracelet . . .

'What's going on, Brook?'

Brook turned to face Copeland at the door but no words were necessary. As soon as the retired detective saw the picture of his sister in Brook's hand, the Stanforth party photograph in the other, his eyes fell to the floor and he visibly sagged. After what seemed an age he shuffled, ashen-faced, to slump on to his chair.

'I might ask you the same thing,' said Brook, giving the old man little time to gather his thoughts. 'Your sister and Billy Stanforth are in the same photograph on the day of his death.'

Copeland sighed and reached into the desk for a small flask. He poured what smelled like rum into the aluminium cap and drank it straight down. Brook sat opposite, refusing a drink with a swift shake of the head. After another shot of rum, the old man nodded. 'This is a good thing. This is why I gave you the files. I was sure you'd make the connection.'

'I'm flattered by your confidence,' said a deadpan Brook. 'But if you wanted me to review both murders, why didn't you just tell me?'

'I wanted you to—'

'Never mind,' snapped Brook. 'I have a better question.'

'What?'

'When did *you* make the same connection, Clive?'

'Have you read Tilly's file?' mumbled Copeland, ignoring Brook's query.

'I've read it.'

'I want you to find her killer, Brook.'

'Then answer my questions,' demanded Brook. 'Your sister died in nineteen sixty-five, two years after this photograph was taken.'

'Yes.'

'She was only fourteen in this picture.'

'Yes.'

'So she was at the Stanforth house on the day of the party.'

'She was.'

'Then I'll ask again, when did *you* find out she was there?'

'When I reviewed the Stanforth case for the first time in nineteen seventy-eight, I saw those pictures and I knew straight away it was Tilly.'

Brook's brow creased. 'You didn't know until nineteen seventy-eight?'

Copeland took a deep breath. 'You have to remember, I was just a boy when Tilly died. As a kid, all I thought about was football and cars. Tilly was sixteen, a young girl on the verge of womanhood, an adult in so many ways.' He hesitated.

'Go on.'

'Quite often she had to look after me when my parents were out, which she resented.'

'Is this important?' asked Brook.

Copeland nodded. 'You see, it's not that she didn't love me, it's just that I was holding her back when she . . .' He choked on the words.

'When she wanted to be with her boyfriend,' finished Brook.

Copeland nodded again. He looked at the flask of rum but resisted. 'Sometimes she'd say things, funny things, adult things, none of which made much sense to me at the time, they were just . . . odd.'

'And that changed?' asked Brook.

'When I saw that picture in nineteen seventy-eight, I knew. And then those things she said, some of the sudden disappearances, made sense. You see, she was . . .'

When he couldn't finish, Brook stepped in. 'Matilda was Brendan McCleary's other girlfriend.'

'One of them,' smiled Copeland bitterly. 'Though Tilly didn't realise she was just one of the chorus line until the day Billy Stanforth died, you must believe that.'

'She wasn't a virgin when she died,' said Brook.

Copeland hung his head. 'She'd been sexually active for at least a year before she died.'

'How do you know?'

'In nineteen seventy-eight, when I found that picture, I remembered some of the things Tilly had said. I went up to Leeds to see McCleary in prison. I asked him if he was having a sexual relationship with Tilly.'

'And he told you?'

Copeland looked at the floor, shamefaced. 'Not at first.'

'But you persuaded him,' concluded Brook, a grim smile on his face.

Copeland glanced briefly up at Brook's eyes to check he'd not misread the tone. 'Yes,' he said softly, gaze firmly back on the floor. 'It was easier back then.'

'And McCleary told you he and your sister had been having sex.'

'Yes.'

'Must have been quite a shock.'

Copeland smiled weakly. 'You have no idea.'

'For your parents too. Or did they already know about McCleary?'

Copeland's face was wreathed in pain. 'Mum didn't know that scumbag even existed, never mind the idea that Tilly was sexually active. But I think Dad must've known because I remember there'd been words between them a few months before she died.'

'What about?'

'About where she'd go all day. How late she'd stay out.'

'She was still seeing McCleary.'

'Yes. Anyway, by the time I found out, it was academic. Dad had already passed away and I certainly wasn't going to bring it up in front of Mum. It would have killed her. I decided it was better she went to her grave . . .' He couldn't finish the sentence.

'Believing her daughter had been raped and murdered rather than discover she was the willing sexual partner of a convicted killer.'

Copeland suddenly smiled at the bitter joke forming in his mind. 'You make it sound so sordid.' His merriment ceased instantly. 'May I?' He held out his hand and Brook handed back the picture frame which Copeland placed reverently back on the table facing his chair.

'So you didn't realise until nineteen seventy-eight that Tilly must have been running up towards Kirk Langley to meet McCleary the night she disappeared.'

'That's right.'

'Pity you didn't know the year before,' observed Brook.

Copeland's eyes widened in confusion. 'How so?'

'Nineteen seventy-seven was the first time you reviewed your sister's murder, wasn't it? As a CID officer.'

Copeland stared. 'Walter Laird signed off on that review.'

'But you did all the investigating,' said Brook.

Copeland nodded. 'Walter told you.'

'Actually it's common knowledge,' replied Brook. 'Laird just confirmed it.'

A lowering of eyes before Copeland nodded. 'Yes, nineteen seventy-seven was the first year I was able to investigate my sister's murder. As a DS.'

'And if you'd known about McCleary and your sister it would have helped your review, no?'

Copeland smiled sadly. 'It would. If only . . .' He halted in midsentence.

'What?'

'If only I'd taken the dog out that night.' Copeland's eyes were back on the floor and Brook had the feeling he was finishing a different sentence. 'It was my turn but Tilly said she wanted to do it. She must have had a date to meet McCleary. I never saw her again.'

Brook pointed at the arm grabbing the dog in the photo. 'So why was Tilly at the Stanforth house that afternoon?'

'She was meeting McCleary.'

'Presumably she wasn't invited to the party,' said Brook.

'Course not,' replied Copeland. 'From what we knew of McCleary, from what Walter Laird found out about that night, we think McCleary arranged to meet Tilly to spite Amelia for some reason, to show her up for some imagined slight. He was, still is, a nasty piece of work.'

'When I interviewed Amelia, Tilly's death came up,' said Brook. 'Now I know why. She must have been livid.'

'I wasn't there,' said Copeland.

'No, but you spoke to Amelia about Tilly in nineteen seventy-eight, when you were reviewing her brother's case.'

'Yes.'

'What was her attitude then?'

'What do you mean?'

Brook waved a hand in the air. 'I only saw Amelia a few days ago but she hadn't forgotten about Brendan and his other girlfriend. And with your sister turning up at Billy's party, I can understand why.'

'You're right. She was still bitter in nineteen seventy-eight,' conceded Copeland. 'About Tilly, yes, but more about the way McCleary had treated her, I think.' He looked up sharply. 'You have to believe that Tilly wouldn't have known about Amelia and she didn't stay when she found out. She wasn't there when Billy Stanforth was killed. She came back home that afternoon. Otherwise, Walter would never . . .'

'Would never have been able to keep her name out of it,' finished Brook.

'No.'

'And that's why her name wasn't *relevant* to the inquiry, why he drummed it into all those children to forget Tilly was ever there, that they weren't to mention her name.'

'It was easy,' said Copeland. 'Kids did what policemen told them in those days.'

'But why would Laird go to all that trouble to distort an inquiry like that?' said Brook.

'Because Walter Laird was, is, a friend of the family, long before I joined the force. He lived just a few doors away in the early sixties, knew Mum and Dad well. And he always dropped in presents at Christmas. Small things like liquorice for me and Tilly. Maybe chocolates for Mum and Dad.'

'So in suppressing Tilly's name from the investigation, Laird wasn't protecting Sam Bannon, he was protecting your family.'

'And Tilly's good name. Don't you see? She wasn't involved,' insisted Copeland. 'Her being there *wasn't* relevant. But to have her name linked with scum like McCleary . . . you've no idea what that could've done to her reputation in nineteen sixty-three.'

'And at the time, you knew nothing about it,' said Brook.

'I was a child. I wasn't told. I couldn't have kept that quiet.'

'But you say your father knew.'

'Yes. I found out subsequently that Walter had told Dad, warned him so he could keep an eye on Tilly, try and keep her away from McCleary. It only made sense years later.'

'I see.' Brook shook his head in dismay. 'So many secrets, Clive. This is what happens when you start down that road.'

'I know. Walter regrets it but it didn't seem a big deal at the time because Tilly wasn't connected to the fire . . .'

'She was connected to the statements witnesses wanted to make,' said Brook emphatically.

'He did it for Tilly's sake, for her reputation. He went out on a limb for our family. He could have lost his job.'

'And that's why you're in his debt.'

'Yes.'

'And why you told him I was investigating the Stanforth case,' said Brook. 'It wasn't just professional courtesy.'

'It was both.' Brook grunted doubtfully before Copeland resumed. 'You've got to understand, Brook. He was more than a friend to me, he was a hero, a great copper and I wanted to be like him, a big-time detective solving cases. He helped my career. I owe him a lot.'

'So it would seem.' Brook tapped a finger on his chin. 'OK. Here's what I can't fathom. Walter Laird would have known you were reviewing your sister's death in nineteen seventy-seven.'

'Of course,' said Copeland. 'He signed off on it.'

'Against all regulations.'

'He did it out of—'

'Loyalty and friendship,' finished Brook, his voice clipped. 'I heard you the first time. But tell me this. Why didn't Laird tell *you* about your sister's relationship with McCleary and her presence at the Stanforth party *before* you reviewed her case in nineteen seventy-seven? You were no longer a child, you were a colleague.'

Copeland hung his head, his voice becoming difficult to hear. He took another cap of rum. 'God, I wish he had. But we're talking twelve years after she died. Walter assumed I already knew. After

Tilly's death, Dad told Walter he was going to tell me about McCleary but he never did.'

'I see,' said Brook, shaking his head. 'What a mess,' he murmured eventually. Copeland didn't deny it. 'What about Sam Bannon?'

'What about him?'

'How does an experienced DCI like Bannon allow a detective constable to manipulate witnesses and an entire investigation like that?'

'Because in nineteen sixty-three Bannon wasn't around a lot of the time.'

'But he was the SIO on a murder,' insisted Brook. 'He left the conduct of a murder inquiry to a detective constable? I don't believe it.' He thought of Noble. 'A DS, maybe.'

Copeland sighed. 'Sam Bannon was a great copper, Brook, but by December nineteen sixty-three he was a broken man.'

'Because his wife had died,' suggested Brook.

'You know about that?'

'I'm re-investigating the case, remember?'

Copeland smiled. 'This is why I gave you Tilly's file, Brook – your thoroughness. I checked your record on major cases and I don't care what Charlton or any of the dickheads at this nick say. You're streets ahead of them.'

'That's very gratifying,' replied Brook.

'You're angry.' Copeland's expression hardened. 'I suppose it's understandable. Does that mean you won't look into Tilly's death?'

'You were telling me about Bannon's wife,' insisted Brook.

'I need to know Tilly's in good hands, Brook.' Copeland waited, breath held. 'I won't be around forever.'

'Too much time has passed, Clive. I'm not a miracle worker.'

'Please tell me you'll try,' said Copeland. 'I'm begging you.'

Brook exhaled, trying to keep the irritation out of his voice. He hated conversations in which people needed careful handling. This was the point he normally stepped away and gestured for Noble to take over. His detective sergeant always knew how to manage the emotionally challenged. 'I'll do my best,' he replied, an approximation of a sympathetic smile pulling at the corners of his mouth. 'First things first.'

Placated, Copeland continued. 'Sam's wife had died in childbirth a few months before the Stanforth fire and he hadn't got over it. Walter told me Sam would put in appearances and try to do his job but he just wasn't up to it. He was still grieving. Also he had a newborn baby to look after.'

'The baby survived?' said Brook.

'She did,' smiled Copeland. 'Little Rosie was a battler. And with no mother and a broken-hearted father, she needed to be.'

'Rosie,' repeated Brook slowly. The notebook in his pocket jammed against his thigh, goading him to check a detail.

'Rose Emily Bannon.'

Brook was silent for a moment. 'And that's when Laird began to cover for Bannon's absences.'

'That's right,' said Copeland. 'Walter loved that man. He would have done anything for him. And it wasn't hard. Walter may have been just a DC but he was a damn good detective. I saw that at first hand when I signed up. He made DS in no time – DI too.' Copeland shook his head. 'The sad thing is, despite Walter's help, Bannon never really recovered and it became harder to shield him from scrutiny, especially if cases were in the public eye.'

'Like Tilly's murder two years later.'

'Exactly,' nodded Copeland. 'By the time Tilly was killed, Bannon was becoming erratic. Fortunately Walter was a DS, he could cope. He had to. Bannon was little help.'

'But Bannon's name is on all the reports,' argued Brook.

'Because Walter protected him, made sure he kept a profile, made him sign all the paperwork to make it look right. But Bannon was taking more and more time off, sitting at home alone, dwelling on things, drinking. You, of all people, must know what happens when you take it home with you.' Copeland glanced up at Brook. 'With that thing you had.'

'Mental breakdown,' said Brook softly. 'Call it what it is.'

'Right,' said Copeland. 'You managed to recover. Sam didn't. His mind started to go and, eventually, Brass started to notice. I never saw Bannon in his prime, only the remnants of the man. Tragic to see. The drinking took over and he began to unravel. I mean we all like a drink,' Copeland lifted his flask. 'Hell, sometimes we need more than one but control is everything, right? We have our loved ones to consider – wives, daughters. I only have Tilly and she's dead but that's still enough for me to keep a lid on it.'

'But Bannon had a daughter to see to,' reasoned Brook.

'It made no difference,' replied Copeland. 'He couldn't get back to what he was after his wife died. Tragic.' Copeland stood to stretch his legs. 'You asked me about the Pied Piper.'

Brook was taken aback. 'Yes.'

'That was a product of Bannon's decline.' He looked hard at Brook to ensure the clarity of his message. 'When he began to be overlooked for big cases he started brooding about his unsolveds and even incidents he knew nothing about. By the early seventies, he was drinking a lot. I was still a raw DC but I saw it with my own eyes. He'd retired but sometimes he'd wander into the station, smelling of drink, and try to take files away with him.'

'You didn't give them to him.'

'Walter did,' admitted Copeland. 'At first. He thought Sam might do some good, see something they'd missed.'

'Like the Stanforth murder?'

'Exactly,' said Copeland. 'Sam had the file for a couple of years after he retired. I mean he'd been a DCI . . .'

'Was Jeff Ward one of the files he wanted?' asked Brook.

'The file on my desk.' Copeland nodded. 'He wanted it but Sam had retired by the time the Ward boy was killed and Walter kept him at arm's length. It didn't stop him asking for it. By that time he was obsessed.'

'I see.'

'I don't know if I should tell you this but somehow Sam managed to turn up at the crime scene the same morning the body was found, only a few minutes after Walter.'

'Really? How did Bannon even know there'd been a murder if he was a civilian?'

'Sam said he was monitoring police chatter on the radio,' said Copeland. 'He said he was *expecting* a kill on December the twenty-second, waiting for it, like he knew it would happen.'

'Because it was the tenth anniversary of Billy Stanforth's death,' said Brook.

'Correct.'

'He was right,' said Brook.

'He was insane,' snapped Copeland.

'So what happened that morning?'

Copeland shook his head. 'It broke Walter's heart to see him. Sam was drunk and he looked like a tramp. And by now even Walter had had enough and he had Sam escorted away. I mean, there was snow on the ground, footprints to be preserved.' He shook his head. 'It made no difference. And because he'd somehow predicted Ward's murder, Bannon's mania got worse. He latched on to the Ward killing, looking into it on his own time. He wouldn't stop.'

'And so he came up with the theory of a serial killer murdering teenage boys on Billy Stanforth's birthday,' said Brook.

'He even came up with the name – the Pied Piper – because of the way Stanforth and Ward had been coaxed away from their homes.'

'It's pretty tenuous,' said Brook.

'You don't need to tell me,' said Copeland.

'Did Bannon ever say why the Pied Piper killed these particular boys?' asked Brook.

'No,' replied Copeland. 'But that's because he didn't know, if you ask me. It was just a product of his ailing mind.'

'Mind if I take a look at the Ward file?'

'Be my guest.' Copeland rummaged in his desk and slid a green folder across the table.

Brook opened the file then looked at Copeland. 'Ten years is a long time between kills, Clive.'

'Exactly what Walter told him,' agreed Copeland. 'Where's the escalation, right? It's absurd. Serials can't control themselves for that long. They need to chase the high of that first kill. And another thing – you'd expect the MOs to be the same with a series like that but the two kills were completely different.'

'Maybe there were others before Jeff Ward,' suggested Brook.

'That's what Bannon thought,' said Copeland. 'Before he retired he began to look for other suspicious deaths of teenage boys – same date, different years.' But Christ, this is Derby not Detroit and it didn't take Sam long to find out there were no suspicious deaths for *any* teenage boys on that date in any of the intervening years. Not a single teenage boy murdered on December the twenty-second.' He shrugged. 'But he wouldn't see reason. It was tragic to watch.' Copeland fixed his eye on Brook. 'You know how Bannon died?'

'A shed fire,' said Brook.

'Just like Billy Stanforth,' said Copeland, significantly. 'Though it was more than a shed, more like a summer house, as I remember. Bannon used it as a study, kept all his papers there, all his notes, all his ravings about the Pied Piper pinned up on the walls. Worst of all he even had a camp bed and a small stove in there. I mean, he had a daughter and a big house twenty yards away but he *chose* to live in that shed, even had his meals there. He was completely fixated.'

'It happens,' said Brook, quietly. 'And if he was drinking heavily, accidents can happen.'

Copeland grunted. 'Is that what Walter told you?'

'You're saying it wasn't an accident?' snapped Brook. Copeland hesitated. 'Clive, if you want me to look into Matilda's death you have to be completely honest with me.'

Copeland paused. 'This stays between you and me, Brook.'

Brook grimaced. 'More secrets?'

Copeland's face hardened. 'This is ancient history, Brook. Trust me. I need your word this goes no further.'

Reluctantly Brook relented. 'As long as no laws were broken.'

'Bent maybe.'

'Clive . . .'

'Walter was protecting his friend.'

Brook sighed. 'He seems to do a lot of that.'

'That's because he's a good man and loyal.'

'I'll take your word for it.'

'I know how it sounds but hear me out, you'll understand.' Copeland gathered his thoughts. 'It was December the twentieth, nineteen seventy-eight, two days before Billy Stanforth's birthday. Bannon was convinced the Pied Piper was about to strike.'

'Changing from a ten-year cycle to five,' pointed out Brook.

'Ah, but by that time Bannon had convinced himself that Francesca Stanforth was part of the pattern, even though she died an adult and her death was officially squared away as an accident. But because she'd drowned in a bath on December the twenty-second, five years after Billy, Sam enrolled her into his profile.'

'It's been suggested to me that Francesca might have committed suicide,' said Brook.

Copeland opened his arms. 'Same difference. It's still not murder.'

Brook rubbed his chin. 'And there was no murder on Billy's birthday in nineteen seventy-eight either.'

Copeland smiled in sudden admiration. 'You already checked.'

'I did,' said Brook. 'Bannon was wrong.'

'Thank you,' said Copeland. 'But that didn't stop him networking all his old contacts in the run-up, claiming his imaginary serial killer was about to kill again.' Copeland shrugged. 'Sadly he died before he could be proved wrong.'

'What happened on the night Bannon died?' asked Brook.

'Sam phoned Walter.' Copeland hesitated. 'To tell him he'd worked it out.'

'Worked what out?'

'The name of the boy that was going to die.'

'What? Two days before?' exclaimed Brook. 'Who?'

'Sam said his name was Harry Pritchett.'

'Harry Pritchett? How could he possibly . . . ?' Brook stopped. 'Did Harry Pritchett go missing?'

'How did you know?' said Copeland.

'There were no suspicious deaths on the twenty-second that year,' reasoned Brook. 'But if a missing person died and the body was never found, it might still fit the profile. No body means no murder, at least not one you can put on the books.'

'I'm impressed,' conceded Copeland. 'You're right. The Pritchett boy had disappeared.'

'When?'

'The week before but, Brook, Sam was wrong. There was no body because there was no murder,' insisted Copeland. 'Harry Pritchett walked away from home on December the fifteenth, nineteen seventy-eight, and was never seen again. Not in Derby anyway.'

'Then in theory he could have been abducted and murdered by the Pied Piper,' argued Brook.

'In theory,' admitted Copeland. 'But do I need to tell you how many kids go missing every year, especially from broken homes?'

'And was Pritchett's broken?'

'It was. His father was Irish, mother from Derby. Sean Pritchett had moved back to North London and tried to get custody the year before Harry disappeared. That's where Harry ended up, I reckon, although Sean Pritchett would never come clean. He travelled back up when his son went missing, went through the motions of being a concerned father for a while then eventually returned to Kilburn. My guess is he'd snatched Harry and stashed him with relatives down there until things blew over.'

'What were his grounds for custody?'

'He said the mother was unfit. They'd had another kid, a daughter who died when she ran under a car three months after father and mother had split up. Pritchett said she was negligent and he didn't want his son living with her.'

'But Bannon didn't think it was a custody battle,' said Brook.

'Course not,' scoffed Copeland. 'According to Bannon, the Pied Piper had snatched Harry to be his next victim.' Copeland was scornful of Brook's serious expression. 'He was raving. And drunk, according to Walter. Paranoid too.'

'Paranoid?'

'Bannon said his house was being watched and he was concerned for Rosie. He was gibbering like a madman that the Pied Piper was out to get him.' Copeland made sure he had Brook's full attention for his next utterance. 'When Walter didn't take him seriously, that's when Bannon threatened to kill himself.'

Brook was sombre. He could tell where this was heading. 'Go on.'

'That last night Walter managed to calm him down, told him to make some coffee and he'd come round in the morning and listen to everything he had to say, if only he'd stop drinking and get some sleep.' Copeland was sombre. 'That was the last conversation they ever had. Walter rang me at four the next morning to tell me the news. He picked me up and we went to Bannon's house. Another ex-colleague of Bannon's was already there – DS Bell. He talked us through what happened. The fire investigator had told Bell the blaze had been deliberately started from *inside* the shed. There was an empty petrol can and a camping stove under the desk where he would've sat. The nozzle of the stove was jammed open as though someone had turned it on and lit it. That's where the fire started.'

'Sam Bannon killed himself.'

'That's what happened.'

'Suicide note?'

'Not that we found.'

'Then why not murder?' argued Brook. 'Maybe he *was* being watched.'

'It couldn't have been murder, Brook. The door wasn't locked or barred, inside or out. Sam wasn't trapped. He could have got out at any time. He just chose not to.'

'You don't know that.'

'He'd become obsessed with the Pied Piper and chose to die like the Stanforth boy,' insisted Copeland. 'Even the way he died defined his obsession.'

'That's speculation.'

'No it isn't,' shouted Copeland. 'Listen. Bannon was face down when they found him.'

'That's not unusual,' argued Brook. 'The smoke often kills people first and they collapse—'

'And burn later,' finished Copeland. 'Yes, I know. But when that happens and a victim is face down on the floor, that part of their body is partially protected from the flames.'

'So?'

'So when they turned Bannon over, his front was burned just as badly as the back of him.' Copeland paused to let Brook catch up to the implication. 'You see, Brook, he was sitting at the desk when he set fire to himself.'

'Maybe he was drunk and had an accident.'

'He'd been drinking. But too drunk to crash out of a flimsy burning building when you're on fire? I doubt it. But either way, it's still not murder.'

Brook thought it through. 'So why did Laird tell me it was an accident if it was suicide?'

'Because he persuaded the investigator to fudge his report so it could be interpreted either way. That way Bannon's kid could get looked after; financially, I mean.'

'More facts massaged,' sighed Brook.

'Walter was helping a friend, Brook. To most people that's a natural reaction,' he added, with a hint of censure.

'And the investigator went along?'

Copeland shrugged. 'Why wouldn't he? A favour from one service to another.'

Brook shook his head. 'It's fraud, Clive.'

'Jesus, you're a father,' Copeland spat. 'Do you think the insurance companies were out of pocket? Fuck, no.'

Brook winced. 'Easy, Clive.'

'I bet they still turned a huge profit that year,' continued Copeland. 'But if Bannon's death was certified as suicide, his life insurance would have been invalidated and Rosie would've been left penniless.'

'But Laird had no right—'

'Sam Bannon was a friend and colleague with a kid who was

suddenly an orphan. There wasn't time to debate it. What would you have done, Brook? Tell me.'

'A crime was committed for financial gain.'

'Not Walter's gain,' shouted Copeland. 'Get off your high horse. Without that money, Rosie would have been homeless.' Copeland sat back, calmer now. 'It wasn't just the money, Brook. You're a father. Work it out for yourself. Walter didn't want little Rosie growing up with that stigma, that shame gnawing at her, knowing that her father had topped himself rather than live with his daughter another day.'

Brook was silenced, remembering his angry conversation with his daughter only a few months before about Terri's attempted suicide in her late teens. Leaving a loved one to pick up the pieces after self-destruction was the ultimate betrayal, the final kick in the teeth. He conceded with no more than a drop of the eyes. 'I suppose . . . I can understand,' he mumbled.

'Welcome to the human race,' said Copeland, sarcastically.

'Save the smugness, Clive,' replied Brook quietly. 'If this wasn't ancient history I'd already be banging on Charlton's door. Laird has let down the force. Not to mention your sister.'

'Matilda?' exclaimed Copeland, making a stab at indignation. 'What the hell are you talking about?'

'What Walter Laird did in nineteen sixty-three, had ongoing consequences. The fact that Matilda was Brendan McCleary's girl-friend at the time of Billy Stanforth's death was material evidence.'

'But I had no idea until nineteen seventy-eight,' responded Copeland.

'But Laird did,' said Brook, banging a fist on Copeland's desk. 'He knew in nineteen sixty-three and he knew two years later, when he and Bannon investigated your sister's death. It was material then, maybe even crucial, and McCleary should have been inter-viewed.'

'He was interviewed.'

'By who? Bannon?'

'No.'

'No, because Laird had to keep Bannon in the dark about Matilda's relationship with McCleary or compromise his actions in the Stanforth inquiry,' continued Brook. 'Laird was trapped in his own deceit, forced to conceal pertinent information.'

'That may be so but Walter did interview McCleary about Tilly's death,' replied Copeland.

'But it's not in the file, Clive,' said Brook. 'It couldn't be, could it? There's nothing in there about Amelia either.'

'Amelia?' Copeland was puzzled. 'What would Amelia have to do with my sister's death?'

'Are you so blinkered, Clive? Why would McCleary kill his girlfriend? Amelia had a much stronger motive than Brendan.'

'Jealousy?' Copeland drew a breath, reluctant not to concede the point. 'I can't believe she killed Tilly.'

'What we believe as detectives is determined by the facts, Clive,' insisted Brook. 'And there are no facts, no interviews, no alibis, not a single mention of two potential suspects in your sister's murder book because of your friend's dishonesty. There couldn't be or Walter Laird would have had to explain to superiors how McCleary and Amelia Stanforth came to be suspects in your sister's death despite living three miles away from Mackworth and seven miles from Osmaston Park, yet not owning or having access to a car.'

Copeland was silent, complicit in the deceit. 'Think what you like about me, Brook, but Walter Laird did his job. I'm convinced of that. He knew McCleary's history with Tilly and he went after him hard. Brendan McCleary *was* interviewed. McCleary told me as much when I visited him in prison.'

'And Amelia?'

Copeland hung his head.

Brook laughed without humour. 'I see. The webs we weave, Clive.'

'Walter did everything possible to find Tilly's killer.'

'Everything that didn't shine a light on his past deception,' said Brook. He shook his head. 'It must have been frustrating for Walter, being hamstrung like that.'

Copeland was confused. 'And what does that mean?'

'Your sister died, Clive. McCleary would be the perfect fit for her murder,' explained Brook. 'But poor Walter couldn't pin Tilly's death on her boyfriend without damaging his own reputation.'

'I don't—'

'Haven't you noticed?' continued Brook. 'Laird seems to have a particular bee in his bonnet about McCleary.'

'In what way?' asked Copeland.

'He had McCleary in the frame for Billy Stanforth but couldn't prove it,' replied Brook. 'And the year after, he went after him again.'

'Sixty-four? You mean the Charlotte Dilkes drowning?'

'You've reviewed the files,' said Brook. 'Laird was all over McCleary *and* Amelia, trying to implicate them in Charlotte's death. But he couldn't swing that one either.'

'I wasn't there, Brook. You'll have to ask Walter.'

'Ask Walter?' repeated Brook. 'I don't need to ask Walter about Brendan McCleary. He's even got him in the frame for Scott Wheeler's abduction.'

'That's because McCleary's a villain,' insisted Copeland. 'And Walter has no time for villains.' There was silence for a while until Copeland glanced at his sister in the picture frame. 'Which just leaves Tilly.' He looked at Brook. 'Do you want to do this now?'

'It's late,' replied Brook softly. 'And this place is like a tomb at night.'

'Then let's get comfortable. Come back to my house. I can answer all the questions about her there.'

'I can't. I have another call to make.' Brook didn't elaborate. 'Meantime, I need you to phone Walter Laird. He didn't believe you'd let me near your sister's file and wouldn't talk to me about her.'

'I know everything Walter knows and more but yes, I'll speak to him.'

'Thank you.'

'But it's still his case,' said Copeland. 'If he doesn't want to talk, he won't. You'll have to make do with me.'

'He'll talk to me,' said Brook, smiling suddenly.

'Why so sure?'

'Because I have something he wants.'

Copeland waited for an explanation that didn't arrive before handing Brook an address card. 'Come and see me as soon as you're ready.'

'You live in Shirley,' said Brook, staring at the card. 'Next to Osmaston Park.'

Copeland avoided the unspoken question. 'Mornings are best. I'm up by six.'

Brook stared at him, wondering whether to ask. He decided against it. 'Six it is.' Copeland frowned in confusion. 'I'm up at four,' explained Brook.

When he was sure Copeland was on his way to the car park, Brook fumbled for his notebook and glanced briefly at a page of his notes then returned to his office to check a further detail from Sam Bannon's personnel file.

Noble was still at his desk sifting through reports when Brook popped his head round the door. His head sagged on to his hands, telling Brook all he needed to know about progress on Scott Wheeler. After a curt greeting, Brook removed the three cartons of cigarettes from his old desk.

'I knew it wouldn't last,' crowed Noble, glad to be able to crack a smile.

'What can I say?' conceded Brook.

'How's progress at the CCU?' asked Noble, still grinning. He seemed light-headed with exhaustion. 'Any *potential resolution*?'

Brook shook his head. 'I'm dealing with memory and perception stretching back half a century, John. Even if I could guarantee witnesses weren't lying to me, I can't ensure they recall events correctly.' He took a breath and voiced what was beginning to gnaw at him. 'Know what's worse? You start by looking at the facts but eventually all you end up doing is looking at the quality of the investigation.'

'Tough beat.'

'Tough beat,' echoed Brook.

He left Noble and walked silently down to reception, for once oblivious to who was on duty. He caught sight of a new flyer with Scott Wheeler's happy face on it above the hotline phone number and the banner HAVE YOU SEEN SCOTT?

Brook picked one up and slid it into the Jeff Ward file under his arm and left the building, brooding.

Scott Wheeler – missing person.

Twenty-One

EDNA SPENCER PUT ANOTHER CUSHION behind her back to ease the pain in her hip but it was no use. After shifting position several times, she rocked back and forth for impetus, then pushed her walking stick firmly down on to the floor and got to her feet with all the strength she could muster in her arms. Regaining her breath, in what passed for a standing position she rubbed her hip, one hand holding on to the mantelpiece for security. Gradually the pain eased.

Whilst there she took the opportunity to glance lovingly at the fading picture of her younger self and her late husband in pride of place above the fire. The Christmas card from her son and daughter-in-law stood next to it.

'Still here, Eric my love,' she said, a sad smile counteracting the tear of pain in her eye. 'Bet you thought I'd be with you years ago, didn't you, my darling?' She felt the heat from the middle grille of the gas fire on her polyester slacks. 'I'll be with you soon enough, my love.' She laid a light peck on his yellowing image, arm in arm with her younger self, standing in the vast allotment at the back of their former home.

Edna tarried a while, warming her body and soul at the thought of a past she visited more and more – she and her husband working the allotment all hours of the day, all days of the year with barely a pause when baby Stephen came along. Only three days after delivery, the baby was introduced to Edna and Eric's pride and joy, where he would sleep for hours in his pram, shaded from the sun by a parasol, while they toiled over summer fruit and vegetables.

During the preparatory work of the winter months, Stephen would snooze contentedly in the lean-to shed, warmed by a few burning sticks in the pot-bellied stove. It was a wonderful time. Eric had spoken of it often since his death and she always dreamed that when God saw fit to take her to his bosom, the allotment would be the place where she and Eric would spend eternity together.

How she missed those times when she could talk with her beloved husband beyond the grave, take comfort from his presence, always keen to chat with her about the earth's bounty.

What would he think now that fresh produce was a distant memory to her? Would he be angry? No, Eric was never ill-tempered, even when the cancer had ravaged him, denying him his one true pleasure – a life lived in tune with the seasons. Often, during the final months, Edna would take a basket of fruit or vegetables into the bedroom and proudly show him what he no longer had the strength to help nurture, nor even the capacity to chew in his liquid meals. Did he ever show resentment? Did he rail against a God that taunted him so? Not once. Not ever.

In fact, Eric insisted she show him every harvest, every dirt-crusted root vegetable, drew succour from her account of the day's labours then gave her tips for the next season's planting that he knew he wouldn't see. He once even chided her for spending too much time caring for him when she should have been labouring in the soil, cultivating nature's gifts.

Even after his death, Eric had said he understood why she'd had to sell their beloved house in Overdale Road so she could afford to live on her meagre pension, abandoning the allotment she loved.

And now her diet consisted of biscuits and cream cheese sandwiches leavened only by the occasional bag of chips when she could muster the energy to visit the local chip shop.

Once the owner used to sneak half a battered cod into her order without her knowing and, back in her sheltered flat, when she unwrapped her meal and bit down on the snow-white vinegary flesh, she used to think she'd died and gone to heaven. That was before that foreign gentleman had taken over the business and turned it into a burger and pizza takeaway, doubling the prices into the bargain.

Edna shuffled across her cramped living room to look out at the bleak weather outside. The nights were getting longer and the temperature colder but at least her little flat, two rooms and a kitchenette, were easy to heat on a low setting. She wondered what the weather was like where her son and his wife were. Hot, they said in their Christmas cards which always had a kangaroo on the front as though she was a simpleton who couldn't grasp where they'd gone without clues.

She peered through the condensation of her ground-floor window at her woebegone herb planter on the sill outside. The herbs she nurtured so carefully in summer were just blackened stumps in the harshness of winter but, even in the hot months, the sun rarely visited her window and Edna was lucky if she could cultivate a spray of parsley to liven up her sandwiches.

She dropped the veil over the outside world and made her way back to her chair. Before easing herself down, she opened her weekly bottle of stout, her only luxury throughout the year. On Christmas Eve, if she'd been very careful with her pension, she'd get the annual council minibus to Asda and treat herself to a chicken leg, a packet of value mince pies and a half bottle of Emva Cream to celebrate the birth of the baby Jesus on Christmas Day.

'Lord, don't let me endure another winter on my own,' Edna muttered to the ceiling, holding back her tears in case God took against her selfishness. 'Take me now, Lord. Take me now.' She turned on her TV for company, took a sip of stout and depressed a heavy thumb down on the failing remote then sat back in as much comfort as her body would allow, before a soft knocking on the front door turned her head.

Brook drove away from St Mary's Wharf as light rain began to fall. Instead of turning off the inner ring road at Friar Gate and taking the Ashbourne Road towards home, Brook stayed on until Abbey Street where he took a right up to Burton Road. Crossing the ring road to the smart suburb of Littleover, he took a left turn before the lights and pulled up outside a large house halfway down. He checked the address against his notes.

He stepped from the car, pulling his coat tight against the damp, and examined the solid old building. It had three storeys with tall, old-fashioned, wooden-framed windows, looking out on a cramped but well-tended front garden. To the side, a wide drive wound past an old garage and round the back of the house, disappearing into the dark beyond.

Brook jogged up the stone steps to the front door and hammered on the heavy knocker. He fancied he could hear music somewhere at the back of the house – the brain-damaging pulse beloved of teenagers everywhere. He knocked again.

A hall light shone through the door's stained glass and a shadow was thrown across. A short female figure, face in darkness, pulled open the door and contemplated Brook. She reached to her left to flick on the outside light.

'Mrs Shah?' inquired Brook.

Despite her name, the woman was Caucasian, close to Brook's age, maybe late forties, with short bleached blond hair showing a touch of black root. She had a pleasant enough face, round with smooth skin, light-grey eyes and a strong nose.

'Inspector Brook,' replied the woman. 'I'm flattered.'

Brook had no head for names and faces but houses he remembered – unlike people, they didn't require anything of him – and he was certain he'd never been to the address before. 'Have we met?'

'I saw you in the papers,' she said. 'Your reputation precedes you.'

'I'm sorry to hear that,' said Brook.

Mrs Shah smiled reluctantly. 'Don't be. Like I said, I'm flattered.' Her voice was deadpan, suggesting the opposite. 'I don't usually get the brush-off from someone of your rank.'

'The brush-off?' repeated Brook.

'Inspector Laird used to send round some pimple-faced lackey to warn me about wasting police time. Now I get a DI.'

'Inspector Laird retired.'

'I know,' she said. 'His glove-puppet, DS Copeland, took over and others followed. And now the job's yours.'

'I don't—'

'It's cold, Inspector, so if there's nothing else, I'll consider myself warned.' She stood back to close the door.

'You've offered information about the Pied Piper before?' said Brook.

She tilted her head to give him a withering look. 'You know I have or you wouldn't be here.'

'When?'

'Like you don't know.'

'Humour me,' replied Brook. 'I'm still learning the ropes – this is my first brush-off.'

She considered Brook through pursed lips, not sure how to take him. 'Very well. Yes, I used to try and warn you lot every five years. That's the Pied Piper's cycle. Or it was until he stopped.'

'And you think he's started again.'

She pulled a simpleton's face. 'D'uh. There's a teenage boy missing, in case you hadn't noticed.'

Brook contemplated her. 'You're Rosie Bannon, Sam Bannon's daughter.'

'Guilty as charged. Didn't they brief you properly?'

'No,' answered Brook. 'And there is no *they*.'

'Then how did you know who I am?'

'This was your father's house,' said Brook. 'And the address you left when you phoned the hotline.'

'You should be a detective,' she sneered. Brook managed his one-note laugh. 'Well,' she continued, brusquely, 'message delivered. If there's nothing else . . .'

'May I speak now?'

She studied Brook with the manner of someone used to having her trust in people betrayed. 'You're moving on to stage two already?

Fine. Go to the papers. See if I care. I'm not ashamed of my past and you can quote me. My son already knows about it, I don't have a job to lose and I don't give a monkey's for the opinions of my neighbours. Got it?'

Brook made to speak but she slammed the door in his face. 'Goodnight,' he said to the door.

Brook dozed off on the sofa after his third read-through of the Jeff Ward file but woke soon after for a fourth. It was a heart-rending case. The boy's death had been a hard blow for a family already recovering from the death of their other son, Donny, who had drowned two months earlier in the River Dove, during a family day out to the Peak District.

Elder son Jeff, presumably still traumatised by his brother's death, had walked away from the house in deep snow, following a set of footprints on to Allestree Park Golf Course. The killer's footprints were small enough to belong to a child. Interestingly, it seemed Jeff Ward had tried to obliterate all traces of them as he followed them to his doom. Why?

Brook was drawn again to one particular crime scene photograph which gave him the shivers. An abandoned balloon, sporting the face of Dennis the Menace, was trapped in the branches of a bare tree. According to the caption the tree stood at the fringes of the ninth green on which the body of Jeff Ward was discovered. According to the file, the balloon, or one identical to it, had belonged to Jeff's drowned brother. More puzzling yet, the parents had last seen Donny's balloon trapped in the branches of a different tree, overlooking the spot on the River Dove where their younger son had drowned. *A child's balloon, perhaps belonging to a child who kills.*

'Spooky.' Brook closed the file, hauling himself up to go to bed – he wanted to be at Copeland's house at six the next morning.

He heard the shot a split second before the glass shattered and was on the ground as soon as he felt the impact of flying shards. Once on the floor, Brook scrambled round to the side table and switched off the lamp, before manoeuvring himself to the broken window and peering carefully over the sill. Another shot rang out, chewing at the wood of the sill by Brook's head and he decided on the better part of valour and sank back to the floor.

A moment later he heard the throaty roar of an engine, tyres squealing, and he bounded up to sprint for the front door. At the gate, Brook could only watch as the lights of the vehicle receded from view.

He turned to race back inside for his own keys, gathered them up and ran towards the BMW, slowing in frustration when he saw the flat tyre.

Scott Wheeler dragged himself to the pipe sticking down into his chamber from the surface, biting down on the searing pain from the worst of the many rashes along his groin and all the way round his buttocks. He inclined his neck to take a breath of fresh air. The cold chilled him so he pulled his blanket tighter, dislodging soil into his mouth.

He gripped the blanket under his chin, not daring to feel along his groin with his hand to assess the damage that lying in his own urine and faeces had done. The last time Scott had tried to examine the affected area his fingertips had been dotted with blood when withdrawn. Somehow that had transferred the bacteria to his face and now the edge of his mouth had erupted in sores. The only course open to him now was to keep as still as possible to avoid breaking the skin and dislodging the scabs. Ignoring the stabbing pains was not an option and gritting his teeth against them only caused more discomfort around his mouth.

The stinging in Scott's groin had worsened overnight. The skin was broken and infected, and for the first time Scott had felt like vomiting because his vision was becoming woozy and blurred.

An earwig dropped into his mouth which he spat out with an instinctive upward jerk of the head, loosening more soil to trickle on to his head. He pushed the back of a hand across his face to flick away the debris and brushed through his dry, itchy scalp, which suddenly felt alive with insects feeding on his skin.

The earwig wriggled along his fetid, sweat-encrusted neck and underneath his clothing. Scott shivered when it touched his skin but he managed to manoeuvre into a position where he could depress his elbows to the floor with enough force to squash the invader. Eventually, with a sickening pop, the creepy-crawly stopped moving against his skin and Scott was able to lie still, panting. Invariably such mini-dramas brought more tears and more tears meant more salt to sting his cracked lips.

He opened his eyes to the dim circular glow at the other end of the pipe. It must be morning again. How many days? He couldn't be sure. *Eight, nine. Gotta keep score. Like Tom Hanks on that island.*

'Day nine,' he intoned in his best Geordie accent, his face cracking into a painful smile. The tears arrived with it but he blinked them away to stop the salt falling on to his lips.

That's it! Pretend like I'm on Big Brother. *Cameras are watching me. People see me here. People can vote for me. Gotta hang tough. Won't get no votes if people think I'm gay. No more crying.*

He wiped his eyes with a sleeve and drank in the hope offered by the distant dawn. The sky was grey and damp but Scott didn't mind that. Not like he used to. Stopping in all day, playing on his Xbox when he could have been outside in the fresh air, moving around, running, jumping? Never again. Outside was everything now. His present, his treasured past and hopefully his future. Without this small globe of light to sustain him he knew he would be either dead from the fumes of his piss and shit or completely off his trolley. Then again, maybe he already was.

Water dripped from the pipe and Scott inclined his head to place his mouth under the drips. He was getting good at slithering. He couldn't stand, couldn't sit up and initially the effort to lie still had him first sobbing in frustration then screaming until his vocal chords seemed to shatter. But nobody had heard him. Nobody came to this place.

Place? Where was he? It wasn't Heaven, that's for sure. But it weren't Hell neither. He'd heard birds singing, seen them darting across the sky. And when the wind got up and whistled down the pipe he fancied he could hear the music of the air rushing through grass and trees above him.

As his underpants had filled, not moving had become the better option so as not to feel the squelch of filth against his damp, sore skin, imagining every itch and tickle to be an insect feeding on his body waste before laying eggs in his skin, to break out days later into thousands of baby insects also looking to feed . . .

Stop. No thinking. Thinking was bad. Feeling was worse. It weakened him. Scott shuddered and licked greedily at the raindrops to occupy his mind. Got to preserve his supplies. He'd downed one of the bottles of water straight after he'd woken up that first night and shouted himself hoarse to summon help. But then, when no one came, when no one responded to his desperate cries, he'd realised the need to eke out his provisions.

He stared at the distant glow of the sky. How far was it? Five feet? Six? He couldn't be sure but to try and force his way to the surface was impossible. He'd tried before, pushing against the boards of his prison, dislodging earth to fill his shrinking tomb, choking on soil and stones.

That wasn't the plan. That wasn't what they wanted. He'd worked it out. If they'd wanted him dead, they could have merked him straight off. Easy. But whoever put him down here didn't want him dead. Not yet anyway.

'Josh!' he croaked. His voice was hoarse from all the screaming and shouting. 'Anybody,' he murmured with no expectation of a response. It was no use. Josh wouldn't come. Josh had led him here, had betrayed him to others, and this is where he had to stay until they thought he was ready – ready to say sorry to his friend.

'Didn't mean it, Josh,' he muttered. Another tear leaked from the corner of an eye. *Don't cry. Makes me thirsty and I gotta preserve the water.*

He felt around for the bag of food and reassured himself with a quick count. Two bottles left. That first night, when he'd calmed down enough to feel around in the dark, he'd found the bags by the dim light from the pipe. There was a torch and spare batteries and when he'd finally flicked it on, the light had banished his cares for one brief moment of ecstasy. *Like scoring the last-minute winner in the Champions League final.* But seeing the limits of his new existence quickly doused his mood and Scott had turned off the torch to save the batteries.

But he'd seen enough to understand his diminished world and, as his strength had waned, he'd accepted it. And he had the torch. He could see enough to find the food and drink left for him. Someone wanted him to live a while yet. Six small bottles of water that he could just about tip into his mouth without dislodging more soil. A carrier bag full of biscuits and apples. The apples were gone. He didn't know how long they'd last so he'd eaten them first, which hadn't helped his diarrhoea. Had to be done. Despite the problems with his digestion, Scott knew the biscuits would keep. Eat the fresh food first. Then the dry.

'See, I'm smart, you fucker,' he croaked, his throat raw, his glands swollen. He looked at the grey blanket of cloud seething across the small disc of his life and another tear pricked the corner of his eye. 'I'm smart.'

Twenty-Two

Tuesday, 18 December 2012

THE NEXT AFTERNOON, BROOK SIGNED the paperwork and bade goodbye to the glazier who'd replaced his window. He hadn't slept a wink and trudged wearily inside to make tea and wash his hands from changing the tyre. Although he'd missed his appointment with Copeland, Brook didn't take out his phone to ring the number on the card, instead thumbing one of the two numbers he kept on speed dial.

'John. It's me. I was shot at last night.'

'Shot at? Where?'

'The cottage.'

'Are you—'

'I'm fine.'

'Who?'

Brook hesitated. 'I'm not sure. But I think it was a rifle.'

'A rifle? Think it could have been McCleary?'

Again Brook paused before answering. 'It's possible.'

'Why the hell would he want to shoot you?'

'I don't know, John,' said Brook. 'He's on the run and I suppose he could be angry. And thanks to me he's now a suspected paedophile.'

Noble was quiet for a moment. 'He wouldn't know you were responsible for that.'

'Maybe not. But I was in the papers the day we searched his flat. Or maybe he saw us there.'

'I can—'

'No. I don't want this to become an incident, John, so keep it off the grid. The last thing I need is more publicity.'

'But this is serious.'

'We can't be sure it's McCleary and I don't want Ford putting a target on his head.'

'But if he shot at a police officer . . .'

'If,' said Brook. 'We don't know it was him.'

'Maybe it was a warning shot.'

'Or maybe it was someone else, someone who intended the shooting to make us intensify the search for McCleary.'

'What does that mean?'

Brook sighed. 'Haven't you noticed, John? McCleary is the perfect fall guy for Scott Wheeler's abduction.'

'That's because he's a violent offender.'

'Forty years ago.'

'And a secret paedo.'

'I'm still not convinced.'

'You think McCleary's being set up?'

'I don't know. But if McCleary did fire those shots, he's making things very easy for someone.'

'But if he took the boy . . .'

'If McCleary did take Scott Wheeler and stashed him somewhere, then gets himself killed by an armed unit, we might never find the boy. But if McCleary didn't take him and the boy is never found, no one's ever going to believe he's innocent if he's dead.'

'So you think whoever took Scott planted the kiddie porn in McCleary's flat to point us in a different direction.'

'The only thing I know for sure is those pictures weren't planted by Scott's abductor.'

'Why so certain?'

'Because if you've abducted a child, you must have more damning evidence to plant than a few dirty pictures.'

'Like an item of Scott's clothing,' agreed Noble. 'I see that. What do you want me to do?'

'Nothing,' replied Brook. 'We don't want Ford getting trigger happy. And if McCleary has taken Scott and hidden him somewhere, we need him alive to show us where.'

Brook rang off and prepared to ring his daughter but was unsure what to say. If he mentioned the shooting, that might guarantee a visit and he didn't want Terri anywhere near him if someone was taking pot shots at him. Instead, with a heavy heart, he sent a perfunctory text to say he'd changed his plans and wanted to be alone at Christmas.

'I'm sorry, Terri,' he mumbled.

Rosie Shah opened her front door and frowned. 'What now?'

Brook returned her expression with interest. 'I got shot at last night.'

She was both astonished and angry. 'And you think I had something to do with it.'

'No,' answered Brook. 'But I'm reviewing your father's old cases and I think somebody wants me to stop.'

Rosie Shah stared at him, the frost in her manner beginning to thaw. 'Why did I call the hotline? I should've known . . .' She blew out her cheeks. 'You'd better come in.'

She stood aside and ushered Brook into the light, warm-coloured hall, the smell of spicy food and baking permeating the air. Brook could hear the same throbbing music he'd heard the night before.

A large portrait photograph of a beautiful woman hung on the wall. Facially, she looked a little like Rosie but her hair and make-up were from a different era. She was heavily pregnant.

'My mother,' Rosie explained, seeing Brook's glance. She jabbed a finger towards her mother's womb. 'And that's me. Excuse me,' she said, pausing at the foot of a dark wooden staircase, filling her lungs and raising her face to the upper storeys. 'Ollie,' she shouted, her stentorian voice belying her slight frame. The music stopped seconds later. 'Volume control,' she bellowed a decibel lower.

Brook heard a muffled male voice answer with, 'Please!'

'Please and thank you,' said Rosie, darting a glance at Brook. The music started again at a lower volume and she ushered Brook into a bright warm kitchen where the smell of baking was even stronger. Having forgotten to eat the night before, the aroma had an immediate effect on Brook's production of saliva and his stomach began to grumble in case his brain hadn't taken the hint.

'That's the trouble with kids,' she smiled, clicking on a kettle. 'You teach them good manners and they hold you to the same standards. I sometimes wonder if it wouldn't just be easier to leave them to work it out for themselves.' A shadow of something personal darkened her face for a second before the smile resumed. 'Tea?'

'Please. And thank you,' Brook added drily. She gave him the ghost of a smile in return. 'You mentioned ex-DCI Copeland last night, Mrs Shah.'

'Was he the one shooting at you?' she asked, half-serious.

Brook raised a stern eyebrow. 'No.'

'And you weren't really shot at because you came to see me, were you?' she continued. 'That was just to inveigle your way in.'

'Inveigle?' echoed Brook. 'Mrs Shah—'

'Please don't keep reminding me of my ex. My name's Rosie.'

'Rosie,' repeated Brook sternly. 'Why on earth would I need to *inveigle* myself into your house? You rang the Scott Wheeler hotline with information about his disappearance. People who do that are inviting a visit from CID.'

'I've already had plenty of those down the years,' she said.

'From Clive Copeland, you said.'

She hesitated, wondering whether to submit to questioning. 'He called once in the early days when he was a detective sergeant. Then DS Ford. The names change. The message doesn't.'

'Forget about the Pied Piper,' said Brook.

'There you go.' She pointed a finger at him. 'You haven't even changed the wording.'

'Presumably they say they're concerned about the damage you might be doing to your father's reputation,' suggested Brook.

She narrowed her eyes at him. 'You sure they didn't send you?' Brook didn't answer. She poured hot water into a teapot. 'You'll have to have Darjeeling, I'm afraid. I won't have anything else in the house. A hangover from my years in Bengal.'

'Fine,' replied Brook. He took a look around, noticing now the oddments of knick-knacks with an Asian theme. 'I've never been to India.'

'Go,' she said. 'It's a real eye-opener. A good place to find yourself, metaphysically speaking.'

'And did you?'

She smiled. 'I think so. Problem is I also found a husband and when that didn't work, and I realised I was pregnant, it was goodbye to globetrotting and hello to parental responsibility.' The oven alarm sounded. 'Speaking of which . . .'

Having opened the oven door, allowing more of the delicious aromas to taunt Brook, she removed a pizza on to a large plate as a slim teenage boy, pale brown skin and jet-black gelled hair, concealing dark features, shuffled through the door. He was in regulation teenage uniform, as strictly enforced as if he were in the army. Worn jeans covered bare feet and were held up only by his thighs, too-small torn T-shirt hanging loosely showed his skinny midriff and designer underpants, the only nod to materialism displaying the label as required by teenage law.

He walked into the kitchen as though Brook were invisible and approached the pizza plate. His face fell. 'This isn't Cheese Feast.'

'Oh, dear,' said Rosie Shah laconically. 'Better throw it away then. I've got some sprouts I can microwave for you.'

'Fun-ny,' he said sarcastically, turning to leave with his plate. He stopped cold at the kitchen door, returning with a look of impatience to place the plate back on the counter.

With a sly glance at Brook, Rosie rifled through a drawer for a mezzaluna and sliced the pizza into segments. 'I've got some salad to go . . .'

But Ollie was already on his way again, without having looked at Brook once.

'Thank you,' she prompted.

A muffled repetition trailed away. A moment later the music began again.

'Do you have kids, Inspector?' she inquired, pouring tea through a strainer. 'Or do I need to explain what just happened?'

Brook emitted his one-note laugh. 'A grown-up daughter.'

She smiled at him. 'Then you'll know.' She pushed a milk-free tea towards him.

Brook managed to maintain the remnants of good cheer on his face despite the tug of guilt and regret. Although recently reconciled with Terri, Brook had missed almost her entire childhood after the divorce.

'You also mentioned your past last night.'

She looked suspiciously at Brook as she had the day before. 'A few drugs when I was younger. *Finding* myself.'

'And they threatened you with that?'

'It was all very polite, you understand, never any unpleasantness. But yes, a word in the ear of a friendly reporter was the usual tactic. I told them to publish and be damned. They never did.'

'And now?'

'Now? As soon as the Wheeler boy went missing I told my son everything about my past drug use before I rang the hotline, so don't waste your breath.'

'What did he say?'

'Ollie?' Rosie shook her head. 'He thought it was cool. Kids today, eh?' Her confident façade began to crumble and Brook could see painful memories playing across the surface. 'If this good cop routine is a new approach . . .'

'Mrs Shah. Rosie,' Brook corrected himself. 'I was given your name and address by a colleague looking into Scott Wheeler's disappearance. You claimed to know something about a serial killer called the Pied Piper who abducted young boys. I'm not interested in your background and I'm not here to warn you off.'

She eyed him. 'Keep talking.'

'I'm re-investigating two murders that occurred in the sixties, murders that were under the command of DCI Sam Bannon, your father.' Her eyes bored into him. 'During my research, I found a reference to the Pied Piper actually *on* a folder that belonged to one of those cases. It was in your father's handwriting.'

'Go on.' Her voice was little more than a squeak and her eyes were filling.

'It's almost impossible to make any headway on the two cases because the remaining witnesses are either too old or too unwilling to help me. And I'm sad to say that your father's old colleagues belong in both those groups. They may feel they have a legitimate reason to close a door on the past but I've been given a job to do and I'm going to do it, no matter where it takes me. Will you help me?'

She nodded imperceptibly and tears of relief fell on to her smiling lips. 'Thank you,' she croaked, reaching for a roll of kitchen towel. 'You're the first . . .'

'Before you get too grateful, you need to understand something,' said Brook. 'If my inquiries find your father criminally at fault in any way—'

'Criminal? What do you mean?'

Brook paused, wondering whether to risk their new-found accord. 'Your father was retired. He was a heavy drinker too. Yet somehow he uncovered a serial killer that no one else knew existed.'

'So?' retorted Rosie, aggressively.

Brook was beginning to wish he'd said nothing but now he'd opened the door, he had to step through it. 'He also had mental health issues.'

'Dad was under stress because of what he knew and because he couldn't prove it,' she explained. 'It unbalanced him sometimes. What are you driving at?'

'OK,' said Brook. 'Playing devil's advocate, you understand: if someone with a mental illness had *invented* a killer and people took no notice . . .' Brook halted to let her fill in the blanks.

She looked at him in horror. 'You think Dad killed one of those boys to make his theory look plausible?' She was stunned but Brook could see the alien thought had lodged in her mind. 'So the boy in the snow, Jeff Ward . . . you think . . .'

'The possibility occurred, yes.'

'But why would Dad invent the Pied Piper?'

Brook shrugged. 'I don't know. Why do the mentally ill do anything?'

'How could you even think—'

'By looking at the bare facts,' said Brook.

'Such as?'

'Fact one – experienced detectives dismissed your father's theory of an unknown killer out of hand.'

'That's because there was no concrete evidence,' she said before realising she'd delivered fact two.

Brook held his hands open. She was making his case for him. 'Fact three, your father showed up at the crime scene the same morning Jeff Ward's body was discovered.'

'He was listening in to the police frequency,' she countered, but the doubt had taken hold.

'You know that for certain?'

She took a sharp breath. 'I was only ten when the Ward boy died.'

'Is that a no?'

Rosie lapsed into silence for a few minutes. 'Did Laird and the others tell you Dad had killed that boy?'

'The opposite. As far as they're concerned, your father was a hero who'd fallen on hard times. Walter Laird was very protective of him.'

'Was he?' She seemed genuinely surprised. 'So, all these years they really might have been warning me off to protect Dad's reputation?'

'Is it so surprising?'

'When you put it like that, I guess not,' she said mournfully.

'I just thought you should know that I'm after the truth and not a vindication of anyone's . . . position.'

She nodded finally. 'OK. I've waited a long time for the truth to come out and I'm not going to stop now.' She took a deep breath.

'This is a shock. I think I need a proper drink.' She took a bottle of white wine from the fridge and gestured at Brook, who shook his head.

She poured a full glass and attempted a pallid smile. 'Dad didn't kill that boy. You'll see.' She plucked a set of keys from a nail. 'Come with me. I've got something to show you.'

Brook followed Rosie Shah through the gathering darkness of a winter's afternoon, alternating between watching his footing and gazing at the large wooden building looming out of the shadows. 'Your father died in a fire in this garden.'

'In a shed identical to this one,' she said over her shoulder. She hesitated. 'I had it rebuilt exactly as it was.'

Brook trained his eyes on the back of her head, fresh doubts surfacing.

'You can say it,' she said defensively.

'Say what?'

'That I'm weird,' answered Rosie. 'That I'm obsessed like my dad.' Brook decided not to comment.

When Rosie stepped on to the low wooden veranda, the whole structure creaked. She grinned at Brook's sombre expression. 'Is this creeping you out?' Brook didn't answer. 'It's not like he died in *this* shed.' Rosie unlocked the pine door with two keys and walked into the blackness.

She snapped on a lamp on top of a large desk, throwing jagged shadows on to the walls.

'This is also a close copy of his desk,' she said, trailing a loving hand across the leather top. 'Everything is the same. Even the phone.' She picked it up and brandished it at Brook. 'It works too. Like I said, I had everything rebuilt exactly as it was. Mostly from memory. And a few photographs.'

Brook looked around. The place was more like a mobile home or a holiday cabin. The desk sat in the middle of the first room but there was still space for a fridge and a microwave against the back wall. Another door led off to a smaller room and Brook could see the end of a camp bed there. He turned his gaze on the desk, its surface covered in dozens of picture frames, all but one containing photographs of Rosie's mother. The odd one out was an old photograph of a handsome young Sam Bannon, leaning with a young Walter Laird on an old-fashioned Jaguar, both smiling happily for the camera.

'Dad had thousands of pictures of Mum. The one you saw in the hall was his favourite.'

'There are no pictures of you,' Brook observed, playing responsible parent for a moment. 'Even as a baby.'

'You *are* a detective.' She laughed flippantly but couldn't hold the mood. 'Why would he have pictures of me? I killed the only person he ever loved.'

Brook looked at her but she wouldn't make eye contact. 'Your mother died in childbirth, Rosie. It could happen to anyone.'

'It didn't happen to anyone, it happened to my mum. And Dad never forgave me.'

'You can't possibly know that. Or say that he didn't love you.'

'If he did love me, he had a funny way of showing it,' she said. 'He never even held me. Not once.'

Brook tore a page from his unwritten autobiography and read it out. 'Men have funny ways of showing things, Rosie. Especially love. And he was a copper. It's hard in our line of work to let things affect us. Sometimes we bury our affections down deep so they can't be used against us. Remember that when you think of your father.'

She shrugged but seemed pleased at Brook's words.

'Do you remember much about the night he died?' asked Brook.

'Not much. Officially it was an accident though, much later, one of Dad's colleagues told me it was suicide. He said they put the thumbscrews on the chief fire investigator to change his findings so the insurance paid out.'

'Who told you that?'

'Does it matter?'

'Your father's friends committed fraud,' said Brook. 'Telling you was a risk.'

'It was Detective Sergeant Bell, if you must know. He was in charge that night, though Walter Laird called the shots when he got here.'

'When did Bell tell you?'

'Three years later. That's when I knew for certain Dad didn't love me. He'd rather kill himself than spend another day with me.'

'He was ill,' said Brook.

She nodded. 'Yes, he was. And I was alone in the world – an orphan at fifteen, a mother I never knew and an unhinged father who committed suicide.' Rosie lowered her head but bounced out of her reverie a second later. 'But hey, when I was eighteen, I was rich. And ten years after Dad died, I used some of the money to rebuild Dad's shed, everything as it was. Like a memorial,' she said, her lip beginning to quiver.

Brook looked around. 'This isn't healthy, Rosie.'

She ignored him and waved a hand at her surroundings. 'This is how it looked the day he died.' She nodded over Brook's shoulder. 'Except that wall was covered in documents and photographs. His Pied Piper wall, he called it.' Brook turned to look. The pine wall was bare.

He turned back to her, silent for a moment, searching for the right question. It wasn't hard. 'Why?'

'The shed?' Rosie considered the question as though for the first time. 'My first shrink told me I was in denial about Dad's death, turning back the clock to when he was alive. My second said I was trying to please a ghost. Who knows? But it seemed like a good idea at the time.' She studied Brook. 'I know it must seem weird and I can see that with hindsight.' She laughed suddenly. 'Though in one way I'm glad I did it because when Walter Laird and Clive Copeland saw it they thought I was off my trolley.'

'And why was that good?'

'Because being a fruitcake, they no longer thought I was a threat and they stopped visiting, socially at least.'

'Why would they think you were a threat?'

'Because Dad didn't really kill himself and it wasn't an accident. Somebody murdered him and I think they were involved.'

'Can you prove that?'

'No, I can't. You said it yourself – there's never been any concrete proof. But my window was open and I did hear something that night.'

'What?'

'Dad was arguing with someone.'

'Are you sure your dad wasn't talking on the phone? It would be the middle of the night.'

'I heard another man's voice.'

'Your father rang Walter that night,' said Brook. 'They spoke about the Pied Piper.'

'It wasn't on the phone. The other man asked Dad why he had official documents on the shed wall. They argued. I heard them.'

'Official documents?' repeated Brook.

'Exactly,' grinned Rosie. 'Who would know they were official documents except another policeman?'

'What documents?'

'His Pied Piper documents. Dad had all the incident reports, witness statements, autopsy reports, photographs of victims, newspaper coverage of all the kills.'

'And they were destroyed in the fire.'

'Yes . . .' Rosie smiled and reached out to flick on a pair of spotlights trained on the bare wall. 'And no.'

Puzzled, Brook's eyes followed her to the desk drawer from which she pulled out a cheap wooden doorknob and moved to the wall. On closer inspection, Brook noticed a small screw, incongruously jutting out from the pine boards next to the door jamb as though someone had miscalculated the depth of the wood from the other side. She twisted the doorknob on to the inverted screw and when it was tight, pulled it. The whole partition was a false front on hinges and it swung away from the door jamb all the way to the adjoining wall, where Rosie fastened the hinged board in place.

The recessed wall and the inside surface of the false wall were covered in papers, photographs, copies of police reports, documents and newspaper pages. Brook's jaw dropped.

'The history of the Pied Piper,' Rosie announced grandly. 'The timeline of a killer who doesn't exist.'

Brendan McCleary readied a bin bag. He brushed a little dirt from the trainers and placed them in the bottom of the bag. Next he folded up the hoodie as neatly as he could. Before putting it on top of the trainers, he held it to his face and took a deep breath. He nodded in satisfaction and placed it in the bag. Next the tracksuit bottoms. He held the trousers up first to get an idea of size then folded them into the bag. They were a bit creased but that was to be expected.

It was time. He slung the bag over his shoulder and stepped out into the black night, cloudy and grey. There wasn't an artificial light to be seen anywhere on the horizon.

Perfect.

Picking his way carefully across the field, McCleary unlocked the Land Rover and threw the bag of clothes into the boot. The loaded rifle was already there.

Brook shivered, feeling the bite of winter on his cheeks, in his bones. He looked across at Rosie who was lighting a stove attached to a gas bottle to warm the place.

'They said Dad was crazy,' she said. 'Now you must think the same about me.'

'You did all this?'

'Who else? In fact I've made a few additions since Dad died.'

Brook approached the display to examine the multitude of papers pinned neatly to it. He recognised many of the documents from the Billy Stanforth file, though they didn't appear to be originals. Besides police reports and other official documents, there were yellowed newspaper pages splashing the various stories and photographs and maps pertaining to the case as they'd appeared in the local press.

'Look familiar?' asked Rosie, sitting on the desk to observe Brook. 'It's not the same as Dad's Pied Piper display. But I've done my best.'

'These aren't original reports.'

'They're copies. Dad was always meticulous about having duplicate paperwork. The amusing thing is that a lot of this stuff was copied by Walter Laird when Dad was still on his game.'

'But if he kept them in the original shed, why weren't they destroyed in the fire?'

'They were. But newspapers can be replaced.'

'And the police papers?'

She smiled. 'Those are copies of copies. Just before he died, Dad took everything off the wall and photocopied it at the library. The photocopies got burned when he died; but the original copies, if that makes sense, were in a steel box hidden in the house. And only he and I knew where. See, Dad knew he was in danger. He was getting close to the Pied Piper and he knew he could end up dead.'

'Murdered by the Pied Piper?' offered Brook, sceptically.

She shrugged. 'Or those protecting him.'

Brook lowered his head.

'What?' demanded Rosie.

'That's a huge leap, Rosie. Firstly, the fire investigator said it was suicide . . .'

'Suicide can be faked. Especially by people who know what they're doing.'

'You're suggesting police officers conspired to kill your father, a fellow officer and a friend. Why?'

'To protect the Pied Piper.'

'A killer that nobody knows exists, Rosie. Same question. Why would senior detectives in Derby want to protect a child killer to the extent that they'd kill one of their own? It's very hard to believe.'

She took a sip of wine. 'That I don't know,' she conceded. 'But they all lied at the inquest.'

'I know they did. And they shouldn't have. But they persuaded the fire investigator to fudge his report so you and your father wouldn't be saddled with the financial and emotional stigma of his suicide. They thought they were doing the right thing.'

'I never cared about the money.'

'You might if you'd been left penniless.' Brook stared at her for a while, gathering his thoughts. *Bannon had mental problems. Is his daughter the same?* He turned back to the papers on Billy Stanforth's death, looking at each in turn. Bannon had even managed to get copies of the photographs taken of the partygoers by Bert Stanforth on the day of the fire.

'What's this?' Brook pulled an unfamiliar document from its Blu-Tack fastening. It was a letter from the Chief Constable of Derbyshire delivering an official warning to DCI Bannon about his conduct following a complaint by a harassed witness. It was dated 1969. He showed it to Rosie.

'Dad had a couple of those.'

'I didn't see them on his personnel file.'

'Presumably they expire or something, like driving endorsements,' suggested Rosie. She became animated. 'Or maybe someone's removed them deliberately.'

'Let's not think everything's a conspiracy,' sighed Brook.

'So you don't think it's significant.'

'The fact your father kept it in his documents must mean something,' conceded Brook. 'But what's it doing with the Stanforth papers? This letter was issued six years after Billy's death.' He found his answer at the bottom of the page. The complainant was Billy Stanforth's mother.

'Ruth Stanforth complained about your father's conduct in nineteen sixty-nine,' mused Brook. He turned to Rosie. 'Any idea why?'

Rosie shook her head. 'I don't know for sure but he got that after he went to the funeral.'

'Which funeral?' demanded Brook.

Rosie pointed further along the wall. 'That one.'

Brook approached the jaundiced copy of the local paper dated 23 December 1968. The headline read, TRAGIC TWIN DIES ON BIRTHDAY. It was the story of Francesca Stanforth's accidental death, slipping and hitting her head on the side of the bath and drowning after consuming a bottle of spirits.

'Billy Stanforth's sister?' Brook raised a doubtful eyebrow at Rosie.

'I don't know why Dad kept her death in the sequence. I think he thought it might be important because she died on Billy's birthday. And hers. She was only eighteen.'

'So five years after Billy's murder, your father went to Francesca Stanforth's funeral and offended her mother. How?'

'He didn't say.'

'If he was mentally unbalanced it could be anything,' suggested Brook.

'Yeah, maybe he dropped his trousers and waved his dick around in the church,' retorted Rosie, sarcastically.

Brook's expression soured but he didn't rise to the bait. 'Whatever your father did, I'm not sure this belongs in Billy's murder book.' Nevertheless he returned the letter to its place on the wall. 'Though finding out why it was issued could change that. And maybe tell us why your father saw fit to include reports of Francesca Stanforth's death in his sequence.'

'That's always puzzled me,' put in Rosie. 'The Pied Piper likes young boys.'

'Perhaps he was looking for a death that fitted his theory,' suggested Brook.

'Could be.'

'I don't see any papers from the Matilda Copeland case.'

'Clive Copeland's sister? That was nineteen sixty-five – not part of the Pied Piper's cycle.'

'I know but it's one of the cold cases I'm looking into.' Brook stroked his chin. 'And there *was* a connection to the Stanforth murder that your father may not have known about at the time. You know the details?'

'Dad mentioned it sometimes. Poor girl. Walter Laird was distraught, apparently. He knew the Copeland family. Clive was just a boy and took it hard.'

'I know,' said Brook. 'He's still consumed by her death after all these years.'

'And that's unhealthy, right?' snapped Rosie, defiantly.

Again Brook didn't rise to the bait. 'What did your father say about it?'

Rosie became hesitant. 'He told me he felt guilty because he was in a bad way when she disappeared – it was a few days after Mum and Dad's wedding anniversary and he was off work, drinking a lot. Walter Laird pretty much ran the show solo though he got Dad to sign all the paperwork to keep up appearances.'

'How did your father feel about that?' asked Brook.

'Bad. But Walter Laird was already a DS and Dad rated him to do the case justice. Unfortunately, because Laird knew the girl, it became more personal for him.'

'What do you mean?'

'Dad couldn't help and Laird resented it more because he couldn't make any headway on it. It was around that time he started losing faith in Dad.'

'You can see his point, Rosie.'

'I suppose,' she conceded. 'I do remember one thing Dad said about that case.'

'What?'

She hesitated. 'I don't know if I should tell you.'

'That's why you should,' replied Brook.

She considered. 'A few days after they discovered Matilda Copeland's body, Dad made an effort and drove up to the lake where they found her.'

'Osmaston Park.'

'That's right. Dad had just parked up and was walking over to talk to Walter and DS Bell, who were interviewing the estate's two gamekeepers. I don't remember their names.'

'John Briggs and Colin Ealy.'

'If you say so.' Again she hesitated. 'Don't take this wrong but Dad spotted one of them looking over at him.'

'Looking over at him? How?'

'I don't know, sort of funny somehow. Staring. Dad wondered if he knew him from somewhere but he was pretty sure he didn't. And neither gamekeeper had a criminal record so he didn't know them from work.'

'Maybe he recognised your father from the crime scene,' said Brook, bracing for a reaction.

'Oh, so now Dad killed Matilda Copeland as well,' said Rosie angrily. 'I might have known you'd twist it. It's a good job I know you're wrong.'

'You have to admit it's pretty odd.'

'Why couldn't he have seen Dad in the papers?' argued Rosie. 'Dad was always getting his picture in. That's how I knew you.'

'Which gamekeeper?' said Brook, to change the subject. 'Briggs or Ealy?'

Rosie took a sullen slug of white wine. 'I don't know the names,' she finally answered, 'but it was the young one, the one that ran off.'

'Colin Ealy?' said Brook. She shrugged. 'What happened then?'

'Nothing,' she replied. 'That was it. Though Dad knew then the lad was suspect. When he disappeared the next day that seemed to confirm it.'

'Did your father think Ealy had killed Matilda Copeland?'

'I don't think so,' she said. 'He reckoned it was some weirdo neighbour living on the Mackworth Estate. And Walter Laird was pretty keen on him too.'

'Trevor Taylor?' offered Brook, rubbing his eyes, lack of sleep beginning to catch up.

'I can't remember. But Laird got nowhere with it. See, he was nothing without Dad there to do the thinking.' She was beginning to slur her words. She raised her wine glass to her lips but then put it aside. 'You look tired,' she said to Brook. 'You should take a nap. There's a bed in there.'

Brook studied her. The adrenalin had left her and she seemed to be brooding. 'I'm OK. And I'm sorry you've had to confront unpleasant thoughts about your father.'

She didn't reply for a while. 'How about a coffee then?' When Brook nodded she slid off her chair and left the shed.

* * *

Sharmayne moved her thumb expertly around her iPhone keypad, sometimes grinning, sometimes laughing at texts and pictures from friends. The building was quiet and she had the night to herself, her headphones thumping and her head moving to the beat. A light on her panel distracted her. With a sigh, she removed her headphones and depressed a button. 'Are you OK, Mrs Pinchbeck?'

A querulous voice answered. 'There's a man again.'

'What's that, dear?'

'He was here. The prowler. Outside my window. I saw him. Hurry.'

'OK, my love. Craig's on his way.' Sharmayne blew out her cheeks and flicked at another button. 'Craig. You there? Get your arse over to Jessica's room asap and throw a bucket of water over the daft cow. The old bat thinks she's seen a prowler again.'

Brook drained his coffee, not taking his eyes from the document-covered wall. The bulk of the papers belonged to the 1963 Stanforth case because Bannon was the SIO on that inquiry and had better access to the files.

The papers under the other dates on the Pied Piper's five-year cycle were much less dense and consisted mainly of local newspaper articles. Under the label for 1968 were several front pages reporting the tragic death of Francesca Stanforth on 22 December and her funeral in January 1969. As her death wasn't the subject of a murder inquiry, there were precious few police reports although Bannon had managed to obtain a copy of the autopsy report, declaring her death an accident.

The same paucity of documents was true of Jeff Ward in 1973. By now Bannon had retired from the force and had been compelled to rely exclusively on newspaper stories and whatever he picked up on police frequencies. Brook sifted through all the newspaper content, examining the different photographs, trying to find something of interest. The grieving family took centre stage in most pictures, as did snaps of both dead Ward boys, smiling into the camera.

'Not much here,' mumbled Brook, comparing it to the Ward file he'd read the night before.

Slumped on a chair, Rosie stirred at the sound of Brook's voice. 'Like I said, Dad was out of the loop and couldn't get his hands on police papers. He tried to tell them Ward was killed by the Pied Piper but they wouldn't listen.'

Brook returned his gaze to the wall. The next date label, five years after Jeff Ward, was 1978. Three more labels were arranged in columns around the wall and rose in five-year intervals until 1993. Each label had a Missing Persons leaflet pinned underneath, a young teenage boy frozen in time on the cover. Police documents were conspicuous by their absence.

Brook moved to the 1978 section where there were two sets of newsprint, one front page dealing with ex-DCI Bannon's accidental death in a fire, the larger batch concerning the continuing search for a missing boy, Harry Pritchett, who'd vanished the week before.

'Missing persons,' said Brook. 'No body. No murder inquiry.'

'Clever, right?' Rosie grinned. 'After Jeff Ward, the Pied Piper must have known Dad was getting close. He changed his MO. Instead of killing the boys, he abducted them and killed them later but kept the corpses hidden. Or else he destroyed them with acid or something.'

'Nineteen seventy-eight, Harry Pritchett. Nineteen eighty-three, Davie Whatmore. Nineteen eighty-eight, Callum Clarke,' Brook read aloud. He flicked up a stray newspaper covering the Callum Clarke photograph before letting it fall. 'So all these boys are technically still missing.'

'Correct,' answered Rosie. 'And with Dad gone, no one will ever know they were killed.'

'Copeland was listening to him at least,' observed Brook. 'He knew about Harry Pritchett.'

'What did he say?'

'The general feeling was Pritchett's father abducted Harry and took him to London when he couldn't get custody.'

'Bullshit,' said Rosie. 'There'd be a trail. Pritchett's dad wouldn't have the skills to hide his son forever. The Piper took him.'

'And hid him?'

'Exactly,' she replied emphatically. 'Harry Pritchett disappeared the week before Dad died. And when Dad realised what was happening, he found as much background on Harry Pritchett as he could and told everyone who'd take his calls.' She lowered her eyes. 'And that's why he died. Coincidence?' she challenged Brook. 'I don't think so.'

'So all these papers after nineteen seventy-three are your work,' noted Brook.

'That's right,' she said. 'The day after the fire, I bought all the newspapers carrying reports of Dad's death. And when I rebuilt the shed ten years later, I hunted down all the back issues for the other cases. After that, everything you see was collected by me. All the way to nineteen ninety-three – when the killing stopped.'

'Stopped?'

'Actually it stopped in nineteen eighty-eight,' said Rosie, looking at the floor. 'I just didn't realise for another five years.'

Brook fixed his eyes on the 1993 column. LUCKY JIM FOUND SAFE AND WELL screamed the headline.

'James Stroud was the only Derby boy who went missing that December,' explained Rosie. 'They found him wandering the streets of London, stoned off his tits.' She shot Brook an apologetic glance. 'As we ex-junkies used to say.'

'So he hadn't been killed or abducted, he *had* actually run away from home.'

'Right.' Rosie nodded briefly at the previous column. 'The Clarke boy was the last.'

Brook turned to the 1988 disappearance. Callum Clarke. Went missing on 22 December 1988 and was never seen again.

'December the twenty-second?' said Brook. 'That's late.'

'What do you mean?' mumbled Rosie.

'In nineteen seventy-eight, Harry Pritchett disappeared on the fifteenth. Five years later, Davie Whatmore went missing on . . .'

Brook squinted at the fading newsprint with difficulty in the dim light, 'December the twelfth, nineteen eighty-three. But Callum didn't vanish until the twenty-second, the day the Pied Piper is supposed to kill his victims.'

'I see what you mean,' said Rosie.

'Callum Clarke went missing on his way home from school after breaking up for the Christmas holidays,' read Brook.

'Tragic case,' said Rosie, tight-lipped. 'His family lived not far away. The final victim of the Pied Piper.'

Brook glanced at her then at the brand-new column, headed 2012. Scott Wheeler's face stared back at him. 'Until now.'

'It's getting late, of course you must stay,' insisted Rosie, nodding at the small room off to the side. 'The bed's already made up.'

Brook thought about trying to sleep in the gloom of his windowless office at St Mary's. He didn't want to drive back to his cottage, especially with an unknown gunman on the loose. 'You'd trust me with all your father's papers in here?'

Rosie smiled. 'I have copies of everything.'

'Thanks for the vote of confidence.'

She grinned and handed him the shed keys. 'So? What do you think?' She waved an arm at the wall.

Brook looked beyond her to the new batch of papers assembled under the date label 2012. On crisp newsprint, the headlines, 'WHERE IS SCOTT?' above a picture of the missing boy and 'HAVE YOU SEEN THIS MAN?' beside a picture of grizzled ex-con Brendan McCleary.

'I don't know, Rosie, and that's the truth,' said Brook, untying a shoe. 'Twenty-four years is a long time between kills, never mind five.'

'Maybe the Piper moved away for a while,' she suggested.

'Unlikely. In a series like this, wherever those bodies are, the killer will want to be near them.'

'Why?'

Brook considered her curious face. 'A variety of reasons. And none of them pleasant.'

She nodded slowly at him, assimilating his meaning, deciding not to press for more information. 'There's always prison. He could have been out of circulation.'

'You're quite good at this, aren't you?' said Brook.

'I've had to be,' she said, moving to the door. She nodded at the picture of McCleary on the wall. 'And if my dad was right . . .'

'Then our current suspect is innocent because he was behind bars when all the boys were taken,' said Brook, removing his other shoe.

'You're quite good at this, aren't you?' Rosie smiled.

'Why *twenty twelve*?' said Brook.

'What do you mean?'

'Well, if this is the Pied Piper, he's a year early,' said Brook. 'By rights, he shouldn't be striking until *next* December.'

Rosie shrugged. 'Maybe he's starting a new sequence.'

'Or maybe he's getting too old and this is his swansong,' said Brook. 'It's also possible—'

'Inspector,' interrupted Rosie, moving to the door. 'Get some sleep.'

Brook nodded. 'You're right.' She left a little unsteadily and Brook sat at the desk for five minutes, his mood grave. It was nearly one in the morning. 'I may not be as good as I used to be, Rosie. But even I know your father didn't have a crystal ball.' He turned off the lamp and padded through to the tiny single bed and, with a huge sigh, lay down on it fully dressed.

Twenty-Three

Wednesday, 19 December 2012 – early hours

I N THE MIDDLE OF THE night, Brook felt the vibration of his phone. After the second pulse, he realised it wasn't a text but didn't move to answer. Eyes closed, he was prepared to ignore it when he realised it might be Terri ringing about Christmas.

He opened his eyes, blearily checking the display. It wasn't Terri or Noble, the only two numbers on his contact list. He sank back on to the pillow, yawning.

Against his better judgement, but in accordance with parents everywhere, Brook pressed the answer button. Terri could be calling on a friend's mobile even at that time. Of course, it might also be his *Good Friends* at BT ringing from India to hammer home their Season's Greetings with an unbeatable offer.

'Hello.' There was a pause before he received an answer.

'Hello,' replied a male voice. 'Who's this?'

'Don't you know what time it is?' answered Brook, moving his thumb to ring off.

'Brook, is that you?'

Puzzled, Brook returned the phone to his ear. 'Who is this and what are you selling?'

'It is you, Brook. I'd recognise your toffee-nosed voice anywhere.'

Now Brook recognised the caller. 'Ford? How did you get this number?'

'Nice to talk to you too.'

'What the hell do you want?'

'That's a very good question, Brook.'

Brook let himself out quietly and double-locked the door. Instead of returning to the house, he walked across the damp lawn to the drive that would take him back to the street. Once on the asphalt, Brook glanced up at a light at the top of the house. Framed in the glow was Ollie Shah, staring down at Brook as he picked his way towards the road.

'Now he sees me.'

A few minutes later, Brook pulled over to the kerb in Mount Street and parked in front of the ambulance to walk the few steps to Edna Spencer's front door. Two orange-bibbed support workers were standing in a circle with the ambulance driver, chatting over cigarettes and stamping their feet to keep warm. As he approached, they followed his progress and Brook saw the condensation of their breath increase as they muttered something in his direction.

'Detective Inspector,' said one of them in greeting, barely able to suppress a snigger.

Brook couldn't remember his name but for once didn't agonise over his failings.

'Valued support worker,' he responded dismissively on the way past.

The unnamed support worker did not appreciate Brook's jibe about their relative status. 'Think we've got nothing better to do than stand around here waiting for you to sign off on a suicide?' he called after him.

'I don't think about you at all,' retorted Brook over his shoulder, to the amusement of the man's co-workers. Brook continued towards the ground-floor flat, pulling out a pair of latex gloves and feeling rather pleased with his reply.

Before he could get through the front door, DI Ford emerged. 'Brook. You didn't need to come round.'

'I was close by. Is Noble in there?'

'He's following up a lead on McCleary,' said Ford. 'We're just finishing up.'

'I thought I'd come and take a look for myself, if that's OK?'

Ford's smile was as genuine as he could manage but he didn't stand aside. 'No need, Brook. You've explained how Edna came to have your number. And I do remember her from the Stanforth inquiry now.'

'You reviewed Billy Stanforth's murder?' asked Brook.

Ford waved a hand. 'Not really. I carried DCI Copeland's coat when he interviewed the old dear once, after she'd moved to Derby.'

'When was this?'

'Many moons ago.' A grin formed on Ford's lined face. 'So don't fret, Brook, that's a case even good coppers haven't cracked.'

'That's odd,' said Brook, a tight smile forming. 'I'm close to an arrest.'

Ford's fake bonhomie fell to its death. He braced himself as though Brook might try to push past. 'Well, I've eliminated you from our inquiries, Inspector,' he said loudly for the benefit of the assembled support workers.

Brook heard approving laughter behind him and resisted the temptation to turn. There was an awkward pause while each waited for the other to move. 'So can I go in or not?'

'Like I said, there's no need,' said Ford. 'Clear suicide – case closed.' Ford stood his ground. 'My case.'

'Involving a witness in *my* case,' flashed back Brook.

Ford glared at Brook, eventually coming to a decision. 'Know what? Do what you want, Brook. Be a jerk and waste everyone's time.' He moved past Brook. 'Cooper can sleep-walk you through it.' He marched towards his car, shouting across at the knot of freezing workers. 'Sorry, you'll have to wait, fellas. DI Brook wants to have a gander.'

Brook didn't wait to hear the moaning and pushed through the door. Edna Spencer's body was immediately visible, sitting in the same armchair Brook had last seen her but now even the limited movements available to her that day had gone with her to eternity.

DC Cooper turned, surprised to see Brook. 'Sir?' He had been leaning against a wall but stood off at Brook's approach then turned back to the pale corpse of the old woman, eyes shut tight as though counting down to a round of hide and seek. 'DI Ford's gone home.'

'I saw him . . . Dave,' replied Brook stiffly, pleased to be able to remember Cooper's first name from their time on the Deity case. He moved to watch the kneeling scene of crime officer go through his routine. He bagged an empty glass then peered through the plastic bag at the spray of white grains pooled at the bottom.

'Suicide,' murmured Cooper. 'Name's Edna . . .'

'I know her,' said Brook.

'Course,' nodded Cooper. 'She had your number.'

'Has the PS done a preliminary?'

'Higginbottom's been and gone. No sign of violence on her. And traces of something in the dregs of a glass of stout. Sleeping pills, looks like,' said Cooper. 'There was an empty pill bottle on the floor. No label. Must have been old tabs – they save them up specially.'

Brook stepped forward to peer down at the old woman. As he moved, he noticed the red standby light on the TV in the corner, gazed at it for a second then dropped to scour the floor. With two fingers he retrieved the remote from next to Edna's armchair. 'Evidence bag.' Cooper obliged and Brook dropped the remote into the plastic bag and handed it to Cooper, who seemed at a loss what to do with it.

Then Brook lifted the upturned picture frame on her lap with a latex hand. Edna's youthful smile beamed out at Brook. She was arm in arm with her late husband who proudly held a large marrow in his hands as if it was a baby. He compared the face of the happy woman in the shot with that of the slackened corpse sitting before him now. 'I was here a few days ago.'

'How was the old girl?'

'Lonely. In pain.' Brook placed the frame back on her lap.

Cooper nodded. 'Makes sense then.' He looked gloomily around the tiny flat. 'Truth be told, if I ever have to live like this, I'll be taking the same way out, pain or not. There isn't room to swing a cat.'

Brook nodded grimly before walking into the tiny kitchen where he'd poured himself tea on his last visit.

'Nothing in the kitchen,' Cooper called after him. 'If you can call it that. I've given the bedroom a quick once-over. Bed's made and the room's spotless.'

Brook paused at the sink. A single cup and saucer, stained with tea dregs, sat in the stainless steel bowl, a dirty spoon beside the cup.

Returning to the tiny lounge, Brook began opening drawers and rummaging through the detritus of a life in retreat. He found hundreds of unsorted photographs amongst old birthday and Christmas cards.

'The cards are from her son, Stephen,' said Cooper, when Brook examined one. 'Though we're not sure where he lives yet.'

'He lives in Australia, Dave.'

Cooper's face creased in confusion and even the SOCO stopped what he was doing and looked up to listen.

Brook indicated the pair of Christmas cards on the mantelpiece. One was old and had seen many Yuletides. *From her dead husband, no doubt. Like Terri's – brought out every year in the absence of a replacement.* The newer one had a kangaroo on the front. He held up several older cards from the drawer. 'Sydney Opera House, crocodiles, Aboriginal designs.'

DC Cooper smiled. 'Right.' He took out a pen and made a note.

Brook pulled out more drawers – ironed handkerchiefs, odd gloves, scarves, a bag of old coins containing pennies, halfpennies and threepenny bits.

'Why do old people keep those when they can't use them?' said Cooper.

Brook looked up briefly. 'She's holding on to the past, Dave. It was a time when she was happy.'

Cooper smiled patiently. He was hoping to get this over and get home to a warm bed but still Brook searched. Another drawer contained the meagre medical supplies a pensioner surviving on the margins could afford – cheap aspirin and antacid lozenges, a few dog-eared sticking plasters and a roll of grubby elasticated bandages studded with safety pins.

'No pills,' Brook muttered. He opened more drawers filled with pens, drawing pins, crossword books, puzzle magazines and packets of seeds for a variety of herbs.

Brook broke off to gaze at the desultory Christmas streamers and the minute fake tree off in one corner. Was this the future that beckoned all elderly partners of the deceased? A life of penury lived out in a bare room with only the local newsagent for daily conversation. For once Brook took some comfort from his gender. For a change, men got the sweet deal. Shorter life expectancy. Men didn't linger when decay summoned. A short illness, a quick death and a tearful send-off, assuming there was anyone left to care. *Hallelujah*.

'What about paperwork?' prompted Brook. 'I don't see any cash or utility bills.'

'Not seen any.'

'You've checked the safe?' asked Brook.

'Safe?' Cooper's mouth creased in amusement.

Brook knelt beside the frail corpse of Edna Spencer, sitting upright in her chair, head lolling slightly to the side. 'Your parents are still alive, I take it.'

'They are. Though Dad's a bit . . .'

'You've got this to come then.'

'What?'

'Well, if Edna's anything like my mother . . .' Brook slid a hand down the side of the armchair and felt around before plucking out a large brown envelope and tossing it to Cooper. 'The safe,' Brook said as he stood. 'If you're old, you literally sit on your valuables. You don't use banks because you can't get to them. You pay all your bills in cash at the post office when you collect your pension and never get behind in case you die and your reputation is besmirched by debt.'

Cooper rummaged in the straining envelope, hearing the chink of coins at the bottom.

'You'll find upcoming bills in envelopes with the exact money tucked inside. If I were a betting man, I'm guessing you'll also find a fully paid-up funeral policy down there too.'

Cooper discharged a little laugh and held out a document to show Brook. GUARANTEED FUNERAL PLAN. 'Bang on.'

'Sad, isn't it?' said Brook, looking at Edna's slackened face. 'Old people prepare everything so when they go they won't be a burden.'

'Makes our job easier when it's this tidy,' said Cooper.

'You call this tidy?' Brook eyed the young detective, wondering when to break the bad news. He took a final three-sixty around the room. No pictures of the son, interestingly. Not on display at least. Two cards on the mantel. Brook picked up the old one, yellowed and warped, propped against the chimney breast to stay upright.

'With you forever, my darling Edna. All my love, Eric.' Sombre, Brook put the card back on the mantel.

The SOCO stood off his haunches, pulling off his gloves. 'I'm done, Coop. You can take her away.'

'Thanks.' Cooper moved towards the door.

'Wait,' said Brook. 'Get a team in here. I want the whole place dusted, including the TV remote and the crockery in the sink. The killer may have touched them.'

'Killer?' exclaimed Cooper. 'I don't understand. DI Ford has already called it – suicide.'

Brook stared at the young detective, tight-lipped, his reaction expected. 'Someone else was here. Mrs Spencer was murdered.'

Cooper was still not processing the information. 'Murdered?' The SOCO stood mute, waiting for a winner. 'There's no direct evidence of that,' reasoned Cooper.

'But there's plenty of indirect evidence,' said Brook. When Cooper splayed his hands for clarification, Brook continued, realising the absurdity of what he was about to say. 'For one thing, she left the TV on standby.'

Cooper's head spun round to the television in disbelief. 'The TV?'

'Trust me,' said Brook. 'If she was going to kill herself, she would have switched off every single appliance at the plug to avoid running up a bill. There's also an unwashed teacup in the sink. She wouldn't leave that. It's slovenly.'

The SOCO smirked but muffled it quickly while Cooper just stared, his forehead creased in confusion. 'But who would want to murder the old girl?'

'I don't know, Dave,' said Brook patiently. 'That's what a murder inquiry is for.'

'You think it was McCleary because he lives in the next block,' offered Cooper.

'Is that why DI Ford got the call?' asked Brook.

Cooper nodded. 'The old girl and McCleary go way back. DI Ford thought maybe she knew where he was hiding and McCleary wanted to shut her up. But he discounted it straight away because—'

'DI Ford's right,' conceded Brook. 'McCleary would've killed her with his hands. Somebody a little more subtle was here but the result's the same.'

Cooper hesitated. 'I don't know, sir. DI Ford said . . .'

'DC Cooper . . . Dave.' Brook smiled to reassure. 'I wouldn't be in here if Frank hadn't asked me to take a look.'

'And?'

'And he told me to do what I want.' Brook pointed an emphatic digit at Cooper. 'Those were his exact words. Now get a full team in here and talk to the next-door neighbour, find out if she heard anything.'

It was gone five o'clock in the morning when Brook left the sheltered flat of Edna Spencer. He was mentally and physically exhausted. Having considered his options on the way back to the BMW, Brook drove the ten miles out to the attractive village of Shirley and parked across the road from his destination. Rosie Shah's shed keys were on the passenger seat so Brook opened the glove compartment to throw them in. The forgotten junk mail from Brendan McCleary's flat was still there and Brook took out the three envelopes to flick through before disposal. One letter offered cheap dry-cleaning, one was from the Caravan Club and the other was advertising the benefits of satellite television. Brook tossed them on the passenger seat. Then he set the alarm on his mobile, closed his eyes and fell promptly to sleep.

Forty-five minutes later Brook woke to the beeping alarm. He turned off his phone and looked over to the house. There was a faint light on downstairs so Brook roused himself to walk across the frosty road and knock on the door.

Copeland's puzzled expression gave way to relief and he checked his watch. 'Brook. Six o'clock. You weren't kidding. Expected you yesterday.'

Brook decided not to mention the shooting. 'Something came up.'

'Come in. You look shattered.'

'I'm fine,' replied Brook.

'This job will do that to you,' continued Copeland, as though Brook hadn't said anything.

Copeland showed Brook through the house to a conservatory facing out on to open countryside and gestured him to one of three ample armchairs before returning to the kitchen to make tea. No plants, no cane furniture, no glass-topped tables. Copeland was clearly and resolutely single.

Brook slumped in the chair, staring blankly out at the dark sky, threatening clouds billowed on the murky horizon. He could just make out the trees that formed the boundary of the Osmaston Park Estate half a mile away.

Copeland returned with a mug for Brook. 'Can I make you a bacon sandwich?'

'This is fine,' replied Brook, taking a life-giving sip of the milky brown liquid.

'Like the house?'

'Very nice,' said Brook mechanically. 'No view of the lake though.'

Copeland tried to smile. 'Believe me, if there was a house with a view of the lake, I'd be living there.'

Brook raised an eyebrow. 'And does it help, living so close to where Tilly was found?'

Copeland shook his head. 'Not any more. When I bought this place thirty years ago I thought it might. But it's a long time to stare out of a window, looking for ghosts.'

'Amelia Stanforth did it for longer,' said Brook.

'True.' Copeland took a deep breath and tried to get to business. 'I spoke to Walter and told him you had my blessing to look into Tilly's death.'

'What did he say?'

Copeland hesitated before finding the right words. 'He's not happy but he'll try to answer your questions.'

'Try?'

'He's an old man . . .'

'And his memory's not so good,' finished Brook. 'Yes, he said.'

'I hope you don't mind, I mentioned you knew about the mix-up.'

'What mix-up?'

'Him thinking I already knew about Tilly and Brendan McCleary when I reviewed her case in seventy-seven.'

Brook took a thoughtful sip of tea. 'How did he react?'

'He's worried you'll make a song and dance over nothing.'

Brook grunted. 'He had seniority. Let him worry.'

'Look, protecting Tilly's good name didn't compromise either investigation, Brook. I wish you'd accept that.'

Brook decided to change tack. The bond between Laird and Copeland was too strong for a frontal assault. 'I re-read your sister's file.'

'Anything jump out at you?'

'Should it?'

Copeland shrugged. 'I just thought . . . a fresh pair of eyes.'

'I noticed a lack of information about Tilly's boyfriends.' Brook's smile was tight. 'That all makes sense now, though.'

Copeland didn't rise to the bait. 'Anything else?'

'The daunting number of potential suspects.'

'I know.'

'I called on one of them,' said Brook, watching his host for a response. 'The shopkeeper's surviving son, where Matilda worked.'

Copeland nodded uncomfortably. 'Winston Barney.'

Brook watched Copeland to turn up the heat; silence was his favourite weapon and, as Barney had refused to be interviewed, his only one. Copeland was the first to crack.

'I'm prepared for anything you throw at me, Brook. I have no excuses. I only hope you can understand what I was going through.' Still Brook said nothing. 'The first time I got my hands on Tilly's file . . . I . . .'

'You were overenthusiastic,' put in Brook drily to move things along.

Copeland put a hand to his brow. 'That's putting it mildly. You see, I'd waited twelve years – years of pent-up frustration – waiting for the chance to do something meaningful for Tilly, something in an official capacity. And when I got that opportunity, I admit I went at it like a bull in a china shop.'

'And that included intimidating witnesses,' said Brook.

A pause. 'Yes.'

'Physically?'

'Sometimes.'

'Winston Barney? His brother Arthur?' offered Brook.

'The father too, I think. I forget. I'm not proud, Brook. But I wouldn't be the first copper to cut a corner or two.' Copeland's accusatory glance found its mark.

'And there it is,' nodded Brook, standing. 'I wonder it took you so long.'

Copeland stood to block Brook's exit. 'I shouldn't have said that, I'm sorry. Please don't go. I meant no offence.'

'Two things you should know about me, Clive,' said Brook, still on his feet. 'First, I never take offence. Second, I won't be played.'

'Played?'

'If you think for one minute that my disciplinary record can be used to shut me up if I find something irregular—'

'No,' insisted Copeland. 'I never thought that. I'm sorry. Please sit.'

After a suitable pause to drive the point home, Brook sank back into the armchair.

'It's just . . . reliving the past is difficult, facing up to what I did, the kind of copper it made me,' said Copeland, also sitting now that Brook was back in his chair. 'I'm very ashamed and I'd apologise to Barney . . . if I could.'

'I don't think that's wise.'

'No.'

'Was he ever a credible suspect?'

'There were no witnesses to the actual abduction, Brook, so at some point they all were. Arthur, Winston, their father Derek. The gamekeepers . . .'

'John Briggs and Colin Ealy.'

'Yes.'

'Your neighbour, Trevor Taylor.'

Copeland looked out at the lightening sky. 'Him too.'

'But not Brendan McCleary.'

Copeland's voice tightened, expecting more disapproval about the cover-up. 'Not in nineteen seventy-seven, as I only found out about him and Tilly the year after. And with Ealy still in the wind, I concentrated on the Mackworth witnesses.'

'Plenty of those that night,' said Brook.

'Yes.'

'And Trevor Taylor was the last to see her alive, running up the lane towards Kirk Langley.'

'He was,' agreed Copeland.

'The files imply that Laird and Bannon were keen on Taylor,' said Brook.

'They were. Apart from being *last to see*, all the other witnesses placed Tilly on the estate.'

'And he was a single man with his own home,' added Brook. 'Privacy, if needed.'

'Exactly,' agreed Copeland. 'He looked every bit the prime suspect. I'd known him since I was a kid and he was always a bit weird. A loner, low intelligence, probably low self-esteem too—'

'But he didn't have any transport,' put in Brook.

'His mother had a car,' replied Copeland.

'I didn't see any paperwork on that,' said Brook softly. 'Wasn't she interviewed?'

'Of course,' said Copeland. 'According to Walter, Mrs Taylor said the car hadn't been out of her garage for months.'

'So why is there no record of that in the file?'

'I was a kid at the time,' answered Copeland. 'You'll have to ask Walter.'

'Let's hope he can remember.'

'That's unnecessary, Brook,' protested Copeland. 'Tilly died forty-seven years ago. In cases this cold, often whole files have been misplaced. I'm afraid it's the nature of the beast.'

Brook shrugged. 'So, according to Walter, did he believe Taylor's mother about the car?'

'Not without corroboration,' replied Copeland. 'But Taylor was put on the back burner because suddenly they had a better suspect.'

'Colin Ealy,' suggested Brook.

'Right,' said Copeland. 'He disappeared. A young lad working as an assistant gamekeeper, on his own for much of the time, access to transport – it looked all over bar the shouting.'

'But it wasn't.'

Copeland took a deep breath. 'In hindsight, no.'

'What about the van?'

'Ealy was using it the night Tilly disappeared.'

'According to Briggs?'

'True,' said Copeland. 'But the work log backed him up. Ealy had signed for the van. He was shifting logs from the park until late that night. Nobody saw him, though Briggs said the logs had been moved as directed.'

'He could have moved them the day after,' proposed Brook.

'True.'

'And the van?'

'The techs worked it over pretty thoroughly but found nothing to connect Ealy to my sister. And no forensics at his parents' house either.'

Brook drained his tea. 'So why do *you* think Colin Ealy ran?'

Copeland shrugged. 'I don't know. If he didn't kill Tilly . . .'

'What did John Briggs think?'

'You've read the file. Briggs was in the dark. He'd worked with Ealy for about a year. Said he was hard-working and reliable. A bit of a dreamer. Not the brightest.'

'Anything else?'

Copeland hesitated. 'Briggs did say one thing which may not be in the file. He said Ealy was very nervous all of a sudden. The day before he disappeared, Briggs said the lad became agitated and edgy.'

'Do you know how hard Laird went at him?' asked Brook.

'Pretty hard according to Walter.'

'And Briggs?'

'The same.'

'And what about you twelve years later?' asked Brook.

Copeland hung his head briefly. 'I gave Briggs a hard time, I won't deny it.'

'Is that code for an assault?'

Copeland's face betrayed anger but he controlled it. 'I want to make something clear, Brook. I didn't assault Briggs. Or the Barneys, for that matter. I stepped over the line with them, yes. But the most I did was put the fear of God into them that if they lied to me they'd never see the light of day again. The only time I laid hands on them was maybe to grab some lapels to stick my face into theirs but I never hit them, Brook. And that's the truth.'

'That's a comfort then.'

Copeland couldn't contain himself any longer. 'My sister was murdered, Brook. Possibly raped as well . . .'

'Which is why you shouldn't have been anywhere near it, Clive,' retorted Brook forcefully. 'Your judgement was impaired.'

'Don't you think I know that?' shouted Copeland. The atmosphere crackled in the ensuing silence and Copeland's whole body was stiff with tension. He sank back into his chair, defeated. 'Of course I knew but by then it was too late. I was young and driven. I had my sister's killer to find. What would you have done if it had been your daughter?'

'I don't know,' conceded Brook. 'But it doesn't justify—'

'I'm not justifying anything,' insisted Copeland. 'I know what I did was wrong. And if you talk to anyone connected to Tilly's case who still wants to make a complaint, I'll cop to it. I know I've no career to lose, but I still have my reputation and I'll put that on the line if you want me to make amends, even now. You see, I've learned my lesson the hard way, Brook. The more I wanted Tilly's killer, the harder I went at people, the less likely the chances I was going to find him. I realised that, over time.'

'So you changed tack,' said Brook.

'I was grinding to a halt and one day it hit me,' sighed Copeland. 'I knew if I didn't take all the emotion out of it, I couldn't function. That's when I became more methodical, compiling background, doing the legwork. You've seen the file.'

'It's impressive,' said Brook. 'No doubt about that.'

'Thank you.'

'But it was too late, wasn't it?'

Copeland lowered his face and nodded. 'The damage was already done. The Barneys wouldn't speak to me freely, not without legal counsel present. And John Briggs was scared to death of saying anything in case it was the wrong thing.'

'Wrong thing?'

'About Ealy,' said Copeland. 'You see, I thought maybe Briggs knew where Colin Ealy had gone, maybe even helped him get away to Scotland.'

'Scotland. Right.' Brook's smile was involuntary.

'What?' queried Copeland.

310

'Forgive me. But an unsophisticated seventeen-year-old boy running away to a remote part of Scotland and hoping to blend in. I don't think so.'

'People don't always do what you expect.'

Brook conceded with a shrug. 'But why Scotland?'

'My guess was that Ealy, being a woodsman, thought he could survive better in the wilds than in a big city,' said Copeland.

'Your guess or Walter's?'

'Does it matter? We don't pick our evidence, Brook. When the national alert went out, that's where Ealy was seen. Someone rang in a tip.'

'And Laird went to Scotland to follow it up.'

'Yes.'

'But it came to nothing.' Brook nodded, deep in thought. 'You went too.'

'I took some annual leave in Crianlarich,' said Copeland, shrugging. 'Well, why not? And it *was* very beautiful, very wild.'

'But you were looking for Colin Ealy.'

'Of course.' Copeland took a sip of tea. 'But I didn't find him.'

'Weren't you worried Brass might get wind that you were looking for your sister's killer?'

'How? I was the only one reviewing the case. And I wasn't stupid enough to traipse up to Scotland during working hours. I was on leave.'

Brook was quiet for a moment. 'Tell me about the night Matilda disappeared.'

'Tuesday, thirty-first of August nineteen sixty-five,' announced Copeland, as if he was reciting mathematical tables in school. 'An ordinary night. Tilly was her usual bubbly self. It was still light when she called Ebony and said she was taking the dog out. The dog came back. Tilly didn't. The rest is in the file. She was seen walking around the estate with Ebony and then running up Radbourne Lane without him.'

'By Trevor Taylor.'

'Yes.'

'Can you remember how Matilda seemed before she left?'

'If you mean did she seem preoccupied by thoughts of meeting her prohibited boyfriend, the answer's no,' said Copeland. 'But then I was a young boy. Such subtleties passed me by.'

'Your parents noticed nothing?'

'Nothing they ever communicated to me. Or Walter.'

'You asked him?' said Brook.

'When I was old enough.'

'When you went to see McCleary in prison . . .' began Brook, feeling no need to finish the sentence.

Copeland nodded. 'Yes, he confirmed they were meeting that night.'

'Where?'

'Halfway between Mackworth and Kirk Langley.'

'But your sister never arrived.'

'No,' mumbled Copeland.

'According to McCleary.'

'You said it yourself,' said Copeland. 'He didn't have a car. His father didn't. I had no reason to lay Tilly's death at his door.'

'Nor Trevor Taylor's neither.'

'What do you mean?' said Copeland.

'Taylor became a suspect because he was the last to see Matilda,' said Brook. 'When you found out about McCleary, you must have taken Taylor out of your calculations.'

'Why?'

'Because Taylor's sighting suddenly made sense.'

'It doesn't mean he couldn't have gone after her and killed her.'

'Before helpfully telling the police he'd seen her?' Brook smiled. 'Not very bright.'

Copeland's sullen shrug conceded the point. 'He wasn't bright and he was still a creep.'

'With access to his mother's car,' added Brook.

Copeland was tight-lipped. 'Yes.'

'Pity there was no proof against him then,' concluded Brook.

'There was one thing, though you could hardly call it evidence.'

'Go on.'

'Two days before, Walter had cleared the last of his stuff from his house and dropped the keys off with Dad.'

'His house?'

'I told you. He was a neighbour and a friend. He moved out the weekend before Tilly disappeared.'

'So there was an empty house on your road?' said Brook, surprised. 'That wasn't in the file.'

'Because it wasn't relevant, Brook.'

Brook slowly lifted his eyes to Copeland. 'Not relevant?'

'I mean it was looked into. Dad had Walter's house keys in case of emergency, a burst pipe or something. When the new owners moved in, he was to hand them over. So when Tilly went missing, the empty house was checked. There were no signs of a break-in, nothing out of place. No one had lured Tilly there. Besides, she was seen running towards Kirk Langley, remember.'

'I remember,' said Brook. 'What time did your father ring the police?'

'I don't know,' said Copeland. 'About ten thirty, I think. After he'd been round the estate looking for her. The police arrived fifteen minutes later.'

'And CID?'

'They called Walter around midnight but only because my dad insisted,' said Copeland. 'The uniforms wanted to wait and see until the morning. Walter came round straight away.'

'But not Bannon,' said Brook.

'I only saw the uniformed officers and Walter. Later, when I was older, I asked. Walter would only tell me Bannon was indisposed when the call came through.'

'Meaning?'

Copeland opened his hands to offer a choice. 'Drunk? Depressed? Take your pick.'

'So Walter ran the investigation on his own.'

'Most of the time,' nodded Copeland. 'He was used to it by then. And he was a top DS.'

'You were telling me about two days before her disappearance,' prompted Brook.

'Yes, so when Walter dropped off the keys with my dad, Tilly was just taking out the dog. It was the Sunday before, about eight thirty.' Copeland hesitated. When he continued, his voice had dropped down the register. 'When Walter drove away, he passed Tilly and looked back at her in the rear-view mirror and Trevor Taylor was walking behind her on the way to the pub, looking at her.'

'Looking at her?'

'Looking at her in a way that lonely single men look at beautiful young girls. Walter said it sent a shiver down his spine.'

Brook nodded slowly. 'You're right. That's not evidence.'

'Maybe not,' said Copeland. 'But Taylor was a loner, an oddball. He was a prime suspect with good reason.'

'So Taylor killed Matilda and twelve years later, overcome by guilt, committed suicide by jumping off a railway bridge. Is that the theory?' Brook stared at the glass-panelled roof of the conservatory as though reading the words from it. 'That's quite a gestation period for guilt.'

'Thirteen years,' corrected Copeland. 'Taylor died in nineteen seventy-eight and the coroner concluded it could have been accidental. He'd been drinking.'

'So he had,' agreed Brook. 'So when exactly did he die?'

'Is it important?'

'Humour me.'

Copeland's brow furrowed. 'January, February, I think. I remember when we scraped him up off the track, the ground was frozen solid. I can check.'

'No, that's near enough,' said Brook. 'So it was a few months before you reviewed the Stanforth murder.'

'Yes.'

'And found out about Tilly and McCleary.'

'Yes.' Copeland shook his head. 'Taylor's poor mother. There wasn't much of her son to identify.'

'You spoke to her.'

'Someone had to.'

'That was good of you,' said Brook. 'I would have delegated. And how did Taylor seem to you when you spoke to him the previous year?'

'How do you mean?'

'I'm presuming you re-interviewed him as part of your review.'

'Of course.'

'Well. Did he seem suicidal to you?'

'Honestly, no,' said Copeland. 'He stuck to his story, his account, word for word. But I went at him hard and—'

'Raking it all up again may have triggered something in him,' finished Brook. 'Yes. I can see how it would.' He lapsed into silence.

Copeland brandished his cup. 'More tea?'

'No thanks.' After deliberation Brook announced, 'I spoke to Rosie Bannon.'

'I see.'

'You don't seem surprised.'

'I expect you to be thorough but she should come with a health warning, Brook. She's a drug addict and she has her father's delusional genes. You should give her a wide berth.'

'She didn't seem delusional, Clive. Obsessed maybe.'

'Like her father then.'

'People in glass houses . . .'

Copeland raised a hand. 'Fair comment. But really, Brook, this Pied Piper fantasy . . .'

'She doesn't think it is.'

'Two young boys murdered on the same day ten years apart,' sneered Copeland. 'That's hardly a compelling pattern.'

'What about Billy's sister, Francesca?'

'Her death was squared away as an accident, Brook. Which just leaves two unsolved murders ten years apart – Billy Stanforth and Jeff Ward.'

'If that's where it ended,' said Brook. 'Rosie seems to think the Pied Piper is still active.'

Copeland pursed his lips. 'Like I said, delusional.'

'After Jeff Ward, she says her father got close to catching him. From nineteen seventy-eight, she thinks the Pied Piper started abducting the boys instead, killing them in secret to stay under the radar.'

'Harry Pritchett again.' Said Copeland.

'There were other plausible disappearances after Pritchett.'

'Don't get dragged into her fantasies, Brook,' said Copeland. 'Look what happened to Sam.'

'Look what happened to Scott Wheeler,' replied Brook.

Copeland shook his head. 'Harry and Scott are not dead until their bodies show up. Just because they're missing doesn't mean they've been killed and it certainly doesn't mean there's a series. Teenagers go missing all the time, Brook. And if you're looking for suspects . . .' Copeland looked sharply up at Brook, then away. 'Never mind.'

'No, tell me,' said Brook.

Copeland took a huge breath. 'I shouldn't say this, and Walter would have my guts if he heard me, but when Sam Bannon turned up at the Jeff Ward crime scene, just after Walter had arrived, I was suspicious. I even suggested to Walter that maybe Bannon was schizo. That a part of his personality had murdered Jeff Ward and, out of guilt, the other half was trying to catch his killer. Like two different halves of the same twisted psyche. I don't suppose you considered that, did you?'

'Actually I did,' said Brook. 'I still am.'

'Glad to hear it,' sniffed Copeland. 'And, of course, if Bannon was a killer, it would also explain his method of suicide.'

'How so?'

'Isn't it obvious?' said Copeland. 'He died like Billy Stanforth, burned to death in a shed – a parting shot to convince Walter and me the Pied Piper was real.'

'What did Walter say to that?'

Copeland smiled. 'I prefer not to repeat the language he used. Let's just say he wouldn't accept it.'

'And now?'

'Look, I don't believe Sam Bannon was a child killer, not for a second,' said Copeland. 'But patterns can be found if you're looking for them, Brook, especially if you're mentally unstable.'

'I know.' Brook wondered what Copeland would say if he knew about Colin Ealy recognising Bannon at Osmaston Park Lake. He decided that was a conversation for another time. He clambered wearily to his feet. 'OK. If there's nothing else you can tell me . . .'

'If I think of anything I only have to walk across the corridor,' smiled Copeland. 'You're always there. I've noticed and I made sure Charlton knows it too.'

Brook inclined his head to approximate thanks.

Copeland stood and grabbed Brook's hand. 'I can't thank you enough for doing this, Brook.'

Brook tried to smile in return. 'I haven't done anything yet.'

As Brook clambered wearily into his car, a clear blue dawn was breaking in the east. As he sank into the driver's seat, his phone vibrated. Brook checked the display and braced himself.

'You're up early, John.'

Even across the ether, Brook could sense Noble's annoyance. 'Have you any idea of the earache I've just had from DI Ford?'

'What about?' asked Brook innocently.

Noble wasn't playing. 'He's seething.'

'Is this about Edna Spencer?'

'Yes, this is about Edna Spencer. Ford is fuming and he's every right to be.'

'He shouldn't be too hard on himself, John,' said Brook. 'It wasn't obvious to the untrained eye.'

'That's not funny. And I doubt Charlton will be laughing either when Ford sees him.'

'Knowing Charlton, I've got until lunchtime then,' said Brook.

'It's still not funny.'

'No, you're right,' said Brook. 'A boy's life is at stake . . .'

'What's Scott Wheeler got to do with it? I'm talking about Edna Spencer and you calling out a full SOCO team.'

'I know.'

'Then what do you mean about Scott?'

Brook sighed, uncertain he should raise expectations. 'What if I told you there's a slim chance he could still be alive, John?'

'How do you know?'

'Something cropped up in my cold case work. There might be a connection.'

'Is this something to do with that Pied Piper tip we logged?'

'That's right – a serial killer who doesn't exist.'

'Then why think there is one?' demanded Noble.

'Because a dead copper spotted a pattern of young boys dying, enticed into danger somehow and killed.'

'But how could a serial killer go undetected?'

'Because he stopped leaving us the bodies, John,' explained Brook. 'That dead copper got close before he died. And now the Pied Piper takes the boys and they're never seen again.' It sounded absurd when he said it. 'Or that's the theory.'

'So instead of a murder we have a missing teenager who could have run away from home . . .'

'And he draws a fraction of the attention.'

There was silence while Noble thought it through. 'It has a certain logic. But if there's a chance, we should take it to Charlton.'

'Not now,' said Brook. 'It's a huge long shot and the Chief won't buy it.'

'He won't if you don't tell him,' replied Noble.

'I've got to go.'

'What?' exclaimed Noble. 'You can't just leave me dangling like this.'

'I have to,' said Brook. 'If I come in, I'm going to be explaining myself to Ford and Charlton, and if Charlton doesn't bite I could end up suspended again. Or worse.'

'That bothers you now?'

'Only because it would render me impotent,' said Brook. 'And if this killer exists, the Wheeler boy's got less than three days to live.'

'Three days?'

'I haven't got time to explain, John.'

There was a long silence at the other end of the line. 'What can I do?'

'Nothing.'

'But—'

'John, you've been passed over for promotion because of me. Don't compromise yourself further. I'm turning off my phone. That should keep Ford and Charlton off my back for a while . . .'

'You've got to give me something,' pleaded Noble.

Brook paused. 'Edna Spencer knew something and she died because of it. The killer was too careful. You won't find anything at the scene. But dig deep into the old girl's background. There's something in there that got her killed.'

Brook rang off and turned the ignition. He was sorely tempted to risk driving back to the cottage and sink into a coma for the rest of the day. But he remembered the keys to Rosie Shah's shed and made the shorter journey back into town. He let himself into Sam Bannon's replica shed and climbed on to the small camp bed in a state of near collapse.

Twenty-Four

BROOK WAS WOKEN BY THE sound of crockery in the main room of the shed.

'Brunch,' called out Rosie. 'Get it while it's hot.'

Brook opened his eyes, swung his legs off the bed and hobbled into the main room, shoes in hand, yawning all the way to the desk. The smell of cooked bacon made Brook almost hallucinate with hunger. 'This looks good. What time is it?'

'It's one in the afternoon,' she said.

'Really?'

'Ollie tells me you left in the middle of the night.'

'He's very observant,' said Brook diplomatically.

'Why?'

'The policeman's lot,' he said, taking a large bite from the bacon sandwich, followed quickly by another.

'Did you sleep?'

'Like the dead,' answered Brook, with mouth full.

'Had a chance to mull over what we discussed?' she inquired, nodding towards the Pied Piper wall.

'Not yet,' replied Brook, without looking up. 'But I will.'

Rosie narrowed her eyes at him. 'There's a problem, isn't there?'

Brook looked at her. 'Can we do this later? I'm barely awake.'

'Tell me now,' said Rosie. 'I'm a grown-up.'

Brook sighed and replaced the half-eaten sandwich on the plate.

'The problem is, if the Pied Piper exists then we have two confirmed kills and two dead bodies, exactly ten years apart.'

'Stanforth and Ward,' agreed Rosie warily.

'Maybe you can say three kills if, like your father, you put Francesca Stanforth into the mix.' Brook spoke slowly.

'OK,' said Rosie.

'But in nineteen seventy-eight, five years after Jeff Ward's murder, the Pied Piper changes his MO and abducts Harry Pritchett in the lead-up to December the twenty-second because he doesn't want to leave a body and draw attention to the sequence.'

'Still no argument here,' she said. Her arms were crossed. *Not a good sign.*

Brook paused, hoping she'd work it out before he had to voice it. 'The problem is your father flagged up this change of MO the week before the twenty-second and died two days *before* the anniversary passed.' He stared at her to gauge her reaction. 'So how did he know the MO was about to change before it actually did?'

Rosie was silent for a minute then shook her head. 'I don't know.' She became defensive suddenly. 'You're not still suggesting Dad had something to do with these murders, are you?'

'And try to get former colleagues involved in the case? That doesn't make sense unless...' He left the sentence for her to finish.

'Unless he was insane,' she said, her face tight. 'Brook, for the last time, Dad was not crazy.'

Brook splayed his hands. *We're just talking.* 'OK, if we accept that your father was sane – troubled, obsessed but sane ...'

'I'll settle for that.'

'There is a way round it, a reason he could have expected a change in the MO before it happened.'

'And what's that?'

He sighed. 'Not only did your father know who the Pied Piper was, the Pied Piper knew he knew and realised he had to alter his method. When Harry Pritchett disappeared, your father realised what was happening.'

Rosie was speechless for a second then shook her head. 'But if Dad knew his identity, why didn't he tell someone?'

'Maybe he couldn't prove it,' offered Brook.

'What does that matter? He would still tell *someone* in case anything happened to him,' pleaded Rosie. Brook smiled quietly, waiting for her to catch up. When she did, the violence of her emotion took him aback. 'Jesus. He did tell someone. That's what got him killed.'

Later that afternoon, Brook parked the BMW in the former pub car park in Rawson Green and retrieved the tightly packed carrier bag from the boot.

Braced for a cool reception, Brook knocked on the plastic door two minutes later, hoping he wouldn't have to talk his way past Laird junior. A moment passed before the door opened as far as the chain allowed. Walter Laird's beady eye gazed balefully back at him.

'Brook.'

'Walter,' said Brook cheerfully. 'How are you?'

Laird tapped his chest and cleared his throat. 'I'm not feeling so good this afternoon.'

'Did Clive ring you?' said Brook, still grinning as hard as he could manage.

'Aye, but I'm not up to it, lad. We'll have to do this another time.' The door began to close.

'So you'll not be wanting these then?' Brook drew one of the cigarette cartons from the carrier and waggled it in front of Laird. 'Peace offering.'

The old man's eyes lit up and he looked greedily at the carton and the other four hundred cigarettes in the bag. He held a hand through the chained door for the box of delights. 'Very nice of you.'

Brook pulled the carton out of range, his smile rebuking Laird for misunderstanding the terms and conditions. With a resigned sigh, Laird drew back the chain and snatched at the first ingot of death, scuttling back inside to the warmth, clawing at the cellophane as he moved. Brook followed and sat down at the table as Laird lit up with a moan of pleasure then fell back into his armchair, face wreathed in ecstasy. 'Can't afford to buy these beauties usually. Thanks, Brook.' He looked furtively across at Brook, who was still clutching the bag but relaxed when the younger man leaned over and dropped the rest of the bounty in his lap.

'Any danger of a cup of tea?' asked Brook, deprived of his usual flask and suffering withdrawal.

'Just made a fresh pot,' replied Laird with a nod to the tiny kitchen. Brook poured the tea and returned with two chipped mugs.

For the first time, Laird considered Brook with a kindly face as he took a mug of tea from him. 'I've misjudged you, lad. Showing respect – it's appreciated.' His smile died slightly when Brook fished out his notebook. 'And now you want to ask me about poor Tilly.' His head lowered. 'Aye. Terrible business.' He took a long draw and exhaled towards the hearth.

'Did Clive tell you what we spoke about?' asked Brook.

Laird nodded.

'Everything?'

'Everything,' confirmed Laird. 'And you were right. I lied but I did it for a friend and I won't apologise for that.'

'Which friend are we talking about?' asked Brook. 'Sam Bannon or Clive Copeland's father?'

'Both,' snapped Laird. 'It's called loyalty.'

'Some might call it deceit.'

'And some would call it an honest mistake,' retorted Laird, trying not to lose his good mood.

'We all make mistakes, Walter, but some of us learn from them.'

'What does that mean?'

'You suppressed evidence in the Stanforth inquiry.'

'I told you before, Tilly being at the Stanforth house that day was not relevant.'

'Maybe not,' said Brook. 'But that act of suppression became very relevant when Tilly died two years later. Potential suspects had to be ignored because of what you did.'

'They weren't ignored,' protested Laird. 'Didn't Clive tell you?'

'They were ignored *officially*.'

'I interviewed McCleary *and* Amelia Stanforth in nineteen sixty-five . . .'

'But you couldn't put it on the record because you'd painted yourself into a corner two years earlier.'

Laird hung his head. 'I can't deny that,' he said. 'But I did my job and all the right people were spoken to.'

'Trevor Taylor?'

'Especially Trevor Taylor,' snarled Laird, sucking on his cigarette. 'He killed Matilda, I'm sure of it. He gave me the shivers every time I saw him. Fucking pervert.'

'And is that what you told Clive when he joined the force?'

'Clive didn't need telling,' said Laird. 'Everyone who lived on the Mackworth Estate knew he was a wrong 'un.'

'But you couldn't prove it.'

'No. But he was the last to see Tilly alive, running up towards the heath.'

'Towards Kirk Langley.'

'Yes,' answered Laird quietly. He stubbed out his cigarette and lit another immediately, his hand shaky.

'Towards a rendezvous with Brendan McCleary.'

'So it seems,' said Laird.

'But she never made it.'

'No.' Laird shook his head. 'Poor kid. Taylor probably followed her and had his way with her . . .'

'And borrowed his mother's car to move her body,' said Brook.

'We could never prove that.'

'We'll come back to that,' said Brook. 'Clive said you saw Taylor a couple of days before Matilda disappeared.' Laird's brow furrowed. 'You were moving house.'

'That's right,' said Laird, pointing a finger, his face brightening. 'I'd cleared up all the odds and sods from the house and I left the spare keys with George, Clive's dad. Asked him to keep an eye on the place until the new owners moved in.' He shook his head. 'It was getting late and Tilly had just taken the dog out. When I drove past, I looked back in the mirror and Taylor was right behind her, drooling all over her like the dirty old bastard he was. Made me sick to my stomach when I thought about it later.'

'Presumably you went after him hard when Matilda's body was found.'

A ghost of a smile crossed Laird's face. 'I'll say. And I dare say we might have cracked him if that gamekeeper hadn't done a runner. We wasted a lot of time and resources trying to connect Colin Ealy to Tilly.'

'So you don't think Ealy killed Matilda.'

Laird took a long pull on his new cigarette. 'I couldn't say for sure. But it seems a bit of a stretch putting Ealy so far from his place of work on a Tuesday night at the exact time Tilly Copeland walked past. And what little I saw of him, he didn't seem the type. Not like Taylor.'

'Or Brendan McCleary,' added Brook.

Laird shot him a sidelong glance. 'No.'

'You and Sam made a big thing about transport in your paperwork. Presumably you cleared McCleary and Amelia Stanforth on those grounds. *Unofficially.*'

'Right,' said Laird through pursed lips.

'But then Taylor didn't have a car either, did he?' said Brook. 'For a body dump in Osmaston he'd need a vehicle.'

'His mother had one.'

'But you couldn't prove Taylor borrowed it the night Matilda disappeared,' stated Brook.

Laird's features darkened. He knew what was coming. 'Not according to the mother. I interviewed her.'

Brook nodded. 'That's what Clive said. Only I can't find a report of that conversation either.'

'It were near fifty years ago, lad,' said Laird, finally losing patience. 'Papers get lost, destroyed. The old battleaxe said the car hadn't been out of the garage and we couldn't find a neighbour to say different, you'll have to take my word.'

Brook nodded. 'But by this time the focus had switched to Colin Ealy.'

'The minute he disappeared we thought we'd cracked it,' said Laird. 'He had transport and he knew the dump site. So we went over the van for a week and put out a nationwide alert. We tested everything he ever owned – and retested when DNA rode over the horizon. We got nothing, Brook. No connection to Tilly. No fibres, no prints, no DNA.'

'But he remained a suspect.'

'Oh, aye,' conceded Laird. 'But only because he'd dropped out of sight. If he came back tomorrow we'd still have had a job to convict without a confession.'

'Why do you think Ealy disappeared if there was no evidence against him?'

'I've tried to figure it out for nearly half a century, lad.' The old man shook his head. 'I couldn't tell you.'

'Was it because he got scared when he recognised DCI Bannon at the lake?'

Laird's eyes widened. 'Who told you that?'

'I can't tell you.'

'Never mind. I can guess,' snarled Laird. 'You've spoken to Graham Bell, haven't you? Jesus, Brook. Bell never made it past DS because he was useless and Sam Bannon said so when he came up for promotion. That's why Belly always had it in for Sam. Always had something to say when Sam was on the sick.' He took a long draw on his cigarette. 'What did he tell you?'

Brook, pleased to be able to keep Rosie out of it, decided against contradiction. 'That Ealy saw Bannon arrive at the lake and became edgy because he'd recognised him.'

'That's because Sam was always in the papers,' replied an exasperated Laird. 'Look, Ealy didn't see anybody the night Matilda's body was dumped or he would have mentioned it before then, whether he knew who it was or not. Jesus! I can't believe you rang Australia to talk to that shithead.'

Brook shrugged. 'So Bell's lying.'

The old man hesitated. 'He's exaggerating.'

'Then there *was* a reaction to Bannon.'

Laird was quiet until, 'Yes. But you can't mention this to Clive. He'll get the wrong idea. And that's not why Ealy did a runner.'

'Why then?'

'For God's sake, Brook. Why not? He was a seventeen-year-old kid, good-looking. He probably wanted to see the world.'

Brook smiled. 'So he headed for the wilds of Scotland.'

'You know about that?'

'It's in the file.'

Laird laughed. 'Clive's left nothing out. You've got to hand it to him.' He looked into his mind's eye. 'Crianlarich. I went there. Nice place, if you like it remote. There'd been a phone call, a report that Ealy had been seen but by the time I got there the bird had flown.' He shook his head. 'Clive took a couple of holidays there as well, looking for Ealy, and we're talking fifteen years after the sighting. Poor sod. He thought about little else but Tilly before and after he joined CID.'

Brook drank his tea without taking his eyes from Laird. 'Did you find out how Ealy got away?'

'He disappeared.'

'And left his van behind,' said Brook. 'Didn't that strike you as odd? I mean he must have got to Scotland somehow.'

'Maybe he took the train . . .'

'But how did he get to the station? Was he noticed buying a ticket? How many people saw him on his journey? How many remembered him arriving somewhere so remote, a young Englishman in the wilds of Scotland?'

Laird stared hard at Brook. 'I don't know. We never found a witness. Maybe someone gave him a lift.'

'John Briggs?'

'He said not.'

Brook didn't come back with more questions and the two men considered each other across the waves of blue-grey poison drifting on the air between them.

Investigating the investigation. Tough beat.

'Is that it?' inquired Laird, almost cheerful now. He'd answered all Brook's questions and was six hundred fags up on the deal.

'The night Sam Bannon died, he called you.'

Laird closed his eyes. 'I don't want to talk about Sam. It's too painful.'

'Then I'll be brief,' insisted Brook. 'He called you.'

Laird sighed. 'He did. I wish I'd . . .' He shook his head, unable to go on.

'You wish you'd done something differently,' suggested Brook. Laird nodded. 'But he was out of his head.'

'Raving. I tried to calm him,' said Laird.

'What was he raving about? The Pied Piper?'

Laird looked at Brook, his eyes narrowing. 'You've been talking to that junkie, Rosie Bannon, I can tell.' No answer from Brook. 'That bitch! I should never . . .'

Brook raised an eyebrow when Laird halted. 'You should never have perverted the course of another inquiry to help her out. I agree. Funnily enough she said the same. She didn't want the insurance money.'

'It's easy to say that when you've got plenty.' Laird's lip curled. 'Besides, the money didn't matter to me either. I was helping my friend save his reputation.'

'Decent of you.' Brook paused for effect. 'So tell me what you thought about Sam's Pied Piper theory.' To his surprise Laird threw back his head and laughed.

'Not you an' all. I thought you had brains, Brook. That fantasy was dreamt up by a sick man and kept alive by a drug addict with too much time and money on her hands. I should have let her make her own way.'

'Is that why you had her warned off?'

'She was wasting police time and dragging her father's reputation into the mud,' growled Laird. 'There is no Pied Piper. We had two boys murdered on the same day ten years apart. That's not a serial, it's a coincidence.'

'And Harry Pritchett?'

'Who?'

'The boy who went missing in nineteen seventy-eight, the week before Sam died.'

'Is he dead too?' crowed Laird. 'Where's the body then?'

'Hidden,' said Brook hesitantly. 'Maybe.'

'That's bloody convenient,' sneered Laird.

'Did Sam tell you Pritchett was the next kill?'

'There was no kill because there wasn't a body,' insisted Laird. He panted, getting his breath back. 'Look, the Pritchett lad was missing. Still is. So Sam signed him up to his fantasy.'

'There were others. Davie Whatmore in nineteen eighty-three. Callum Clarke in eighty-eight. And now Scott Wheeler. They all disappeared on or just before Billy Stanforth's birthday.'

Laird laughed again. 'Scott Wheeler? What's this now? The twenty-odd-year itch. Listen to yourself, Brook. Scott Wheeler's dead. Brendan McCleary took him, raped him, killed him and buried him somewhere. When you find that scumbag, you'll find Scott Wheeler.'

'Sam Bannon knew who the Pied Piper was, didn't he?'

'Give it a rest, Brook. It's time you went.'

'He worked it out.'

'Bullshit.'

'He worked it out and he knew he was in danger,' said Brook. 'He knew someone was watching the house.'

'Sam was paranoid, I'll give you that,' said Laird. 'The poor man had lost the plot.'

'He told you he was being watched?'

'Yes, he told me,' retorted Laird. 'Said the Piper was after him and Rosie. He wanted me to look after her if anything happened.'

'Something did happen,' said Brook. 'Bannon died.'

'Think I don't know?' shouted Laird. 'My best friend finally flipped out and killed himself, leaving his daughter to fend for herself. But still I helped him out, and her, *because* he was my friend.'

Brook was silent for a few moments before making his concession. 'OK, let's say I accept that Bannon was unbalanced.'

'That's putting it mildly.'

'Just the same, he must have told you about the Pied Piper.'

'Told me what?'

'Told you who he was.'

'He was unbalanced, you said yourself.'

'That doesn't mean he couldn't give you a name, no matter how insane you thought he was.'

'There is no Pied Piper,' Laird croaked. 'He told me nothing. And if he had, I wouldn't have listened. I'd had enough and put the phone down on him.' He ran a shaky, liver-spotted hand through his thinning white hair. A tear followed the irregular contours of Laird's cheek as it rolled unevenly down his face. 'Are you happy now? I let him down. I wasn't there for him when he needed me. Now I've answered more than my share of questions and I think you should leave.' He jammed a thumb and finger up to his eyes, panting with emotion.

Brook sat motionless for a moment but then stood. 'I'll see myself out.'

Laird looked up to plead with Brook. 'Don't come back until you've found Brendan McCleary and put him back behind bars.'

It was already dark when Brook parked in the overflow car park of St Agatha's and hurried through the light rain to reception. Sharmayne, the girl on duty from his last visit, was at the desk but instead of a look of polite inquiry, her face betrayed alarm and relief.

'Inspector Brook. Thank God. You got the messages then?'

'Messages?'

'We've been ringing you all morning but your phone was off. Amelia Stanforth's gone.'

Brook hung his head. 'I'm sorry to hear that.'

'No, I don't mean dead, I mean she's disappeared.'

'What? When?'

'We're not sure. When the nurse went to wake her this morning her room was empty. The staff are searching the grounds but there's no sign yet.'

'Maybe she made a bolt for the village?' suggested Brook. 'You said that happens sometimes.'

'Not during the night,' replied Sharmayne. 'And there's something else. One of our residents reported a prowler a while back and she says she saw him again last night.'

'If there was a break-in you should've called nine nine nine.'

'There wasn't a break-in,' said Sharmayne. 'The French window in Amelia's room was unlocked from the inside as though she let someone in. Also some of her clothes and a bag are gone. There's another thing.' Sharmayne cast around the surface of her desk, picking up an opened envelope and handing it to Brook. 'We found this on her bedside table.'

Brook pulled out the paper. It was a confirmation slip for a coach ticket from Derby to London at six o'clock that morning. 'Arriving in London at nine twenty,' he read out.

'If that's where she's gone, she'll already be there,' said Sharmayne. 'What should we do?'

'You didn't call the police?'

'She's not a prisoner,' said Sharmayne. 'She's a free agent. They all are.'

Brook closed his eyes to think while Sharmayne prattled on.

'She's here by choice and if she wants to leave—'

'Is she on medication?' interrupted Brook.

'Of course. She has a bad heart and takes tablets for blood pressure. They're gone too.'

'OK. Finish searching the grounds,' said Brook. 'But if there was a prowler, you can't be sure she left voluntarily so if you don't find her, report her missing.'

Back in his car, Brook sat and thought it through. *First Edna, now Amelia* . . . Instead of finishing the list, he turned the ignition.

* * *

'Mr Mullen,' shouted Brook, pounding on the front door, the smell of dog excrement assaulting his nostrils. He heard the stairlift apparatus clunking into life and stopped knocking. It seemed to take an age to descend so Brook stepped along the crumbling path to his right to gaze at the rear of the house for something to do. In the dark, he spied a decaying old shed barely standing in the far corner of the back garden, almost engulfed in the branches of an overgrown tree. There was a rusted padlock on the door. The path to the shed was nearly undetectable under the assault of uncontrolled mosses, grass and weeds. Brook could only imagine what the rest of the garden was like. For the first time he understood the logic of Walter Laird's maintenance-free yard.

The whine of machinery ceased and Brook returned to face Edward Mullen at the front door. The old man stared back sullenly.

'Inspector.'

'Mr Mullen. Sorry to disturb you again. I thought you ought to know, Edna Spencer was found dead yesterday.'

'Dead?'

'I'm afraid so.'

Mullen shook his head. 'Poor Edna. I should say I'm sorry but she was in a lot of pain. And after her husband passed—'

'She was murdered,' announced Brook.

Mullen's bony hand shot to his mouth. 'What? Are you sure?'

'There's no doubt.'

Mullen blew out his cheeks. 'This is a shock.' He stared at the ground, regaining his breath. He made to close the door. 'Thank you for telling me, Inspector.'

'That's not the main reason I'm here,' said Brook.

'I don't understand,' said Mullen.

'I need to ask a quick question.'

Mullen blinked and nodded. 'Very well.'

'You remember DCI Bannon? He was the senior investigating—'

'I remember him,' inserted Mullen. He smiled suddenly. 'Was that the question?'

'No,' was Brook's abrupt reply. 'Bannon was at Francesca Stanforth's funeral.'

Mullen was surprised. 'Francesca?'

'That's right,' echoed Brook. 'Amelia told me you were there too.'

Mullen stepped back from the door. 'You'd better come in.'

'I don't—'

'It's cold,' interrupted Mullen.

Brook dutifully walked into the dark lounge. Mullen closed the door and hastily lit a couple of candles. The wood burner was glowing faintly. Brook sat at Mullen's request.

'What about her funeral?' said the old man, levering himself down opposite Brook.

'At some point during or after the service, DCI Bannon spoke to Billy's mother.'

'Mrs Stanforth?'

'That's right. It would have been quite an animated conversation, maybe even an argument, because Mrs Stanforth complained about Bannon's behaviour in writing and he received a reprimand.'

Mullen steepled his hands under his nose. 'Yes. I remember the incident. There was some shouting.'

'Can you remember what it was about and what Bannon said?' asked Brook.

Mullen narrowed his eyes. 'It's a long time ago. Did you ask Amelia?'

Brook hesitated. 'I can't. She's missing.'

Mullen's jaw dropped in shock. 'Missing? What do you mean?'

'She wasn't in her room this morning,' said Brook. 'She may have gone on a trip.'

'A trip?' said Mullen. 'On her own?'

'We're not sure.'

'That doesn't sound right, Inspector.'

'No,' agreed Brook. 'We're looking into it.'

'I see. Well, I hope—'

'Mr Mullen,' said Brook sharply. 'DCI Bannon.'

Mullen stared at Brook before rocking himself upright to go to the cupboard where he extracted the half-full bottle of port. He poured himself a small glass and gestured towards Brook who declined with a shake of the head. 'The Chief Inspector asked Mrs Stanforth if she'd seen Brendan McCleary the night Billy died. In fact he seemed most insistent that she had. He badgered her until he was asked to leave.'

'I see,' said Brook, nodding. 'And Mrs Stanforth denied it?'

'When she'd stopped crying, yes. Does that help?'

Brook smiled minutely and got to his feet. 'That's a big help. Thank you.'

'I don't see how,' said Mullen.

Brook hesitated. 'I now know that Francesca Stanforth was murdered.'

'Murdered?' exclaimed Mullen. 'But her death was supposed to be an accident.'

'Accidents can be faked,' said Brook. 'Especially with heavy drinkers.'

'Can you prove it?'

'I can certainly try.'

'Who?' inquired Mullen. 'Brendan?'

'Who else?' Brook moved towards the door. 'Thank you. I won't trouble you further.'

'I'd appreciate that,' said Mullen. 'I don't want to rake all this over again. Billy's birthday is near.'

'I understand,' replied Brook.

'Inspector, wait.' Mullen stared at Brook. He took a sharp breath and held a hand to shield his eyes as though in pain. 'I think I ought to warn you. There's somebody with you.'

Brook was puzzled. 'No, I'm quite alone.'

'I don't mean in the car. I mean with you now, a spirit shadowing you.' Mullen closed his eyes and gripped his throat.

Brook's eyes glazed over. 'This is all very entertaining,' he said drily.

Mullen opened his eyes wide. 'Your companion . . .'

'In case you weren't aware, I'm not impressed by this mumbo-jumbo.'

Mullen ignored Brook. 'He's trying to speak but it's difficult.'

'I'm not surprised,' said Brook.

'He wants to know what happened to him,' explained Mullen.

'Don't we all,' said Brook. 'I'll see myself out.' He marched to the front door. 'Give my love to Marilyn Monroe,' he added over his shoulder.

'Do you know anyone called Floyd?' said Mullen urgently at Brook's retreating frame.

Brook halted halfway across the threshold. He turned slowly back. 'Floyd?'

'Floyd.' Mullen smiled beatifically at Brook. 'Tall, black male, well-built. He'd have been about thirty-five years old when he died. Did you know someone by that name?'

Brook's eyes burned into Mullen's. 'Yes, I knew somebody by that name. Many years ago. In London.'

'And he died a violent death?'

'You've done some research into my past,' said Brook sourly. 'Congratulations.'

'Research?' said Mullen. 'No, I merely report what I see.'

'For a fee,' snapped Brook. 'And I'm not buying.'

'I told you, I can't turn it on and off.'

'You should make more effort.'

'Don't you want to know how he died?' smiled Mullen.

'I know how he died,' said Brook.

'There's blood on his teeth, in his mouth,' Mullen offered.

'There would be,' said Brook. 'Floyd Wrigley had his throat cut. He was the victim of a serial killer called the Reaper in nineteen ninety-one. And those facts are a matter of public record.'

'Then why does he cling to you for answers, Inspector?' said Mullen.

'Maybe because I found the body.'

'That must be it,' nodded Mullen. 'I'll say goodbye then. I don't expect I'll be seeing you again.'

Brook turned to march towards his car, his mind replaying their conversation. He could feel the old man's eyes following his every step. Light rain was beginning to fall.

'Inspector!' shouted Mullen from the doorway. Brook turned to listen, his car keys in his hand. 'You must meet a lot of bad people,' said the old man. 'And I'm not one to judge.'

Brook held his eyes for a moment before climbing into the driver's seat.

Mullen watched him drive away before closing the door on the world. Shivering, he returned to the warm lounge and took another sip of his drink, looking across the long oak table towards the chessboard, now shorn of combatants as the endgame approached.

Brook was sombre when he pulled up at the cottage an hour later. After lighting the wood burner, he sat down with a larger than usual malt and plucked a book from a dusty bottom shelf. *In Search of the Reaper* was Brian Burton's woefully inaccurate volume that attempted to make sense of the murder of a family in Derby several years previously. Three members of the Wallis family had been slaughtered in their own home by the Reaper, a serial killer who had been active since his first strikes in London in 1990 and 1991.

Brook had tried and failed to bring the Reaper to justice as a DS in the Met. Then, when the Reaper had apparently followed Brook to his new posting in Derby many years later, he'd tried to catch him again as a detective inspector. All files remained open and, officially, the serial killer was still at large.

After burning his throat with a large swallow of whisky, Brook flicked through the index to find the name Floyd Wrigley. Wrigley, a drug addict and dealer, had died in '91 in his poky flat in Brixton. His wife and daughter had died with him, their throats cut by the Reaper.

Brook had been first on the scene and, according to Burton's third-hand account, had found the family dead in their home.

'A matter of public record,' said Brook, journeying back to that unhappy time and remembering the girl Wrigley had violated and butchered, so long dead. *Laura Maples*. The sight of her decaying, rat-infested corpse had invaded his dreams for years.

He drained his glass and fetched a pen, underlined the name Floyd Wrigley in Burton's book then bent down the page. He slipped out to the car and threw the book into the boot and brought back the three pieces of junk mail taken from McCleary's flat, binning the first two. The third held his attention for a moment. He tore open the envelope and examined the contents before consigning them to the refuse with the others.

Twenty-Five

S COTT GENTLY OPENED HIS EYES to blackness and blinked rapidly to be sure they were open at all. Now, instead of waking with a start, Scott had adjusted, had gradually come to accept his situation, even in his sleep. No longer did he move to sit bolt upright when semi-conscious, no longer did he loose off a shout of despair. His life had changed, his environment had been reduced to an underground box with no way out and he had trained himself to ignore the screaming in his aching limbs and chafing skin, to keep perfect stillness as his default position.

It helped that he was growing weaker by the hour. Now it was easier to preserve the integrity of his tiny cell, to prevent the roof collapsing and the soil engulfing him forever. The urge to move, to stand and to turn was ebbing away as his breathing shortened. It would soon be over. He was almost glad. He moved a hand to rustle blindly in the plastic bag, fumbling for the final packet of biscuits and counting them out with his thumb like an abacus. Seven biscuits. And not even chocolate. He managed a bitter smile but the tears followed soon after, the salty liquid almost a welcome tide, carrying grit and other irritants away from his eyeballs.

He had only one thought now. Trapped, barely able to breathe or move, he could concentrate on only one thing: do whatever it took to survive in one form or another. He'd seen the light. Friendly faces beckoning him to the other side. Even Josh, the friend he'd betrayed.

Scott thumbed the scar on his palm at the thought of his dead friend. *Omerta. Blood brothers. We'll be brothers in death at least.*

No, he would survive. Those miners on the other side of the world had survived for months and they got out fine. Better than fine. They were celebrities. On the telly every night, everyone wanting to speak to them, everyone thinking they were great. Ladies and gentlemen, the heroes of the hour. Loud screaming. Girls in the audience. Be like winning the lottery . . .

'Scott!'

Scott snapped his neck to stare up to the top of the pipe. A face. A voice. Their eyes met and hope surged through him.

'I'm here. Get me out, please. Hurry. Get me out. I want my mum. I want to go home.' The flimsy barriers of stoicism inside the boy were washed away like a sandcastle at high tide and Scott sobbed uncontrollably, his limbs quivering, almost salivating with the prospect of movement. 'Please, please, hurry.' Blinking away the bitter tears, Scott glimpsed the man's eyes at the other end of the pipe. His black eyes were creased in merriment, nodding faintly with satisfaction.

'You're hanging on,' he said. 'That's good. You've been down there a long time.'

'Get me out of here,' shouted Scott.

'Not long now, Scoot,' said the man's voice, his face creasing at Scott's reaction.

'Who are you?' demanded Scott. 'Why have you done this to me?'

'Don't you know, Scoot?'

'Get me out of here now or my dad will kill you.'

'Brrr,' said the voice, breaking into a long low chuckle. 'You're scary.'

'Please. Get me out,' screamed Scott, happy to beg.

'You'll be out in a day or two,' said the voice.

'Mr Stapleton?' shouted Scott in shock. 'Is that you?'

'What if it is?' said the voice.

Scott couldn't look at him. 'I . . . I'm sorry about Josh. It wasn't my fault.'

'Wasn't it?' The chuckle broke out again. 'I saw what you did to him.'

The aggression returned to Scott, adrenalin summoned from somewhere. 'I didn't do nothing.'

'That's a double negative.'

'Let me out, you bastard. You can't do this to me . . .'

The face grinned one last time before disappearing and Scott could see only a pair of hands either side of the pipe.

'No, don't leave me,' screamed Scott. He was hoarse and his throat felt as if it was on fire. 'Don't leave me,' he begged as the tears began again.

'I'm not leaving you,' said the voice, sounding more distant. 'I'm getting you out of there.'

Scott's face deformed in horror when he saw the hands stretch something over the end of the pipe. The breeze disappeared and although he could still see the sky and the hands working, his vision was distorted. Then he realised what it was. That stuff his mum used to keep food fresh. 'No. Don't. Please. Don't. I can't breathe. I can't breathe.'

'Course you can,' said the man. 'For a couple of days at least.' When the man had finished wrapping the clingfilm over the end of the air pipe, he waved a hand across the boy's disfigured vision in ostentatious farewell, ignoring the muffled pleas and screaming that dwindled to silence the further he walked away.

At five the next morning after a restless night of familiar dreams, Brook left his cottage wearing his walking gear, carrying shoes and a torch. He dropped them into the boot and drove out of Hartington through the dark and dank village streets.

A little over half an hour later, he pulled into the grounds of St Agatha's Care Home, this time happy to park the car as far from the ivy-covered building as possible. Gently closing the driver's door,

Brook flicked on the torch and strode out of the car park to cross the deserted main road.

On the far side, he clambered on to a convenient stile and, balancing on top, surveyed the boggy field with his torch. Locating what appeared to be firmer ground, he jumped and landed with a slither before picking his way carefully to higher, drier pastures then set about climbing up and over the shoulder of land.

Half a mile of sustained walking later, Brook reached the crest of the hill and scoured the hillside in the pale light. He tramped around several fields without success before his eyes alighted on a ruined outhouse in the distance.

Five minutes later, Brook approached the outhouse and, when he was almost upon it, caught sight of a caravan beyond, nestling in the lea of a crumbling wall. Beyond that an old Land Rover sat hard by the other side of a second crumbling wall. He turned off the torch and, at reduced speed, crept noiselessly towards the settlement, taking care where he placed his feet as he drew near.

A wisp of wood smoke rose from the dying embers of a brazier fire, confirming habitation. A blackened cooking pot sat on the ground nearby. Apart from the faint glow of coals at the bottom of the rusting, punctured oil drum, the only other light came from the moon peeping occasionally between the clouds.

Almost at the caravan, Brook's attention was attracted to the highest wall of the ruined outhouse. Four dead rabbits had been hung by their feet on a length of twine. Their bloodied heads were draining into plastic bags, intermittent black drips trickling through holes and down the stone on to the manure-rich ground.

In the shadow of the caravan, Brook took a breath and placed a gloved hand on the door. Too late he heard movement over his shoulder and before he could turn, a gun barrel was jammed into the back of his head.

'Don't turn round, copper,' said a deeply gravelled voice.

Brook's breath steamed hard in the cold air. 'Take it easy, Brendan.'

The gun barrel tapped Brook sharply on the back of the head. 'Shut it. And put your hands up.'

'Where's Amelia?'

This time the butt of a rifle caught Brook squarely on the side of his head and he staggered forward against the caravan. The man then grabbed Brook's coat collar to fling him on to the cold wet ground.

'I said shut it,' he spat with real venom.

Brook scrambled on to his knees, turning to face Brendan McCleary, rubbing his ear. The old man's face was in shadow under an Australian bushman's hat but the rifle at his waist was impossible to miss. 'Hands up, I said.'

Brook clambered to his feet. 'Put that down, Brendan. I can't help you if you threaten a police officer.'

McCleary took off the hat and threw it to the ground. His unkempt grey hair stuck out from his balding head. His crooked, blackened teeth appeared in a grin that split his whiskered jowls. He raised the gun to take aim.

'You mean like telling everyone I'm a nonce. That your idea of help?'

'That *wasn't* my idea,' said Brook.

'Bollocks. You were there. I saw you. You and that young copper planting that filth in my place,' McCleary snarled, shaking his head. 'Kids. Little boys.' He struck a fist into his chest, animated in his sudden rush of anger. 'Now everyone thinks I'm a beast.'

'We didn't put it there, we just found it. And you're right, we knew it was suspicious but DI Ford wouldn't listen.'

'Ford,' said McCleary, his lip curling. 'One of Laird's lackeys. He did the press conference.' The rifle lowered slightly.

'That's right,' said Brook, trying to soothe. 'It's his case but Noble, the other officer you saw, is trying to put him straight.'

'I don't know nowt about that missing lad,' said McCleary, lifting the rifle again.

'I know,' said Brook, his hands now in front of his chest, pacifying. He stared at the rifle, wishing he'd paid more attention in weapons seminars. 'Now put the gun down so I can help you.'

McCleary looked at the weapon and back at Brook. 'Help me? I don't think so, copper. See this. I shouldn't have guns. It says on my licence. But the beaks don't understand. I need 'em for rabbits. I don't have much money, see.'

'What is it?' asked Brook. 'An air rifle?'

McCleary's expression was contemptuous. 'Do I look like a ten-year-old? It's a twenty-two semi-auto, same as the one you got from my flat. It'll do you plenty of damage, no messin'.'

'How many rifles have you got?' asked Brook.

'Two,' growled McCleary. 'For rabbits.'

'We didn't find the other one, Brendan,' said Brook, lowering his hands slightly. 'It wasn't in your flat. Someone must have taken it. Someone who planted those pictures.'

'Someone took it?' McCleary was confused. 'Who?'

'We don't know,' said Brook.

'Then how did you know I was armed?' said McCleary, becoming agitated. 'It said in the papers.'

'We found an empty box of cartridges.'

'It don't mean I'm going to shoot people,' said McCleary.

'I know,' agreed Brook. 'But they won't take any chances . . .' Brook left out the rest of the sentence. *With a convicted killer*.

'With my sort, you mean,' seethed McCleary. 'You never let us forget, do you? Whatever happened to second chances? In the papers—'

'Forget the papers,' said Brook. 'They don't know you. And, if you give me that gun, I can speak to them – tell them you're not dangerous.'

'Give you the gun?' repeated McCleary, incredulous. 'I look like an idiot to you?'

'Can I put my hands down at least?'

McCleary studied Brook. 'No. Get on your knees.'

'Brendan . . .'

'Do it,' shouted McCleary, tightening his grip on the rifle.

Brook knelt slowly. 'You have to listen. Whoever planted those pictures took your rifle. They used it to shoot at my house.'

'Shoot at your house? What are you on about? I don't even know where you live.'

'I know,' said Brook. 'It was somebody else, someone lining you up to take the blame for Scott Wheeler. If you don't give me the gun, they're going to kill you and then you'll always be a beast. I can help if you trust me.'

McCleary managed a warped smile. 'Trust a copper? No chance.' He shrugged apologetically. 'I'm sorry, Brook. I've never killed a man before. Not sober, at least. It's nothing personal.' He lifted the rifle to take aim.

'Why start now?' asked Brook.

'I've got guns, haven't I? With my sheet it won't be a fine, even when that kid does turn up safe.'

'The guns are fixable, Brendan.'

'Don't talk me down, copper,' shouted McCleary. 'I blew my dad's head off and sure as shit I'll do the same to you.'

'You're making a serious mistake, Brendan.'

'It's serious for you, Brook, because I'm not going back in the box. Not even for a year on a gun charge.'

'It needn't come to that.' Brook clambered back to his feet.

'What are you doing?' shouted McCleary. 'Get back on your knees.'

Brook stood upright, his arms to his side. 'You're not a cold-blooded killer, Brendan.'

'You know different, copper.'

Brook shrugged. 'Well, if I'm wrong, at least I die on my feet.'

Both men stood completely frozen, McCleary with his hand on the trigger, Brook staring at the barrel. The wind picked up and buffeted both men but still neither moved.

Eventually Brook took a step closer. 'You need to give me that rifle, Brendan.'

'Stay back.'

Brook took another step. 'Give me the rifle or shoot.' He watched McCleary's finger snake around the trigger and tighten.

'Brendan!'

McCleary lowered the rifle and both men turned. Amelia Stanforth stood in the doorway of the caravan, a look of horror on her face.

'That's enough.' Amelia marched across to Brendan, her face stern. She looked incongruous in hoodie and tracksuit. 'Give him the rifle.'

'Amelia . . .'

'Don't argue, Bren. Give it to him.' She shook her head in disbelief. 'We finally get a chance at a life together . . .'

'Amelia, I—'

'You boys and your silly guns.'

Shamefaced, McCleary handed Brook the rifle. Not sure how to make it safe, Brook simply pointed it at the ground.

Amelia handed Brook and McCleary cups of tea and sat with them on the banquette in the caravan's small dining area. Rain began to hammer against the fibreglass roof but at least the sun was up. Somewhere.

'How did you find us?' asked Amelia.

Brook nodded at McCleary. 'There was a letter from the Caravan Club in Brendan's flat. And on my first visit to the care home, I remembered the wood smoke and the gunshots.'

McCleary looked sheepish under Amelia's fleeting look. 'I got a free twelve-month membership when I got the caravan, love. They don't bloody leave you alone.'

'Didn't you see I had a ticket to London?' Amelia asked Brook.

'That was neat,' said Brook. 'But you should have bought two. I couldn't see you making a break on your own. That's when I realised Brendan was the prowler.'

'That Jessica,' said Amelia, shaking her head. 'If she didn't eat so much cheese, she'd be able to sleep at night. Well, this is a pretty pickle. What do we do now, Inspector?'

'I'm not going back in the box,' bristled McCleary. 'Not for a day. I didn't touch that boy and that kiddie porn ain't mine.'

'I know.' Brook took a sip of tea and tried to think. 'This is my fault. I flagged up your name to the Wheeler task force.'

'But if someone was planting evidence against my Bren, his name would've come up sooner or later,' said Amelia. 'Wouldn't it?'

'Yes, it would.' Brook smiled at her. 'I'm sorry for underestimating you, Amelia.'

'I'm old,' she replied. 'It comes with the territory. And *I'm* sorry for acting gaga. You have a nice face. I should've trusted you.'

'Why?' said Brook. 'The way your brother's case has been mishandled over the years, you had every reason not to.' He hesitated, glancing between the pair. 'So you do remember Matilda Copeland.'

Brendan looked uncomfortable. Amelia grabbed his hand in hers. 'Of course,' she said. 'And I didn't blame the poor lass falling for my Bren.' She glanced at the awkward, untidy figure, gripping his hand. 'It's all water under the bridge now. If you want to be happy, sometimes you have to forgive even if you can't forget.' She smiled at McCleary who managed to hold her eyes for a second.

'I don't deserve you, Amelia Stanforth,' he mumbled.

'You do now,' she replied, patting his rough hand.

'I have to ask, Brendan,' said Brook. 'Were you meeting Matilda the night she was abducted?'

McCleary nodded, eyes glued to the table. 'Halfway – Brickyard Wood on the common. She never showed. I wasn't best pleased but I didn't think anything of it because she didn't always manage to get away. Her dad watched her every move after DS Laird tipped him the wink about me, even two years after Billy died.'

'And were you and Matilda...' Brook hesitated, looking solicitously at Amelia.

'Yes, they were sexually active,' replied Amelia matter-of-factly. Brendan tried to bury his head in his chest.

'And did she say anything in the months before she died?' asked Brook.

'About what?'

'Men looking at her sexually, making her uncomfortable when she was around them.'

'Not really,' said McCleary, shaking his head. 'Except that neighbour of hers.'

'Trevor Taylor?'

'I know the name now,' replied McCleary. 'But she never said it. She knew if she told me who he was, I'd end up decking him.'

'What did this neighbour do?'

'What you just said. Looking at her all sly, like. Gave her the willies, she said.' Still McCleary studied the table when talking about his former love. Brook glanced at Amelia, gripping McCleary's calloused hand, eyes glued to her man. So much love, so much strength drawn from adversity.

Brook slid out from the banquette to his feet. 'I can't let you keep the rifle. Will you have enough food?'

'For a few days,' answered McCleary uncertainly. 'You're not taking me in?'

Brook took a breath, still not sure of his reasoning. 'No.'

'Won't you get into trouble?' asked Amelia.

Brook shrugged. 'No one knows I'm here.'

'Well, they won't find out from us,' she said, also standing. 'Thank you, Inspector. We treasure every day together.'

'Making up for lost time?'

Amelia shook her head. 'Think of it like that and you waste even more time.'

Brook was taken aback when she stepped in to hug him, unsure where to put his hands. Eventually he settled for a stroke of her bony shoulder.

Picking up the rifle, Brook made for the door. 'One final question, Amelia, I hope not too painful,' said Brook softly. She smiled minutely and Brook needed no further prompting. 'Your sister Francesca . . . at her funeral, there was a policeman, DCI Bannon.'

'I remember,' said Amelia. 'He was horrible to Mum.'

'I think I already know the answer, but can you tell me why?'

* * *

A few minutes after eight o'clock, Brook arrived back at the car. The sun was beginning to burn off the morning mist. He placed the rifle in the boot, changed his shoes and socks and sat in the driver's seat. He turned his phone on and, ignoring the vibrations of at least a dozen missed calls and texts, began composing a message to Noble, agonising over its content before deciding to keep it simple.

McCleary no longer armed. Downgrade search if you can.

A second later the phone vibrated. 'John?'

'Inspector Brook.' Chief Superintendent Charlton's voice. Brook hesitated. 'I know you're there, Brook,' said Charlton impatiently.

Brook plumped for breezy. 'Hello, sir. I thought you were DS Noble.'

'Never mind that,' interrupted Charlton. 'What's this about McCleary?'

'McCleary?' answered Brook. 'What about him?'

'You've seen him.'

'No, sir.'

'You're lying. I read your text.'

Brook took a deep breath. 'Yes, sir.'

'So tell me where he is.'

'I can't do that, sir.'

'I beg your pardon?'

'McCleary is a harmless ex-convict. He's got nothing to do with Scott Wheeler.'

'That's not your call, Brook. Now tell me where he is or you're finished at Derby CID.'

Brook thought hard, looking for a way round. There wasn't one. 'Very well. I resign.'

'What?' exclaimed Charlton. 'You're throwing in the towel to protect a convicted killer? You could face charges.'

Brook prepared to ring off but then he thought about Scott Wheeler. It would be hard enough to do what needed to be done without losing his warrant card. A better strategy offered itself. 'You're right, sir. I'm coming in. Your office in half an hour.'

'Just a bloody minute . . .'

Forty minutes later, Brook knocked and entered Charlton's office. The Chief Superintendent looked up from behind his desk while three other heads turned and looked at Brook. There were no other empty chairs available and Brook was forced to stand.

Charlton stared at Brook without expression while Copeland and Noble avoided eye contact. DI Ford, however, could barely disguise his contempt and he leapt up to confront Brook.

'Where's my suspect?'

'Sit down, Frank,' ordered Charlton.

'Brook's taking the piss . . .'

'Sit down,' Charlton repeated. 'There's a right way to do this.' Ford returned reluctantly to his chair.

'Well, Brook. Are you going to tell us where McCleary is?' asked Charlton, his voice clipped.

'McCleary didn't take Scott Wheeler.'

'That's not for you to say,' Ford spluttered, squirming in his seat.

Charlton grimaced, as though confirming what he already knew. 'What gives you the right to interfere with an active case by withholding information from a colleague? I want your resignation on my desk by the end of the day.'

'About fucking time,' snarled Ford.

Brook could see the unhappy faces of Copeland and Noble. Worse, he could also see Scott Wheeler smiling on a leaflet on Charlton's corkboard. His career might be over but without Charlton behind him, a boy might lose his life and he knew he had to gamble.

'I think Scott Wheeler's alive and I think I know who abducted him.'

Charlton looked up at Brook, his hands clasped in front of his face to hide his surprise. 'We're listening.'

'You're not taking that seriously?' cried Ford.

'Frank . . .'

'Brook's blowing smoke in your face to save his arse,' insisted Ford.

349

'There's a child in danger, Frank,' said Charlton. 'A boy that you and Noble have failed to find.' Ford looked angrily at Charlton but kept his counsel. 'If Brook knows something . . .'

'The only thing I know for certain is McCleary is a blind alley,' said Brook. 'He didn't take the Wheeler boy.'

'He's a paedophile and a killer,' spat Ford. 'And what's more he's armed.'

'He's not armed because I took his rifle,' said Brook. 'It's in my car. He's also not a paedophile and I'm even beginning to doubt that he's a killer.'

'What's that supposed to mean?' snarled Ford.

'Never mind,' said Brook.

'It is possible the pornography was planted, sir,' said Noble. He felt the sudden heat from Ford's glare on the side of his face. 'It was very easy to find.'

'But DI Ford's right,' said a serious Copeland. 'McCleary served twenty years for killing his old man. He pleaded guilty and took the full hit. There's never been any bleating about a miscarriage, even from him.'

'There wouldn't be if he thought he *was* guilty,' replied Brook, beginning to wish he hadn't thrown this hand grenade into the conversation.

'Make sense, Brook,' said Charlton quietly. 'Your career depends on it. Ancient history has no bearing on how we proceed.'

'You're wrong,' said Brook. 'Ancient history is all too relevant in this case because Scott Wheeler's abductor was identified by the SIO in one of my cold cases. It's the Pied Piper.'

'Not this Sam Bannon rubbish again,' sighed Copeland.

'Sam Bannon?' exclaimed Ford, laughing in disbelief. 'He died in nineteen seventy-eight.'

'And went to his grave believing there was an unknown serial killer abducting and murdering young boys,' replied Brook.

'What young boys?' demanded Ford. 'When?'

'There's been a . . . respite but essentially a boy died every fifth year up to nineteen eighty-eight.'

There was stunned silence, particularly from Ford and Charlton.

'Jesus Christ,' laughed Ford eventually. 'You're crazier than Bannon was.' He looked at Charlton for a similar response but his expression darkened when it didn't arrive.

'You think this Pied Piper took Scott Wheeler?' asked Charlton.

'This is bullshit!' said Ford.

Brook hesitated, unsure about nailing his colours to the mast but decided he had no choice. 'I do.'

'And if this Pied Piper exists, what makes you think Scott Wheeler is still alive?'

'Because he keeps them alive and kills them on December the twenty-second,' said Copeland.

'You know about this, Clive?' asked Charlton.

'I know Bannon's fantasy inside out,' Copeland answered. 'And that's exactly what it is – a fantasy.'

'It's bullshit, that's what it is,' said Ford.

Copeland turned to Brook. 'Frank's right. The whole idea is insane.'

'I know,' said Brook. 'And that was Sam's biggest problem.' He hesitated. 'His other problem was nobody believed him because he was mentally unbalanced.' He hesitated. 'So disturbed that I think he may have murdered your sister.'

'What?' said Charlton.

'Sam Bannon murder Tilly?' exclaimed Copeland. 'You can't be serious.'

'I wouldn't joke about a thing like that, Clive,' said Brook.

Copeland narrowed his eyes to concentrate. 'Can you prove it?'

'I think so.'

'Sir, aren't we getting off the subject . . .' began Ford, only to be silenced by Charlton's hand.

'I want to hear this, Frank,' said Charlton, waving a hand for Brook to elaborate.

'Colin Ealy was a gamekeeper on the wooded estate where Matilda's body was found,' Brook explained for Charlton's benefit.

Oddly, he seemed to take the information in his stride. 'When Bannon drove out to Osmaston Park Lake a few days after Matilda's body was recovered, Ealy recognised him. Sam was aware of it. Others were too. Walter Laird and DS Graham Bell both noticed but said nothing to protect their boss. The next day Ealy dropped out of sight.'

'He ran off to Scotland,' said Copeland, still in shock. 'He was seen.'

'I don't think so,' said Brook quietly. 'I think Sam killed him that same night to shut him up. Either the sighting in Scotland was a mistake or a deliberate attempt by Sam to throw the inquiry off the scent.'

Charlton was sombre. He looked at Copeland. 'What do you think, Clive?'

Ford was aghast. 'You're not buying into this? What about hijacking my case and concealing the whereabouts of my suspect?'

'Frank,' said Charlton, 'would you and DS Noble leave us for a moment?' Noble pushed back his chair and headed for the door.

'I'd like DS Noble to stay,' said Brook. He declined to elaborate with Ford present but the senior detective needed no explanation.

'Oh, I see,' said Ford, sneering at Noble. 'You been keeping Brook in the loop behind my back, have you, Johnny boy?' Ford's scowl followed Noble back to his chair. 'And you wonder why you're still a DS.'

Brook turned on Ford. 'Sergeant Noble has behaved impeccably.'

'Not another fucking word from you,' spat Ford, standing to poke a digit into Brook's chest. 'You're a fucking nut job.'

Brook pushed Ford back to arm's length before Copeland and Noble jumped in to hold back the senior man.

'You're finished, Brook,' screamed Ford, struggling to get to Brook. As usual, Brook's response was a wide grin, which wound Ford up further. 'You hear me? Finished.'

'That's enough, Frank,' shouted Charlton above the scuffle. 'I have to explore every avenue if it helps us find a missing boy. You had your chance. Please leave.'

Emboldened by his sense of grievance, his face like thunder, his fists balling, Ford made another attempt to move against Brook but Copeland and Noble wouldn't budge.

'You piece of shit,' shouted Ford, eyes bulging with sudden fury. 'You should've been drummed out of CID years ago.'

'Get out,' Charlton roared at Ford. 'And close the door behind you.'

All four detectives froze at the unaccustomed violence in Charlton's voice. Then all eyes turned to Ford. A moment later, the veteran detective snorted his disdain and stomped towards the door. He turned and extended his scorn to Charlton. 'Why we bend over backwards for this washed-up . . .' He shook his head in disgust and slammed the door on his exit.

Charlton looked after Ford, briefly assessing the diplomatic effort required to bring him back into the fold. He turned to Copeland. 'Sam Bannon, Clive?'

Copeland shook his head. 'I don't know. Not in a million years did I suspect . . .'

'Why would a DCI abduct Tilly, a girl he doesn't know, and kill her?' demanded Charlton.

'Why do people do anything?' said Brook, puzzled by Charlton's easy familiarity with the case. *Tilly?* 'He wasn't in his right mind. His wife had died and he was unbalanced by her death. My guess is he saw Matilda walking up the common to meet her boyfriend and stopped to pick her up.'

'And then?' asked Charlton.

'Then?' Brook opened his hands. 'Maybe something happened, something triggered inside him and he lost his head. Perhaps he tried to kiss her and she resisted. Maybe she screamed or promised to tell someone and Bannon just snapped. Whatever happened, he killed Tilly then drove to Osmaston and dumped her body in the lake where he was seen by Colin Ealy.'

Copeland stared. 'And you have proof.'

Brook sighed. 'Shouldn't we be concentrating on Scott right now?'

'Your credibility in this division is zero, Brook,' said Charlton. 'I'm not letting you loose on another officer's case until I know I can trust you. Now do you have proof or not?'

'Not yet,' said Brook. 'But I've got a good idea where to find it.'

Darkness had fallen when Charlton speared a look of contempt towards Brook, caught in the reflected shimmer of the two arc lights trained on the lake.

'Why do I listen to you, Brook? Whenever I give you a chance, I end up with egg on my face and a bloody great hole in my budget.'

Brook decided silence was the best answer. He'd gambled and lost.

'What really disgusts me is holding out hope for a missing boy just to save your career. On my desk, tomorrow,' said Charlton, feeling no need to qualify the remark. 'And give the whereabouts of Brendan McCleary to Noble. Now! Or you'll be losing your liberty as well as your career.'

Charlton squelched away from the edge of the lake towards the Osmaston Park access road and its line of awkwardly parked vehicles. Brook watched him leave, disconsolate not about his own failings but the hope of resolution he'd given Copeland. The divers had been searching for several hours now and failing light combined with plummeting temperatures would soon curtail their work in the water.

Unable to watch, Copeland had stayed, hunched in his car, saucer-eyed as he contemplated the end of a near fifty-year search and then, when failure loomed, sat reflecting on its continuation. Brook exchanged a dejected glance with Noble, walked to Copeland's car and got into the passenger seat.

'I'm sorry, Clive,' he said. 'I thought . . .'

Copeland turned to him with a thin smile. 'Don't be sorry. At least you're doing something, trying something.'

'I don't think Charlton will be quite so forgiving.'

'Leave Charlton to me,' said Copeland quietly.

Brook studied him in the gloom. 'You have influence?' Copeland shrugged. 'That day when you and Charlton were arguing about

354

letting me work a particular case, it was Matilda's, wasn't it?' Copeland nodded. 'And you insisted I be put on it.'

Copeland turned to him. 'I told you, Brook. Everything I read told me you were the best man for the job.'

'But Charlton doesn't think that.'

'In his heart of hearts, I think he does,' said Copeland.

'He's got a funny way of showing it.'

'That's just his way.'

'Sounds like you know him well.'

'All my life.' Copeland smiled apologetically at Brook. 'He's my nephew on my mother's side,' he explained.

'Your nephew?' said Brook. 'You mean—'

'Yes,' interjected Copeland. 'Tilly was his aunt – would've been. He missed her by a year.'

Brook looked off into the black woods, mist beginning to snake along the ground. So much now made sense.

'Why here?' said Copeland suddenly.

'The lake? It's perfect,' said Brook, rousing himself to dredge up his failed theory. 'Who'd look for a body in a place that had so recently been thoroughly searched?'

'Especially if somebody knows to weigh the second body down.' Copeland nodded. 'Yes, I see that.'

'It seemed to make sense when I thought of it,' said Brook. 'Except for one thing.'

'What was that?'

'Something Walter Laird said. If Ealy saw Bannon the night Matilda's body was dumped, there should've been a report that he'd seen *someone* but there wasn't.'

'Maybe Ealy didn't realise he'd seen anyone until Bannon came to the lake that day,' suggested Copeland.

'Or the report got mislaid,' countered Brook.

'That's possible. It's been a long time.' Copeland shook his head. 'What I don't understand is why Walter didn't tell me.'

'He was protecting his friend,' said Brook. 'And now it looks like he had good reason.'

The two detectives were startled by an urgent hammering on the window.

Charlton finished tying his shoes and picked up his dirty wellington boots. He'd tried to scrape off all the mud on some bracken but it was impossible in the pitch black so he made do with laying the boots on an old newspaper.

He slammed the boot but before he could tiptoe delicately round to the driver's door, a noise off in the darkness turned him round. It was Brook.

'Don't bother to apologise, Brook. Because of you, I've got a senior officer to placate—'

'Sir,' interrupted Brook. 'They've found a body.'

'I owe you an apology, Brook,' said Charlton, gazing down at the skull by the light of a flashlight.

'No need, sir,' said Brook. 'We all get overwrought when cases get personal.'

Charlton's head darted towards Brook then over at Copeland who seemed to be in a trance. 'Yes we do,' he conceded, putting a consoling arm on Copeland's shoulder. 'It's over, Clive.'

'Fractured skull, would you say?' said Copeland, ignoring Charlton. He knelt to touch the large crack in the back of the skull.

'Looks that way,' said Brook. 'Bannon must have caught Ealy off guard and hit him with something when his back was turned.'

'When his back was turned,' echoed Copeland. He looked up as though about to ask a question then seemed to think better of it. 'Yes.' He glanced towards his colleagues. 'Well, it's been a long day.' He marched away like a robot towards the access road.

'He's in shock,' said Brook to Charlton.

'It's been a long time,' said Charlton. 'Are you staying?'

Brook shook his head. 'I've still got Scott Wheeler to find and his time's almost up.'

'OK, Brook,' said Charlton. 'You've got my attention. Tell me.'

'I have to do this alone.'

'Do what?'

'I can't tell you.'

'Because it involves breaking the law,' sighed Charlton.

'Maybe a slight bend.' Brook waited, his lips pursed. He knew he'd get the go-ahead – finding the missing boy would be a massive feather in Charlton's cap.

'Deniable?' asked a weary Charlton. Brook nodded. 'And after that?'

'If I'm right, I'll need a large search team prepared to move on my say-so. Dogs, helicopters, the lot.'

'Where?'

'I don't know. Hopefully—'

'Wait, you don't have any idea where Scott is?' said Charlton, his expression showing pain.

'None,' replied Brook.

Charlton closed his eyes and rubbed a gloved hand over his brow. 'What do you need from me?'

'I just need you to be ready. And Sergeant Noble.'

With a resigned sigh, Charlton gave Brook a sideways glance. 'Take him. It's his case, after all.'

Brook returned to his vehicle in the dark. Clive Copeland's car was gone.

'Clive gone home?' he called over to Noble.

Noble nodded. 'He looked exhausted.'

'I bet.'

'Must be weird finding a killer you've been hunting for that long. Then suddenly it's over.'

'It'll never be over,' said Brook.

'What do you mean?'

'To Clive, this isn't a result because he can never face his sister's killer.' After a moment's silence, Brook cleared his head with a long pull of oxygen. 'Speaking of killers, John. We've got work to do.'

'The Pied Piper?' inquired Noble. At Brook's slight nod, he smiled in the gloom.

357

Brook hesitated. 'I may have to get a little . . . creative with how I proceed,' he said.

'You mean you're going to break the law.'

'If you'd rather—'

'Let's go get him, sir. There's a young lad who should be with his family.'

Twenty-Six

Friday, 21 December 2012 – early hours

EDWARD MULLEN WOKE TO THE high-pitched whine of the smoke alarm, leapt out of bed and ran along the landing. Stepping over the stairlift at the top, he bounded down the stairs and, from the bottom step, peered warily through the smoke. Adjusting his eyes to the gloom, he was surprised to see the bucket of water no longer behind the door but standing half-empty against the back wall. Further, burnt newspaper was floating in the water, doubtless the source of the flames.

With the alarm at its loudest, Mullen moved smartly to the door, his bare feet squelching on the sodden carpet. Reaching out a hand, he opened the door to waft away the lingering smoke. After a moment, the smoke cleared and the alarm fell silent and Mullen refastened the door, leaving the key in the lock.

Mullen's breathing began to slow as his brain picked up the pace. In the pitch black, he spun round, his squinting eyes alighting upon a foreign object in the living room, a shadowy figure sitting motionless at the dining table.

'Is that how it was with Joshua and Scott?' said a male voice Mullen recognised.

Mullen stared at the indistinct outline then back at the locked door. 'How did you get in?'

'I broke in,' replied the voice, without embarrassment.

Mullen paused to process the information, saying nothing. Shivering, he padded into the room and reached for an old cardigan on the back of a chair, slipped it over his pyjamas then pulled a box of matches from the pocket to light a candle. Its meagre light trembled to reveal his uninvited guest and Mullen stared into Brook's cold eyes. 'I thought we had an understanding.'

'I asked you about Joshua and Scott,' said Brook. 'If you're having trouble with your memory, it was October the thirty-first last year, the night Joshua Stapleton was murdered.'

Mullen was sombre. 'I remember perfectly. It was trick or treat night – an evening of dread for respectable homeowners everywhere.'

'And you had no treats to offer them,' put in Brook. No response this time. 'And so they pushed a burning rag through your letter box.'

'They did,' replied Mullen evenly. 'Only back then I didn't have a bucket of water to douse the flames or an alarm to wake me. I could have been killed.'

'But you weren't,' replied Brook. 'It must have helped being so nimble, especially for a man with a stick and a stairlift.'

'The lift was for my mother,' explained Mullen, finally cracking a smile. 'I've always been sound of limb.'

'If not of mind.'

Mullen grinned. 'Ouch.'

Brook's face was impassive, determined. 'So you're able to leave the house whenever you like.'

Mullen shrugged. 'I haven't exaggerated my difficulties with people but I can get around as I please. Nights are best.'

'And when you'd put out the fire, you went out that night,' continued Brook. 'In search of the perpetrators.'

Mullen hesitated. 'Yes.'

'And decided to come out of retirement.'

'Retirement?'

'You were . . . are the Pied Piper,' said Brook.

Mullen's smile was modesty itself. He lit another candle. 'DCI Bannon's name for me.' He moved to the wood burner and threw on

360

newspaper and a few sticks and revived the glowing ashes with another match. 'I suppose it accurately sums up what I do.'

'Then why kill again after nearly a quarter of a century?' asked Brook. 'Or have you never stopped?'

'Oh no, I stopped.' Mullen continued lighting candles, warming to the conversation. Brook followed his progress around the room. In the burgeoning light Brook saw the place setting in front of him then the whole table – a dozen party plates and beakers, brightly coloured napkins on top. A Sara Lee birthday cake sat in its box in the middle of the table. After another candle, he noticed the tired, old-fashioned birthday cards on the mantel and the large banner tied across the hearth. *HAPPY BIRTHDAY BILLY.*

'I had no intention of killing again, no need,' continued Mullen, blowing out a match and moving to sit opposite Brook. 'Billy had more than enough company to see him through eternity.' Mullen's face hardened. 'But when those two little *shits* imposed themselves on my life, I couldn't help myself.'

'Old habits?' suggested Brook.

'Something like that,' chuckled Mullen.

'So you followed them?'

'Only to see who they were,' explained Mullen quickly. 'I had no thought of harvesting one of them.'

Harvesting! 'But all that changed the moment you saw Scott kill his friend.'

Mullen's eyebrow arched in surprise. 'You know?'

'I do now,' said Brook.

Mullen nodded. 'Not before time.'

'You seem annoyed.'

'You would be too,' said Mullen. 'Seeing a life taken so . . . thoughtlessly. No sense to it.'

'Your killing is different,' said Brook.

'Very,' replied Mullen, raising an index finger. 'Seeing that animal Scott behaving like that . . . it was sickening. The Stapleton boy was no angel but he didn't deserve to die like that.'

'And Scott does,' said Brook.

'Absolutely,' retorted Mullen, indignant. 'He's a killer and I only harvest the guilty, Brook. I only select those with no thought for others.'

'So Scott selected himself by killing his friend.'

'You understand perfectly,' smiled Mullen.

'Far from it, he's a thirteen-year-old boy,' said Brook.

'Thirteen. Thirty. What does it matter?'

'Quite a lot under the law.'

'The law,' laughed Mullen. 'After what you've done, you're getting on a very high horse. No matter. Think me a monster, if you must, Brook, but when Billy needed company, I never once considered taking the innocent, only the guilty. Francesca, Jeff Ward and the others, they all had it coming.'

'Because someone close to them had died.'

'Died?' exclaimed Mullen. 'That's a polite way of putting it. Every child I've taken has killed, has deliberately taken another life.'

Brook studied him. 'You know that for a fact?'

'Not for a court of law,' replied Mullen. 'But I know it.'

'Because you see their victims in a vision,' said Brook contemptuously.

'That's right,' said Mullen, unabashed. 'Except for Scott. I was a live spectator to his fall from grace.'

'Francesca too, I think.'

Mullen was puzzled. 'What do you mean?'

'You told me once that she killed Billy,' said Brook. 'You were there that night. You must have seen her do it.'

'What do you think I am?' said Mullen, his eyes blazing. 'My friend died in agony. If I'd seen her lock Billy in that shed, I would have moved heaven and earth to stop her.'

'Then how did you know what she'd done?'

'I saw her, of course,' said Mullen. 'Not then. Years later.' The pain etched on his face turned to pleasure. 'I saw Billy again. He was with her, do you see?'

'No, I don't see,' snapped Brook. 'Any more than you do.'

'I sometimes wish you were right.' Mullen hauled himself to his feet and moved to the cabinet, extracted the near-empty bottle of port and poured himself a small glass. 'When my family moved to Derby after Billy died I didn't see anyone from Kirk Langley for years. I tried to forget what happened to my friend. Then, when I was sixteen, I had an accident. I fell from a tree branch and hit my head and my life changed forever. That's when I began seeing things.'

'Ghosts,' mocked Brook.

'Not ghosts,' protested Mullen. 'Imprints of people's lives that have been snuffed out by lethal violence.'

'The unquiet grave?'

'Exactly, Brook. The victims of violence attach themselves to their killer forever and I could see them. It was driving me insane until I realised what I was looking at. Stepfathers with their abused and murdered children, old people with a spouse they'd suffocated with a pillow, young men walking next to the drunk they'd stabbed. I nearly went mad.

'But one marvellous day I met Francesca again and I saw Billy. She was outside a pub in town, drunk at eleven thirty in the morning. Billy was with her. At first I thought I was dreaming. The friend I'd lost was there before my eyes.' Mullen laughed without humour. 'I even shouted across to him. He didn't respond, of course, and Francesca was too drunk to understand. But I wasn't. And I realised what I was seeing.'

'When was this?'

'About six months before I killed her. That's when I got the idea.' Mullen took a sip of port and stared off into the shadows. 'That's when I knew Francesca had killed my friend and suddenly I saw my path back to Billy.' He looked at Brook, his eyes shining with zeal. 'If I became a killer, if I killed Fran, then she would be with me forever and, if there was a God in heaven, Billy would be with me too.'

'If he was an *imprint*, wouldn't he be horribly burned?' said Brook.

'I wondered about that too,' said Mullen. 'But, no. You see he died of smoke inhalation, before the flames consumed his body. That's why he didn't scream.'

'And so you killed Francesca on Billy's birthday.'

'It seemed appropriate somehow,' said Mullen. 'I was giving him the gift of my friendship for eternity – no more traipsing beside his killer, lost and confused in perpetuity. Apart from that, I was no killer so I worried about covering my tracks. I figured if the police became suspicious that Fran's death wasn't an accident, dying on her brother's birthday might tip them towards suicide. Especially with her drinking.' He raised an eyebrow. 'It seems I needn't have worried. The police didn't give it a second look.' Mullen broke into a huge grin. 'It was all so easy. I was nervous naturally but as soon as the last bubble of oxygen had left her mouth, there they all were beside me. One big happy family, Francesca, Billy, Charlotte . . .'

'Charlotte Dilkes?' exclaimed Brook, narrowing his eyes.

'Of course. Didn't I say?'

'You mean Francesca . . .'

Mullen nodded. 'Drowned poor Charlotte, yes.'

'Why?'

'I can't be sure but my impression is that Charlotte saw the padlock key in Fran's hand while the rest of us stood around watching Billy burn. The silly girl didn't realise the significance until later and instead of telling an adult, she confronted Francesca.'

'And Jeff Ward?' said Brook. 'What was his crime?'

'Jeff had a younger brother. Donny,' said Mullen. 'He drowned in a river but it was Jeff who pushed him under. I'd harvested two killers, two more companions for Billy, two murders avenged. And, of course, I had the pattern of dates going now, so that was fun.'

'Fun?' repeated Brook. 'You're insane.'

'If it's crazy to remove two souls who killed siblings out of petty jealousy, bring on the straitjacket,' said Mullen.

'You couldn't know that for sure,' said Brook. 'You had no evidence.'

'Evidence,' spat Mullen. 'I have better than that. I can find the killers of people the police don't even know are dead. Don't talk to me about evidence when you lot can't even arrest Scott Wheeler for killing his friend.'

'It wasn't my case,' replied Brook, on the back foot suddenly.

'And a killer escapes punishment. Well, my justice is not that random, Inspector,' said Mullen. 'I convicted Jeff Ward the first time I clapped eyes on him. His brother Donny walked beside him. When he drowned he was wearing a Dennis the Menace jumper – it was so wet and heavy, it almost covered his knees, the poor little mite.'

'And the balloon?'

'He must have been clutching it in his hand before he went in the water,' said Mullen, shaking his head. 'Can you imagine anything so pathetic? A little boy, dead forever and only his killer to know he'd been murdered.'

'That's why you impersonate the victim,' said Brook. 'To get the killer's attention.'

Mullen was surprised and delighted. 'You worked it out. Yes, I bought the same clothes as Donny, even managed to find the balloon, and all I had to do was wait for Billy's birthday.' Mullen grinned at the memory. 'The murdering little swine's eyes nearly popped out of their sockets and he would've followed me to hell to hide what he'd done. You've read the case file?'

Brook nodded.

'Does it mention how he obliterated all my footprints in the snow, thinking they were Donny's? There's guilt for you.'

Brook was impassive. Mullen was in the zone and Brook didn't want to staunch the flow. 'And Harry Pritchett's sister?'

'They thought she'd run in front of a car.' Mullen shook his head. 'But one little push changes everything. I think Harry was sorry he'd done it. That was something.' He drained his glass, looking sadly towards the fire. 'Then there was Davie Whatmore's baby brother who was supposed to have succumbed to cot death.'

'Have you considered that you might just be crazy?' said Brook softly.

'Of course,' said Mullen. 'But doesn't considering it make me sane? Besides, I stopped at will.' Mullen paused. 'Just like you.'

'Until Scott,' retorted Brook, not rising to the bait.

'Until Scott,' conceded the old man. He raised a finger. 'But would a lunatic stop at all? Could he? The opposite, I think. The mentally deranged killer can't stop, not until he's caught. No impulse control, you see. That's not me. Or you.' Mullen was suddenly sombre. 'I only took those who deserved it, Brook, and I've no reason to doubt that you did the same. From what I've seen, Floyd was a killer too.'

'You don't know anything about me,' said Brook.

'On the contrary. I know you're a killer. Like me.'

Brook was silent.

'No denial?' teased Mullen.

'I won't dignify it with a denial,' said Brook. 'Floyd Wrigley's death—'

'Is a matter of public record,' smiled Mullen. 'I know. And you were there.' Brook didn't answer. 'And you were hunting a serial killer. The Reaper. But you found Floyd. Another killer. And you decided to act. After all, for a man of your talents, it must have been easy to chalk up his murder to the man you were hunting.'

Brook's power of speech had deserted him. With a deep breath he found his voice. 'You're guessing. It was over twenty years ago. You can't possibly know Floyd was a killer.'

'Can't I?' Mullen's expression was one of supreme confidence. 'So did you kill the girl who walks with him as well? I'm shocked. I assumed Floyd had slaughtered her before you extracted vengeance.'

Brook was startled, unable to breathe, but he managed to pant an inquiry. 'Girl?'

'There's a young girl with him in her own unquiet grave,' said Mullen. 'She's had terrible violence done to her. Please tell me that wasn't you, Inspector.'

Brook stared at Mullen, stony-faced. *Laura.*

'Would you like me to tell you her name?' asked Mullen, solicitously.

Brook shook his head. There was silence now. Brook had more questions but they could wait. There was only one issue now. 'That changes nothing. Where's Scott?'

'That's enough for tonight,' said Mullen. 'I'm tired. I think you should leave.'

'I can't do that,' said Brook. 'I won't let you kill another child, no matter what he's done.'

'And I can't let you have him,' said Mullen, standing. 'Not now. Everything's prepared.'

'Tell me where he is,' insisted Brook.

'He's close.'

Brook sat up. *Present tense*. 'In the house?'

'Don't be stupid.'

'But he's alive.'

Mullen looked around the room, smiling and nodding as though greeting friends at a party. 'For a while yet, I think. But he'll be along. They both will.'

'*They?*' repeated Brook.

'Scott's bringing Joshua with him. Keep up. They're together forever. Like you and Floyd. And the girl. You didn't kill her, did you? But she's in your dreams, I'll wager.'

'Where is Scott?' said Brook, managing to inject urgency into his request.

'You're becoming repetitive, Inspector. Your thoughts should be for his victim and the degrading way he died.'

'If it was so degrading why did you watch it happen and do nothing?'

'It may have escaped your notice but I'm an old man,' protested Mullen in an injured tone. 'I wasn't going to get between Scott and his prey. The boy's an animal.'

'But it took Josh hours to die.'

'His neck was broken. There was nothing I could do.'

'You could have called an ambulance.'

'Why? The boy was nothing to me,' said Mullen. 'If he'd had his way, I would have burned to death. I let things take their natural

367

course and waited for justice to be done.' He laughed. 'But instead of arresting Scott, you pinned it on some bewildered tramp who happened to be dossing at the house.'

'It wasn't my case,' repeated Brook, feeling the need for distance from DI Ford.

'It's academic now. Justice is near.'

'An eye for an eye?'

'I'm not a vigilante, Brook.' The old man's cold eyes goaded. 'Not like you. But every time I saw my blackened door and Scott Wheeler's grinning face in the paper, I felt the pull of the Piper, enticing me to one last kill.' He laughed. 'And I've got to be honest, playing Joshua was the most fun – he was much nearer my height and build, especially in the dark. Jeff's brother too. The others were harder. I had to improvise. But Scott was careless. He allowed me to see the living victim, made it easy for me. I could impersonate Josh's mannerisms and body language as well as wear the clothes. I could become Joshua's double.' Mullen laughed, warming to the memory. 'You should have seen Scott's face when he saw me that night. It was like he'd seen a ghost.'

'You mean an imprint,' said Brook, sourly.

Mullen smiled. 'You're getting the idea.'

'So the others,' prompted Brook. 'The ones that were harder to take. Did you send them a letter like Scott's?'

'You saw that?' said Mullen eagerly. 'What did you think?'

'A message from a dead friend,' said Brook. 'Hard to ignore.'

'I cut the letters out of the paper from the day Joshua died,' grinned Mullen. 'For added effect.'

'We noticed,' said Brook. 'Taken from the stack of old editions I found in your kitchen, no doubt.' He smiled for the first time. 'Exhibit A.'

'I'm a hoarder, it's true.' Mullen was not put off his stride. 'My own worst enemy – newspapers, candles, teenage boys.'

'Tell me where he is, Mullen. If he's alive, I can help you. You're not well.'

'If you'd seen just *one* of the victims, you wouldn't say that.'

'Spare me the fake sympathy,' said Brook.

Mullen's expression hardened. 'I'm not made of stone, Brook. And if you'd seen Scott on Whitaker Road a few nights after he killed Joshua, you'd thank me for what I'm doing. The house was due for demolition and he went there and he watched where his friend died and I saw the cruel smirk on his face. He'd got away with it.' Mullen grinned with satisfaction. 'It was a pleasure slipping that letter into his pocket the week before I harvested him. And I can guarantee he hasn't smiled from that day to this.'

'Hasn't he? Well, explain this,' said Brook. 'If Scott was such an animal, how did a frail old man like you manage to *harvest* him that night?'

Mullen tapped his skull. 'Because his mind was gone, Brook. That's why I gave him the letter. That's what psychological warfare does to you. Like chess. Scott was a nervous wreck, always looking over his shoulder, jumping out of his skin at every loud noise. He only needed one more push to be a gibbering idiot and, when he saw me in Joshua's clothes, he was finished. It was just a question of leading him where I wanted him.'

'Where was that?'

'Please stop asking.'

'No,' barked Brook. 'Tell me where he is.'

'I'll let you know as soon as he joins us.'

'I want him alive. Give him to me and I'll see that he pays for Joshua's death.'

'Really? Like you paid for Floyd Wrigley's?'

Brook was silent.

Mullen smiled in genuine sympathy. 'We shouldn't be arguing, Inspector. We provide a public service. We're brothers-in-arms, you and I.'

'We're nothing of the kind,' snorted Brook. 'You don't know me or what I've done.'

'Think that if it gives you comfort.' Mullen smiled. 'But I warned you secrets can't be kept from me.' He took a sip of port. 'Floyd will always be with you, Inspector. He belongs to you and has done since

369

the day you killed him. Think yourself lucky you can't see him. For some of my clients, even that was no consolation. They couldn't handle it.'

'Floyd Wrigley was a pimp who prostituted his ten-year-old daughter so he could buy drugs,' said Brook softly, staring into space.

'You don't need to explain. I'm sure he deserved it.'

'He was also a rapist and a murderer.'

Mullen hesitated, the port bottle in his hand. 'But you couldn't prove it. You see, I understand. It's not so hard to kill killers, to make them suffer for eternity. We're equals, you and I. Whatever you've done in the distant past, I won't judge you.'

'You're in no position to judge.'

Mullen smiled back at Brook. 'Conversely, neither are you.'

Brook emitted his one-note laugh. 'You're wrong, Mullen. I do judge you. I made a mistake that I've regretted every day of my life but you, you kill children in cold blood and smile about it.'

'Be careful with that lofty tone,' said Mullen coldly. 'You've got a lot more to lose than me.'

'Less than you think,' replied Brook, a thin smile deforming his lips.

Mullen hesitated. 'I mean it. You have no right to look down on me.'

'I don't look down on you,' replied Brook. 'Now where's Scott?'

'About to meet the fate that all killers deserve.'

'Tell me where he is, Edward,' said Brook tenderly. 'If we save him I'll help you.'

'Go home, Brook,' said Mullen. 'This doesn't concern you.'

'It's all that concerns me.'

'Then you're going to be disappointed,' said Mullen. 'Scott's body will never be found. Not while I'm alive, at least. Now I'd like you to leave, Inspector. I have a birthday party to organise and I'm tired.'

'A party for a dead boy,' said Brook. 'Just listen to yourself.'

'I do little else, Inspector,' said Mullen.

Brook nodded at the table. 'Quite a crowd you're expecting.'

'They're already here,' answered Mullen, gesturing around the room. 'They never leave.'

'Where's Sam Bannon so I can wave?' asked Brook.

'Sam Bannon?' said Mullen, his eyes narrowing. 'Why would he be here?'

'Because he worked out what you were doing when Harry Pritchett disappeared and came after you,' said Brook.

'That was impressive, given his health,' admitted Mullen. 'But why would I kill Bannon?' Mullen's expression told its own story.

Why kill a madman, believed by nobody? Brook began to harbour his first doubts but decided he had to play his hand for all it was worth. 'Because he knew you were the Pied Piper.'

'So what?' said Mullen. 'Harry was safely hidden away and Sam Bannon was losing his mind. Not one of his colleagues believed a word he said. He couldn't prove a thing, especially as he was working to a flawed hypothesis.'

Brook was silent for a moment, thinking it through. 'Billy?'

Mullen nodded. 'Exactly. For Bannon's Pied Piper theory to make sense I must have killed Billy and to prove I killed Billy he needed to break my alibi for the night he died.'

'But he couldn't break it,' said Brook softly. 'Your alibi was genuine.'

'I didn't kill my friend,' said Mullen, holding out his hands. 'I said so all along but Bannon wouldn't accept it. He kept badgering Mrs Stanforth, even at her daughter's funeral.' He glanced at Brook. 'I'm sorry I lied about that but you were starting to ask the right questions so I thought it better to draw you away.'

'No apology needed,' said Brook. 'That lie confirmed you were the Pied Piper.'

'How?' said a puzzled Mullen.

'I spoke to Amelia.'

'Amelia?' Mullen was startled. 'You've seen her? Is she all right?'

'She's fine,' said Brook.

'I'm glad. And she remembered Bannon harassing her mother about me?'

'Like it was yesterday,' said Brook, suddenly deep in thought.

'Well.' Mullen shrugged, eyeing the empty bottle of port with regret. 'Now we've established our mutual interest, what does it matter?'

'How do you know Sam Bannon's colleagues didn't believe him?' asked Brook.

Mullen's hesitation betrayed a false step. Eventually he answered. 'They didn't come after me, did they?'

'No, they didn't.' An unexpected smile creased Brook's lips as he found his mark. 'One visit,' he murmured.

'Pardon.'

'One visit from experienced detectives and then they left you alone. In fact, some didn't even bother interviewing you at all.'

'I don't know what you're talking about,' replied Mullen.

'Rosie was right. You've been protected all along,' said Brook, warming to his theme. 'By someone like you, someone with secrets and a mutual interest in self-preservation.'

'Why would I need protection?'

'Because you're a killer,' said Brook.

'We both are,' said Mullen.

'You can drop this fantasy now,' said Brook. 'Because if you could really see ghosts, the imprints of murder victims, you'd know that Sam Bannon killed twice.'

Mullen's face creased with consternation. 'What? When?'

'Nineteen sixty-five,' said Brook, smiling. 'Didn't see those *imprints*, did you?'

'I don't believe it.' Mullen stared at Brook. Suddenly he broke into an unsettling grin. 'No, you're right, I missed those.'

Mullen's self-assurance unnerved Brook so he reached for his final round of ammunition.

'And your moral posturing is in tatters after killing Edna.' Brook watched closely, no great confidence in his accusation but Mullen was taken aback.

After a beat, the old man's surprise gave way to admiration. 'I'm impressed. How did you know? I made it look like suicide.'

'I'm a trained detective,' replied Brook. 'I told you she was murdered and the natural question was to ask how. You didn't. But more than that, Edna would never leave a dirty teacup in the sink if she was going to commit suicide. You should have known that much. That's not how your generation do things.'

'I underestimated you, Brook,' said Mullen thoughtfully.

'So much for harvesting the guilty.'

'I'm not ashamed, Brook. Yes, Edna's here with us because that's what she wanted. She's happy here.'

'Why would she be happy?' demanded Brook.

'Because she wanted me to kill her.'

'I don't believe it,' said Brook. 'You're saying it was a mercy killing?'

'No, Edna was in a lot of pain but she could handle that,' replied Mullen. 'It was her mental suffering she wanted to end. You see, she wanted me to *help* her the way I helped her husband when he was dying.'

'Assisted suicide?' exclaimed Brook. 'You're lying. Edna Spencer was a Catholic. Her husband too.'

'But their devotion dwindled when they realised how their God had abandoned them,' said Mullen. 'Edna couldn't stand to see Eric suffering. They were my friends so I helped him on his way. That meant he could cling to me. When Eric was gone, I was able to tell Edna that he was with me, that he was safe, that he loved her.'

'She was a client?'

'She was a friend,' said Mullen. 'And when the time was right, Edna wanted me to do the same for her so she and Eric could both be together for the rest of time.'

'With you?'

'A small price to pay.'

'In your little stable of ghosts.'

'If that's how you want to describe it.'

Brook shook his head. 'A mercy killer. I don't think so. You killed Edna because she knew you'd taken Scott.'

Mullen's eyes narrowed. 'Not so.'

'You couldn't let her live. She might have given you up.'

'No.'

'She knew something that could harm you and you killed her because she was a threat.'

'She wanted my help,' insisted Mullen. 'Why won't you believe me?'

'"No child deserves to die." Edna's last words to me,' said Brook. 'She knew what you were, Mullen – a child killer. Maybe she did turn a blind eye because she thought you were some kind of link to her husband but that was about to change.'

'You're guessing.'

'Am I? She was on the verge of telling me. She couldn't stand the thought of another boy suffering. Instead, she spoke to you to tell you to stop and you killed her for it.'

'All the effort you've put into these wild allegations and you can't prove any of it, can you?' smirked Mullen. 'Curiously, I have Sam Bannon to thank for forcing me to make myself bombproof.'

Brook's eyes bored into Mullen. 'You're not bombproof yet. We're still working the forensics on Edna's flat and if they find something—'

'They won't.'

'If they do—'

'If they do, you will bury it,' said Mullen, bringing a fist down on to the table. 'Because when it comes to making accusations of murder, your hands are tied.'

'As others have been before me?' asked Brook. Mullen opened his mouth to speak but closed it again. 'One visit,' continued Brook. 'Did they think I wouldn't notice? Did you?'

'Go home, Brook,' said Mullen.

'Do you think your ghost stories will stop me from putting you away?'

'Without a doubt,' said Mullen. 'You've got too much to lose.'

'It'd be my word against yours and who'd believe you?'

'Can you take that chance?' countered a grinning Mullen. 'Read the papers, Brook. You're not well-liked. Something else we have in common. There'll be plenty of takers if you force me to turn you in.'

Brook didn't answer for a while, simply staring thoughtfully at Mullen. 'Where's Scott?' he said eventually.

'Do I have to call the police?' demanded Mullen.

'Your friends can't help you any more,' said Brook. 'You need professional help.'

'Then for your sake, let's hope I don't get it,' said Mullen. 'Now I need you to leave. I'm tired and I've got a busy day ahead.' He stood to draw matters to a close.

Brook considered him for a moment before also getting to his feet. He walked solemnly to the front door.

Mullen's friendly smile returned. 'Don't worry, Brook. I never betray a confidence.'

Brook opened the door, turning back to Mullen for the last time. His eyes alighted on the oak table. The chessboard was bare.

Mullen followed his glance to the empty board then grinned back at Brook. 'Game over, Brook. You lose.'

Brook took a step across the threshold before shouting, 'Sergeant!'

Mullen's face drained. 'What are you doing?'

Noble walked through the door and held a document in front of Mullen. 'Mr Edward Mullen, we have a warrant to search your property. Please step aside.'

Mullen snatched the warrant and glared at Brook. 'You'll be sorry for this.'

Brook ignored him. 'I'll take the upstairs, John. You do downstairs.' He pulled out his mobile as he trotted to the first floor. 'Sir? DI Brook. I need that team now.'

Mullen sat resentfully at the table in front of the chessboard unable to do little more than stare at the heavy curtains. All around him uniformed officers poked around the room, some searching shelves and cabinets, others pulling up the ancient carpet to check the integrity of the floorboards. DS Noble and DC Cooper sifted through the untidy bookcase. Other officers did similar work in the kitchen and adjacent dining room.

'It might help if we had more light,' said Cooper. 'Is this guy Batman or what?'

'Eyes on the prize, Dave,' reproached Noble. 'We're looking for a lost kid, remember.'

Chief Superintendent Charlton walked through the front door at that moment, getting his bearings and looking round in distaste at the furnishings and general state of decay.

Mullen jumped up to speak to him but was held down by a uniformed constable. 'Are you in charge?'

Charlton nodded in acknowledgement.

'I want to swear out a complaint or whatever it is I need to do,' said Mullen. 'This is an outrage. I'm an intensely private man and Detective Inspector Brook broke into my home and interrogated me against my will.'

'That's a very serious charge,' said Charlton. 'Broke in how?'

'Through the front door. He knocked over my water bucket.'

Charlton backtracked to the front door to examine the locks. 'I don't see any damage.' He patted the sopping wet doormat with a shoe and, confused, glanced up at Noble who made a circular sign against his head with a finger. *Crazy.*

'He's a policeman, isn't he?' protested Mullen. 'He must have skeleton keys or something.'

'Sergeant?' said Charlton.

'Total rubbish, sir,' said Noble. 'DI Brook and I knocked on the door and served the warrant together.'

'He's lying,' spat Mullen.

'Another serious charge,' said Charlton, not taking his eyes from Noble. The detective sergeant blanched under his searching gaze.

'I don't even know what I'm supposed to have done,' protested Mullen, again failing to get to his feet.

'Calm down, sir,' said Charlton. 'You'll get a hearing once we finish our business.'

'But you've no right,' protested Mullen. 'And no evidence of wrongdoing. At least tell me what you want.'

Brook came down the stairs, his expression severe. He didn't need to speak but shook his head briefly at Charlton for good measure. Charlton pursed his lips but resolved not to interrogate Brook in front of a civilian.

'John?' ventured Brook. Noble shook his head in turn and Brook turned away to mask his frustration.

'Perhaps it's good that you're here, after all,' said Mullen, a smile forming.

'Sir?' inquired Charlton.

'I should tell you that on an earlier visit, DI Brook confessed to me that he's a murderer.' Mullen looked cheerfully round the gathering to gauge reaction, his eyes landing finally on Brook's impassive features.

'Murderer?' said Charlton.

'You heard me,' confirmed Mullen, pointing at Brook. 'Him. See, he's not bothering to deny it.'

'What are you talking about, sir?' asked Charlton.

'In nineteen ninety-one, when DI Brook was serving in London, he encountered a black man named Floyd Wrigley, during a case. And when he couldn't prove this man was a killer, Brook executed him.'

'Executed?' Charlton looked at every face, baffled.

'Cut his throat,' added Mullen with relish.

There was complete silence for half a minute as six law enforcement officers contemplated the slight figure of Mullen before them. Noble broke the silence, his emerging grin turning into laughter which the others, Charlton aside, echoed.

'What are you laughing at?' cried Mullen. 'Didn't you hear what I said? Brook is a murderer. And you can check what I say.'

'How do you know this?' asked Charlton, looking from Mullen to Brook, fighting his own nascent smile.

'There *was* a Floyd Wrigley involved in the original Reaper inquiry in London, sir,' said Noble. 'I've read about it.'

'The Reaper case! Yes,' said Mullen, turning to look gleefully at Brook.

'Is that true?' Charlton asked Brook.

'About Floyd Wrigley?' said Brook. 'Yes, sir, Mr Mullen's correct. Wrigley did live in Brixton and his throat was cut. It's public knowledge. He and his family were killed by the Reaper.'

'Brian Burton wrote a book about the case after the Reaper struck in Derby,' put in Noble.

'Brian Burton, yes,' nodded Charlton uncertainly. 'I remember it.'

Mullen's confidence turned to confusion when he saw the pity in the expressions of his audience. He turned to see DC Cooper behind him, holding aloft a book in his gloved hands. It was called *In Search of the Reaper*, by Brian Burton.

'Is this the book?' said Cooper.

'That's the one,' confirmed Noble.

Mullen turned back to Brook, his face draining of blood. 'Where did you get that?'

'It was on your bookshelves, sir,' said Cooper.

'That's a lie!' said Mullen, trying again to stand but being pushed down again. 'Brook brought that with him or else one of you planted it.'

'How many allegations are you going to make tonight, sir?' said Charlton.

'I've never owned that book,' said Mullen. To Brook he said, 'You planted it. Admit it.'

'You need help, Mr Mullen,' said Brook.

'Hang on, there's a page marked,' said Cooper. He opened the book and showed the page to Charlton who stared at the underlined name of Floyd Wrigley.

'Mr Mullen,' said Charlton quietly, taking the book and showing the page to the old man. 'When you level false accusations against any of my officers, I guarantee I'll come at you with everything the law allows.'

'That's not my book, I tell you,' Mullen spluttered.

'It was on your shelf, in your home.' Mullen was silent. After a pause, Charlton continued. 'So, we'll forget the wild allegations, shall we, sir? Before you get into any more trouble.'

Mullen opened his mouth to speak but thought better of it. He glared at Brook. Brook held his gaze before glancing at the chess-board then back again. His meaning didn't escape Mullen. *Game over.*

Mullen stared back at him. *OK, I've lost a battle but I'm winning the war.* 'Very well. But I want you out of here,' he insisted, dredging up a semblance of indignation. 'I've done nothing wrong.'

Charlton couldn't argue. He looked round at Brook. 'Is there anything more?'

'There's a shed at the back of the house,' said Brook, glancing at Mullen. His slender hopes were dashed when a confident smile began to spread across the elderly man's face.

'And then will you leave?' said Mullen.

'Certainly, sir,' said Charlton smoothly, already plotting a course back to being the helpful public servant rather than law enforcer.

Mullen got grudgingly to his feet and, feigning disability, hobbled to the rear of the house to pluck a bunch of keys from a hook.

The senior officers of the search party trooped through the back door after Mullen, Brook in tow, his heart heavy. As Brook had surmised on his previous visit, the garden at the rear was a jungle, with grass and weeds above waist height. The overgrown path had to be negotiated with care, torches trained on the ground to avoid animal excrement and slugs. At the ramshackle shed, Noble took the padlock key from Mullen, unlocked it and pulled open the flimsy door.

The blades of a helicopter roared overhead and a strong searchlight illuminated the scene. Brook glanced at Charlton.

'Ours,' said the Chief Superintendent.

Three lights shone into the shed and Noble squeezed himself inside, head stooped. He walked to the far end of the shed, knocking forlornly on walls, ceiling and floor with a knuckle. The structure was virtually empty and when Noble returned he had only a shiny new spade and garden fork to show for his search.

'Gardening tools,' said Mullen, trying to keep the smugness in check. 'Satisfied?'

'Well, that's it,' said Charlton, turning away. 'I'm sorry you were inconvenienced, sir.'

'Inconvenienced?' cried Mullen above the roar of the helicopter. 'I've been violated and you haven't heard the last—'

'Wait!' said Brook. All heads turned.

'What?' said Charlton.

'The spade.'

'What of it?' demanded Charlton.

'It's new,' pointed out Brook.

'And?'

'Right. Why does he need a spade at all?' said Noble. 'He's not using it in this garden.'

Charlton turned to Mullen. Brook was thrilled to see anxiety spread across the old man's face. 'Well, sir. Do you have an explanation?'

Before Mullen could answer, Noble spoke. 'Sir, DI Brook asked me to look into Edna Spencer's affairs.'

'Edna Spencer?' answered Charlton. 'What has—?'

'Years ago, she and her husband lived a few streets away in Overdale Road.'

'So?' said Charlton.

'So, behind Overdale Road there are garden allotments and the Spencers had one that backed on to their house,' continued Noble. 'They even had a gate put in, I think.'

'She moved to Mount Street years ago,' said Brook.

'But she kept the allotment,' said Noble. 'It's still in her name and the annual subscription is renewed every year. It was in her financial records.'

'That's why Mullen killed her,' said Brook, looking at the old man's deathly white features for confirmation. 'He's got the allotment and that's where the bodies are buried.'

'I didn't kill anyone,' shouted Mullen. 'But DI Brook did. And he's not the only copper I know . . .' Brook gestured Cooper to escort Mullen back to the house. 'No, you've got to listen to me,' shouted Mullen, before he was led out of earshot.

'I thought the allotment was searched when Wheeler went missing,' said Charlton.

'It was,' confirmed Noble. 'Every shed. Every greenhouse.'

'You don't use a spade to hide people in a shed,' said Brook.

Charlton nodded. 'Does the warrant cover it?'

Noble nodded. 'House and grounds.'

'Get the dogs.'

Twenty-Seven

I T WAS FOUR IN THE morning yet still Clive Copeland sat on in his
dark conservatory, oblivious to the passage of time. When he
did look up, his eyes found the treeline of Osmaston Park and
beyond it the lake, in which his sister's body had floated for four
summer nights almost five decades ago.

He lifted his hand and with it the gun, examined it as though for
the first time, almost in wonder. He caressed the stock, stroked the
muzzle and ejected the clip, checking it for the hundredth time,
before heaving it back up into the handle. Without looking at it,
Copeland flicked the safety catch on and off with his thumb.

The phone rang somewhere in the house but aside from a brief
dart of the eyes, Copeland didn't react. It tripped over to answering
machine.

'Sir, this is DC Cooper. We're in Normanton and we think we
may have caught a break on the Scott Wheeler case. It ties into
some of your old inquiries so DI Brook thought you might want to
be here.' Cooper gave directions to the allotment and hung up.

The machine cut out but Copeland remained motionless. He
raised the gun with two hands and simulated taking a shot out into
the night then stood to gather up his car keys from a table.

The owner of Edna Spencer's old home on Overdale Road was
already at the front door, alerted by the helicopter overhead. His
curiosity turned to concern when a delegation of police officers
opened his gate and marched up to his house.

'Sir, we need access to your back garden.' After Charlton had quickly explained the situation and been granted the permissions he needed, he gestured several uniformed officers towards the rear of the house, two of them with sniffer dogs. Brook, Noble and Cooper followed.

The bottom of the back garden allowed no admittance to the allotment but the constables set to work removing the old doors and planks which barred the way where once there'd been a gate.

'Why isn't Ford here?' asked Brook.

'Dave rang him but he wasn't in,' said Noble.

'And Clive?'

'Same.'

The obstructions were cleared and the dog handlers led the way into the dark allotment beyond. The helicopter moved overhead to illuminate the ground.

There were no sheds or greenhouses in this part of the allotment, just a cordon of overgrown fruit trees, making it difficult to see the ground from outside and above. Looking across the terrain, Brook was the first to spot the sawn-off drainpipe protruding a few feet from the soil. 'Over here,' he shouted, running over to it. The aperture at the top of the pipe had been covered with clingfilm, now damp with condensation. Brook tore it off and recoiled from the harsh stench of ammonia. He shone a torch down its length. He could see what looked like an arm. It was inert and covered in filth.

'Scott!' shouted Brook. No movement. He stepped back to examine the area around the pipe.

'Is he there?' pleaded Charlton.

Brook nodded. 'He's there.'

'Alive?'

Brook didn't answer. One of the search team readied a spade but Brook threw an arm across him. 'Wait. The ground's untouched. It could take ages to get through and if we dig on top we might bring the whole lot down on him.' Brook took the spade from him and began probing around the plot. 'There has to be an easier way.'

Like Brook, the officers with spades began probing around the site, their breath steaming in the sharp air. Meanwhile, Charlton leaned over to Cooper. 'Get back to the house and take Mullen into custody.' He looked back at Brook jabbing the spade gingerly into the soil around the pipe. 'And get the paramedics in here, stat.'

Brook hit something metallic with the point of the spade. 'Here.'

Charlton, Noble and Cooper watched Brook and the search team carefully but quickly lift dirt away from around the pipe. Brook glanced around at his surroundings as he worked. At the edge of the helicopter searchlight he saw two other plastic pipes standing proud from the ground. They were older and weathered. Still digging, he gestured across to Noble who nodded in grim comprehension.

A moment later, one of the search team fell to his knees, shouting. He uncovered a metal handle, brushing dirt away from it. Brook knelt down to help and the pair pulled it firmly upwards. A large heavy board began to move and the pair recoiled as one from the stench. Other bodies bent to hoist the board further skywards. At forty-five degrees, large sods of freezing wet soil began to slide off until the assembled officers were able to propel the board, its air pipe still attached, away from the hole.

Everyone blanched at the aroma of human waste emanating from the boy and each member of the search team shared a look of horror with a colleague. The boy was covered in dirt, crawling with insects and his blackened, motionless form was wasted and unrecognisable. What parts were visible showed his skin like parchment, cracked and infected.

'Scott,' shouted Noble, jumping down into the foul-smelling grave and brushing dirt away from the boy's mouth and nose. A paramedic arrived beside him to check the boy's airways. Noble placed a finger against Scott's neck as more paramedics ran towards them.

'I've got a pulse,' shouted Noble, suddenly hoarse with the release of tension.

The paramedics eased Noble out of the way and jumped down to tend to the boy, forcing a mask over his uncovered mouth and nose. After massaging the boy's chest and his extremities for thirty seconds or more, the rapt audience sighed with relief at a cough and a splutter. Scott's lungs began to fill with oxygen and the paramedics prepared to heave Scott on to a gurney.

In the harsh light, Noble's face began to quiver. He pushed the back of his hand across his mouth to staunch the flow before gazing across at Brook. 'Thank you,' he mouthed before the tears began to fall.

Brook nodded, tight-lipped, his own sangfroid beginning to crumble. He felt Charlton's gloved hand slap him on the shoulder and stay there as they watched the boy being hurried to the ambulance.

'That goes for all of us.' Charlton's face was creased with happiness. 'Damen.'

Back on the concrete of Overdale Road, Charlton and the CID officers were greeted by Brian Burton and a photographer now alerted to the drama taking place. Cameras flashed and Charlton basked in the limelight but wasn't too self-satisfied to forget Brook. He turned to grab his arm and hold it aloft. 'Here's your hero, Brian. DI Brook saved Scott Wheeler's life.'

Burton tried to smile as he recorded the quote in his notebook. Brook tried not to, as he watched the journalist making notes, his teeth grinding in frustration.

And your third-rate book saved mine, Brian.

Half an hour later the adrenalin of the chase had evaporated and Brook, Charlton and the others began to feel the rigours of a long day and night. Edward Mullen had been taken to St Mary's Wharf for processing and SOCO teams were commencing the grisly business of excavating Mullen's allotment for further victims. Noble had left with the ambulance after ringing Scott's mother with news of her son's survival.

Fortunately the cold drizzle had kept most sightseers away but both local and national TV and press had joined Brian Burton at the newly erected crime scene perimeter where Charlton had made various statements to the media.

Before he left for the night he made sure of a parting word with Brook. 'You've filled up the mortuary today, Brook,' said Charlton, declining to mention the detrimental effect on budgets. 'And you've taken a serial killer out of circulation. The citizens of Derby are grateful. Go home and get some rest.'

Brook nodded and shuffled away in apparent compliance, dragging his weary body back to his car outside Mullen's house, refusing all requests for an interview.

As he slid into the driver's seat, Brook glanced across at Mullen's decomposing home, its appearance befitting the evil that had been hatched there. Blue-suited technicians were already beginning the process of taking Edward Mullen's life apart, to bureaucratise and render banal the details of his sad and twisted life. Brook was glad to leave them to it and embark on his short journey.

He pulled his car into Rosie Shah's drive but instead of jogging up the steps and pounding on the door, he crept into the back garden and let himself into the shed. He flicked on the desk lamp and stared at the Pied Piper wall, its mass of papers still waving in the draught from his entrance. One newspaper strained enough to finally pull its drawing pin from the wood and clattered to the floor.

Brook stooped to pick it up. It was a 1978 edition. Harry Pritchett's doomed grin stared back at him. It was a page he hadn't seen before – a picture of Harry behind a chessboard, his black combatants scattered in the Sicilian Defence.

Brook shook his head. 'Insane,' he mumbled, pinning the yellowing print back in place.

'Who's insane?' asked Rosie from the door of the small bedroom.

Brook was startled. 'Rosie! I'm sorry. I thought you'd be asleep in the house.'

Rosie stepped into the main room. She was fully dressed. 'What are you doing here?'

'I was in the neighbourhood . . .' he hesitated, 'and I needed to get a couple of hours' sleep.'

'Don't you have a bed at home?' she teased.

Brook hesitated. 'I also needed to speak to you before anyone else does.'

Her face registered the gravity of Brook's tone. 'What is it?'

'There have been developments,' he said softly. He plumped for the good news first. 'We found Scott Wheeler.'

'Alive?'

Brook nodded.

Rosie's face creased with joy. 'That's marvellous. Is it something to do with that bloody helicopter keeping everyone up?'

Again Brook nodded, his face drawn.

'And the Pied Piper?'

He sighed, picking his words. 'I can't discuss it but it looks promising.'

Her face erupted in tears and she ran towards him, throwing her arms round his neck. 'I don't believe it,' she spluttered. 'After all these years.' Her hands stroked his neck, pulling and hugging him, the emotion shaking her body to its core. Finally she pulled away from his unyielding frame and stared into his ashen face.

'What's wrong?'

'We found another body late yesterday – the skeleton of a young male in Osmaston Park Lake. We think it's Colin Ealy.'

Rosie's hand flew to her mouth. 'Oh, my God. The gamekeeper.'

'The gamekeeper,' repeated Brook. 'He didn't run away. He never left Derbyshire.'

Rosie couldn't mistake his tone and her face hardened. 'And why did you feel an urgent need to tell me this?'

'Because Colin Ealy knew something about Matilda Copeland's murder and was killed for it.'

'I don't understand.'

'Whoever abducted and killed Matilda was seen by Ealy. He was scared. Maybe he tried to run but someone cracked open his skull when his back was turned.' Brook stared at Rosie, his expression grim. 'Then, alive or dead, he was placed inside an old crime scene body bag and weighed down with stones by someone who knew what he was doing. A professional,' he added pointedly. 'Then he was dropped into the deepest part of the lake, probably from one of the boats the gamekeepers used.'

To Brook's surprise, Rosie suddenly smiled. 'And you think my dad killed the gamekeeper because he recognised him from the night the girl's body was dumped.'

'Walter Laird confirmed your story about the day your father visited the lake. Reluctantly, I might add.'

Rosie laughed now, shaking her head for good measure. 'You're wrong.'

'Rosie, I understand—'

'No you don't. Dad wasn't at the lake that night—'

'Rosie—'

'Because he didn't abduct Matilda Copeland.'

'You don't know that. Your dad was in turmoil, you said it yourself.'

'But he couldn't possibly have been at the lake.'

'Why not?'

'Because he was pissed out of his head in the Half Moon up the road.'

'Rosie, you were only two years old.'

'You remember I told you about Dad's disciplinary record.'

'Yes,' said Brook doubtfully.

'I told you he'd got a couple of written warnings about his behaviour. One was for harassing Ruth Stanforth at her daughter's funeral; the other was for getting drunk and into a scuffle at his local on the night Matilda Copeland disappeared. That's why Walter Laird had to take the call on his own. So, you see, Colin Ealy couldn't have seen my dad at Osmaston Park Lake the night Matilda was dumped. He was drunk. He could barely walk, never mind abduct and kill a young girl.'

Brook's mind was racing as parts of the jigsaw fought to rearrange themselves in his brain. 'Are you sure?'

'Absolutely certain. He was drinking in the local from opening time to last orders and beyond. After the fight, the landlord closed up and walked Dad home with a friend. He even helped my aunt put him to bed. I remember her saying it was well past midnight.'

Brook stood there unmoving so Rosie grabbed him by the wrist and pulled him to the desk. She opened a drawer and after a few moments' rummaging, extracted a document and thrust it at Brook. It was another disciplinary letter. Sam Bannon had got falling-down drunk and into an altercation with another customer in the Half Moon public house in Littleover on 31 August 1965, the night Matilda Copeland had been abducted. He received a formal reprimand about his conduct.

Brook lowered his hand and stared at the disc of light on the desk. His eyes came to rest on the photograph of the young Walter Laird and Sam Bannon leaning on Bannon's Jaguar. Brook's eyes closed in realisation.

. . . when his back was turned . . .

'Brook? Are you OK?'

He opened his eyes to look at Rosie. There were questions he wanted to ask her to confirm what now made sense but he knew he didn't have the time. Instead he smiled. 'I'm glad.'

'I'm so glad you're glad,' said Rosie haughtily. 'You're going?'

'I have to.'

'But—'

'The dead will keep a little longer, Rosie. I have to see to the living.'

Brook ran to his car, his fatigue forgotten. He pointed the car at the inner ring road and fifteen minutes later squealed to a halt outside Clive Copeland's village home.

Unlike his previous visit, there was no sign of life and the house was dark. Brook hurried through light rain to bang on the door. A censored light came on but nothing else stirred. The drive was empty. Copeland's car was gone.

Brook jogged back to his car, feeling his phone vibrate in his pocket.

'John. How's the boy?'

'Stable. Are you home yet?'

'No, why?'

'I meant to tell you, Terri rang me.'

'When?'

'A few days ago, after you were shot at. She wanted to know what was wrong when you brushed her off for Christmas so she rang me to get a straighter answer.'

'What did you tell her?'

'The truth,' said Noble. 'I said you were safe and I'd let her know when things were back to normal. I texted her five minutes ago, so expect a call.'

'I suppose I should thank you,' said Brook after a pause.

Noble laughed. 'No, just don't lie to her next time. She's a grown woman.'

'Right,' said Brook feebly. He jumped behind the wheel and turned the ignition. 'I can't talk now . . .'

'There's something else, something bothering me.'

'John, I've got to go.'

'It's about Josh Stapleton's murder and the Pied Piper.'

Brook was turning the car round but stopped in mid-arc to listen to Noble. 'I'm listening.'

Twenty minutes later, Brook screeched to a halt in the dark and mounted a kerb outside the house. Not bothering to lock his car, he ran through the rain towards Laird's terraced cottage and came to a halt at the plastic door with its funeral-urn knocker. Panting, he knocked on the urn whilst looking for movement inside. A faint light was visible through the mottled glass so Brook opened the unlocked door and hurried inside.

The single-bar fire was on and Brook could see the gnarled hand of Walter Laird gripping the arm of his chair. 'Walter.' No response. 'Laird. It's me. Brook.'

Brook walked to the chair and pulled it round.

Laird's head tilted back to stare glassily up at him. Blood shone above his left eyebrow. He struggled to speak. 'Brook. Thank God. I thought it were our Darren.'

'Darren?'

With a flick of his eyes, Laird pointed Brook in the direction of the kitchen from where a voice sounded, calm and resigned. 'He's worried his son might turn up and get himself killed trying to stop me.'

Brook turned to see Copeland step from the shadows. He carried a gun. 'Clive. You worked it out.'

'That's right, Brook. I worked it out,' said Copeland, a bitter smile twisting his face. 'Only took me forty-seven years. And me a DCI. Pathetic.'

'He was your hero, Clive,' said Brook softly, trying not to stare at the gun. 'We blind ourselves to their faults.'

'Well, I'm not blind now,' replied Copeland.

'It was the car, wasn't it?' said Brook. 'That's what Colin Ealy recognised, not Sam.'

'The Jaguar Mark X,' confirmed Copeland.

'Ealy hadn't seen a man the night Matilda's body was dumped, that's why there was no report of a sighting. But he *had* seen a car, he just didn't realise it until he saw Bannon pull up in the Jaguar. But Bannon wasn't driving it the night your sister disappeared, am I right? He couldn't have been. He was falling-down drunk in a pub.'

'Was he?' said Copeland. 'I wouldn't know about that.' He gestured at Laird with his gun. The old man lowered his head. 'I only know that Walter loved that car. He often borrowed it. He had it that week to help him move.' Copeland's breathing revealed a quiver of deep-seated tension. 'He even turned up in it after we reported Tilly missing on the night . . . after he'd . . .' Copeland bit down on his emotions but felt no need to complete the sentence.

'And after Ealy recognised the car, who would he tell?' continued Brook, edging closer to Copeland. 'Not Sam Bannon, obviously, not the owner of the car, but another policeman, someone he could trust . . .'

'Someone he *thought* he could trust,' said Copeland, staring at Laird. 'That's why Walter killed him.'

'He had no choice,' said Brook. 'If Ealy mentioned the car to someone else, it wouldn't take long to piece together. Must have been quite a shock, Walter, having to work so fast.' No response. Brook eased himself a few more inches towards Copeland. 'What did you do, Walter? Arrange to meet Ealy at the lake that night? Tell him not to speak to a soul until a case could be built against Sam Bannon. Must have been difficult.'

'I doubt that,' sneered Copeland. 'Walter's got a silver tongue.'

'Still, so much to organise,' continued Brook. 'Rustling up a body bag without arousing suspicion. Can't have been easy. There was already a convenient boat at the lake for the gamekeepers' use. That was useful. You'd need it to get the body to the deepest part of the lake. I'm guessing you arrived early to hide the body bag, making sure you weren't seen. Then, when Ealy appeared and his back was turned, you let him have it.'

Laird grunted in derision. 'You're off your rockers, the pair of you.'

'It wasn't the most satisfactory outcome because there was no evidence that Ealy killed Matilda,' said Brook. 'That would have sealed it. And you still had her clothes.'

'Why didn't you use them to incriminate Ealy, Walter?' barked Copeland.

'Oh, he would have if he could,' said Brook. 'But the van and the workshop had already been searched, remember. It would look suspicious if an item of your sister's clothing turned up after that. No, better that Ealy just disappeared. And when the time was right, Walter could fake a sighting in Scotland to keep the pot boiling.'

'You bastard,' said Copeland. 'That boy trusted you, Walter. Tilly too. And you murdered them.'

Brook took another step towards Copeland. 'And Ealy wouldn't have turned his back on Sam Bannon, not after seeing him get out of the Jaguar . . .'

'I like you,' growled Copeland, turning to Brook. 'But if you take another step towards me, don't kid yourself I won't use this. I'd try to wing you but I'm no marksman.'

'Clive, this isn't—'

'Sit over there,' ordered Copeland, gesturing at a wooden chair. 'Palms on the table.'

Brook hesitated, assessing his options before retreating past Laird to the cramped dining table. He placed his hands flat. 'You can't do this, Clive. It doesn't count unless the killer faces justice. Your words.'

'He'll get justice,' said Copeland, touching a hand to his crucifix under his shirt. 'An eye for an eye – his life for Tilly's.'

'But you won't be taking his life, Clive,' said Brook sadly, 'because he's already lived it. Don't you see? If you kill him he gets away with it.' Copeland turned to hear Brook. 'He doesn't have to face his shame. He doesn't lose his dignity. The only thing Walter has left is his reputation and that's what we have to take. That's why we need a confession.'

'And how admissible do you think a confession would be with a gun to my head,' snorted Laird, resurrecting a little aggression. 'Dream on, Brook. I confess to nothing and there's no proof I killed anyone.'

'Don't speak, Walter,' said Copeland, raising the gun and gripping it hard then glancing over at Brook. 'Walter's right. It's been too long. There's no proof. No corroboration. He has to die or he gets clean away with it.'

'You're wrong,' said Brook. 'We got the evidence earlier tonight – a confession.'

'I told you. I'm confessing to nowt,' croaked Laird.

'You don't have to,' said Brook. 'We've got a witness and enough for a charge.'

'Don't bother talking me down, Brook,' said Copeland. 'We both know there are no witnesses.'

'Hear that, Brook?' cackled Laird. 'Clive doesn't believe you.'

'I told you to shut up, Walter.' Copeland stepped across to put the barrel of the gun against Laird's temple.

But instead of cowering, the old man cackled. 'Go ahead. Shoot, if you're man enough. But I want a final cigarette. Allow me that at least.' His chest continued to heave with merriment and Copeland's calm demeanour began to disintegrate.

'You murdering bastard . . .'

Brook stood quickly, hands raised, and sidled to the fireplace. 'He's provoking you, Clive. He wants you to shoot him because he doesn't want to go to prison.'

'Sit down, Brook,' shouted Copeland, pointing the gun at him.

'Take it easy.' Brook lowered his hand towards a pack of cigarettes and a lighter. 'Put the gun down, Clive. Listen to me for the time it takes Walter to smoke a cigarette and if you're not convinced, I'll walk out and leave him to you.' After a brief hesitation, Copeland nodded. Brook took out a cigarette and put it in his mouth, lit up and passed it to Laird. The old man took a long draw of the poison into his lungs.

'Tick-tock, Brook,' said Copeland.

'If you kill him, he takes your life as well as Tilly's.'

Copeland lifted the gun and snaked a finger round the trigger. 'Think I give a shit about my life after I let down my sister like that.'

'Tilly wouldn't want you to sacrifice your life for hers,' said Brook. 'Think about that.'

'My life? That was over the day she died, Brook,' said Copeland. 'Tick-tock.'

'OK,' said Brook, trying to think. 'Shoot him now and he dies quick and clean.'

'You said that already.'

'But look around, Clive,' urged Brook. 'As miserable as his life is now, can you imagine how much worse it would be in prison? He'd be in a living hell, scared and alone, an ex-copper who murdered a child and was complicit in the deaths of other children.'

'Other children?' Copeland lowered the gun and stared at Brook.

'We found Scott Wheeler alive a few hours ago,' said Brook.

'Alive?' exclaimed Copeland. 'Where?'

'Do you want to tell him, Walter?' demanded Brook. Laird grunted, eyes resolutely on the floor. 'No? Well, perhaps you don't know about that part of Mullen's method. Scott was buried in an underground vault in an allotment near Mullen's home.' Brook spoke slowly to Copeland, being sure to leave nothing out. 'We found him just in time and arrested Edward Mullen for kidnapping and attempted murder. We'll be charging him with the murders of Jeff Ward in nineteen seventy-three, Harry Pritchett in nineteen seventy-eight and maybe other missing boys buried in the same allotment, an allotment which once belonged to Edna Spencer. He killed her too.'

'Edward Mullen?' said Copeland, shaking his head. 'Walter always steered me away . . .'

'He would,' said Brook, watching Laird's confidence drain away. 'And you weren't the only one. You see, Mullen and Walter had a mutual interest in turning a blind eye to each other's crimes. But now we have Mullen in custody, he's no longer under any obligation to protect Walter. He's confessed to his crimes and he's implicated Walter,' Brook lied with all the conviction he could muster. 'Mullen is the Pied Piper, a killer of children. Sam Bannon was right, Clive.'

'My God,' said Copeland, narrowing his eyes at Laird. 'All those years I poured scorn on Sam, on your say-so.'

'There's more,' said Brook. 'Walter's a serial killer in his own right.'

'What?' exclaimed Copeland.

'You're off your head,' snarled Laird.

'Am I?' asked Brook. 'You abducted and killed Tilly in nineteen sixty-five. You killed Colin Ealy to cover your tracks. And when Sam Bannon began to close in on Mullen, you were forced to kill him too.'

'That's a lie,' shouted Laird. 'Sam was my friend.'

'Yes, he was,' said Brook. 'But when Mullen told you Bannon was getting close, he warned you that if he went down, you were going with him.'

'It's not true,' snapped Laird. 'And no one's going to take the word of a nutcase like Mullen.'

Copeland was confused. 'He's right. Why the hell would Walter kill his best friend on Mullen's say-so?'

'Because Mullen knew Walter had murdered your sister, Clive. And one word to you . . .'

Copeland was silent, staring grimly into space. To Brook's dismay he didn't ask the question.

'Don't you want to know how he knew?' asked Brook finally. Copeland nodded, without looking up. Brook took a breath to voice the absurd. 'Mullen thinks he has a gift. He thinks he can see the dead.'

'See what I mean?' crowed Laird. 'Who's going to believe that shit?'

'He thinks murder victims are bound to their killers in the afterlife and he can see them, trapped, asking for answers about what happened to them.'

Laird grunted. 'Listen to yourself.'

'And you believed him?' asked Copeland, finally meeting Brook's eyes.

Brook hesitated. 'Course not. But I believe Mullen said enough to convince Walter. After that, Walter's guilty conscience did the rest.'

'But when did Mullen find out about Walter?' asked Copeland. 'Not on the Stanforth inquiry. Tilly and Colin Ealy were still alive.'

'Two years after Walter had killed Tilly, he was reviewing the Stanforth case with Sam in nineteen sixty-seven. They went to interview Mullen. I'm guessing when Mullen was alone with Walter he said just enough to make Walter believe his secret was known. It always struck me as odd that Mullen had been interviewed so rarely since Billy's death. Walter only made that one visit to his home in Normanton. One visit. He never went back again. And he persuaded every other officer reviewing the case to take Mullen out of their calculations. Most of them did.'

'But Sam didn't,' said Copeland softly.

'No,' replied Brook. 'Despite all his problems, Sam gradually came to believe something was wrong about Mullen. And the idea took root that he was a killer.'

'So Mullen killed Billy Stanforth,' said Copeland.

'No, that's the irony,' said Brook. 'That's what Bannon could never get round, why he couldn't fit Mullen into his Pied Piper theory and bring him to justice. That, and his deteriorating mental health, meant no one would listen. All his allegations about the Pied Piper and Mullen fell on deaf ears.'

'Lucky for Mullen,' said Copeland.

'Even luckier for Walter,' said Brook, turning to him. 'With Walter's reputation, no one would question his loyalty to Sam and no one would doubt the pain it caused him to paint Bannon as a mentally unstable burn-out.'

'You don't know what the hell you're talking about,' spat Laird.

'Don't I?' said Brook. 'You knew Bannon was getting close because Mullen told you he was. And when Bannon phoned you two days before Harry Pritchett was scheduled to die, you knew you had to act. Bannon had to die. And it was easy. Sam was unstable, a drunkard. Everyone knew he was fixated on catching a killer who'd burned a boy to death in a shed. What better way to deal with your friend than to fake a suicide using the Pied Piper's own method? It would look like the final sad act of a deranged mind.'

'All that phoney concern about Bannon's reputation and his kid,' growled Copeland, his face sour. 'You sick, shameful old bastard.'

Brook was pleased to see Copeland lower the gun. *Keep talking until Noble arrives.* 'There's more yet, Clive. Walter didn't just kill people to protect himself. He went out of his way to ruin the lives of innocent people.'

'More bullshit,' sneered Laird, taking another long draw of his cigarette. There was silence now, except for the crackle of the burning tobacco. Brook watched Laird tight-lipped. Still no admission of guilt. He pressed on.

'You deny planting those pornographic pictures in Brendan McCleary's flat?' asked Brook.

Laird opened his arms wide, gesturing down at his withered legs, almost spitting in his vehemence. 'Look at me, Brook. I can barely get to the kitchen.'

'But your son could have done it,' answered Brook. Laird looked for the words but didn't answer. 'Did you spin him some yarn about the greater good, about the end justifying the means? I hope so, for his sake, Walter. With luck, he hasn't been poisoned by years of your toxic hatred.'

'Leave my Darren out of this,' blurted Laird, finally showing some emotion.

'Why would Walter want to set up McCleary?' said Copeland.

'Walter has been trying to destroy Brendan McCleary ever since Billy Stanforth burned to death in nineteen sixty-three. He couldn't pin that on him so the year after Billy died, he tried again.'

'That's because the lowlife killed Charlotte Dilkes,' insisted Laird.

'No, he didn't,' answered Brook. 'Though you tried hard enough to prove it. And I dare say you would've put him away for Tilly's murder the year after that, if doing so wouldn't have exposed more of your dishonesty.'

'Bullshit,' mumbled Laird. It was a token effort. The flame of defiance was dying.

'I can't prove you killed Malcolm McCleary but—'

'Malcolm McCleary?' exclaimed Copeland, looking from one to the other.

'Oh, yes,' continued Brook.

'You're mental,' growled Laird out of the side of his mouth.

'Am I?' Brook shrugged. 'Maybe I am overreaching but it seems the obvious move, having tried and failed to pin three murders on Brendan. Why not just take the initiative and frame him? And you were used to killing by nineteen sixty-nine. It was easy.'

'If Walter murdered Malcolm McCleary, why didn't Brendan ever contest the verdict?' argued Copeland.

'Because it was the perfect fit,' said Brook. 'Like the rest of the world, even Brendan assumed he was guilty. He hated his father. He was drunk that night and couldn't remember anything. The perfect set-up.' He turned to Laird stewing in his armchair, his cigarette burned down to the filter. 'No denial.'

'I'm not dignifying this bullshit,' replied Laird. 'McCleary's a fucking paedo and a criminal.'

'You say that and yet Brendan's most serious crime in your eyes was to have fallen for Clive's sister,' said Brook. 'Matilda, the pretty girl you lusted after, as you might, seeing her every day, walking down the street to school, or later to her work in Barney's store. She told Brendan that one of her neighbours gave her the creeps but wouldn't say who. Everyone thought it was Trevor Taylor but it was you. But she didn't pay any attention to you, did she? Not the kind you wanted anyway.'

'You're sick,' said Laird.

'You were obsessed by her, Walter,' continued Brook. 'You wanted her but couldn't have her. And maybe that would have been that except for one thing that turned the screw. Not only could you not have her but she was giving herself to someone like Brendan – a petty criminal. And that's why you hated McCleary.' Brook flicked an eye at Copeland. The anger had gone and only sadness remained. The gun was still in his hand but forgotten.

'But I was engaged, remember,' protested Laird, jamming a finger into his chest. 'I had it on tap. Why would I lust after a little girl?'

'Who knows why we obsess over anything,' said Brook. 'But you lusted after Matilda and she rubbed salt in the wound by treating you like the old man you were – a neighbour, an uncle figure, in the background. Worse, she was in love with a handsome boy, a rogue desired by girls and admired by boys.

'To you, Walter, McCleary and his father were the antithesis of everything you stood for. And the idea that young girls, especially the young girl of your sick dreams, should give themselves to such a boy mortified you – you, a valued, upstanding public servant set against McCleary, an uncouth yob.'

Laird gestured for another cigarette but Brook ignored him.

'But a teenage girl doesn't fall in love with social status, Walter,' continued Brook. 'And maybe you would've forgotten about the pair of them if one dark December night hadn't presented you with a final opportunity, the chance you needed to draw yourself closer to the family, to Matilda.'

'Billy Stanforth,' said Copeland.

'Exactly,' said Brook. 'After Billy's death, you were able to show Matilda that you existed by keeping her name out of the inquiry. You proved your love for her and you wanted payback. The family was in your debt and, in your sick dreams, Matilda was too. She owed you.'

Laird was sullen but managed to resurrect a little belligerence. 'You can't prove any of this nonsense.'

'Thanks to Mullen I can,' countered Brook, trying to keep the confident edge in his voice. If Laird didn't crack soon, they'd have nothing. He played his last card. 'You're going to prison for the rest of your life, Walter. Stripped of respect, stripped of dignity. You raped and murdered a child and you killed a fellow officer. And when you get to prison, both sides of the system will be feeding on your soul.'

From somewhere a smile invaded Laird's features. He fixed Copeland with a stare. 'Edward Mullen?' laughed the old man. 'You've met him, Clive. Surely you don't buy this shit. He's an even bigger nutter than Brook. No one will believe a word Mullen says. It's not proper evidence like fingerprints. Eh, Clive? Haven't I always helped you when you've been up against it? Put the gun away, lad, and we'll say no more about it.'

'I loved you like a father, Walter.' A tear meandered down Copeland's cheek but he ignored it. He slumped on to the back of a chair, his shoulders sagging, his hands hanging. The gun was almost falling out of his hand. He seemed on the point of collapse.

'Walter Laird,' announced Brook. 'You're under arrest for murder.'

A car pulled up outside.

'There's DS Noble,' said Brook, approaching Copeland. 'Clive?'

Copeland looked down at the gun and flicked the safety catch back on before pocketing it. He glared at Laird, who cast his eyes to the floor in defeat. 'You killed my Tilly and you're going to burn in hell, even if I have to take you there myself.'

'I need you to give me the gun, Clive,' said Brook.

'Last chance for justice, Clive,' panted Laird. Copeland ignored him and stood to leave, turning his back.

'Clive, give me the gun,' said Brook, arm outstretched.

'Yeah, give him the gun so I can tell you how I raped your sister.'

Copeland swivelled. 'Shut up.'

'That bitch owed me,' shouted Laird at Copeland's retreating frame. 'I saved her from a criminal. I saved your family from humiliation.'

'That's enough, Walter,' warned Brook. 'Clive, the gun.'

'She paid no attention to me,' ranted Laird. 'Me, a man to respect, to look up to, and she chose that fucking pikey over me.'

'Give me the gun, Clive,' said Brook firmly, his hand held in front of Copeland.

Laird laughed, finding his script. 'She owed me so I fucked her and when she started snivelling I choked the life—'

'Clive!' Copeland was pulling the gun from his pocket, moving towards Laird.

'Shut up, you dirty bastard!' screamed Copeland.

'Clive, don't,' shouted Brook trying to interpose himself between Copeland and the old man. 'That's what he wants. Give me the gun.'

Copeland pushed Brook aside with surprising strength and raised the gun.

'You haven't got the fucking balls,' goaded Laird. 'You fucking cry baby. Want to know something else? When I answered the call, that slut's clothes were in the boot of the Jag all the time I was—'

A shot rang out and, for a second, everything except cascading glass was frozen in time. The explosion rolled around the room, assaulting the eardrums of its occupants. Eventually Copeland's gun hand lowered as he contemplated the inert figure of his aged mentor, white-knuckled, gripping the armchair, unshaven face wide-eyed in shock.

A second later, Copeland crumpled to the floor and Brook fell on top of him, pulling at his shirt as the scarlet stain rippled outwards from his chest.

'Clive.'

Copeland's eyes were lifeless but his arms and legs attempted movement, futile and uncoordinated, as though swimming in tar.

The shattered door was kicked open and Darren Laird, rifle in hand, advanced towards them until he in turn froze, looking in astonishment at Brook. He scrunched across the broken glass towards the stricken Copeland.

'Oh, Jesus,' he said, aghast. 'It's Clive Copeland.' He turned round to his father. 'I saw the gun, Dad. I thought . . . Oh, Jesus. What have I done?'

'Put the rifle down, Darren,' said Brook, his bloodstained hands raised to pacify. 'He's alive. Ring for an ambulance.'

'Shoot DI Brook, son,' said Laird.

Darren was astonished. 'What?'

'They came here to kill me, son. Now shoot him.'

'He's lying, Darren,' said Brook. 'We came to arrest him.'

'Shoot him!' repeated Laird, struggling to his feet. 'They're armed.'

'You're arresting my dad?' queried Darren.

'What are you waiting for, son? Shoot.'

'Your father raped and murdered Clive's sister.'

'He's lying,' spat Laird. 'Shoot him.'

Darren shook his head. 'Matilda Copeland? What's he saying, Dad?'

'Your father raped and murdered her,' insisted Brook.

'N-no, that's not right,' argued Darren. 'Brendan McCleary killed her.'

'You've got it, son,' soothed Laird. 'Now shoot Brook. We can sort it later.'

'He can't shoot me, Walter,' said Brook. 'Darren's a policeman, like me.'

'Yes he can. Now do it,' screamed the old man, shuffling towards his son. 'Or give me the rifle and let me do it.'

'Dad, I don't understand. What's going on?'

'Darren,' said Brook, getting to his feet and feeling for his phone. 'I'm phoning for an ambulance. Put the gun down. Your father's under arrest.'

'Shoot him, lad, before it's too late.'

'Dad, I can't.'

Laird was only feet from the rifle. 'You just shot a copper, son. If you don't act now, you'll be behind bars with the scum of the earth.'

'You made a mistake, Darren,' soothed Brook, dialling. 'You saw a gun. You reacted. Honest mistake. We can fix it but we've got to get an ambulance for Clive.'

'He also took a pot shot at you, Brook,' snarled Laird. 'How you going to fix that?'

'Dad.'

'We're in deep shit, you lily-livered little pansy, so shoot or give me that gun.' He reached Darren and grabbed the rifle from him, turning unsteadily to train it on Brook. 'Call yourself a man,' he hissed at his son.

Brook stood, hands outstretched, the voice of the emergency operator audible from the mobile. 'How many more, Walter?'

'Shoe's on the other foot now, you smug southern bastard.'

'Tilly, Colin Ealy, Malcolm McCleary, Sam Bannon. Four dead, Walter.'

'What's he talking about, Dad?'

'Shut up, lad. You too, Brook.' He wiggled the rifle at Brook. 'Move out to the kitchen. There's enough to clean up in here.'

'No,' said Brook. 'Do it here. Then your son will have to drag us both out to the back garden to bury.'

'Dad?'

'Please yourself.' As Laird levelled the rifle, Darren wrenched it

403

away from him and pushed him away. Laird lost his balance and fell to the ground.

'You do it then,' he snarled angrily.

'No, Dad,' said Darren. 'I've done enough shit for you. I'll not kill a copper.'

'Son,' Laird pleaded. 'Shoot him. For me.'

'I can't,' replied Darren, gesturing at Brook to speak to the operator.

'All right,' screamed Laird, trying to sit upright. 'Then for pity's sake shoot me, you cowardly little cunt.'

Twenty-Eight

BROOK SAT IN THE AMBULANCE, hunched with tension, while the paramedics worked. The frenzy of their efforts had diminished since the first urgent minutes in Laird's cramped little house. One peeled away from Copeland's inert form to speak softly to Brook.

'He's stable but it's touch and go.'

Brook nodded. He was beyond exhaustion, too tired to speak, not that there was anything to say.

'Brook.' The croak from Copeland was barely audible.

Brook manoeuvred closer to the trolley, glancing at the paramedic.

The younger man shrugged back at him. 'Can't hurt.'

Copeland's eyes were vaguely open but unable to focus. He lifted a shaking bloodied hand and fumbled for his crucifix. Brook grabbed the hand and guided it to the small silver cross under his spattered shirt. He took Copeland's other hand to let him know he wasn't alone.

Copeland's smile was sightless. He spoke again but Brook couldn't pick it up. An infant's squeeze of his hand drew Brook to crouch over his friend, turning his ear to Copeland's stained mouth. 'Tilly says thank you,' he mouthed under the mask feeding him oxygen.

'Save your strength. You're going to be . . .' Brook choked on the lie. If he couldn't be straight with a friend standing at the gates of heaven, when could he? 'Save your strength,' he repeated.

Copeland nodded minutely and mouthed something else. Brook patted him on the shoulder but Copeland wouldn't be denied. He withdrew his hand from Brook's and pushed the oxygen mask aside. 'He. Couldn't. Even. Drive.'

Brook pushed the mask back over his mouth. 'It's OK, Clive. I already know.'

Copeland pulled him back towards his mouth, trying to speak. 'Priest.'

'He's coming,' said Brook above the noise of the siren. He leaned in again. 'He's coming.'

The trolley was hurtling down the corridor, Brook trailing in its wake. They passed an intersecting corridor and Brook slithered to a halt and grabbed a man talking to a nurse.

'Father. Come with me now.'

'But—'

'Don't argue,' insisted Brook. 'My friend wants to make his peace with God.'

'What religion is he?'

Brook snorted. 'Does it matter?'

The priest prepared a counter-argument but thought better of it. 'No. Lead on.'

Brook held Copeland's cold hand for the longest time, aware of nothing but a strange peace washing over him. They were alone in the cubicle, the frenzy of the trauma team long past, the tubes and machines disconnected and inert.

Finally Brook blinked as though coming out of a coma. He unfastened the necklace of Copeland's crucifix, examined it briefly then dropped it in his own pocket.

'I hope you're where you want to be, Clive.'

Brook gazed at his bloodied right hand before plunging it into the water. He cleaned the caked blood from between his fingers, and stared at himself in the small mirror. With his bloodshot eyes, he looked like death but after several handfuls of cold water over his face, he felt fresher. He emerged from the toilets and dragged himself to sit on the chair next to Noble. Copeland's body was a dozen feet away being prepared for the mortuary.

'You OK?' asked Noble, handing him a beaker of hospital coffee.

'I will be after a week's sleep,' replied Brook, too weary even to grimace at the coffee.

'Quite a caseload you've cleared these last few days.'

'Quite a caseload,' echoed Brook. 'Pity the results don't reflect so well on the force.'

'Hardly your fault,' said Noble. 'You did everything by the book.'

Brook turned to Noble, opening his mouth to speak.

'Everything,' repeated Noble.

Brook nodded his thanks and stared down at his drink. It was the colour of dishwater.

'I'm sorry about Clive,' said Noble.

'Yep,' mumbled Brook.

'Walter Laird,' said Noble, shaking his head. 'How the hell did he get away with it?'

'Different era, John,' said Brook. 'The cult of the personality. Charismatic coppers could do whatever they liked back then. It helped that Laird was running most of the investigations he misdirected. Matilda Copeland, Malcolm McCleary, Jeff Ward. And even if he wasn't in charge, a word in the ear from an experienced officer like Laird could pervert any inquiry.'

'Incredible,' said Noble. 'Maybe we shouldn't complain about the PSD looking over our shoulders, keeping us honest.'

Brook smiled. 'I wouldn't start that conversation in the canteen.'

Noble grunted and looked across to the shrouded cubicle where Copeland lay. 'At least Copeland got justice for his sister.'

'There is no justice, John. There's only ever retribution and, if we're very lucky, redemption.'

Noble narrowed his eyes at Brook, unsure of his meaning. He realised now was a good time to focus on unpleasant reality. 'When I spoke to you earlier . . .'

Brook took a sip of the bitter coffee and returned his eyes to the floor. 'You're right. All Mullen's kills were in December. And if Noel Williams didn't push Josh Stapleton off that landing, someone else must have.'

'I'm right, am I?' Noble cracked a humourless laugh. 'You suspected it could be Scott from the off, didn't you?'

Brook sighed. Noble was going to need handling. 'It's easier from the outside looking in, John. You get too close and it can be hard to see things right in front of you. You had a lot on your plate as well as Ford making all the wrong moves.' He shrugged. 'But you got there in the end.'

'It'll be a tough sell to Charlton,' said Noble.

'Most things are,' replied Brook. 'How is Scott?'

'He'll live,' said Noble. 'Mentally scarred though, I reckon.'

'He'll fit right in then,' said Brook. 'How will you go at him?'

'Thought I'd give it time, let him get healthier first. Get a statement from Mullen then ask Scott to ID him.'

'Good idea,' said Brook quietly.

'Once I've thrown Mullen into the mix, I can bring up the Stapleton boy's murder; maybe even tell him we're re-opening. Hopefully he'll fold like a pair of twos.'

Brook took another sip of coffee. 'And if he doesn't?'

Noble was sombre. 'Scott's young,' he said reluctantly. 'We could offer his brief a deal, cushion the blow a bit.' He sighed. 'It's just . . .'

'The Stapletons, I know,' said Brook. He looked at Noble. 'Their son is still dead, John. There are no winners. With murder, everybody loses.'

When Noble had gone, Brook went searching for signs to the hospital chapel. There weren't any. Now, those of religious inclination were offered the multipurpose Faith Centre.

Brook stepped inside. There was calmness here, a peace that Brook tried to breathe deep into his exhausted body.

The priest who'd received Copeland's final confession was

kneeling before the altar, head bent in prayer. On hearing Brook's approach he raised his head, half-turned then stepped back from the altar to make the sign of the cross.

'Father Christopher.'

'Inspector Brook.'

'I wanted to thank you. Clive can go to his maker with a clean slate.'

The priest's smile widened in modesty. 'Glad I was able to help.' He studied Brook. 'You're not a religious man yourself.'

'Is it that obvious?' said Brook, fingering the crucifix in his pocket.

'*Clean slate*. You see confession as something transactional,' said Father Christopher. 'A bargain entered into between a worshipper and a deity.'

'That *is* why confession was dreamt up,' replied Brook, sitting on the bench furthest from the cross. 'Salvation for a fee.'

'That's a very cynical way of looking at it,' said the priest, with the patience reserved for unbelievers. 'And we don't charge these days.' The priest considered Brook and sat on the bench beside him. 'Would you like to pray, my son?'

Brook laughed without amusement. 'I haven't prayed since I was a child.'

'And what did you pray for?' asked Father Christopher with a smile. 'Toys? Sweets?'

'I prayed for my father,' said Brook, turning to face him. 'I didn't want God to let him die in pain. He was a miner in Barnsley.'

'But he died anyway.'

Brook smiled as though it was self-evident.

'Black lung?'

'How did you know?'

'My father was a miner in Nottingham,' replied the priest. 'His lungs killed him in his fifties.'

'And did you accept your father's death as part of God's great plan?' asked Brook, with an unintended touch of bile.

'Prayer isn't just about asking for favours, my son. If it were, there wouldn't be *any* death in the world.'

'You're mixing with the wrong people, Father,' said Brook. 'The people I deal with wish death on others on a daily basis.'

'Why are you here?' asked Father Christopher, lowering his eyes. 'You know I can't discuss your friend's . . .'

'No need. I know what Clive told you,' said Brook.

'I still can't . . .'

'His name was Trevor Taylor,' said Brook finally. Father Christopher's expression neither confirmed nor denied. 'Clive thought he deserved to die.'

'And did he?' asked Father Christopher.

'Is that the sort of question a priest should ask?' said Brook.

'It's the sort of question a man asks and I'm a man first.'

'Then, no,' replied Brook softly. 'Clive killed an innocent man. Does that make a difference?'

'Not to God.'

Brook looked at the priest. 'And to you?'

Christopher smiled. 'I'm a poor sinner like you, Inspector. I feel the impulse for vengeance when a child is murdered and I doubt the Lord when injustice flourishes. We're all weak.'

'But you overcome it,' said Brook.

'Usually.'

Brook was pleased with the answer. 'What would you have said to Clive if he hadn't been dying?'

'I can't discuss what Clive—'

'Hypothetically then,' said Brook. 'A man tells you he's killed another man. What do you say to him?'

'Did the man deserve to die?'

'Clive thought Taylor killed his sister.'

'I'm not talking about Clive,' said the priest, his eyes burning into Brook's. 'We're speaking hypothetically, remember.'

Brook's gaze dropped. After a moment, 'Yes, he deserved it.'

'Very well,' said Father Christopher. 'I would tell that person to be ready to make reparation before God—'

Brook got to his feet. 'I should be going.'

'But I would also tell him that, in asking the question, he had already shown God he could be saved.'

'Anything else?' asked Brook.

'I would ask if he performed good works to make amends for what he'd done.'

'He tries to,' said Brook.

'Then he must continue. And when he is ready to save his soul, God will be waiting for him.'

Brook walked away but turned at the exit. 'Where will he be waiting?'

'God is everywhere,' smiled Father Christopher. 'But I'll be at St Alban's Church on Roe Farm Lane.'

'What denomination is that?'

Father Christopher held Brook's gaze. 'Does it matter?'

Twenty-Nine

23 December 2012

'WHAT A MESS,' SAID CHARLTON, looking through Walter Laird's statement. He glanced up at Brook. 'And there's no doubt?'

'None.'

'All those years Clive worked with Laird. He thought he was a god . . .'

'Hero worship is never healthy,' said Brook. 'Especially for the worshipper.'

'And with that kind of blind devotion, Laird would have no trouble skewing plenty of inquiries, I suppose.' Charlton threw the statement on his desk and went to look out of the window. 'Why confess to McCleary's father?'

'Sir?'

'Aunt Tilly, Sam Bannon and that gamekeeper. Good clearances. But Malcolm McCleary – it's water under the bridge. Brendan did the time without complaint. Who needs to know?'

Brook decided his response was better left unsaid.

'Brendan served twenty years for a crime he didn't commit,' explained Charlton, thinking Brook hadn't understood. 'That will draw a big pay-off and it'll be open season for all the lefties in the media.'

'I'm sure Brendan would prefer the time back,' said Brook drily.

'Mmmm.' Charlton narrowed his eyes at Brook. 'How did you get all this out of the old sod?' he asked, picking up the statement again and waving it at Brook. 'I mean there's not a lot to back all this up. If he'd taken the Fifth, we'd have had a tough sell to the DPP.'

Taken the Fifth? Are you American? Brook stared beyond Charlton's head to avoid voicing the question. 'He was keen to make a clean breast of things,' Brook lied.

'Without inducement?' countered Charlton suspiciously.

Brook hesitated. 'We decided there was scope for lesser charges against his son in return for Walter's full and frank cooperation.'

'Lesser charges?'

'It was suggested to his brief that we wouldn't oppose a plea of voluntary manslaughter with a recommendation for leniency.'

'Voluntary manslaughter?' said Charlton, aghast. 'He shot and killed a former police officer.'

'And he will go to prison,' argued Brook. 'But when Darren arrived at the scene he acted out of protective instinct towards a parent.'

'Even so . . .'

'Sir,' snapped Brook. 'Clive had a gun. He was armed and prepared to kill Darren's father. And maybe even me, if I'd got in the way.'

'Ah, yes, the gun.' Charlton's acceptance was grudging. 'I suppose it's better that Clive's little aberration doesn't come out – as we're playing ball.'

'It may yet come out but if we're not contesting the plea, their barrister may not need to bring it up.'

'I still don't like it,' said Charlton.

'Justice is blind, sir.'

'What does that mean?'

Brook tried to pick his words with care. 'Your uncle and Walter Laird were very tight in the seventies and eighties.'

'And?'

Brook sighed. 'I got to know Clive over the last two weeks. He had his secrets and they caused him pain. More than his sister's death could account for.'

'Are you suggesting what I think you're suggesting?' said Charlton, ready to take offence.

'"He couldn't even drive",' said Brook.

'What? Who couldn't drive?'

Brook reached into a pocket and pulled out a dog-eared sheet. He unfolded it and dropped it on Charlton's desk. 'Trevor Taylor couldn't drive.'

'Clive's neighbour?' said Charlton. Puzzled, he read the report. 'This is an interview with Taylor's mother.' Brook nodded. 'Where did you find it?'

'Hidden in Walter Laird's papers,' answered Brook. 'Trevor Taylor couldn't possibly have abducted Matilda and driven her to Osmaston Park Lake. He didn't know how. But by removing this from Matilda's file, Walter kept Taylor in Clive's sights. Then, in nineteen seventy-seven, Walter wound Clive up like a clockwork toy and let him loose on Matilda's case. He withheld that document and filled Clive's head with tales about Trevor Taylor's deviancy and how he escaped justice.'

'Do I want to hear any more?' said Charlton, tight-lipped.

'There is no more,' said Brook. 'Trevor Taylor fell to his death from a bridge that winter and Clive finally got to speak to Taylor's mother.'

'And she told him what was in this document,' mumbled Charlton, shaking his head. 'Why did Laird do it?'

'To have something on Clive, sidetrack him, make him spend time covering his own tracks instead of looking for Matilda's killer. Take your pick.'

'An insurance policy.' Charlton nodded. 'Poor Clive.' He picked up the dog-eared document. 'So what am I going to do with this report?'

Brook stared hard into Charlton's eyes for longer than was comfortable. 'What report?'

Eventually Charlton's eyes lowered. He folded the document into his breast pocket and returned his attention to Walter Laird's statement.

'You're right, Brook,' said Charlton in his most businesslike voice. 'Without an accommodation, this bad apple could say anything about events surrounding the Pied Piper, or anything else for that matter.' He paused to look up at Brook. 'Walter won't survive his sentence and this concession is a fair price to close the book on that period.'

Charlton's demeanour changed when his eye fell on the front page of that afternoon's *Derby Telegraph*, celebrating the safe return of Scott Wheeler to his parents. The lead picture showed Charlton addressing the media. He looked authoritative and commanding. *And no hint of smugness*, he thought smugly, nodding solemnly.

'Yes. We must accentuate the positive. We've done a lot of good here.' Charlton looked across at Brook, who didn't seem to be accentuating as positively as himself. 'And don't think I'll forget your role in all this,' he said. 'You're finally due that promotion. Clive was right about you.'

Brook hadn't realised that being in Charlton's good books was just as uncomfortable as being in the bad. 'Sir . . .' he began.

'No, don't be modest. Your skills deserve wider recognition.'

'DS Noble deserves all the plaudits, sir.'

'Very generous of you, I'm sure,' replied Charlton. 'Which reminds me. How are he and Ford getting on with Mullen?'

'Not one word since his arrest,' said Noble. 'I think he's working up to an insanity plea.'

'It might even be true,' said Brook.

'But if I'm to move against Scott, I need Mullen to make a statement about Josh Stapleton's death,' said Noble. Brook detected something in his voice and glanced across. Noble smiled. 'Well, you know him best.'

'But it's your case, John,' said Brook.

'Are you worried he might start making wild allegations again?'

'No. But he thinks I planted evidence in his house.'

'But you didn't,' said Noble softly. 'So there's nothing to worry about, is there?'

Brook didn't answer.

'All right, if you could just watch the monitor,' said Noble. 'Give us some pointers. We'd like to wrap it before Christmas – for the sake of the families.' Noble waited, a plaintive expression on his face. 'Christmas is a terrible time . . .'

'When?'

'We're taking another punt now,' smiled Noble.

'I don't know why you need me,' said Brook. 'You've got the bodies. Just charge him and move him on.'

'We would,' said Noble. 'But we're missing one.'

'Missing one?'

'We've only got two bodies,' explained Noble. 'Three under-ground chambers – two with bodies and one for Scott. But if the Pied Piper material is right, there should be another victim, right?'

'Harry Pritchett, Davie Whatmore and Callum Clarke.'

'We're still digging up the allotment and the back garden. So far only the two and there's nothing on infrared,' said Noble.

'Any ID on the two you have got?' asked Brook.

'Waiting on DNA,' said Noble.

Brook trained his eyes firmly on Mullen as the interview began. He hadn't seen him since that highly charged night at his house and he'd changed. Now the old man's expression was completely blank, almost catatonic, staring absently off into space, even when his solicitor tried to speak in his ear. *Maybe he has lost his mind.*

Ford strutted around making the introductions for the tape, while Noble sat down sifting through the documents and evidence Ford would use against the suspect.

But after fifteen minutes, Ford's hectoring had produced barely a blink from Mullen, The DI sat down and looked across at Noble, tagging him into play.

'Mr Mullen, I want you to look at these pictures,' began Noble, his voice soft and sympathetic, respectful – a contrast to Ford's old-school bluster. He pulled a series of dated glossy portrait photographs from an envelope. 'This is twelve-year-old Harry Pritchett who went missing on December the fifteenth, nineteen seventy-eight. He was last seen walking home after a game of football. He lived in Stimpson Road which is no more than a mile from your home. He hasn't been seen to this day.'

Mullen didn't react or move a muscle.

Noble peeled another photograph from the stack. 'This is thirteen-year-old Davie Whatmore. He was last seen on December the twelfth, nineteen eighty-three, walking across Markeaton Park, near the pond. He lived on Old Road, again just a mile from your house.' Pause. No reaction.

Brook wondered why Mullen's solicitor hadn't tried to call a halt, maybe even ask for a doctor to examine Mullen. *He must be receiving instruction. There's nothing wrong with Mullen.*

'This is thirteen-year-old Callum Clarke,' continued Noble. Mullen's eyes darted briefly to the photograph then away.

Brook craned closer to the monitor. 'What was that?' He watched intently as the old man reassembled his mask of impassivity.

'Callum was last seen walking home in Littleover on December the twenty-second, nineteen eighty-eight,' continued Noble. 'He lived less than half a mile from your home.'

Again, Mullen's eyes shifted to the photograph and back, too quick for Noble to see it.

'Callum Clarke,' murmured Brook, thinking it through. 'He must be special. He must be the missing body, John.'

'Mr Mullen, the only thing the families want from you at this moment is to know what's happened to their sons. If they're dead, they want to grieve; they want to take their children home and lay them to rest so that they can mourn them properly and get on with their lives—'

'After you wrecked them, you sick bastard,' inserted Ford.

Noble looked across at his senior officer and the solicitor muttered something. Ford put up his hands in apology. Brook kept his eyes on Mullen, torn between the monitor and going next door to help.

'You're going to be confined for the rest of your life, Mr Mullen,' Noble continued. 'Nothing will alter that and nothing will bring these boys back. But if you have any shred of decency left in you, give these families the peace they deserve.'

No response. Noble looked up in despair at the camera but after a pause carried on. 'Sir, would you at least tell us which boys were buried in your allotment? We'll find out eventually so it can't hurt to tell us that.' Pause. No reaction. 'Would you at least tell us where the third boy is buried?'

Again, quick as a fox, Mullen's eye flashed across to the picture of Callum Clarke but, again, he did not reply. But this time Noble noticed the involuntary glance and picked up Callum Clarke's photograph.

'That's it, John,' mumbled Brook.

'Callum is the third boy, right?' said Noble. 'Is he buried somewhere else? Where, Edward? Where did you bury Callum?'

Brook's eyes narrowed. 'Not where, John, but *why* did he bury him somewhere else?' Brook scraped back the chair when it hit him. 'It's the twenty-second, John. He changed his MO. He killed Callum on Billy's birthday and buried him where he harvested him.'

Noble was beginning to lose patience. He pulled out a picture of Jeff Ward. 'You strangled Jeff Ward to death on December the twenty-second, nineteen seventy-three, but left the body. After that, you changed your method. You abducted the boys and started burying them alive, letting them die slowly until the twenty-second, your friend's birthday. I've seen the banner and the cards and the cake. These boys are birthday presents to your friend Billy, aren't they?' Noble stood behind Mullen, silently blowing out his cheeks in exasperation.

'Why did you take Callum Clarke so late?' persevered Noble.

'Very good, John,' murmured Brook. 'Stay on that.'

'Was it a last-minute kill?' continued Noble. 'Bit of a panic? Is that it? Is that why you buried him somewhere else?' No response. Noble looked over to the camera in frustration. 'Interview suspended.'

* * *

Brook placed the two thin beakers of coffee on the table. Without looking at Mullen or his solicitor, he pulled out two fat candles from his pocket and, after lighting them, put them on the table on a sheet of A4 to catch the wax. He then snapped off the overhead light and turned on the tape to list those present.

'Thanks for my drink,' said the solicitor sarcastically. 'What's with the candles?'

'Mood lighting,' Brook explained. He glanced at Mullen for the first time and slid the coffee towards him but then said nothing further for several minutes, choosing just to gaze at Mullen. The old man wouldn't reciprocate; he sat, arms folded, staring at the wall, his coffee untouched and unacknowledged.

After fifteen minutes, the duty solicitor became agitated, mouthing at Brook to speak or draw the interview to a close.

'I've been asked to have a word, see if I could . . . move things along,' said Brook eventually. No reaction. 'And I brought you something,' he added, as though just remembering. 'From the house.' He pulled a plastic bag from his jacket and took out the travel chess set Mullen had given Billy Stanforth nearly fifty years ago.

Mullen's eyes moved briefly to the set then back to the wall.

Brook opened the case and took out the tiny board. 'Everything's ready for a game.' He swivelled the board between the two of them. 'In light of recent events, I think I should be white.' He picked up the king's pawn and moved it two spaces, looking at Mullen for a reaction. Again, gimlet-eyed Mullen flashed a glance at Brook's opening gambit.

'DI Ford thinks you're insane,' said Brook. 'Sergeant Noble's not so sure but he says he'll go along with it.' He looked up at Mullen. 'But I said no. Edward Mullen is not crazy.'

Brook waited.

'I said Edward Mullen has a gift that the world has failed to understand or appreciate.' Wait and watch. 'I said Edward Mullen has fought his entire life for control of that gift and to throw in the towel and accept a plea of insanity would mean betraying it. To do

419

that would hand ammunition to all those people who have poured scorn on who he is.' Wait and watch. Sip of cold coffee. 'Finally, I said that everyone who dislikes and fears gifted people like Edward Mullen would be delighted to dismiss his talents as the ravings of a delusional—'

'Pawn to king four,' said Mullen, looking up at Brook but making no attempt to move his piece. Brook reached over and moved Mullen's black pawn to block his white pawn. He responded by moving his queen's pawn alongside his king's.

'My pawn takes your queen's pawn,' said Mullen.

Brook removed his pawn and responded by moving out a knight to threaten Mullen's advanced pawn.

'I know what you're doing, Brook.' Mullen's cold eyes finally alighted on Brook. 'You think I'm going to tie my forces in knots defending that pawn while you bring out the heavy artillery.'

Brook smiled as Mullen reached for his cold coffee and took a sip. After putting the beaker down, Mullen scanned the room, an odd smile playing around his lips. Brook resisted the urge to look for Mullen's ghosts.

'It's crowded in here,' said Mullen. He turned to the solicitor. 'You can leave now.'

'I don't advise that,' replied the solicitor.

'You're fired,' said Mullen. 'Get out.'

The solicitor glanced at Brook, happy to register no further objections. He scraped his chair back and made a haughty exit which Brook recorded for the tape.

'OK, Brook. What do you want?' asked Mullen.

'I want you to take responsibility for your actions,' said Brook.

'Like you did,' said Mullen, arching an eyebrow. Brook answered with a cryptic smile, dropping a pen on to a blank interview pad, expecting a repetition of earlier accusations. Instead Mullen became thoughtful. 'You played the game well, Brook.' He was silent for several minutes. Then, 'I have three conditions.'

'I only anticipated one,' said Brook.

'You're slipping,' Mullen mocked. 'You should understand a

brother-in-arms better than that.'

'It's been that sort of case, pitting my wits against a clever opponent,' replied Brook.

Mullen smiled faintly. 'What's my first condition?'

'Easy,' replied Brook. 'You want to serve your sentence in solitary confinement.' Mullen raised an eyebrow, waiting. 'With limited access to the internet.'

'Agreeable?'

'I think so,' said Brook.

'What else do you think I want?' said Mullen. 'No pressure.'

Brook considered the slight old man, thinking through their shared history and Mullen's limited needs. 'A bottle of port at Christmas.'

Mullen nodded. 'Agreeable?'

Brook shrugged. 'Tricky. We might manage a half bottle.'

Mullen dipped his head in acceptance. 'And the third?'

Brook had to admit defeat. 'The third? You've got me there.'

Mullen looked at the table. 'I want to play chess.'

'I think that's what we're doing,' said Brook.

'I don't just mean today,' said Mullen.

'There'll be no problem taking a chess set to prison, Edward,' said Brook, smiling. 'I'm sure board games are encouraged.'

'You've misunderstood,' replied Mullen, fixing Brook with a mocking stare. 'I'll be in solitary, remember.'

It took Brook a second to understand. 'I don't think that will be possible.'

'I'll only need an email address,' said Mullen. 'If I accept a life sentence with good grace, it's only right that you do the same.'

'Forget it. I don't want you in my head.'

'Then, I'm sorry . . .'

Brook's mind was racing. He wanted this settled. 'What about a post office box?' he said quickly. 'I can accept that.'

Mullen considered. 'It'll slow the games down.'

'But that favours you,' said Brook, 'being the inferior player.'

Mullen managed a smile. 'Then I suppose that will have to do.'

The old man picked up the pen, ready to make a statement. 'A life sentence together. And maybe this time I can win.'

'I have a couple of conditions of my own,' said Brook.

'Go on.'

'We've arrested Walter Laird for four murders and he's given us a full confession. He's admitted how he, and he alone, steered investigators away from you, believing you had knowledge of his crimes.' Brook stared hard at Mullen, making sure his message was received. 'So please restrict your statement to your activities as the Pied Piper. Start with why you took Scott.'

Mullen stared back, a half-smile playing around his lips. 'Very well,' he replied softly. 'Then you don't want to know about Sam Bannon's killing spree,' asked Mullen, raising a mocking eyebrow.

Brook's smile tightened. 'OK, Sam was no killer. You were right. I was wrong.'

'What a shame I can't have a recording of that,' said Mullen. 'Never mind. I heard it and I'll treasure the sound. You have a second condition?'

'We need to know what you did with the body of Callum Clarke.'

'What happened?' said Noble, two minutes later. 'Everything was going so well.'

'I'm not sure,' said Brook. 'Play that bit back.'

Noble clicked the mouse and both detectives watched the end of the interview intently.

'We need to know what you did with the body of Callum Clarke.'

Mullen smiled and replaced the pen on the table. 'That, I can't tell you.'

'Not good enough,' said Brook. 'We need to know everything about all the boys you took and why.'

'They were killers,' said Mullen.

'Were they?' said Brook, rustling for a document. 'We've done some research. Every boy you murdered, or attempted to murder, had lost a brother, a sister or a close friend. Every boy except the last one, Callum Clarke in nineteen eighty-eight. The last one before you stopped.' Brook let the silence build for a while.

Mullen's cruel smirk was constant. 'You have a question.'

'Simple. Why Callum?' said Brook. 'He wasn't a killer. Were you desperate? Is that why you *harvested* him on Billy's birthday? Couldn't find anybody to fit your specifications?' Mullen's gaze didn't waver. 'I want full cooperation or the deal's off.'

'I am cooperating,' said Mullen.

'So tell me. Why change your MO for Callum Clarke?'

'I didn't.'

'No answer means no deal,' said Brook. 'No solitary. No port. No chess.'

Mullen shook his head. 'You're an intelligent man, Brook. Let me spell it out for you.' He spoke slowly for emphasis. 'I can't tell you.'

Noble clicked the mouse to close the screen. 'What's he playing at?'

'I'm not sure, John,' said Brook. 'I thought we had him. Sorry.'

'Don't be,' said Noble. 'You got him talking at least. We'll just have to pick it up after Christmas.'

'It'll be easier when you've identified the bodies in the allotment,' said Brook. 'The families have waited a long time; they can wait a few more days.'

Thirty

Christmas Eve 2012

THE NEXT AFTERNOON BROOK TOOK the goose out of the freezer, more in hope than expectation, and drove to Derby with his most expensive bottle of wine in the passenger seat. He pulled up outside Rosie Shah's house forty minutes later and jogged up the steps.

'Damen,' shouted Rosie, opening the door. 'You made it. Come in, come in.' She spotted the car keys in his hand. 'You're driving?'

Brook had his get-out clause handy. 'I'm expecting my daughter over from Manchester. I can only stay an hour or two.'

'Never mind, you're here.' She beamed, a little less brilliantly.

She took him through to the kitchen and introduced him to the handful of friends and neighbours standing around with wine glasses in their hands, chewing on the finger buffet of sandwiches and crisps.

'Everyone, this is my hero, Detective Inspector Damen Brook,' announced Rosie.

The conversation dried as all contemplated Brook. He poured himself a soft drink and nodded awkwardly to all the faces, listening to their names go in one ear and fly out of the other.

Fortunately attention shifted when the kitchen door opened and Ollie came in with a friend, the two teenagers dressed in almost identical fashion, the same clothes and the same hair jutting out in every direction under the influence of the same gel.

'Can we have another beer, Mum?' asked Ollie, at his most charming.

'You're under age, Ollie.' Rosie glared at her son with big eyes, glancing slyly across at Brook. 'Remember?'

'Yeah, OC,' giggled his friend. 'You're under age. Best not be smoking no blow neither,' he added, wagging a censorious finger at him. The pair fell about and Rosie tried to usher them out.

'We're seventeen, Mum,' complained Ollie. 'And it's Christmas.'

'There's a policeman here,' she said, tight-lipped, gesturing Ollie to leave.

'Don't mind me,' said Brook. 'They can rob a bank for all I care. I'm off duty.'

'Is that work duty or parental,' tittered a middle-aged woman with red hair and too much make-up. Brook had forgotten her name already.

'Both,' said Brook, smiling politely.

'See?' protested Ollie. 'Just one more.' He held up a single digit. 'Please.'

Rosie opened two small bottles of lager and shooed the pair away.

'OC?' inquired the red-haired woman.

'Ollie's initials,' explained Rosie, blushing across at Brook for some reason.

'It's also some crappy Yank programme our kids watch,' said one of the men. 'They purposely put on rubbish so we're forced to buy the kids a telly for their bedrooms. Bloody conspiracy, it is.'

Everyone laughed and Brook stood there, a half-smile glued to his face, watching the clock tick round, calculating a polite time to withdraw.

Fortunately, as the other guests got a little drunker, the tension eased and Brook didn't feel quite so self-conscious tacking on to a group and saying nothing, occasionally catching Rosie's attentive eye.

'Toilet,' he mouthed at her and she nodded towards the stairs.

* * *

'Ollie.' Brook nodded at Rosie's son on the stairs.

'Do you see a lot of dead bodies?' quizzed the young man, without embarrassment.

Brook never ceased to be amazed at the guilelessness of youth. 'Some.'

'I'll bet,' he nodded. 'My mum likes you.'

'I like her,' said Brook, smiling awkwardly, looking beyond Ollie for the toilet.

'Are you going to marry her?'

Brook shouldn't have been surprised by such a question but he was. 'Ollie, I just met her.'

'She's lonely,' announced Ollie.

'I'm not sure she'd like you telling people that,' said Brook, beginning to move round the olive-skinned boy but he wouldn't be denied.

'Do you fancy her?'

'You seriously want me to answer that?' asked Brook.

'Why not?'

'You think I'm unsuitable,' smiled Brook, 'because I'm a policeman.'

'No. Grandad was too,' said Ollie. 'I just wanna know. Mum says you've got a lot in common.'

'Does she?'

'Yeah.' Ollie laughed. 'You both like hanging in that creepy shed for one thing.'

'And you don't?'

'That place is dread, man. You won't get me in there with all those stiffs on the wall. Place gives me the shits.' Without further ado Ollie sprinted back into his room, the throbbing music invading the landing for the few seconds his door opened.

Brook found the toilet, a bemused expression on his face. Kids.

When he made his excuses, an hour later, Rosie walked him to the car.

'I was hoping you'd stay longer, Damen,' she said, grabbing his arm. 'You could've slept over.'

'I think I've seen enough of that shed,' said Brook, smiling.

'Maybe not the shed then,' she replied, tilting her head coquettishly to one side.

'My daughter . . .' began Brook as she moved in for a kiss.

Brook was too polite to break away so he implied a joint venture and withdrew at the earliest opportunity, looking affectionately into her eyes. 'Thank you for inviting me.'

'When will I see you?' she purred.

'Soon,' he said, turning towards his car.

Back on the A52 to Hartington, Brook's mobile began to vibrate. He pulled over to answer.

'I took another crack at Mullen this morning,' said Noble. 'No joy, I'm afraid. He won't tell me anything, won't even talk to me.'

'What about DNA on the . . .' Brook's head lifted in shock. 'What did you say?'

'I had another crack . . .'

'After that.'

'No joy . . .'

'He *won't* tell you anything,' said Brook.

'That's what I said.'

'That's not what he said to me,' replied Brook, his pulse quickening. '*Can't*, he said. There's a difference.'

'I don't . . .'

'Mullen spelt it out for me. *I can't tell you.* Those were his exact words, John. Not, I *won't* tell you. Don't you see? He doesn't know where Callum Clarke is buried because he didn't kill him. That's why he kept looking at his picture. It was a surprise. He didn't bat an eyelid at the other two photographs. He knew he'd killed them. But Callum . . .' Brook threw a hand over his eyes to think.

'Are you there?' No answer from Brook. 'Sir, are you there?'

'I'm here,' said Brook quietly. 'John, I need you to check something for me – a name. Then I need you to meet me . . .'

* * *

427

Rosie Shah sipped her white wine sitting on the replica of her father's desk. For once, the spot lamp was trained away from the accumulation of documents pinned to the Pied Piper wall, illuminating only a small bright oval on the blotter. The contents of the documents, waving gently on the wall, were difficult to pick out. As she could probably have identified every one blindfolded, that was just fine by her.

She put down her glass to continue her labours, unpinning the mass of newsprint and photocopies from the pine boards and folding them flat into a box.

'We did it, Dad,' she said, a mix of pride and melancholy in her voice. 'We stopped him.' She gulped back her emotions and continued to deconstruct the display that had dominated her life, folding paper, balling Blu-Tack and throwing drawing pins into the metal bin with a clatter.

Working methodically, Rosie finished removing all papers related to the 1983 disappearance of Davie Whatmore and with a sigh turned to the column marked 1988.

As she reached for the date tag, a noise turned her head. The boards of the veranda were groaning under the weight of a person.

'Ollie?' she called. The only answer was the latch being lifted, followed by the creaking of hinges as the door swung open. 'Who's there?' She reached for the spot lamp and flicked the shade towards the entrance.

'Damen,' she shouted, running to the door to throw her arms round him. 'You came back.' She buried her face in Brook's neck and pulled him to her, only stepping back when Brook didn't reciprocate.

He unhooked her hands from behind his head and held her by the wrists. He glanced at the bare wall in the shadows then back at her. 'What did you do, Rosie?'

'I'm getting healthy like you said,' she replied. 'No more living in the past.'

'What did you do?' said Brook slowly.

She studied his impassive face and retreated to sit on the desk where she picked up her wine. 'I don't know what you mean,' she croaked.

'The OC,' answered Brook. 'Oliver Callum Shah.'

'That's my son's name, yes,' she said defiantly, her voice under the strain of her first doubt.

'Did you think giving your son his name would keep him alive in some way?' said Brook, glancing at the wall.

Rosie took a sharp breath, unable to look at him.

Brook marched over to remove the paper covering Callum Clarke's missing persons poster and ripped his doomed face from the wall. 'That's why Callum's photograph is covered. You can't bear to see his face.'

'I don't know what—'

'Look at it!' demanded Brook, thrusting it under her nose. 'Tell me what happened. Make me understand how you can kill a child. And don't blame the drugs.'

She sat back, looked into the distance and a solitary tear rolled down her cheek. 'It was the last day of the cycle. The twenty-second. I'd waited, I was patient. I scoured the papers, the TV . . .' She shook her head.

'But no boys disappeared,' concluded Brook.

She shook her head and more tears fell. 'The Pied Piper had stopped. Everything my father worked for . . .'

'Your father wanted it to stop,' said Brook coldly. 'That's what he worked for.'

'But if the Piper wasn't caught, if he just stopped and melted into the background, all Dad's efforts, his death, would be wasted,' she sobbed. 'I couldn't let him stop. How could we catch him if he didn't kill again?'

'So you killed a child to keep your father's theory alive,' said Brook.

'Yes,' she said, gulping down on the word.

'You found Callum Clarke and lured him here.'

Rosie nodded. 'I'd been drinking . . .'

'Don't blame the alcohol,' shouted Brook.

'No,' said Rosie.

'What happened?'

'It was the last day and already dark. I saw him alone on the high street looking in shop windows. I had an old bike to give away. It was easy . . .' she managed before the tears continued.

'Easy to kill him?' demanded Brook.

Rosie shook her head.

'Did he beg you, Rosie?'

She nodded again, staring into space. 'I hit him and he looked at me, crying. He was so confused. "Please don't", he said.' She looked at Brook now. 'And I didn't want to. I wanted to take it back but it was too late. So I hit him again and again and again.'

'He's buried under the shed, isn't he?' said Brook. 'That's why you had it built, to cover him over so nobody would ever know.' Her silence was confirmation.

Brook's voice was more sad than angry. 'And nineteen ninety-three?'

She shook her head, her expression bitter. 'I couldn't do it again, not after waking up in tears every night for five years, seeing Callum's face, hearing him beg. If the Pied Piper really had stopped, then so be it – I couldn't kill again. I accepted it.' She blew her nose on a tissue. 'But I never stopped looking. I knew Dad was right. I knew he'd strike again.' She looked up at him, hope in her eyes. 'If I hadn't kept looking you wouldn't have saved the Wheeler boy, that's true, isn't it? Damen. That's true. My tip saved Scott.' Her desperate expression beseeched him for this slender thread of redemption.

Brook nodded. 'Yes, that's true.' She wept and Brook looked at her, a great knot of sorrow tightening in his stomach. 'Let's go.'

Rosie nodded. 'Please tell me it hurts. Tell me it hurts just a little bit.'

'It hurts a lot, Rosie,' said Brook quietly, nodding at the door.

'Before we go, will you hold me?' said Rosie.

Brook sighed. 'Why?'

Her eyes beseeched him. 'Dad never held me.'

Brook moved clumsily towards her and Rosie fell into his arms, pulling him to her in a last act of love and longing.

'I wish . . .' she began.

The veranda boards creaked under another's weight.

'That's Ollie,' said Rosie pushing him away. 'Please tell him to go back to the house.'

'He's going to find out . . .'

'But not yet, Damen, please. I need a minute. Don't let him see me like this.'

Brook put his head through the door. It was Noble. Before he could turn back to Rosie, Brook felt all her weight crash against him and he was pushed against Noble on the veranda. The bolts of the door were rammed noisily home from inside.

'Rosie!' shouted Brook, banging on the door. He heard a frantic scraping sound as something heavy was dragged across the floor. He heaved against the door. There was no give. She'd barricaded the desk against it. 'Rosie! Come out of there. You've got nowhere to go.'

'Look,' said Noble, indicating the small window where flames shot up behind the net curtain and seemed to be spreading quickly.

'There's a gas tank in there,' said Brook.

Noble put an elbow through the glass but shutters were slammed across and bolted at once.

'Help me with the door, John.'

Noble stood shoulder to shoulder with Brook and they both heaved against the door. The wood split but the door, reinforced by the desk, wouldn't buckle. 'Again.' They heaved again. By now smoke was gasping under the door and through gaps in the wood. They continued to crash against the door but it wouldn't move.

'Mum!' screamed Ollie, sprinting into the garden. 'Mum.'

'Get back!' shouted Brook.

Ollie ignored him and put a foot up to the window and tried to kick it open. 'Mum!'

Noble ran across and grabbed Ollie by the waist and wrestled him on to the grass as thicker smoke began to billow from the shed.

'This thing will go up in seconds,' shouted Noble. 'There's no time.'

Brook put his shoulder against the door again. More wood splintered and Brook scrabbled at the shards. 'Help me, John.'

But when Noble returned to the door, Ollie ran screaming to kick at the window again, so Noble broke off and wrestled the boy away from the shed and this time didn't let go.

'You can't save her,' shouted Noble, pacifying the eel-like boy wriggling to be free. A terrible, high-pitched scream rent the air and Brook became more frantic as he finally pulled a board of the door away. But this only increased the intake of air and the fire gained momentum, flames blackening the wooden roof.

'It's too late,' Noble shouted again. The scream was lost under the rattle and hum of the flames and the sobbing complaints of the struggling boy. 'She's gone.'

Finally Brook was forced away from the smoke seething under and through the door, windows and roof. He turned away, eyes streaming, unable to look, his clothes smouldering.

He helped Noble drag the boy further from the flames as a loud explosion blew loose boards into the air and the roof collapsed, allowing more oxygen to fan the flames.

'You killed her,' screamed Ollie at Brook. 'You killed her. I've lost my mum.' His accusations were reduced to indecipherable howls and sobs.

Brook looked at Noble, his eyes as dead as a feeding shark's. He put his hand on Ollie's gelled hair and pulled his head on to his shoulder, gripping him tight, whispering comfort into his ear.

Noble looked over at the pair of them, his expression grim. 'Everybody loses.'

Two hours later Brook and Noble trudged through the knot of firemen, uniformed police and curious onlookers to their vehicles.

Noble spied the Half Moon pub on the High Street and blew out his cheeks. 'I need a drink.' He squirrelled a glance at Brook, walking like a zombie beside him.

'I can't.'

'Can't or won't?' said Noble, with a bitter laugh.

'I'm expecting Terri,' Brook lied.

'I should come out,' suggested Noble. 'Be nice to see her.'

Brook nodded, unable to meet Noble's eyes.

'Rain check on that drink?' said Noble, anticipating Brook's reflex reaction. *Are you American?*

'Rain check,' echoed Brook, oblivious.

Brook drove through the dark, feeling despair and exhaustion washing through him. Christmas Eve and he was going home to an empty house and a cold bed while the rest of the world embraced.

When he saw the Fiat blocking his driveway he nearly wept with joy. He ran into the steamy warmth of the kitchen and into Terri's arms before she'd even had a chance to put down her wine glass.

'Am I glad to see you.'

'What a welcome, Dad,' she said, giggling. She extricated herself from his bear hug to look him over. 'You look terrible and you stink of smoke.'

'There was a fire.'

'A fire?'

'I'm exhausted, Terri,' he said, sagging on to a chair. 'Or I was until I saw you.'

She poured him a glass of wine. 'Thought you had nothing important on.'

'So did I,' replied Brook.

'I've got fish pie in the oven,' she said.

'Great,' said Brook, not registering.

'We've time for a few drinks and you can tell me all about this shooting,' she said with a stern expression. 'Honestly, Dad. I thought I'd done something wrong.'

'I'm sorry,' he replied mechanically, not taking his eyes from her. 'I'm a stupid, selfish old man.'

'No argument here,' she laughed. Brook managed a washed-out

smile. 'Jesus, Dad. You're almost catatonic. What have you been doing?'

He shook his head to consign the last two weeks to the past, feeling the tension begin to fall away. 'I've been investigating the investigators,' he mumbled. 'Tough beat.'

'Well, it's Christmas now, Dad.' She raised her glass, smiling. 'So here's to a better day tomorrow.'

'Yes.' Brook looked up at her and nodded. 'A better day tomorrow.'